Stolen

LESLEY PEARSE

PENGUIN BOOKS

PENGUIN BOOKS

Published by the Penguin Group
Penguin Books Ltd, 80 Strand, London WC2R ORL, England
Penguin Group (USA) Inc., 375 Hudson Street, New York, New York 10014, USA
Penguin Group (Canada), 90 Eglinton Avenue East, Suite 700, Toronto, Ontario, Canada M4P 2Y3
(a division of Pearson Penguin Canada Inc.)
Penguin Ireland, 25 St Stephen's Green, Dublin 2, Ireland (a division of Penguin Books Ltd)
Penguin Group (Australia), 250 Camberwell Road, Camberwell, Victoria 3124, Australia
(a division of Pearson Australia Group Pty Ltd)
Penguin Books India Pvt Ltd, 11 Community Centre, Panchsheel Park, New Delhi – 110 017, India
Penguin Group (NZ), 67 Apollo Drive, Rosedale, North Shore 0632, New Zealand
(a division of Pearson New Zealand Ltd)
Penguin Books (South Africa) (Pty) Ltd, 24 Sturdee Avenue, Rosebank, Johannesburg 2196,
South Africa

Penguin Books Ltd, Registered Offices: 80 Strand, London WC2R ORL, England

www.penguin.com

First published by Michael Joseph 2010
Published in Penguin Books 2010

002

Copyright © Lesley Pearse, 2010
All rights reserved

The moral right of the author has been asserted

Set in 12.5/14.75 pt Garamond MT Std
Typeset by TexTech International
Printed in England by Clays Ltd, St Ives plc

ISBN 978 1 40591 328 7

www.greenpenguin.co.uk

ALWAYS LEARNING   **PEARSON**

Dedication

To the real David Mitchell for your generosity in bidding at a charity auction to be a character in my book. I hope you enjoy reading the fictional account of yourself as much as I enjoyed writing it.

Acknowledgements

Thank you to Sue Hughes at St Richard's Hospital in Chichester for your help and enthusiasm, which were much appreciated.

And a huge thank you to Wayne Ashman in Brighton for all your invaluable help with all things Brighton. It went beyond the call of duty! Beware of talking to ladies on planes in future!

Chapter One

'Leave, Toto!' David shouted when he saw his neighbour's dog pulling at something half in and half out of the water, some three hundred yards further along the shingle beach.

It was six o'clock on a beautiful May morning, too early yet for most residents in Selsey to rise. David Mitchell, who was thirty-two, always came out with his neighbour's terrier at this time of day, taking a run along the coastal path while Toto charged about on the beach.

The dog backed off from whatever it was that he'd found, barking furiously. 'I'm coming!' David shouted and jumped down from the path on to the shingle from where he saw that the object of Toto's attention looked alarmingly like a body.

As he drew closer, David realized to his horror that it was a woman, for her bare legs were still in the sea and as the waves came in they lifted the skirt of her dress and made it billow. Her head was hidden from view until he was almost upon her, then he saw she was young, perhaps in her mid-twenties, slender and pretty with brutally cropped blonde hair.

Assuming she was dead, and afraid the tide might sweep her away before he could report he'd found her,

David bent down and putting his hands beneath her arms began to haul her further up the beach. But as he lifted her, a sound came from her, not quite a cough, more of a sigh, and her eyelids fluttered.

'Who are you?' he asked, dropping down beside her on the shingle and lifting her to a sitting position against his shoulder. He took her wrist and though her skin was like ice, and very wrinkled from submersion in the water, he could feel a faint pulse.

'I've got to run and ring for an ambulance,' he said, when she didn't reply to his question, and he laid her down on her side and used the fleece jacket tied around his waist to cover her.

He wished there was someone else around, for he didn't want to leave her there alone, but the path above the beach was deserted. He wondered what nationality she was, for her blue, high-necked and full-skirted dress was very old-fashioned, like the kind he'd seen in films set in the Fifties. He thought maybe she was from one of the Eastern European countries, but whoever she was and wherever she came from, he felt she'd been ill treated as there were purple marks on her wrists and ankles, as if she'd been restrained. Her hair had been crudely hacked off too, leaving it in uneven clumps.

Ordering Toto to stay with her, he sprinted back up the beach to find a phone box.

'Mystery Girl. Who Is She?'

Dale read out the newspaper headline to the two

other girls in the beauty salon as they had their first cup of coffee of the morning. 'It says she was found yesterday half drowned on the beach and she's lost her memory,' she explained. 'Of course, if they gave us a picture of her maybe someone would recognize her and come forward,' she added sarcastically.

'Maybe she's a rich bitch and her husband got tired of her and slung her overboard from his yacht, like in that Goldie Hawn film,' Michelle suggested. 'Did you ever see it? A poor widower with loads of kids found her, and as she'd lost her memory he made out she was his wife and took her home to look after his family. It was hilarious. She couldn't cook or wash up and the place was a tip.'

All three girls remembered the film *Overboard* and laughed and chatted about it for some time.

'It must be so weird to lose your memory,' Dale mused. 'Imagine not knowing who you are, where you come from or anything. I wonder whether if someone gave you something to eat that you hated before, you'd still hate it?'

The three girls were beauticians in the spa at Marchwood Manor Hotel near Brighton in Sussex. The hotel was well established, but the spa had only opened two weeks earlier, and this was why the newly appointed beauty staff were lounging in one of the treatment rooms drinking coffee and looking at the newspaper instead of attending to clients.

Dale Moore was a Londoner, twenty-five, tall, curvy,

with rather exotic looks as if she were Spanish or Italian, and very much the leader of the group. Michelle from Southampton was a slender blue-eyed blonde of twenty-four. Rosie was the youngest at twenty-three, a plump, sweet-faced brunette from Yorkshire.

Across the reception area was the hairdressing salon. Frankie, April, Guy and Sharon had Radio One on, which suggested they hadn't got clients yet either, for any kind of pop music was a hanging offence if the spa manageress, Marisa De Vere, caught them. She would only tolerate classical music tapes in the salon, and here in the beauty section they could only play special music to promote relaxation. But as Marisa was in London today no one would be doing the endless unnecessary cleaning she insisted on when they had no clients, nor would they stick to her choice of music.

'It says this girl's about twenty-four,' Dale said, going back to the newspaper. 'Found at Selsey by a man walking his dog. They think she'd been in the sea a long time but she had nothing on her to identify her. She was taken to St Richard's Hospital in Chichester.'

'She'll be an illegal immigrant,' Michelle said firmly. 'Come over from France on a boat. Maybe she fell out with whoever was bringing her and they pushed her overboard.'

'She was lucky to survive. The sea in May is still very cold,' Rosie said.

'They think she's English,' Dale said, glancing down at the paper. 'Where is Selsey anyway?'

4

'I haven't a clue,' Rosie said. 'But then, everything south of Birmingham is a mystery to me.'

'It's only about thirty miles from here,' Michelle said. 'We used to have holidays nearby when I was a kid. Does anyone want their nails done? Facial, head massage or pedicure? I'm bored!'

'Enjoy the boredom,' Dale sniggered. 'It's a rare treat not to have Marisa the Slave Driver prowling around.'

Dale had already made an enemy of the spa supervisor. As Dale was a first-class beautician with a great deal of experience under her belt, including a year on a cruise ship, she didn't feel anyone unqualified in her field should be telling her how to do her job.

When the staff first came here to open the salon, they had a three-day induction period to evaluate their ability. Marisa had stood over Dale while she was giving a massage, something Dale hated, and she had pointed out that the only way anyone could really assess a massage was by having one themself. Marisa had taken exception to that and since then she'd been looking for things to take Dale to task about.

Dale was no stranger to conflict with management. She was by her own admission stroppy, self-centred, opinionated, stubborn and liable to shoot her mouth off without thinking first. But she was good at what she did, she treated her clients well, and she worked hard – no one could ever accuse her of being lazy or cutting corners. She certainly wasn't cruel to anyone.

Marisa seemed to take pleasure in being cruel. She'd

mortified Michelle by telling her she had bad breath, had Rosie in tears when she had a spot on her face, and April was told she had body odour in front of everyone in the hairdressing salon. Only Scott the fitness instructor, an old friend of Dale's, escaped the woman's sharp tongue, but then, Marisa clearly fancied him.

She made everyone clean constantly to look busy: mirrors with a high shine had to have a greater one, already spotless surfaces had to be wiped again. She couldn't bear to see anyone twiddling their thumbs, but unfortunately, whenever she did sweep into the spa, it was sod's law that someone was telling a joke, reading a magazine or worse, having a sneaky cigarette outside the door.

'I'll go and ask April if she wants anything done,' Michelle said. 'She was talking earlier about going clubbing tonight. If I do her nails she'll let me go with her and maybe I can stay over at her house.'

Dale smiled. Two years ago she would have been just like Michelle, wanting to experience everything Brighton had to offer, but a year on the cruise ship had made her grow up, or at least consider the damage she was doing to her liver.

Michelle, Rosie, Frankie in the hairdressing salon, Scott and Dale shared a staff bungalow in the hotel grounds with Carlos, a wine waiter from the hotel. They were a bit cut off from Brighton, for the bus service wasn't very good and taxis were expensive, but Michelle was the only one of them who complained. The rest

6

were quite happy to sit about chatting and sometimes sharing a bottle of wine in the evenings.

The sound of the door to the treatment room opening made them all jump, but they relaxed again when they saw it was only Scott.

'Doing nothing, eh?' he said with a broad smile. 'I'll have to report you!'

Dale threw a towel at him. 'For God's sake shag Marisa, maybe she'll become a bit more human if you get her all loved up.'

She and Scott had met on the cruise ship where he was fitness instructor, and she'd taken one look at his green eyes, spiky blond hair and rippling muscles and fancied him madly. But every other woman under seventy on the ship fancied him too, so she decided to be his friend instead. It was perhaps the best decision of her life for they had become really close. Along with Lotte, her cabin mate, they would always go ashore together when the ship docked, and any spare moments they had while at sea, they spent together.

Dale had missed him and Lotte a lot when the cruise ended and they went to their respective homes. Dale got a job in a beautician's near her parents' home in Chiswick, in London, but there was none of the camaraderie with the other staff like she'd had on the ship, in fact some of the girls were real bitches.

This was why when she saw the advertisement for staff needed here, she'd telephoned Scott immediately to see if he was interested, and luckily he was, for he'd been working in a bistro in Truro, in Cornwall, unable to get a job in a gym.

Sadly they'd both lost touch with Lotte. She was a hairdresser and Dale thought she would have loved it here. But she hadn't responded to any of Dale's calls or texts since they left the ship; Scott reported the same. They had to assume that she'd moved on and didn't need them in her life any longer.

'I wouldn't shag Marisa with someone else's,' Scott said laughingly. 'I'd be afraid that mask might crack open and underneath she'd be hideous.'

That remark created great merriment for Marisa's complexion was so perfect it was almost like a porcelain mask. In fact everything about her was perfect, from her size ten figure and her beautifully cut black suits to her jet-black hair which she wore in a single sleek plait which reached the middle of her back. It was so shiny it looked as though it had been sprayed with black lacquer, and Dale had expressed the opinion she wasn't human, just a kind of Stepford Wife who had been bred to run a spa.

'She's actually thirty-eight, not thirty-two as she told Scott,' Rosie said with a mischievous sparkle in her soft brown eyes. Rosie wasn't one for dishing dirt about anyone, but she obviously felt unable to keep this titbit to herself. 'She'd left a life insurance schedule on her desk, I couldn't resist taking a nose. And her middle name is Agatha!'

'Agatha!' Dale exclaimed. 'I thought Marisa was bad

enough. I bet her surname isn't De Vere really, it's probably something yucky like Snelling or Greaseworth.'

Scott folded his arms. 'Do you actually know anyone with the name Greaseworth?' he asked with a touch of sarcasm.

'No, but it would suit her,' Dale laughed. She suddenly clapped her hand over her mouth 'M.A.D. Her initials spell Mad!'

There was a burst of giggles from the other girls.

'I'm going,' Scott said. 'I'll leave you to continue the cattiness while I check no one has drowned in the pool.'

An hour later, when Dale had to take over on the reception desk while Becky went for a coffee, she lit some floating candles in the reception water feature and stood back to admire them.

She was by nature cynical, blunt and hard to please, well known for picking holes in everything, including people. But she had found nothing at Marchwood to criticize; in fact, she thought it was absolutely perfect and beautiful. Even Marisa, however hateful she could be, did a good job making sure she kept everyone on their toes.

The hotel was old-style country house, with antiques, real fires, squishy comfortable sofas and a strong smell of lavender polish. But the spa had the kind of Oriental minimalism that cost a fortune. The central reception area had a pale grey stone floor, with the still pool

9

in the centre, now twinkling with floating candles. Decorations were sparse: a lovely piece of Japanese embroidery in a long thin frame, a few pots of orchids, low seating along the walls. The lighting was concealed, and even the reception desk was pale grey wood with a plate-glass top so it seemed to float above the floor.

From the reception area there were three doors. The one on the right led to the beauty treatment rooms, the middle one led to the gymnasium and the swimming pool and to the left was the hairdressing salon.

Hardly a day had passed since Dale arrived here when she didn't hug herself with delight that she'd found a great job with a future. The spa might not be busy yet, but she knew it soon would be once the marketing people began pushing it. She was well paid, the accommodation was excellent and the other staff were all very nice. She knew from past experience that it was the staff who made or ruined a job. There were around thirty or so of them in both the hotel and the spa, and although she had only really got to know the spa staff, she liked them all.

Fourteen months ago when the year's cruise contract ended, Dale had had a few hundred pounds saved. She intended to start her own salon, but that proved to be far more expensive than she had expected, and to make matters worse she frittered away quite a lot of her savings while thinking what she should do next.

She was only too aware that her parents worried

about her, and she'd certainly given them cause in the past. She'd hung around with low life, flirted with drugs, had an abortion, and until she trained in beauty never stuck at anything for more than a few weeks.

While Dale knew she was over all that now, her parents weren't entirely convinced. Even when she was on the cruise ship, where she had never worked so hard, they took the line that she was living the high life.

So now she felt she had to make this job work for her, to prove she really had grown up and could take responsibility for herself and others. Marchwood felt right. If she could just avoid crossing swords with Marisa, she might even end up running the place.

It got busier later in the day when several guests at the hotel booked various treatments, and it was after eight when Dale, Michelle and Rosie walked back to the bungalow after having dinner in the staff room next to the hotel kitchen.

It was a mild evening and the hotel garden looked beautiful by floodlight. The staff bungalow was hidden away behind some shrubs, and they were all looking forward to warm summer evenings when they could sit outside with a drink.

All of them had been surprised by how good their accommodation was. Most of them had worked in places where they were expected to share a room, and where the food had been awful. But here at Marchwood they each had their own room with a tiny en suite bathroom, and their meals were almost as good as those served to the guests in the hotel.

Frankie was in the lounge reading a paper. He looked up and grinned as they came in. 'I put a bottle of vodka in the fridge a while ago,' he said. 'It should be perfect by now.'

Frankie referred to himself as 'Gay' Frankie, as if his sexual persuasion wasn't immediately obvious by the turquoise streaks in his hair and his flamboyant clothes. Just a few days earlier Rosie had pointed out that whatever you said about Frankie you had to put 'very' in front of it. A very funny man, a very good hairdresser, and so on, for there was nothing mediocre about anything he did or said. Tonight he was wearing a ruffled white shirt which made him look as if he'd stepped out of an old swashbuckling movie.

Rosie collected the vodka and some glasses and by the time Dale had changed her work tunic for jeans and a tee-shirt and gone back to the lounge, Frankie was lighting some candles.

'The light is more flattering,' he said by way of an explanation.

'Don't worry, sweetheart, I fancy you even with harsh electric light,' Scott said.

There was some laughter about this for Frankie had spent the entire first week at Marchwood acting as though he was coming on to Scott. It had only been leg-pulling; Frankie said he couldn't resist because Scott was so obviously heterosexual. Frankie had stopped it now, but Scott had taken over with the teasing.

'Oh, look, Dale,' said Rosie, picking up the newspaper Frankie had been reading. 'They've printed a picture of the girl they found half drowned.'

It was the local evening paper, and presumably by tomorrow the picture would hit the nationals. Dale picked it up and glanced only briefly at the picture, which wasn't a real photograph but a police likeness, but she'd no sooner put it down than she felt compelled to pick it up again and study it a little more closely.

'Who does she remind you of?' she asked Scott, handing the paper to him.

Scott looked. 'Lotte? Same high cheekbones and round eyes. But this one isn't as pretty.'

'That's because she's been to hell and back and her hair's been cut off,' Dale said thoughtfully. 'Besides, it's not a real photo. But just imagine this girl with long, shiny hair, and a smile on her face. Scott, it really could be Lotte!'

'It couldn't be.' Scott shook his head.

'Why not?' Dale asked. 'We know she came from Brighton, she's the right age, and it says the girl is a blue-eyed blonde with a slight build.'

'That description would fit thousands of girls,' Scott said, shaking his head again. He picked the paper up and studied the picture again. 'But you've got a point – if you change the messy hair, she's a dead ringer.'

All the others wanted to know who they were talking about.

'She was a hairdresser on the cruise ship and I shared a cabin with her,' Dale explained. 'I was horrified I'd got to share with her when we first met. She's one of those Alice in Wonderland girls, all big eyes and flowing hair. She was dressed in baby pink, and I thought she'd never read anything but *Hello!*, talk endlessly about conditioners and ring her mum up to find out what was happening in *Coronation Street*. But she wasn't like that, she was just the sweetest, kindest, most brilliant friend I've ever had.'

Dale was surprised that she was publicly admitting how much she liked Lotte. There had been a time in her life when she mistook using someone for having a friend, but Lotte had made her see what real friendship was all about.

'The three of us did everything together,' Scott butted in. 'Not just going ashore for booze-ups, but nights talking together and stuff. But then something terrible happened to her in South America.'

'What?' Rosie and Michelle asked in unison.

Scott looked at Dale for support. They had never discussed whether or not they ought to keep quiet about this matter, but there didn't seem to be any harm in telling the people they shared a home with.

'She was raped,' Dale said quietly, understanding Scott's dilemma.

'Raped? Who by? Someone on the ship?' Michelle asked.

'No, it was some nutter in Ushuaia – that's right down as far south as you can go, the last place before the Antarctic,' Scott explained. 'In broad daylight too! She was never quite the same again, and Dale and I felt terrible that we had left her to go ashore alone.'

'Poor girl,' Frankie said in sympathy. 'So what happened to her when she left the ship? Are you serious that this girl in the paper could be her?'

'She was going home to her parents in Brighton when we said goodbye,' Dale explained. 'We all promised to keep in touch, and I did phone and text her, and so did Scott, but she never replied. I guess Scott and I were unwanted reminders of that terrible ordeal.'

'It's pure coincidence that a year on we've ended up near Brighton too,' Scott added. 'I suppose if so much time hadn't passed since the cruise we'd probably have gone and looked her up. But there didn't seem much point as she didn't appear to want to know.'

'If you think this is her,' Frankie said, pointing at the picture, 'you should ring the police.'

'We'd look pretty silly if it wasn't,' Scott retorted. 'But maybe we ought to get in touch with her parents and just check up on her?'

'Ring them now,' Frankie suggested.

'We haven't got a number for them,' Scott said, 'just an address she gave Dale. We tried to get a number from directory inquiries, but they were ex-directory.'

'We could go tomorrow,' Dale said impulsively. 'I've got no appointments booked till the afternoon, and it's your day off, Scott. We could catch the nine-thirty bus.'

'I'd ring the police,' Frankie said with a disapproving sniff. 'For one thing, her poor parents might be looking at that same picture right now and if they don't know where their daughter is they'll be freaking out. You don't want to walk in on that! And besides, Dale, if Marisa finds out you've bunked off she'll go ape shit.'

'If her parents do think it's Lotte too, then they'll need the comfort of someone who cared about her,' Dale said stubbornly. 'And as for Marisa, you lot aren't going to grass me up, are you?'

'Of course not,' they chorused as one. 'She's not due back till the afternoon, but if she does get back early what will we say?'

'That I had to go to the dentist as I had a bad tooth-ache,' Dale suggested.

'Is it a good idea to go barging in on her parents?' Scott asked Dale much later that evening just before they went to bed. 'I can understand you wanting to check with them before going to the police. But what if they haven't seen Lotte for a couple of weeks, and haven't seen the picture tonight? They are going to flip with horror and shock and we'll be there in the middle of it. The police know how to handle that sort of thing, we don't.'

'We could just ask for Lotte,' Dale said. 'Make like it's just a social call. If she's off at work then we can just leave a message for her to ring us and leave. But if they haven't seen her for some time, then we either show them the girl in the paper or go straight to the police, depending on how strong we think her folks are.'

Scott shrugged. 'On your head be it if they freak out!'

Chapter Two

'I always imagined Lotte coming from a leafy suburban area,' Dale remarked as the taxi turned off from the seafront into a street of terraced houses with no front gardens. She and Scott had caught the bus into Brighton but then picked up a taxi when they discovered Lotte's road was some distance away.

Scott looked thoughtfully out of the taxi window at the slightly seedy houses. 'Me too! I got the idea her childhood had been very sheltered, playing with dolls on the lawn and board games at night.'

Many of the houses in the street were downmarket guest houses. They had dull paint on their front doors and vases of artificial flowers in their windows, and Dale imagined the breakfasts would be greasy, the beds lumpy, and hot water in short supply. It was only a few streets back from the seafront, but a world apart from the smart hotels there. To Dale it was a reminder that Brighton had once had the reputation of being the place for a 'dirty weekend'; she could imagine all those Mr and Mrs Smiths flocking here in the Forties and Fifties.

Lotte's house, number 12, had nets at the windows and the front door was painted bright yellow. Parked outside was a small white van with 'E. G. Wainwright, plumber. Corgi approved' painted on the side in black.

'Thank God her dad's in,' Scott said as he paid the taxi fare. 'If her mum freaks he'll be there to sort it.'

Dale stopped Scott before he rang the doorbell. 'Just remember we aren't going to shove the picture under their noses! If things look bad we'll just shoot off and leave it to the police.'

Mr Wainwright opened the door to them. He was a tall, slender man of around fifty-five, with the same blue eyes as Lotte but thinning hair. He was wearing jeans and a sweatshirt which were clearly his working clothes as they were worn and stained.

'We worked on the cruise ship with Lotte,' Dale said, then introduced herself and Scott. 'But we haven't heard from her since, so as we are working near here now we thought we'd look her up.'

The man frowned. 'You'd better come in. The wife's out the back doing a spot of weeding, I'll get her.'

He led them down the narrow hall past a closed door which probably led to the lounge, then into a large sunny kitchen-cum-dining room. It was a bit old-fashioned, with green cupboards and patterned Formica worktops, but very neat and tidy.

Through the patio door they could see a small but very pretty and well-cared-for garden. Mrs Wainwright was bending down weeding a bed of tulips.

Mr Wainwright went out to her. As she straightened

up to listen to what her husband was saying, she looked back at the kitchen.

'She's a lot older than my mum,' Dale said in surprise. 'She looks well over sixty. And they obviously haven't seen the picture in the paper, or at least don't believe it's her, or her dad would have said something.'

Scott didn't have a chance to reply because the couple were coming indoors. Mrs Wainwright was plump and around five feet four, her face heavily lined and her short hair snow-white. She wore the kind of acrylic slacks and sweater normally associated with much older women, but she had a sprightly step, covering the twenty yards or so very quickly.

'We're sorry to interrupt your gardening,' Dale began. 'But Scott and I wanted to get in touch with Lotte.'

'You'll have a hard job, she's off on the high seas,' Mrs Wainwright said.

'She signed up for another cruise then?' Dale said in some surprise. Lotte had said she'd never do it again. 'The one we met on ended last year in March. How much longer after that before she went back?'

'Back?' The woman frowned. 'She left Brighton over two years ago and hasn't been back since.'

Dale looked at Scott. She didn't know where to go from there.

'When we left the cruise ship,' Scott took over, speaking slowly as if he was thinking carefully before letting the wrong thing slip, 'she said she was coming back here to you.'

'I don't know why she'd tell you that,' Mrs Wainwright said, turning to the sink to wash her hands. 'She hasn't lived here for years. We've hardly seen or heard from her since she moved out. The only reason she told us she was going to work on a cruise ship was because she wanted us to store some of her things.'

Scott and Dale looked at each other in concern. They had talked over various possible outcomes of this visit, but they hadn't for one moment expected such coldness from Lotte's mother. It was as if she had no interest in her daughter.

'Do you know where she is right now?' Scott asked.

'Haven't a clue,' her father said. 'We had a couple of postcards way back.' He went over to a noticeboard and removed a card. 'This one was from San Francisco, she'd just joined the ship then, and the other was from Trinidad. Nothing since.'

'But she told me she rang you,' Dale said, remembering Christmas and other occasions when Lotte had said she'd rung home. She also said she spoke to her parents after the rape. 'Why would she tell me that if it wasn't true?'

'She was always a compulsive liar,' Mrs Wainwright said sharply. 'I expect she told you her favourite Cinderella story too, that we were mean to her, that no one cares about her. That's her usual bleat.'

Dale was not only shocked that Mrs Wainwright could tell a complete stranger private family business, she also felt angry that the woman was maligning someone she cared for.

'Lotte never "bleated" about anything,' she retorted. 'But now we've met you I'd guess she was ashamed that she had such uncaring parents and never had any intention of coming home to you. If I'd known the situation with you, I would've taken her home to my mother.'

'What's it got to do with you?' Mrs Wainwright asked, sticking out her lip. 'I don't like your attitude, my girl!'

'I think I ought to explain we feel especially protective towards Lotte because she was raped in South America,' Scott said, looking from the wife to the husband. He paused for a couple of seconds, expecting they would gasp with shock. But they didn't, only stared at him blankly. 'It was a terrible thing, it shocked everyone on the ship,' he went on. 'It happened in broad daylight, the man was a total stranger to her. I take it she didn't tell you?'

Dale looked at Mrs Wainwright, fully expecting her to burst into tears. But she didn't, she just stood there in the middle of her kitchen, seemingly as unconcerned as if they'd just told her Lotte had dyed her hair red.

'She'll have made that up,' she said after a second or two's thought. 'She always tried to get my attention any way she could.'

'What?' Dale exclaimed, unable to believe the woman could say such a thing. 'Mrs Wainwright, the man was caught in the act! A couple who were guests on the ship heard her screams and ran to her. She was examined by the ship's doctor who confirmed it. The man hit her, terrified her even before he attacked her. And you think she would make that up?'

To give Mr Wainwright his due, he did look shaken and he took a couple of steps closer to his wife, almost as if seeking her protection. But she just stood there looking at Dale with a cynical expression.

'Good God, woman! Is your heart made of stone?' Dale said contemptuously.

'At least we know now why she didn't tell you.' Scott shook his head in disbelief. 'She knew you'd be like this, didn't she?'

He looked at them expectantly, hoping for a denial, but none came. 'Why don't you care?' he asked and pointed to the wall in the dining alcove which had at least twenty photographs of Lotte as a little girl. 'How can you keep all those pictures up there, look at them every day, but not care where she is or what has happened to her?'

'That isn't Lotte,' Mr Wainwright exclaimed indignantly. 'That's our Fleur. She was taken from us when she was ten. I can't imagine why you'd think it was Lotte, Fleur was pretty and so talented.'

Dale's mouth fell open as it dawned on her what this strange, cold couple were all about.

'Was Fleur older or younger?' she asked.

'Older by four years,' Mr Wainwright said. 'It broke our hearts when she died. She was so special, she could dance and sing, she won so many competitions. As pretty as a picture too, smart as new paint, and everyone loved her.'

'And you were angry that you were left with just Lotte?' Dale said with sarcastic incredulity.

'Don't you take that tone with me, my girl!' Mrs Wainwright snapped. 'She could never measure up to her older sister, not in talent, looks or brains.'

'Excuse me, but Lotte is one of the prettiest, kindest, most hardworking girls I've ever met,' Dale retorted, her voice rising in indignation. 'She's a star in her own right. How could you be so cruel as to shut her out?'

'So she did tell you some tall tales about us then?' Mrs Wainwright stepped nearer to Dale, her mouth pursed with malice.

'Oh yes, Mrs Wainwright! She told me some tall tales all right. She portrayed you as loving parents and her childhood idyllic,' Dale said, sticking her face right up into the older woman's. 'My God, I understand now why she couldn't bear to come home. I wouldn't either with parents like you.'

Scott pulled the newspaper from his pocket, smoothed it out and shoved it at Mr Wainwright. 'Is that Lotte?' he asked.

The man took the paper in both hands and frowned as he looked at it. 'I don't know. It's like her, but then I haven't seen her for over two years.'

Scott explained curtly what was known about the girl found on the beach. 'We think it is Lotte, though we hoped you'd be able to say otherwise. So now we must go to the police and tell them.'

Dale hesitated before making for the door. She had

had many blazing rows with her own mother, and there had been things said on both sides which weren't very nice. Dale wanted to believe this was the case with Mrs Wainwright, and that once the enormity of what had happened to Lotte filtered through to her, normal maternal instincts would kick in.

But the older woman's face remained cold and tense. There was no way she was going to back down and show some emotion.

'I daresay the police will be right round to see you,' Scott said. 'You should of course be heading down to the station to see them, and then on to the hospital to see your daughter. But we'll tell the police how little you care about her!'

Once outside the house Dale exploded. 'What evil bastards! I can't believe anyone could be that unmoved by their daughter's rape and possible attempted murder. Poor, poor Lotte!'

Scott's lip trembled with sorrow for Lotte and indignation that anyone could be so callous. 'You know, I thought it was odd that her parents didn't come to Southampton to meet her off the ship. That's what mine would have done if one of my sisters was raped. In fact, I think they would've chartered a helicopter to lift her off right after it happened.'

'My mum asked if Mrs Wainwright had come to the ship,' Dale said. 'I kind of glossed over it. I pointed out that Lotte had another month on the ship after the rape, and therefore she was beginning to get over it. Mum said it wasn't something you got over in a month.'

Down at the police station Dale and Scott were ushered into an interview room with a CID officer. He was a short, wiry man of about forty with thinning brown hair.

Dale got out a couple of photographs of Lotte she'd taken on the cruise, gave them to him and explained that she thought this was the mystery girl found on the beach.

'There were several calls last night and again this morning from people claiming they knew the identity of the girl,' the officer said as he studied the pictures. 'Most had no substance to them, but we have to check them all out. If you'll bear with me while I take down some details, and if you don't mind leaving us these other photographs, we'll look into it.'

The man kept them less than fifteen minutes. All he wanted at this stage of the investigation was to know where they last saw Lotte, their relationship with her, and the names and addresses of any friends or family known to them.

'We don't know much about her life before the cruise,' Dale said sadly, suddenly ashamed she hadn't asked Lotte more about herself. 'She is one of those people who would rather listen than talk. She was a hairdresser here in Brighton, but apart from that we know nothing more about her.'

'Now we know what her parents are like we aren't surprised she didn't talk about the past,' Scott added, giving the officer their address and a brief rundown on how they had reacted. 'Don't expect much help from them if this girl on the beach does turn out to be Lotte. They don't appear to care at all.'

Scott stayed on in Brighton as he had some shopping to do, but Dale caught the next bus back to Marchwood, arriving there just after one. The meeting with the Wainwrights had made her feel very anxious and sad, but she put on her uniform and went straight to the spa.

'Anyone miss me?' she asked Rosie who was just finishing off a manicure.

'No. But I'm glad you got back because you've got a facial booked in half an hour's time,' Rosie said with a smile. 'Was the mystery girl your friend?'

'It looks that way but we won't know for sure until the police check it out. Tell you everything later,' Dale said as she opened the appointments book to see what kind of facial her client had booked.

She was putting water into a facial steam bath when Marisa walked into the treatment room.

'I hope you had a good morning in Brighton,' she said, her voice taut with spite. 'Don't bother with the dentist story, I know it's not true.'

Dale gulped. 'OK. I only said that because it was the first thing I thought of. In fact I had to go to the police.

You see, I read in the newspaper that there was a mystery girl found on a beach suffering from amnesia, and I think she's someone I worked with on the cruise ship.'

'Is that so?' Marisa said coldly. 'Wouldn't a phone call have worked just as well? Or you could have let Scott handle it for both of you? I presume he knew her too?'

'I suppose I could have done either of those things, but we thought we ought to go and see the girl's parents first before we contacted the police.'

'I take a dim view of staff who disappear when my back is turned. I need absolute reliability in the spa.'

'I wouldn't have gone if I'd had any bookings,' Dale said. 'And I'm sorry I went without your permission. I could make the time up to you by working my day off.'

'The fact remains that you let me and the whole team down,' Marisa said.

Dale was prepared to eat a certain amount of humble pie, but she thought this had gone on long enough.

'With all due respect, Marisa, this girl found on the beach may have survived an attempted murder or abduction,' she snapped back. 'I was ninety per cent certain I knew who she was. So I had a duty to inform both her parents and the police. It wasn't as if I nipped out for something trivial.'

'You have an unfortunate manner in that you presume you know best about everything,' Marisa responded, her eyes narrowing. 'It may very well be your undoing.'

She turned on her heel and walked away, leaving Dale feeling distinctly uneasy.

The remainder of the day was difficult. Dale was kept busy because there was a wedding at the hotel the next day. Many of the guests on arriving to stay for the weekend and discovering the spa, wanted to have all manner of treatments. Becky the receptionist had booked in two women for inch-loss wraps with Dale, not realizing how long they took. In the end she was forced to run between the two women, while squeezing in a pedicure and a manicure on two others as well.

In an attempt to appease Marisa, for she really didn't want to lose her job, Dale volunteered to stay on until eight that evening. By the time she'd had some supper and got back to the bungalow, all she wanted was her bed. But sleep evaded her, for like the previous night, images of Lotte kept flashing into her mind.

But those images had mainly been of the good times, the crew's parties and days ashore. Now, after learning that her friend didn't have loving parents as she'd always supposed, the images were all of that day when Lotte was raped.

Everything was so vivid still. She could recall waking that morning and sleepily pulling back the curtain without remembering that she was stark naked, or that the ship had docked late on the previous evening in Ushuaia. There, just feet away from her porthole, were men waiting to unload waste and bring on supplies and they all saw her.

She screamed involuntarily and hastily tugged the curtain back over the porthole. But she was too late – the men were all grinning and a couple of them made rude gestures with their fists.

Lotte was lying awake in her bunk and laughed at Dale's predicament.

'You've done it now,' she said. 'They'll be waiting for you when you go ashore.'

Dale could only giggle in embarrassment. She didn't know why she hadn't noticed the ship's engines were quiet, or the noise from the port. If she had, she would've kept the curtains closed as all the staff cabins were so low in the ship they were always on the level with the dock when they went into port.

'I can't wait to go ashore,' Lotte said, bounding out of bed and grabbing her towel to go and have a shower. 'Shame I've got a lot of blowdries to do before I can go. I won't be able to leave until around one. What about you? Any treatments booked?'

'One massage in an hour, that's all, everyone's going off on trips. But I can't face going ashore with you, Lotte. I saw Ushuaia the last time round, and it wasn't very exciting then. Anyway, I'm so tired I just want to go back to bed and stay there all day.'

'That's OK,' Lotte said cheerfully. 'I only want to go and see the old prison and walk about a bit. I don't need anyone with me.'

The girls had a quick breakfast together and then parted, Lotte for the hairdressing salon, Dale to put some washing in a machine before it was time for the massage booked in at the salon.

Dale was sleeping when Lotte came back to the cabin at lunchtime. She was so quiet changing her clothes that Dale only woke when she was about to leave, and sleepily asked her to buy a couple of postcards for her. Lotte was wearing jeans tucked into cowboy boots and a thin pink sweater and she had a light waterproof jacket slung over the top of her shoulder bag. As usual when she wasn't working, her hair was loose. Dale remembered thinking as she went out of the door that it looked like a curtain of shiny molten gold.

Everyone on the ship had to work very long hours, whether they were officers, stewards, cabin maids, barmen, waitresses, entertainers or crew. The passengers were probably completely unaware that the staff numbered the population of a village and that they lived in very cramped conditions in two decks below their cabins.

Furthermore, this huge number of people came from dozens of different countries and cultures, some not even speaking very good English. It was impressed on all of them when they joined the ship that they had to get along with one another, or it would become a nightmare scenario.

Because of this, people tended to party more than they should. Whatever time they finished work, they would want to drink and socialize and it often went on till the early hours. As a result, after a few weeks many of them were so tired they had no alternative but to take to their bunks when they had a few spare hours. Going ashore became less attractive the second time around anyway; the ports down the Chilean coast were small and dull, and although the passengers took coaches further afield to see ranches, whales, penguins and other sights, the staff and crew stayed behind.

So that afternoon, while almost all the passengers were going on boat trips to see the sea lions and sea birds of the Beagle Channel, the remains of the old Ushuaia penal colony and the train the convicts used to haul the wood they chopped, Dale and a good proportion of the staff and crew were sleeping.

Dale was woken by a rapping on her cabin door. When she glanced at her watch she was shocked to see that it was gone seven in the evening.

'Coming!' she yelled as she clambered down from the top bunk. She assumed Lotte had forgotten her key, or else it was Scott wanting some company for dinner.

Opening the door just a crack, she saw it was Atkins, one of the ship's officers, so she hastily snatched up a robe to cover her bra and pants.

'What can I do for you, sir?' she asked as she opened the door properly.

Atkins was a tall, skinny man, around forty-five, with dark hair and a rather stern look about him. Dale had never had an occasion to exchange more than a few pleasantries with him for he dealt with the guests rather than the staff or crew. She couldn't imagine what he wanted with her now.

'There has been an incident in the port,' he began haltingly. 'Lotte Wainwright, your cabin mate, was involved.'

An 'incident' usually meant a fight or something, but she couldn't imagine Lotte becoming involved; she was the kind to run a mile from such things.

'Is Lotte hurt?' she asked.

'She was attacked,' he said baldly.

It was the man's obvious embarrassment that suggested Lotte's injuries were of a delicate nature, and suddenly Dale was frightened. She caught hold of his arm.

'Please, sir, tell me exactly what happened. Was this some kind of sexual attack?'

He hung his head. 'Yes, I'm afraid so. She was raped.'

For a second Dale could only stare open-mouthed at the man. She had a reputation among her friends for being hard and unsympathetic, something she was the first to admit to. But Lotte had an air of fragility about her and a kind of childish innocence that made Dale, and most other people, want to protect her.

'Raped?' she repeated, tears filling her eyes and her legs buckling under her. 'Oh, my God!' she gasped, covering her face with her hands in horror. 'Where is she now?'

'Two of our guests, Mr and Mrs Ramsden, brought her back to the ship. It appears they rescued Lotte from her assailant. Mrs Ramsden hit him over the head with a bottle of wine. They insisted on taking her to their suite. Dr Bailey is with her now and we are awaiting more information from the Ushuaia police. I understand they have apprehended the man.'

Dale tried to pull herself together although she felt dizzy with shock. 'Can I see her?' she asked.

Atkins shook his head. 'She did ask for you to be informed, but Dr Bailey feels she has enough to cope with for now without visitors.'

'But I know her a great deal better than the Ramsdens. We've been best friends and cabin mates for the best part of a year.'

Atkins' face softened. 'I know, but as they rescued her I'm sure she feels secure with them, and Dr Bailey must think so too, otherwise he'd have sent her to the staff sick bay. Now, if you would just get a few of her things together. Nightwear, a change of clothing and toiletries. She's going to stay with the Ramsdens overnight.'

Dale went back into the cabin, leaving Atkins standing at the door.

Lotte was exceptionally tidy-minded. She kept her pyjamas under her pillow, dressing gown behind the door, and everything else neatly folded in the chest of drawers or hanging in the wardrobe. Dale, who was an extremely untidy person herself, had often teased Lotte about it, calling her obsessive, but now, as she effortlessly picked out the things her friend needed, she saw the sense in it and felt guilty about her jibes. She also felt very guilty that she'd let Lotte go ashore alone today.

Dale handed the small packed bag to the officer. 'Will you give her my love and say how sorry I am?' she said, her voice shaking with emotion. 'If there's anything I can do . . .' She broke off as tears overtook her.

'I'll pass on your message,' he said. 'Please be discreet about this, Miss Moore, we don't want the guests to feel threatened or uncomfortable.'

Dale was the kind who would normally rage against such a request, for she was fiery, opinionated and outspoken. She wanted to retort that Lotte must be feeling far more than threatened and uncomfortable, but this one time she kept quiet. Atkins was after all only doing his job.

Dale knew who Fern Ramsden was because she'd given her a facial the day after she and her husband boarded the ship in Santiago, just over a week earlier. Dale hadn't liked the glamorous, statuesque red-headed American much because she seemed terribly full of herself.

But Lotte had done her hair almost daily, either putting it up for a formal evening, or washing and blow-drying it. It seemed to Dale the woman was exceptionally vain to spend so much time on her hair, but then, many of the rich women on the cruise were the same. Whatever Fern Ramsden was or wasn't, however, Dale was impressed she could crack a bottle of wine over a rapist's head, and she was very touched the woman wanted to care for Lotte.

As it was, it was mid-afternoon the following day

before Dale got to see her friend. She had passed a sleepless night worrying about her, and in the early hours of the morning when the engines started up to sail away from Ushuaia, she went up on deck to walk around and try to clear her head.

Lotte was not Dale's usual kind of friend. In fact, when they first met and found they were expected to share a cabin, Dale had been dismayed.

A Barbie Doll was what sprang to mind, for Lotte had the kind of wide blue eyes that usually spelled vacuous, a pixie face framed by pure blonde hair, and she was even wearing a pink fluffy angora jumper, denim mini skirt and pink cowboy boots. Dale imagined her arranging teddy bears on her bunk, constantly phoning home and giggling incessantly.

But it transpired Lotte wasn't vacuous. She might have looked like some people's idea of a stereotypical hairdresser, but she thought deeply, was a great listener, and had more understanding of people's frailties than anyone else Dale had ever met. Her taste in books was quite highbrow; she liked to know what was going on in the world, and always tried to find an English newspaper while in port.

Lotte liked order, Dale was incapable of it, so Lotte elected to keep the cabin neat and tidy, and never once groused about it. She would wash, iron and mend both their clothes, yet there was nothing sanctimonious about her, for she loved drinking, dancing and flirting as much as Dale did.

Many a time they'd seen the early morning sun come up while they were still talking. They'd lied for each other when they couldn't work because they had hangovers, stuck up for each other when they were accused of trying to pinch someone's man, and Dale would never forget how when she had a bad stomach upset Lotte stayed and held the sick bowl for her.

Dale was at the door of the Ramsdens' cabin before nine, desperate to see Lotte before she began her work. She needed the details of what had happened to her friend, and to know she was going to recover. But Fern Ramsden sent her packing, saying Lotte was still asleep.

Dale was probably being irrational in deciding then and there that Fern was a control freak who wanted to keep Lotte all to herself and believed Dale to be a bad influence on her. But the woman had an imperious way of looking at her, with no warmth in her duck egg-blue eyes. Surely any woman would understand how distraught all Lotte's friends were, and particularly Dale who had spent almost a year doing everything with her?

It was OK that Lotte was sleeping, Dale didn't expect the woman to wake her, but just a little information – whether she'd managed to sleep during the night, if she was physically hurt in any way – just woman-to-woman stuff, that was all she wanted.

Dale was back at ten-thirty between clients to be told

Lotte was in the bath. At twelve-thirty she was having a nap. But at four, when Dale was getting angry enough to kick the door down, Fern finally let her in.

Dale had no idea what to expect, but it was an awful shock to see Lotte lying on the couch looking terribly battered and crushed. Not just the hideous black eye, the swollen lip and the stiff movements which spoke of other hidden injuries; it was as if all the joy in her had been snatched away, leaving a frightened, pale wraith in her place.

'Just ten minutes, honey,' Fern commanded.

Fern Ramsden was the kind of woman it would be impossible to overlook. She was around five foot eight, with a voluptuous figure and very good legs. That day she wore a jade-green low-necked sweater dress with a gold chain belt and gold sandals. The colour of the dress enhanced her red hair and her golden tan. While she was probably well over forty, she could easily pass for thirty. But Dale felt irritated by the older woman looking so stunningly attractive when poor Lotte looked so bad; that seemed cruel.

'Oh my God, Lotte, what a terrible thing to happen to you! I can hardly believe it,' Dale blurted out. 'But how are you feeling now? Did you sleep OK? Are you in pain anywhere?'

'She doesn't want questions thrown at her,' Fern interrupted. 'If you want to stay, just sit quietly with her.'

Until then Dale was prepared to believe this woman

was a saint because she'd rescued her friend. But now she was being treated like an irritating child, Dale's gratitude to Fern and her husband faded, and she began to resent her.

She needed to tell Lotte how she felt about the terrible thing that had happened to her, but she couldn't articulate it when the woman was standing close by, timing her visit. All she could do was hold her friend and sob out that she wished she hadn't let her go ashore alone and that she wanted to take care of her.

'That sure is impossible,' Fern chimed in, and now her drawling American accent had a touch of steel to it. 'You gotta work, Dale honey, and Lotte needs rest and quiet if she's to recover.'

'I'll be fine in a day or two,' Lotte said bravely, smoothing back Dale's hair from her face, as if she were the victim who needed comforting. 'I'm on the mend already. Now, don't you worry about me, and give all the girls in the salon my love and apologize for letting all the clients down.'

'But tell me how he did it,' Dale begged her. 'I mean, where were you and how did he get hold of you?'

'That's enough now,' Fern butted in, catching hold of Dale's arm none too gently. 'Lotte doesn't want to relive the whole thing again. Time you went.'

Maybe Fern was right, but by the agonized look in Lotte's eyes as Dale was ushered out, she was sure her friend would rather have talked it through.

*

Dale felt as if she was awake all night reliving the events of that day in Ushuaia, but she must have dropped off to sleep eventually because the ringing of her alarm clock woke her with a start at seven the next morning. She got up immediately, aware that she would need to look bright-eyed and bushy-tailed as many of the wedding party guests were booked in for manicures this morning before the service, and Marisa would be watching her closely.

But she didn't feel like it. Those dreadfully upsetting images of Lotte through the night had left an ache inside her. She was silently praying this girl on the beach wasn't her friend, she'd been through too much already, yet a sixth sense told her it was.

By quarter to eight Dale was in the spa getting her nail trolley set up for the first client, due at eight, when Scott came in dressed in his shorts and singlet for the gym.

They had managed only the briefest of conversations when he got back from Brighton the previous day, and that was about Marisa discovering that Dale had gone out without permission.

'I hope the police contact us today,' he said, rubbing his eyes. 'I can't stand just waiting for news. If that girl on the beach is Lotte, where's she been all this time? Why didn't she ever ring us and tell us where she was?'

Dale went over to him and gave him a hug. His sensitivity was one of his best traits. She doubted many men of his age, especially good-looking ones, would care much about what had happened to a girl who'd only been a friend.

'Maybe we'll find out soon,' she said hopefully.

Chapter Three

Just after three in the afternoon Becky the receptionist came over to Dale while she was giving a client a manicure. 'There's a policeman wants to speak to you,' she said, her sharp features sharper still with pent-up curiosity.

Dale smiled at her client, an attractive brunette in her fifties, and continued to paint her nails. 'Don't worry, he doesn't want to arrest me,' she joked. 'And he can wait until we're finished.'

She turned to Becky. 'Give him a coffee and tell him I'll be five minutes,' she said.

The display of calm was completely false. Dale could barely manage to control her shaking hand to put a sealing coat on her client's nails. 'I expect you saw the story in the news about the woman found on Selsey beach suffering from memory loss?' she said. 'Well, I think she might be a friend of mine. I'm hoping this policeman can either confirm or deny it.'

'Oh, you poor thing!' the woman exclaimed. 'I wouldn't have blamed you if you'd run off and left me only half done.'

'My clients are too important to me to do that,' Dale said silkily, hoping it might get back to Marisa. But making that rather phoney statement reminded her that

Lotte had always really cared deeply for her clients. On Christmas Eve on the cruise she had worked from seven-thirty in the morning till after nine at night without a proper break all day, just to get everyone's hair done. Not for the tips it brought, but just to see her clients' pleasure. She was unique; no other hairdresser cared that much.

Dale fastened her client's wristwatch for her and helped her into her jacket. 'Sit for a while in reception and let your nails harden,' she suggested. 'Becky will get you a cup of coffee if you want one. And have a lovely time tonight. You won't mind if I rush off now, will you?'

The woman thanked her effusively and begged her to go. Dale sped off and was told by Becky that the policeman was waiting for her in the bar.

The bar was closed until five so there was no one there but the plainclothes officer sitting by the window. He was in his mid to late thirties, with wide shoulders, light brown curly hair and a fresh complexion.

'I'm Dale Moore,' she said, holding out her hand. He smiled; his eyes were an unusual tawny colour. At any other time her heart would have leapt for he was very nice-looking.

'Detective Inspector Bryan,' he said, shaking her hand. 'I hope calling on you here didn't upset anyone?'

'I don't care much if it did,' she said, sitting down opposite him. 'Now tell me. Is the girl from the beach my friend Lotte?'

'Yes, she is; her father was able to positively identify her at the hospital,' he said. 'But she hasn't as yet regained any memory – she didn't even know her parents.'

'So you don't know how she got there, or what happened to her?'

'We think it's likely she jumped from a boat. She could of course have been pushed, but it's all a bit mysterious as there were rope marks on her wrists and ankles. You wouldn't expect anyone to remove the bonds if they were intending to push her in! There again, she could have just walked into the sea because she was in some kind of crisis. So until she remembers or we get information from other people who had seen her recently, we're very much in the dark.'

'Is she going to be OK?'

'She is weak, suffering from hypothermia and exhaustion, but her loss of memory is the most troubling aspect.'

'Can I do anything to help?'

Bryan nodded. 'I was hoping you might have some success in stimulating her memory.'

'I'd like to try,' Dale agreed. 'Though you may have to charm the supervisor here to give me permission, that is, if I have to go in working hours.'

'That will be Marisa De Vere?' He arched one eyebrow.

Dale nodded. 'She doesn't like me much already, so please don't give her anything further to hold against me.'

Bryan smiled. 'She was a little frosty when I arrived

here and asked to speak to you. I thought I could take you to the hospital later, as I understand you don't have any more clients this afternoon?'

Dale agreed that was so.

'If you could tell me everything you know of Lotte,' he said, getting out his notepad. 'Her friends other than yourself, family members she kept in touch with, favourite places she might have mentioned. But first, could you confirm the date you last saw her?'

'It was the sixteenth of March, last year.'

'Where was that?'

'On the cruise ship, the morning we were all leaving. She shot off earlier than most of us, around ten in the morning.'

'And she said she was going straight home to her parents in Brighton?'

'That's right, she did,' Dale nodded. 'And I had no reason to doubt it because she was bubbly and excited on the last day. It looks to me now that she must've already arranged to go somewhere else, but I can't imagine why she didn't tell me, she was such an open person normally. Or at least, so I thought until I found out what her parents were like. She kept that from me too.'

'They certainly are a couple of cold fish,' DI Bryan agreed, shaking his head as if bewildered by them.

'Maybe it will be as well if Lotte never remembers about them,' Dale said. 'Or that she was raped in South America.'

The policeman raised his eyebrows quizzically and Dale felt embarrassed.

'Don't tell me you hadn't already found out about that?' she said.

'Yes and no. Mrs Wainwright told me you'd said she was, but she and her husband didn't seem to believe it. I got someone to contact the cruise line for their full report, but until that comes through it would be helpful if you'd tell me about it.'

'It was in Ushuaia in South America, but I only know the bare bones. Lotte didn't tell me anything until a week or more after it happened, and she was still reluctant to talk. She'd gone ashore alone, and apparently the man spoke to her outside a shop. He asked if she would go for a drink with him, or let him show her round. He was South American – I believe he was a native of Ushuaia and not quite the full shilling. Lotte turned him down.'

'Would she have been rude to him?'

Dale shook her head. 'No way, she didn't like to hurt anyone's feelings. Anyway, she cut up the back of town, and the next thing she knows he's coming towards her in a very quiet residential street. He caught hold of her and hauled her back against a shed or garage and hit her when she struggled. He'd got her down on the ground and was actually raping her when Mr and Mrs Ramsden came along. They had apparently heard her scream. I think Mr Ramsden hit the man with a post or something and his wife followed up by breaking a bottle of wine over his head. They got Lotte away and took her back to the ship.'

'She must have been very indebted to these people?' the policeman said.

'Oh, she was. They took care of her in their suite for a week,' Dale said. 'They didn't let anyone else get near her.'

'How did you feel about that?' Bryan asked.

Dale blushed; she felt he'd looked into her soul. 'A bit shut out. I appreciated that Fern, that's Mrs Ramsden, was taking good care of her, but she was so full on, like intense. I couldn't even talk to Lotte alone. And I didn't like the religious stuff either.'

'She was religious?'

'Well, yes. That happy, clappy sort, getting down on your knees and praising God stuff, not the basic Protestant thing. She was very fond of telling Lotte she had to put her trust in Jesus. I felt that if Jesus had been around that day he could have prevented the rape.'

Bryan looked thoughtful. 'How would you describe their attitude to Lotte?'

Dale sucked in her cheeks. 'Well, I'm a bit biased because I resented them not letting me in to see her and that. But it was like they owned her. It made me feel really uncomfortable around them. But then I felt bad thinking that way because I knew they were helping her, and if it hadn't been for them she'd have been stuck in the sick bay without much TLC.'

'And Lotte's views?'

'Oh, she thought they were her doctors, counsellors, friends, parents, all rolled into one. She wouldn't have a word said against them.'

'How long was she with them before she went back to work? She did go back, I assume?'

Dale nodded. 'Yes, a week later.'

'Was she ready for that?' Bryan sounded surprised.

'She'd have got cabin fever without it, I think,' Dale said. 'Hairdressing was more than a job to Lotte, it was her passion; she needed the creativity and her clients. So she returned to share the cabin with me and we went back to most of the old stuff, going ashore, chatting into the night, her doing my hair, me doing her nails.'

'Are you saying she was really over it?'

'No, not at all. She made out she was, went about everything in the same old way, but I could sense her pain just below the surface. It was my opinion that she needed to tell me the details of what happened to truly get over it. By that I mean describing him, how he smelled, exactly what he did and said to her. But she wouldn't. I think that was because she felt a great deal of shame, like it was her fault. Telling me would've done her more good than running up to the Ramsdens' suite for a few prayers!'

He grimaced, and Dale made a despairing gesture with her hands. 'I wouldn't have thought anything of her going off to the ship's chapel, or saying a few silent prayers in bed. But she used to get on her knees in the cabin and say them out loud. It gave me the creeps.'

'And the Ramsdens instigated all this?'

'Completely. She never so much as mentioned God or Jesus until the rape.'

'So she could well have stayed in contact with this couple after she left the ship?'

'I'm sure she did, but they were Americans and going home, so the contact would've been limited to writing letters or phone calls. I mean, she couldn't drop in on them for a cup of tea.'

'Did this couple put her in touch with a religious group?'

Dale stared at him in surprise. 'You don't think she was sucked into one of those crazy sects, do you?'

Bryan smiled. 'It's a possibility we'll be looking into, though I don't know of one operating along the south coast. Was there anyone else on the ship she made friends with and might have gone to?'

Dale thought hard for a couple of minutes. 'No, there was only Scott and me. We were a little unit. She knew lots of other people, she exchanged phone numbers and addresses like we all did, but I can't see her going off with anyone else.'

'So you had absolutely no contact from the day you left the ship, the sixteenth of March 2002?'

'That's right,' Dale agreed. 'She never phoned or even texted me or Scott after we left the ship. I kept on and on leaving messages for her to ring, but after a bit the line seemed dead, like the battery had run out.'

'How would you describe Lotte's character and personality?' he asked.

'She was quiet. The kind that sits back and observes. A giver rather than a taker. A listener not a talker. Kind, sensitive to others' needs, generous and warm.'

'She sounds nice.' Bryan smiled.

'She was lovely. Is lovely,' Dale quickly corrected herself. 'She might look like a Barbie Doll, but she's real and very organized. A bit gullible maybe – back then she took everyone at face value and I don't think she had much idea of her own worth. Of course now I've met her parents, that explains that.'

'Would you call her impetuous?'

'No, not at all.' Dale shook her head. 'She wasn't one for jumping into anything, even buying something impulsively. Definitely not a risk taker! I always had the idea that once she met the right man she'd settle down and have several children and never stray.'

'Did she tell you of any past boyfriends?'

'No. But I got the idea there had been someone important. She wasn't entirely innocent, despite looking as if she'd just stepped out of a fairy tale. She'd definitely had a few lovers. But she wasn't promiscuous either, she never dabbled with anyone on the ship, even though there were lots of guys who fancied her. That's about all I can tell you.'

'That's OK. It's time now I took you and your friend Scott to Chichester to visit her anyway.' Bryan got to his feet. 'I'm sure it will go without saying that she is very weak and still suffering from the effects of being in the sea such a long time. So don't expect too much. I'm hoping that seeing you two will trigger her memory, but it is likely she won't even know you, so please be prepared for that. Now, do you need permission to come with me?'

Dale pulled a face at the prospect of having to ask Marisa. 'We'd better,' she said. 'And I'll need to call Scott. Can we meet you in reception in ten minutes?'

An hour and a half later Scott and Dale were with Lotte in St Richard's Hospital in Chichester. She had been put in a private room on Singleton Ward on the ground floor, with a policeman on duty outside the door.

'Shit!' Scott murmured as he saw the uniformed man. 'I didn't realize they saw this as a really serious crime. They must think she still needs protection.'

If DI Bryan heard what Scott said, he made no comment, but said he would remain outside so they could see Lotte alone.

'You'll be less inhibited without me there,' he said with a smile. 'You'll probably get more out of her too, if you don't stand on ceremony with her. Bring up all your little private jokes, be real. Call me if she starts to remember anything. But don't go on for too long, she badly needs rest.'

Dale gasped involuntarily as they walked into the room, for Lotte looked terrible, almost unrecognizable as the outstandingly pretty girl they'd shared so many good times with. Her hair had been hacked off in lumps, she was very thin, terribly pale and bruised, and the skin on her face was flaking off. Even the big blue eyes they knew so well looked haunted and afraid.

'Do you know us, Lotte?' Dale said, taking her hand. 'I'm Dale and this is Scott. We were your best friends on the cruise ship, we did everything together.'

'Dale and Scott,' Lotte said slowly as if testing the names against anything remaining in her memory bank. She looked searchingly at their two faces and it was clear she didn't know them.

Dale started to talk about the hairdressing salon and the names of the other staff there.

'I used to call you my "slave",' she went on, tears prickling the back of her eyes and her voice shaking. 'I am such a slob, you used to pick my clothes up for me and wash them. You are the best friend I've ever had.'

Lotte squeezed her hand. 'Your voice kind of sounds like I know it,' she said, a look of frustration crossing her face. 'I'm trying so hard to remember something, but there's just shadows, nothing else.'

'It's very early days yet and you're still very weak,' Scott said, bending over to kiss her forehead. 'I used to call you "Barbie Girl".'

Lotte looked hard at Scott for some little time, then sighed. 'It's there, I know it is, but there's something blocking the way.'

'We'll find out what,' Dale assured her. 'We'll come tomorrow with photos we took on the cruise. We'll talk and talk until something gives and you remember everything.'

'My parents came last night,' Lotte said, her eyes misty with unshed tears. 'Well, they said they were my parents, but they didn't mean anything to me. Are you sure that's who they are?'

That remark brought a lump to Dale's throat, for clearly Lotte had picked up on her parents' disinterest even though she probably had no memory of what love or friendship actually meant or felt like. How awful it was going to be for her when she did recover her memory and found she was unwanted by her parents, that she'd been raped, and perhaps someone had even tried to drown her. Perhaps it was better to have no memory if that was what it held.

'It's been a while since they saw you, and you look very different,' Dale said, stroking Lotte's hair back from her forehead. 'Your hair was very long, right down your back and very shiny. You loved the colour pink, and it suited you because you were a very girlie girl.'

'Pink to make the boys wink,' Lotte said with a smile. But then she frowned. 'Why did I say that? It just popped out!'

'I expect that's the way your memory will come back,' Scott said. 'A bit here and there, and one bit will loosen another memory and soon it will be a flood. But you need to sleep and get strong again. We'll come to see you again tomorrow night.'

As DI Bryan walked back with them to the police car they told him everything that had been said. Dale asked him if he'd been in the room when Lotte's parents saw her.

'Yes, sadly,' he said. 'I've never seen a less emotional couple. They didn't touch her once, not a kiss, a squeeze of the hand or a pat on the cheek. Yet they had tears in their eyes when they told me about their other daughter dying. It was all I could do not to slap them round the head and remind them they've got another daughter here who needs care and attention badly.'

'What will happen now?' Dale asked.

'A psychiatrist will be coming in tomorrow morning to see her,' the policeman said. 'Let's hope he has some way of unblocking her memory. We are of course going to run pictures of her in the press again and ask members of the public to come forward if they remember her.'

'What if whatever happened to her was so bad her brain has blocked it out to help her recover?' Dale asked. 'I read somewhere that can be the reason for amnesia.'

'Yes, I believe that is so,' Bryan said. 'And it's very frustrating for us police when we need to know who is responsible for her trauma and apprehend them. But I have it on good authority that this kind of amnesia is not permanent.'

Lotte lay back on the pillows, staring up at the ceiling. It was after eleven now, dark outside and much quieter everywhere. The main lights in the room had been turned off earlier and the nurse had just left the reading lamp above the bed on, turning it away so it didn't shine down on Lotte's face.

People kept asking her how she felt, but she couldn't explain because she had no idea what she felt like before she ended up in the sea. She wanted to sleep for ever, her whole body ached and there were sore patches which the nurse said had been caused by the shingle of the beach. She kept looking at the purple marks on her wrists, wishing she could recall the face of the person who tied her up. The way Dale and Scott had talked to her made her think she must have been a nice person, so why would anyone want to restrain her?

Everything in the room felt oddly familiar, not necessarily as if she'd been in here before, but somewhere just like it. But then she supposed most hospitals were more or less the same.

She found it weird that loss of memory was so selective. It hadn't stopped her being able to speak, read, use a knife and fork or use the toilet, yet when she was told her name, she didn't know that.

'Pink to make the boys wink,' she muttered to herself again. 'Why did that pop into my head?'

She could see the colour pink in her mind's eye, just as she could name the purple flowers in the vase on the window sill as tulips. Her parents had brought those in with them; her mother said they were from their garden. But perhaps she'd also said they were called tulips.

No one had shown her pink, though, she just knew

what the colour was. She reached out for one of the magazines and kept flicking over the pages until she saw a pink dress, pink lipstick and a picture of a room with pink walls.

She continued to turn the pages, and halted suddenly at a picture of a child on a beach. She had a bucket and spade and she was wearing a bikini. Suddenly Lotte remembered.

A pink bikini, pink and white spots with frills across the back of the pants. Her sister had one exactly the same. She even knew it was the summer when she was five and Fleur was nine. They had gone to Camber Sands for the day. Her mother said 'pink to make the boys wink', and Fleur asked why would they want to make boys wink.

As the memory unfurled it was like watching a video. Lotte could see them all getting out of the car in the morning, and her mother piling the picnic and beach stuff into her father's arms so he was almost hidden.

Lotte was given only the buckets and spades to carry. Fleur had the picnic blanket which was rolled up and tied like a big sausage. Mum and Dad carried everything else up over the sand dunes and down on to the beach.

It was her first time on a sandy beach. She loved the way the sand squidged up, warm between her toes, and it was exciting climbing up the big dunes not knowing what was on the other side. But it was even better once they got to the top because they could just slide down the other side to miles of smooth golden sand in both directions. The tide was going out, and it had left small pools of water that were just right for paddling.

Dad hit his hand with the mallet when he was trying to put up the striped canvas windbreak, and Mum laughed at him. He chased her with the mallet, and as Mum ran up on to the dunes to get away from him, he grabbed her by the ankle and pulled her down, laughing at her.

They were like that all day, teasing each other and making jokes. When they went paddling they splashed each other, even though they both had their clothes on. Lotte remembered it was a very long way down to the sea when the tide went right out, and they could see tiny holes in the sand that Dad said were made by winkles.

Fleur sang Madonna's new record, 'Papa Don't Preach', using one of the spades as a microphone as she danced about on the beach. Dad said he wished he'd brought the new cine camera with him, but he'd been afraid of getting sand in it. He said Fleur would have to do it again for them when they got home so he could film it.

Lotte didn't need a cine film to remind her of anything. She could see Fleur, her face flushed with the sun, blonde curly hair caught up in two bunches on either side of her head, like pom-poms. She urged Lotte to jump right across the pools of water left when the tide went out because there might be a human-eating octopus in one.

Down at the sea they held hands and jumped over the waves. Fleur could swim and she tried to teach Lotte by holding her under the tummy while ordering her to move her legs like a frog. She let go several times and Lotte got a mouthful of sea water, but she didn't mind, she was brave when she was with her big sister.

Later that day Fleur tried to teach her how to do a cartwheel. She could do a dozen, one after the other, right down the beach. She could walk on her hands and do back flips, and Lotte wanted to be just like her.

The memory faded sharply, just like a film that was suddenly cut in half. One moment watching Fleur doing back flips, the next nothing. She didn't remember going home, or anything after that.

She didn't mind too much. After all, it was a start, something good to tell the doctor in the morning. Funny though that the couple who said they were her parents were nothing like the happy couple in her memory. They looked like them, only older, but they weren't happy like that any longer. And where was Fleur now? No one had mentioned her.

Chapter Four

The morning after visiting Lotte, Dale walked into the spa and found Marisa waiting for her. One look at the woman's tight expression and she knew it wasn't a social call.

'Can I do something for you, Marisa?' she said as pleasantly as she could. 'I've got time before my first client if you want a manicure or some waxing done.'

'I don't want or need any beauty treatments,' Marisa replied waspishly. 'I came here to say that if you think you and Scott can run out of here whenever you feel like it, just because some girl you once worked with has lost her memory, then you are mistaken. She needs a psychiatrist, not a beautician.'

Dale gave the older woman a scathing look. 'I take it that when you were born you didn't get a visit from the good fairy that doles out compassion?'

'What is that supposed to mean?' Marisa asked.

'Think about it,' Dale snapped, and walked into one of the treatment rooms and shut the door. She hadn't even thought of going to see Lotte during working hours, but it wasn't being told she couldn't which had made her angry, it was that Marisa hadn't even asked how Lotte was.

Dale knew that in the past she'd been fairly careless about people. But she was absolutely certain that she would always have been curious about how someone young and pretty ended up half drowned on a beach. And if the girl had been a friend of people she worked with, she'd have felt involved and sympathetic.

Yet the worst of it was that Dale was sure Marisa was looking for an excuse to sack her. She didn't know why, but the woman had had it in for her since her first day here. She had been harsh to Rosie and Michelle too, at first, but Dale could see that that was to bring them up to the standards she expected in the spa.

Dale knew she had always had that high standard. Marisa couldn't fault her technique, standards of hygiene or client care, she just didn't want her there for some reason.

Marisa had sat in on her interview, but it was Sophia Renato and Quentin Sellers, the joint owners of the hotel, who had presumably selected her from the eighteen hopefuls. They hardly ever came into the spa, and Carlos the wine waiter said they only checked the hotel about once a week and left everything to their managers.

Frankie thought Marisa wanted Dale out because she was confident, bright and a natural leader, and once this became apparent to Renato and Sellers, they might well find it more cost-effective to make her spa manager and get rid of Marisa.

Dale liked the idea that they might think her capable of running the spa, but if truth were told she wouldn't really want the job. It would be too much responsibility and very little more money. She'd rather get a little salon of her own in Brighton where the profits were all hers and she didn't have to work such long hours. But that was in the future. She couldn't afford to make Marisa angry enough to sack her, not yet.

Yet she also felt compelled to help Lotte. How she didn't know, for a sixty-mile round trip to the hospital without a car was going to be difficult. But she was determined to be involved in bringing back her friend's memory and to get her back on her feet, whatever Marisa thought about it.

Scott had said he was going to ask Michael the chef if he could borrow his car to drive over to Chichester tonight. But even if Michael agreed, they wouldn't get there much before eight-thirty, which the hospital might say was too late for visiting. And they couldn't keep that up nightly anyway.

Their transport difficulties were insignificant compared with Lotte's problems, however. Rape was bad enough to deal with, but it looked as if whatever had happened to her in this last year was much worse, or her mind wouldn't have blocked it out. How would she deal with it when her memory came back?

DI Bryan rang later in the afternoon to tell Dale that Lotte wasn't well enough for any more visitors that day. 'I took two old friends of hers over there this afternoon,' he explained. 'They'd come forward after reading about her in the paper. Lotte worked with one of them and she shared his flat with him and his partner for some time.'

'Are they hairdressers?' Dale asked. She remembered Lotte mentioning a gay man she worked with who had become a close friend.

'One of them is, though Lotte didn't recognize either of them,' Bryan said. 'But she had regained a memory of a day on the beach with her parents and sister when she was five.'

'That's a start,' Dale said with some excitement.

'Yes, but I think the strain of it was too much for her,' he replied. 'These guys Simon and Adam were chatting away to her about some of their friends, people she used to work with, and she suddenly had a sort of fit. She couldn't get her breath, it seemed it was a panic attack. We had to call a nurse and we were asked to leave.'

'Is she OK now?' Dale asked.

'Yes, when I rang back a short while ago they said she was resting quietly.'

'Couldn't she be transferred to a hospital near here?' Dale asked. 'It's such a long way for anyone from Brighton to go and visit her.'

'That suggestion was put forward today by the psychiatrist,' Bryan said. 'I think he was thinking mostly of Lotte's parents, though they haven't bothered to ring the ward at St Richard's today to see how she is, so they don't even know she recovered memory about them.'

'I can't see them wanting to take her home with them when she's well enough to leave the hospital. Even if they offered I don't think it would be good for her,' Dale said.

'Simon and Adam suggested she could go to them,' Bryan said.

'Did they now!' Dale said, feeling something ridiculously like jealousy.

'She won't be able to do that unless she regains memories of them,' Bryan said. 'Anyway, tomorrow's another day, maybe we'll have another breakthrough. And the national press and the television companies are running the story about her tomorrow morning, so we should get some more leads.'

Some little while after Dale had put the phone down, she found herself pondering about these friends of Lotte's. Unable to remember the name of the salon where Lotte said they met, she went to ask April, Sharon and Guy who all lived locally if they had any suggestions which one it might be.

'If she said it was the best salon in Brighton, then it would be Kutz,' April said after a moment's thought. 'I trained there. Do you know the name of her friend?'

'Simon or Adam,' Dale replied.

'Oh, that will be Simon Langford! He's a real sweet guy. And he's still there. I spoke to him just last week.'

April was a small, bouncy brunette who often had them in stitches with her tales of working in a hairdressing salon in London's West End. She'd come back to her family in Brighton, as Guy had too, with the intention of saving enough to open her own salon.

'I'll ring there and try and get hold of him,' Dale said. 'I'd really like to meet him.'

At just after eight Dale left Marchwood Manor in a taxi to call on Simon and Adam. She had spoken to Simon briefly on the phone and he said he'd been terribly shocked to see Lotte's picture in the paper and was still totally mystified as to why she hadn't contacted him when she left the cruise ship. He was clearly upset that she hadn't remembered him and his friend Adam that afternoon, and even more so because they'd caused her to have a panic attack. He invited Dale over immediately because he said he was desperate for more information about Lotte.

Simon and Adam's flat was above an antique shop in Meeting House Lane in the North Lanes. It was a quiet backwater, and a wrought-iron spiral staircase led up to the front door which was on a balcony. Dale thought it was the kind of interesting place she'd like to live in herself, right by all the shops and bars, yet only a stone's throw from the seafront.

Simon was tall and thin, with very short brown hair, the tips bleached blond. His ears and nose were too big for him to be called handsome, yet he wasn't unattractive, for his smile was wide and warm and his eyes were a deep dark brown. He wore cream linen trousers held up by braces and a chocolate-brown shirt that matched his eyes.

'I'm really glad you phoned,' he said with genuine warmth. 'It's just a shame Adam's been called out tonight, I know he'll be disappointed he missed you.'

'It's good for me to find out a bit more about Lotte,' Dale said as he beckoned her in. 'Since discovering about her being estranged from her parents I realize I don't know much about her at all.'

'I've been frantic about her for such a long time.' Simon put one hand on his hip in a very camp gesture. 'She was sending me a postcard from every port, but they stopped suddenly.'

Dale could remember Lotte writing postcards; she had assumed they were to her parents.

He showed her into the sitting room, which was very arty with huge navy-blue sofas, stripped floorboards and vast, brightly coloured modern art posters on the walls. He invited her to sit down and offered her a drink.

'Was there any reason she stopped sending the postcards?' he asked as he handed her a glass of white wine. 'Did she find a new man, or was it just 'cos she got involved with new friends?'

Dale sensed his hurt and puzzlement and she felt the kindest thing was to tell him the truth. Lotte needed friends more than ever now, and Simon couldn't really help her without knowing what she'd been through.

'I would've preferred to get around to this a bit more

gently,' Dale said. 'But Lotte didn't stop sending you cards because she lost interest in you, it was because she was raped.'

Simon blanched, and Dale's eyes prickled with tears just the way they always did when she thought about what Lotte had gone through. As she went on to tell Simon the whole story she was overcome with emotion several times; she didn't think the horror of it would ever go away.

'The bastard,' Simon hissed when she'd finished. 'I hope the police strung him up.'

'I think we can safely assume he'll never be capable of raping anyone ever again. They depend on tourism there and the police wouldn't let someone like him put people off going ashore,' Dale said darkly. She blew her nose, wiped her eyes and took a long glug of her wine, before moving on to tell him about Lotte's recovery. 'I believed her when she said she was going home, I had no reason not to.'

Simon had remained silent through most of what she'd told him, then as she drew to the end, he got up and went over to the window. He looked out without speaking for a few moments.

Finally he turned back to her. 'It's obvious she went with someone off the ship. You see, if she hadn't she would've come straight here.'

That didn't sound very logical to Dale. 'Why?' she asked. 'She could've gone absolutely anywhere.'

'She wouldn't, because you can bet your boots that

after what she'd been through she felt much the same about herself as she did when she first came to Kutz,' he said, his brown eyes dull with anxiety. 'She was like a little waif then. You could almost smell the aloneness of her. She'd had no money to buy decent clothes, no one to give her a bit of love. She looked scared of her own shadow. I tell you, if she wasn't made to leave that ship with someone, she would've come running back here as fast as her legs would carry her. This flat would always be her place of safety.'

'How old was she when she came to Kutz then?' Dale asked, touched by his affection for her friend, yet a little jealous too.

'Almost nineteen. When I found out what the bitches she was sharing with were doing to her, I got her to come and live here with Adam and me. She always said that meeting me was like coming out of a dark place into the light. And for us she was our sister, mother, friend and housekeeper all rolled into one. We loved having her with us, she kind of balanced out our lives. That's why I know she would've come back here to see us first if she was hurt, because we were her family.'

'Did you tell DI Bryan this?' Dale asked.

'I tried to, but straight cops tend to see gay men as fanciful airheads. They don't imagine we can form deep and meaningful relationships with women if we don't have sex with them.'

'Bryan didn't come across like that to me,' Dale

retorted. 'What did he say when you told him she must've gone with someone from the ship?'

'I don't think he believed I knew Lotte well enough to make such a statement. You probably don't either?'

'Oh, I do,' Dale assured him. 'You see, you talk about her in the same way as I do, so I know you've seen the same things in her as me.'

Simon's eyes dropped and a blush crept up his neck.

'What is it?' she asked.

'I think I pushed too hard today, and that's why she had the panic attack,' he said. 'You see, I mentioned Mark, and suddenly she couldn't get her breath.'

'Who was Mark?' Dale asked.

'A sailor she fell in love with. But if she remembered him she probably remembered everything else that came before him. That might have been too much for her.'

As Dale was talking to Simon, Lotte was lying still in the hospital bed, her eyes shut, pretending to be asleep so no one would come and talk to her.

Her heart was no longer racing, she wasn't scared or agitated the way she had got when Simon and Adam were here. But that had happened because a sudden deluge of memories came back to her. It was like being hit by a hurricane, and she wasn't even able to reassure Simon that it wasn't anything in particular that he'd said, just that all at once she knew who he was, and all he'd meant to her.

At nineteen she'd sat with him pouring out stuff she'd never told anyone before or since. He was the man who showed her how to deal with it. She was only too happy she could remember his part in her life, for it had been a very important one.

Thanks to Simon she now knew why the hospital room seemed so familiar too. It was like the one Fleur was in just before she died.

Lotte was never actually told there was something wrong with her sister. She could remember being puzzled as to why Fleur stopped going to dancing classes, and that she often didn't go to school and seemed to sleep such a lot. But no one ever explained it.

Perhaps her parents couldn't face up to leukaemia themselves, let alone try to make it clear to their younger child. But not knowing Fleur was ill made all the special treatment she got, the treats, new clothes and toys, trips to anywhere she fancied, seem so terribly unfair.

It was Fleur herself who told her in the end. Lotte had been given a good hiding and sent to bed without any tea for complaining when she was left with a neighbour while Mum and Dad took her sister to London. Fleur crept up to see her with some cake, a bottle of Tizer and a bag of toffees.

'They only took me to a hospital,' she said. 'I had to have some special tests because I've got something wrong with my blood.'

Lotte thought that if she never complained about anything ever again Fleur would get better. But she didn't, she just got weaker, thinner and paler, and each time she was taken into hospital, she stayed longer.

Lotte could remember Fleur's tenth birthday very clearly. A room just like the one she was in now, but filled with flowers, cards, teddy bears, dolls and a cake like Cinderella's coach, with four pink 'My Little Ponies' pulling it. Fleur was so weak she couldn't even blow the candles out, and she asked Lotte to do it for her.

A week later she died.

Lotte was told what had happened by Mrs Broome, the neighbour she was staying with while her parents were at the hospital. Mrs Broome said Jesus had taken Fleur to live with him because she was very special, and that once Lotte went home, she had to be especially good and quiet because her mummy and daddy were very sad.

Lotte went home later that day, and her dad opened the door to her. He picked her up and hugged her, and she remembered his face was all wet with tears.

He put her down and told her to go and see her mother. Lotte stood for a little while in the doorway of the front room, just looking. It always seemed a cold room because it never got any sun. There was a big three-piece suite which was dark red, and in the alcoves on either side of the chimney breast were black wood wall units. Some of the shelves were open, with ornaments and books on; others had sliding glass doors and the best glasses were kept in there.

Her mother was on the sofa, all hunched up, her

head in her hands, and she was kind of rocking herself and making an awful moaning sound.

Lotte went over to her and sat down beside her. There was no response from her mother, who didn't appear to have noticed she was there. So Lotte knelt up beside her and tried to put her small arms around her shoulders.

'You've still got me,' she said.

She remembered what she said so clearly, even after sixteen years, because of the way her mother reacted. She flung her arms out, knocking Lotte to the floor. 'I don't want you, you little brat,' she spat out. 'All I want is my beautiful Fleur.'

Lotte wanted pretty, funny, entertaining Fleur too. There was a big hole in her life where her sister had been; she'd always played with Lotte, read and sung to her. She'd explained things Lotte didn't understand, did her hair, told her stories, and when they went to the shops together, she knew how much change they should get, and the best places to buy anything.

Why didn't anyone understand that she loved and missed Fleur too?

There were so many painful memories in the period after Fleur's death. It seemed as if each day brought new hurts, and Lotte felt bewildered as to why she was constantly being shouted at or punished. But having a belt taken to her backside, and being beaten so hard she couldn't sit down without pain for a couple of weeks, was one of the worst.

Her only crime was being caught playing with Fleur's Barbie Dolls.

'You are not fit to touch her toys,' her mother screamed at her, her face purple and contorted with hatred as she lashed out with the belt. 'Don't you ever go in her room again!'

Lotte's bedroom was a tiny box room with no room for anything more than a single bed and a chest of drawers. But Fleur's room next door to it was at least three times larger and until she'd died they'd always played in there together.

Now it was like a shrine to Fleur. Her mother cleaned and dusted it each week and stayed in there for hours sobbing.

When what would have been Fleur's eleventh birthday came round, all the dolls had their clothes washed and her mother lit candles on a cake and took it in there to sing Happy Birthday to her. She repeated that year after year, but Lotte never had a cake on her birthday, and the present she was given was always just a cardigan or pyjamas. Practical and impersonal.

There were of course no singing or dancing lessons as Fleur had, so Lotte never discovered if she had any talent. Her mother kept her hair cut very short, and bought her very plain, dark-coloured clothes. Young as she was, Lotte soon realized that this was so no one would ever make any favourable comparison between her and Fleur.

Her father wasn't nasty to her, just distant. As he was

a plumber he was often called out on emergencies in the evenings and at weekends. But after Fleur died he hardly ever seemed to be home. As Lotte grew older she sensed he went along with whatever her mother did or said for a quiet life.

But then, her mother was at her absolute worst only when they were alone together. Lotte was often afraid to go home after school because she didn't know what might be awaiting her.

Sometimes it was just a brooding stare, or criticism that she was late or untidy; sometimes she was just ignored. Yet that hurt so much, she felt so dreadfully alone, and she really thought it was because there was something horrible and unlovable about her.

But at other times it was far worse.

Lotte remembered one very wet day when she was about thirteen. She had developed the ability to know when her mother's moods were at their very darkest, just by the atmosphere when she opened the front door. She could feel the tension in the air, smell her anger like something rank and rotten. At these times it was always tempting to run away, and if there had been a friend or relative she felt would take her in and believe what she told them, she would have gone.

But there was no one. She once tried to tell Mrs Broome, their neighbour, but the woman's face tightened up in disbelief and she went straight round and told her mother what Lotte had said. She got beaten with a slipper that day.

So when she sensed trouble that wet day when she was thirteen, she did what she always did and braced herself for the malevolence she knew was to come.

As she came gingerly through the door, she found her mother standing in the hall in the dark pink wool dress that she usually wore only on special occasions. But she clearly wasn't going anywhere special as her hair was a mess and she was wearing her slippers. And even more worrying was the crazed expression on her face.

'You stole some money from my purse,' she spat out. 'I had a ten pound note in there last night and it was gone this morning.'

'I didn't take it,' Lotte said truthfully. She put her school bag down on the floor. 'You can check in there if you like. I haven't got any money.'

She never had any, she didn't get pocket money, another thing which hurt but she never dared bring up.

'You've put that wet bag on my clean floor,' her mother screamed out. 'You're an imbecile – why didn't you die instead of your sister? You're no good for anything.'

Lotte burst into tears. There were a few drops of rain water on the tiles, but they would dry; she didn't think she would get over her mother wishing her dead.

But crying was the worst thing she could do as her mother always took it as weakness.

'That's it – cry! Tears from you don't mean a thing, just crocodile tears. It's bad enough that I've been left with you when my beautiful, talented daughter was taken from me, but you lie to me and steal from me too. God, I despise you!'

Lotte had been called stupid, ugly, ignorant, bad, loathsome and so many other horrible adjectives she thought she ought to have stopped being hurt by them, but to be told that her mother resented being left with her was like a knife through the heart.

'Then call a social worker and get me taken into care!' she shouted back at her mother.

That was the bravest she'd ever been. Normally she didn't dare answer back. But the words had scarcely left her lips when her mother snatched up a walking stick, left behind by a visitor many years ago, from the umbrella stand and brought it down with force on Lotte's head and shoulders. Lotte tried to get away but her mother cornered her behind the front door and rained blows on her back, shoulders and arms, all the time screeching that she was a thief.

She suddenly ran out of steam, dropped the walking stick on the floor and shuffled off to the kitchen. Lotte dragged herself up to her bedroom and wished she could die. She thought if her own mother loathed her, there was no hope that anyone else could ever care for her.

Later it transpired that it was her father who had taken the ten pound note. He'd borrowed it that morning but didn't say anything as her mother was still asleep. But there was no apology for Lotte.

It took a fortnight for the bruises and weals on her body to fade. Her gym teacher stared at them while Lotte was changing, but didn't ask how she got them. For Lotte that was proof no one cared. She gave up hoping for anyone's intervention and made up her mind she would leave home the moment she left school.

She took six GCSEs, did badly in all of them and applied for a job as a chambermaid in the Grand Hotel in Brighton, just because they let their staff live in. She was called for an interview two days before the end of term and was offered a job. It was arranged that she would move in that Sunday and start work on the Monday.

Her mother sniffed when Lotte told her she was going to work at the hotel.

'About right for someone as brainless as you,' she said in her usual cold voice. 'Domestic work is all you're good for.'

Someone in her class arranged a party on the beach to celebrate the exams being over and to say goodbye to those leaving school. Lotte was expected to go, but she knew she couldn't. She had nothing nice to wear and no money either to buy some drink. Besides, she wasn't keen for anyone to find out where she was going to work, in case they reacted like her mother.

Working at the Grand was a bit like pressing her nose up to a toy-shop window. She got to see rich people eating and drinking, wearing expensive clothes and valuable jewellery and arriving in smart cars. There were many conference rooms in the hotel too, which were hired out to all kinds of companies, and she would see girls only a couple of years older than herself organizing seminars, marketing meetings and staff training sessions. They were smart, confident and articulate, which only confirmed in her the belief that she really was stupid, just like her mother had always told her. She didn't bother to daydream about what it might be like to stay in the hotel as a guest, or to have a job where people looked up to her. She really believed she wasn't capable of doing anything more than clean up after people.

But she didn't mind. After all, she could look out of the windows at the sea while she was cleaning her rooms. The colour of the sea changed daily, going from brilliant turquoise when the sun was shining, through greens, greys, and then to black when there was a storm. She loved windy days when the waves were whipped up so high they washed over the promenade, but her favourites were the days with light wind, just enough to make small white horses canter up the beach.

It was good to watch the holidaymakers too. Old couples in their best clothes who would sit for hours in the shelters watching the sea, small children who twitched with excitement as they raced to get down the steps on to the beach. Girls of her own age looking for boys to flirt with, roller skaters, baby-buggy pushers, dog walkers, hugely fat ladies who waddled by eating ice cream, and gay men posing by the promenade railings. She'd been told Brighton was the gay capital of England now, and everyone else in the hotel seemed to know exactly who was gay just by looking at them. But Lotte couldn't tell, not unless they made it very obvious.

She had to share a dark, poorly furnished room in the staff annexe with a Spanish girl who spoke only broken English. She also had to work very hard, but the other staff were friendly, even kindly, and she was far happier than she'd been at home.

One evening while watching her room-mate struggling to blowdry her hair, she offered to do it for her. To Lotte's surprise it turned out really nice, and after that all the girls asked her to do theirs. Word must eventually have reached Gina, the owner of the hairdressing salon in the hotel, because she asked Lotte if she'd like to help her out when she wasn't working.

From almost the first afternoon in Gina's salon, Lotte felt hairdressing was her calling. She loved everything about it – the smell of shampoos and conditioners, the feel of wet hair in her fingers while she washed it, and seeing women who'd come in looking bedraggled and limp-haired go out bouncy and pretty.

Gina was in her late thirties, a buxom blonde who strutted around on very high heels and wore dresses so tight she could've been poured into them, but she had experienced hardships herself in the past. She saw how much Lotte liked the salon, and said she felt that with proper training she had the ability to be a first-class hairdresser.

Lotte didn't have to explain that she couldn't give up working as a chambermaid to train because she needed the room that came with the job, Gina worked that out for herself. So she talked the hotel manager round, suggesting they shared Lotte.

From seven until ten in the morning she would make beds and clean rooms, then spent the rest of the day in hairdressing training. On her day off she had to attend a hairdressing college, and every evening she had to spend an hour turning down beds and changing towels.

Lotte never minded that she had to work a twelve-hour day, and that even on Sunday she would still have chambermaid duties in the morning: she'd come to see the Grand as her home. Anyway, Gina was kind to her, and to be trained properly would mean that one day she could make a good living.

In the two years that followed Lotte plodded on between training with Gina, one day a week at college and the rest of the time cleaning bedrooms and turning down beds. She never went to see her parents, and they never contacted her. At Christmas and on birthdays there wasn't even a card. She had no real social life, just the other live-in staff to chat to over meals and the occasional outing to the pictures or a walk along the promenade after her evening duties were finished.

She often looked at girls of her own age and wondered what it would be like to go dancing, have a boyfriend or even go on holiday. But she earned so little she couldn't afford to buy new clothes, and she spent most of her spare time studying hairdressing magazines. Several of the foreign waiters asked her if she'd be their girlfriend. But she was far too unsure of herself to get involved with anyone, and she usually giggled and ran away.

At almost nineteen she qualified in hairdressing with distinction and won an award for the best student of the year at her college. It was Easter time, and Gina handed her a chocolate egg, a basket of beauty products and an envelope.

Inside the envelope was a letter of introduction to Kutz, Brighton's best hairdressers.

'Don't look so puzzled,' Gina said with a smile. 'You deserve something better than doing shampoo and sets for old ladies on their holiday. I worked with Gerald, the owner of Kutz, years ago, and we're good friends. I've already spoken to him about you, and he's agreed to take you on. This is going to change your life.'

Lotte opened her eyes and came back to the present. Outside her room two nurses were talking in low voices; she thought they were planning a night out.

'Change my life!' Lotte murmured, picturing Gina, the first person to show her some affection and believe she was worth something. She always wore a lot of makeup, her 'warpaint' she called it: thin, pencilled eyebrows, blue iridescent eye shadow and eyelashes thick with clumps of black mascara. She was perhaps a size sixteen, but she always looked kind of sexy, with her low-cut tops and very high heels.

Gina was right, it did change Lotte's life, but not just working at Kutz. It was Simon who waved the magic wand and made things good for her. Perhaps that was why his voice this afternoon penetrated the barrier in her mind and made her remember.

But while she was more than happy to remember Gina, Simon and Adam, three people she owed so much to, she would rather have remained in ignorance about her childhood. The struggles she'd had to overcome that legacy of worthlessness her parents had bequeathed her were painful, embarrassing ones. And she knew by the strange, distant way her mother and father had been with her when they came here to visit her that there couldn't have been any reconciliation between them over the last four years.

The door opened and Janice Easton, the Ward Sister, came in. 'How are you feeling now?' she asked.

'Much better,' Lotte said. Janice had a comforting presence; in her mid-thirties, she had a plump, pretty country girl sort of look, with strawberry-blonde hair and pink cheeks. 'Though I am worried Simon and Adam will feel responsible for causing my panic attack.'

'Well, you needn't be. Anything could have caused it,

but the most likely reason was that they stimulated you into remembering something. Was that so?'

Lotte nodded.

Janice perched on the edge of Lotte's bed, her face alight with interest. 'Do you feel like talking about it?'

Lotte sat up, pulling out a pillow and putting it behind her to lean her back against. She was still very stiff, her limbs ached, and though she'd been told this was most probably because she'd swum for a long time before reaching the beach where she was found, it could also be explained by some other recent, strenuous physical exercise. Her skin was horribly scaly and dry. As for her hair, it felt like steel wool. The nurses had rinsed the worst of the salt water out of it, but it needed a more thorough wash and masses of conditioner to bring it back to normal.

She thought it strange that before the memory of being a hairdresser came back, the feel of her hair hadn't really concerned her. She told Janice this, and the nurse laughed, saying that in the morning she could get in the shower and do it herself.

'So if you remember being a hairdresser, can you tell me how you met those two nice friends of yours?' Janice asked.

Lotte didn't want to tell anyone about her miserable childhood, or even the hardships she'd had working at the Grand. But she didn't mind one bit telling Janice about being taken on by Kutz, Brighton's most prestigious hairdresser.

'It was a really smart salon,' she said with a smile. 'Two floors with everything in shiny black, white and chrome. I expect it's still the same now. But it was pretty terrifying to me then; all the staff were very trendy and I'd been cloistered away in a hotel hairdressing salon with the blue rinse brigade. It didn't help either that I'd just moved into a flat with three other girls who were horrible to me,' she said with a frown.

'Girlie bitchy stuff?' Janice asked.

'Worse than that, they were evil,' Lotte said. 'They used to make me wait to cook my tea until they'd eaten theirs, but they'd leave all the washing up and the whole kitchen would be a mess. They'd use all the hot bath water, never took the rubbish down to the dustbins, I had to do that too. I didn't have any money for nice clothes and they made snide comments about me all the time.'

'And this on top of a new job?' Janice said with sympathy.

Lotte grimaced. 'I felt a freak there too. My one black skirt was well old-fashioned and my white shirt was dingy with age, I can't tell you how inferior I felt. It was horrible.'

'So what changed that?'

'Well, I got home one day to find Mandy and Laura going through my clothes and shrieking with laughter,' Lotte said.

She could visualize everything. The long, narrow passageway had a threadbare red carpet runner, and she was half-way along it, between the sitting room and the bedrooms, when she heard Mandy talking in their room.

'Look at this awful skirt!' she said, and Lotte froze, knowing Mandy was showing one or other of the girls the contents of her wardrobe.

'It's like something a missionary would wear,' Laura chortled. 'And what about this top? Granny or what!'

Lotte wished the floor would open and swallow her up, yet she crept closer and peeped at Mandy and Laura through the crack in the door. They were both glossy, confident girls from middle-class homes who had gone to Sussex University, then decided to stay in the town. Mandy was in advertising, Laura in marketing, and both thought themselves fashion experts.

The skirt in question was dark grey flannel, a mid-calf-length one from the market. Lotte had seen a model wearing one just like it in a fashion magazine and thought it looked great, but she supposed without the right boots and jacket to go with it, perhaps it did look frumpy. As for the checked top, she'd bought it because it was cheap, and soon acknowledged that it was a mistake. She knew she wasn't very good at putting clothes together, but that was because she'd had no practice. When she worked at the hotel she always wore an overall.

'Did you have a go at them?' Janice asked.

'No, I was too scared of them, I suppose. I cried

myself to sleep that night, and I guess I was still blotchy-faced the next morning because Simon asked me what was wrong.'

'And you told him?'

'I burst into tears again and gave him the whole nine yards. He was so kind, he hugged me and said I was to come home with him that night and that he'd cook me dinner and we'd talk it all through.'

Lotte doubted she could explain adequately to anyone how good that night with Simon was. The flat he shared with Adam was just a few hundred yards from the salon, tucked away down a little lane. Lotte thought it was marvellous, right from the first glimpse of the spiral staircase that led to his front door. Adam was a windowdresser but aspired to be an interior designer, and it showed, for the lounge had one bright yellow wall with two large blue sofas against it, and in one corner stood a lamp that was a huge white fibreglass bulldog, complete with spiked collar. She'd never seen anything like it before.

Simon made spaghetti bolognese and talked to her like a big brother.

'You don't believe you're pretty, do you?' he began. 'You've also got a perfect figure, and I bet you don't know that either? But do you want to know why I think people are mean to you?'

Lotte nodded.

'It's because you've got a submissive way of creeping

around with your head down. It invites bullies to have a pop at you; even perfectly nice people are likely to put on you.'

Lotte was astonished and stared at him open-mouthed.

'You've got to be more assertive, stand up straight, look at people directly and don't take any shit from them,' he insisted, wiggling a finger at her. 'Also, you don't wear makeup, your clothes are all too big for you and look like they came from a charity shop, so we've got to fix that. On the plus side you are really sweet to your clients and a great hairdresser, but they want to see a bit of glamour and personality too. We are in the beauty business and we should look the part.'

He said she needed a makeover, and that meant going shopping for new clothes, a more up-to-date hairstyle, and she'd got to learn about makeup.

Strangely, Lotte didn't feel embarrassed by Simon's criticism. He had such a gentle way of making quite incisive observations that she felt cared for rather than insulted.

Adam came in then. He was far more conventional than Simon, with neatly cut dark hair and smart, casual clothes. Lotte would never have guessed he was gay for he looked hunky and muscular, and he had a very deep voice. But he was very welcoming too, and looked sympathetic when Simon explained how things had been for her.

'Simon said you looked scared stiff on your first day at the salon,' he admitted. 'He wanted to bring you home right away, he's such a mother hen. But I said he might scare you even more and he must wait.'

Over the meal and a couple of bottles of wine, both Simon and Adam asked her questions about her past. But there was also a great deal of laughter and Lotte felt relaxed and happy in their company.

She wasn't used to drinking and she got a bit tiddly, so Simon said she'd better stay the night in their spare room. The last thing she remembered thinking before she fell asleep was how funny it was that she'd never admitted anything about herself or her family to anyone before, yet she'd told these two men almost everything.

What Lotte hadn't expected was that Simon would involve everyone in the salon with her makeover. Or that they'd all be so enthusiastic about it. They cut her hair in layers, added two other lighter shades of blonde, plucked her eyebrows, and two of the top stylists instructed her on makeup.

Simon and Jenny, one of the junior stylists, were her shopping advisers, and they took her to shops she'd never even looked in before. They were brutal, not allowing her the loose, drab-coloured clothes she kept straying towards, but forced her into snug-fitting, bright colours, and often what she thought were plain weird clothes.

'Wake up and smell the coffee!' Simon exclaimed

when she asked if the clothes weren't a bit too bright. 'You're gorgeous, why not let the whole world notice you?'

Lotte had no desire for anyone to notice her much, but she soon realized that Simon had a real flair for clothes and knew what was right for her. Each time she came out of the changing cubicle to show him and Jenny another short skirt, tight pair of jeans or a midriff-revealing top, she could see by his face, and the approving glances from other girls, that she was looking good. In one baby pink top and a denim ra-ra skirt she even liked herself.

She would've liked to have bought most of the clothes they made her try, but she couldn't afford them all. In the end she selected three outfits and a pair of shoes, and even that was a whole week's wages. She knew it wouldn't end at that either; now that she'd got the hang of it she'd want more clothes and makeup. She felt wonderful, for the makeover hadn't just altered her appearance, it had changed how everyone treated her. Suddenly she was one of the girls at the salon, not an outsider any more.

Yet even more satisfying was to airily tell her flat-mates she was leaving. Simon had offered her the spare room in his flat.

'You can't just go – what about giving us notice?' Laura gasped as she watched Lotte flinging her few clothes into a plastic bin liner.

'You should have been a little nicer to me then,'

Lotte said, smiling quite confidently because Simon was downstairs waiting for her. 'I don't feel I owe you anything.'

She flung a ten pound note at Laura for her share of the electricity bill as she left. 'By the way,' she said, looking sharply at the girl's bleached hair, 'your roots need doing.'

Lotte only told Janice a very abbreviated and upbeat version of that period in her life; that she'd been very shy when they first met, but Simon had become her friend, brought her out of herself and given her a room in his flat. 'I was so happy living with him and Adam,' she said simply. 'I loved them both like brothers, and I hope I will be able to go and stay with them again once I'm well enough to leave here.'

'I'm sure they'll be thrilled to hear you've remembered where they fit into your life,' Janice said as she stood up, then took Lotte's wrist to take her pulse. 'I don't think it will be long before everything comes back to you.'

After Janice had left the room Lotte thought over what she had remembered and pondered about the four most recent years which were still missing. It seemed to her that these memories were locked inside a series of boxes, and she needed someone to supply the key.

She was sure the dark-haired girl called Dale had been very important to her, and it was so frustrating and scary not knowing why. Dale had told her things, about them sharing a cabin on a cruise ship, trips ashore in places like Buenos Aires and Cape Town, but none of that meant anything. Why couldn't she remember any of it?

'Tell me about this sailor boyfriend of Lotte's,' Dale asked Simon. He'd opened a second bottle of wine and Dale had told him all about how she and Lotte met, and about the good times they'd shared. 'I got the idea there had been someone special just from a certain look she had when people were talking about love affairs, but she never told me anything about him.'

'She met him on her twentieth birthday,' Simon said. 'She had been like a frightened little mouse when she first moved in with us, but within that year she'd become a real doll. I tell you, some guys came into the salon to get their hair cut just to get near her! Lovely hair, pretty face and a body like a top model's. She still wasn't the most confident girl in the world, but she had stuff to say, she could hold her own, and she was liked because she was kind, sunny-natured and very real.

'She'd had a couple of dates, but I guess she wasn't ready to take anything beyond that. Anyway, on her birthday everyone at the salon met up at Loco's night club to celebrate, and Adam and I watched her as she met Mark.'

He paused, his dark eyes a little dreamy. 'It was just like in a movie. They looked at each other across the club, moved together and that was it! Love at first sight. None of us got a look-in with her that night, all she could see was him, so we left them to it. I think they had about ten days together before he had to go back to his ship. We never saw anyone as happy as she was.

'But then he was killed in a road accident.'

'He was killed?' Dale exclaimed. She hadn't been expecting that.

'You can hardly credit fate could be so cruel to her,' Simon said, his eyes glistening with unshed tears. 'She meets the right guy, they fall in love and make plans for the future. But his leave was up, and he's on his way to the station and walks in front of a truck!'

'Poor, poor Lotte! How did she take it?' Dale asked gruffly, for a lump had come up in her throat.

'Badly. She was absolutely prostrate with grief. Adam and I took turns to go on suicide watch,' he said, his voice heavy with emotion. 'We really thought she would attempt to end it all. It wasn't just that he was her first and only love, we reckoned all the other stuff too – her sister's death, her parents rejecting her, and all those growing-up years without a friend in the world – was lumped into it. Adam and I kept telling her we loved her, but for a time it was like she was a rag doll, she didn't respond to anything we said or did. She didn't eat or go to work, she just stayed in bed crying. We didn't know what to do. It was terrible to see.'

'What brought her out of it?' Dale asked.

'Me becoming ill,' Simon said with a glum smile. 'I had some weird virus, I was so weak I couldn't do anything. Adam couldn't take time off work and I was throwing up and stuff and suddenly she got up and started taking care of me.'

Dale sighed. 'That is so like Lotte. Now if it had been me, you wouldn't have roused me out of my misery by needing a nurse. That would have sent me deeper into despair.'

Simon smiled. 'I've got the first postcard she sent me from the cruise somewhere. She said, "Cabin mate is an untidy, selfish bitch, but she's got a certain something about her."'

'She said that about me?' Dale gasped and then laughed. 'She was totally right of course, but I thought she'd write home and say I was cool.'

Simon raised one eyebrow. 'She might be soft-hearted but she's no one's fool. I guess she saw something else in you that she liked. Before long her postcards were full of "we did this" or "we did that."'

'I'm ashamed to admit that I jokingly called her my "slave", because she used to wash my clothes with hers and pick up after me. She used to do this kind of jokey bowing thing to me. But I grew to really love her, I never felt that way about any other girlfriend. I can't bear the thought of all this happening to her.'

'Well, I think, as I've already said, that whoever is responsible for how she ended up was on that cruise ship,' Simon said firmly. 'So come on, Dale, think of all the people she got to know. Was there anyone who would have persuaded or coerced her to go home with them?'

'Well, Fern and Howard Ramsden, the couple who rescued her from the rape and looked after her, are the obvious ones. But they were Americans and they were going home. Besides, they were religious, they wouldn't hold someone against their will.'

'Religious Americans are just about the most likely people to do such a crazy thing,' Simon said, raising his voice a little. 'Maybe the guy is into polygamy, and wanted Lotte for a second wife.'

'That's ridiculous,' Dale said dismissively. 'Those plural-marriage people don't go off on cruises, they live in remote parts of Utah, Montana or Nevada, and marry the children of their friends, women who've been brought up to that way of life.'

'Don't be so sure of that,' Simon said darkly. 'Besides, there's other sects and weird cults in the States that we've never heard of. And our little Lotte, with her complete trust in anyone who appears to love her, would be a sitting duck!'

Dale shuddered. 'Yes, but she didn't end up in America, did she?'

'No, but what if she discovered that's where they were intending to take her?'

Dale felt unable to join in Simon's speculation. She was still staggered that Lotte had never so much as hinted at all the sadness in her past while they were on

93

the cruise. Yet it proved she was tougher than Dale had imagined, for most people would use it to get sympathy. She wondered what more was going to come out about her friend before all this was sorted.

Chapter Five

'Good morning, Lotte,' said Dr Percival as he came charging into her room on Saturday morning without so much as a knock on the door to warn her.

One of the nurses had told Lotte this neurologist had the nickname 'The Bull' and Lotte could see why. He had a bull-like appearance – broad shoulders, a thick neck and large features set in a ruddy complexion. Lotte thought he would look more at home on a rugby pitch than in a hospital ward. Yet the nurse had said he was renowned in his field and that once you got past his bluff manner, he was very likeable.

They chatted for a little while about her general health and Lotte told him about getting some memories back.

'Marvellous,' he said, his grey-blue eyes twinkling. 'So is this making you feel better?'

Lotte agreed it was, though she thought she had a long way to go yet, as there were four years of memory left to recover.

'Then I will try to prompt you,' he said, perching on the edge of the bed. 'What sex was your baby – a boy or girl?'

Lotte looked at him askance. 'Baby?'

'Yes, baby. We found you'd given birth recently when we examined you on admission.'

Lotte felt a cold shudder run down her spine. He had to be mistaken, surely no woman could black out the memory of her own baby? 'I don't know,' she burst out, looking at him in wide-eyed horror. 'I can't have had a baby, can I? Are you absolutely sure?'

The doctor's expression softened. 'You really don't know what's happened to you, do you?' he said, as if until that point he had thought she was faking it.

'I certainly don't know anything about a baby,' Lotte retorted. 'Look, I've told you exactly what's come back to me so far. The rest is just like a closed door. I want to open it, but there is no handle on it. Now you tell me I've had a baby! How long ago was this?' Her voice began to rise in distress at the enormity of what he'd told her. 'Don't you think if I knew I was a mother I'd be desperate to know where and how my child was? Now you're really scaring me!'

'I'm sorry, Lotte, I didn't mean to scare you,' he said soothingly. 'We think the birth was just a couple of months ago, three at the most. We didn't ask you any questions on admission because you were in no fit state to deal with anything, especially if you'd had a stillbirth. But despite the best efforts of the police, social services and many other agencies, no one has been able to throw any light on where you gave birth to this child. It is imperative we find out about him or her, for if it was a live birth it is possible he or she could be alone and uncared for.'

'Oh, my God!' Lotte exclaimed, visualizing a baby lying crying in a cot, wet and hungry. Her eyes filled with tears and she looked pleadingly at the doctor. 'This is getting worse and worse! What can I do to help? Can't you hypnotize me or something to find out more?'

'That only works in films,' he said, patting her hand. 'You have already remembered a great deal, and I'm sure the rest will come back very soon. We have decided though, because of the urgency of the situation, that we must go to the press with this today. Someone out there knows about the baby, and it is imperative we speak to them. Meanwhile you and I can work together, talking through what you have remembered.'

Lotte caught hold of his hand in both of hers, her eyes swimming in tears. 'I have to remember now, for the baby's sake.'

At nearly three on the same day as Lotte was still lying in her hospital bed anxiously wondering how she could have had a baby and yet not remember anything at all about it, David Mitchell, her rescuer, was walking into a pub in Selsey.

He was greeted enthusiastically by Jim Lerner, a foxy-faced man he knew from his gym. 'Hi, Jim,' David responded half-heartedly, as he didn't like the man much, and ordered just a half of lager instead of a pint.

'I hear you found that mystery bird on the beach,' Jim said.

'Yes, that's right,' David admitted. 'It gave me quite a

shock too. I thought she was dead. But I hear she's recovering now.'

'If I found a bird as tasty as that I'd be visiting her in hospital and offering to take care of her when she came out,' Jim said with a broad grin. 'Did you see the picture of her in yesterday's paper?'

David had become a minor celebrity through finding the girl on the beach. He had been door-stepped by the local paper and he was mentioned by name on the television news. He found it embarrassing, for it wasn't as if he'd performed some dramatic rescue, all he'd done was call an ambulance.

He didn't really want to get involved with Jim as the man had only three topics of conversation: the girls he'd bedded, football, and how many pints he could down, but he could see Jim had a newspaper on the bar in front of him and curiosity got the better of him.

'That's not it there, I suppose?' he asked, moving closer.

'Sure is! I brought it in with me to show it round,' Jim replied, opening up the paper and pointing to a picture of a girl in tiny shorts and a sun top. David had to look twice before he saw it was the same girl he'd helped. He hadn't even considered her looks at the time – he was after all afraid she was going to die – but in this picture she looked as gorgeous as any model, and very different from the first police identikit picture.

'Bloody hell!' he exclaimed involuntarily, despite intending to stay cool in front of Jim.

In the four days since David had found the girl he'd thought about her quite a lot, indeed he'd telephoned the hospital twice on the day he found her to make sure she had survived. He really wanted to know her full story too: had she been pushed off a boat, or had she been trying to end her life? Who was she? Was she local?

He paid for his drink and sipped it as he read the article. There was a little more detail in this one, for although the police still didn't know how she came to be washed up on Selsey beach because she had lost her memory, they had found her parents. She was called Lotte Wainwright, a twenty-four-year-old hairdresser from Brighton. This picture of her was taken by a friend while they were working together on a cruise ship. Yet it seemed neither friends nor parents knew where she'd been for the past year since she left the ship. The police were appealing for anyone who had any information about her to come forward.

'A bloke I was working with this morning reckoned his mate used to knock her off,' Jim said as David finished reading.

'Then I hope he went to the police,' David said sharply. He didn't understand why some men had to bring everything to do with women down to the lowest level. 'He might be able to fill in a few blanks for them.'

'Doubt he'll admit to firing blanks,' Jim said, then laughed loudly at his own joke.

'I've got to go,' David said, finishing off his drink.

He'd had enough of Jim for one day, but he thought he might take one bit of his advice and that was to go to the hospital later and see the girl.

It was just before six when David arrived at St Richard's, carrying some flowers and a box of chocolates, and asked at reception which ward Lotte was in. The receptionist was a little flustered as there were lots of people asking her questions, and she said visiting didn't start till six-thirty, but she waved her hand towards Singleton Ward on the ground floor and David assumed that meant he could wait outside the ward.

The corridor of Singleton Ward was deserted. From behind the doors of the different ward rooms came a faint buzz of conversation, the sound of screens being pulled and trolleys wheeled, but the atmosphere was serene; clearly no medical dramas or emergencies were taking place. David walked along the corridor past the men's ward and then the women's where he checked the names of the patients listed outside. She wasn't in there, so he walked on to the single rooms.

There were names on each door except one, but he was reluctant to look through the glass panel to check if Lotte was in there as it seemed an invasion of privacy. So he walked back down the corridor looking for a nurse to ask.

He waylaid one on her way into the men's ward. 'You'll have to check with the policeman outside her door,' she told him briefly before disappearing.

David was puzzled then, for he hadn't seen a policeman

anywhere, but now he came to think about it, there ought to be a guard if someone had tried to drown her by throwing her from a boat.

He was turning to go back to the unlabelled room, when he saw a man about to enter it. He wasn't a doctor as he wasn't wearing a white coat, and clearly not a policeman either or he would have been in uniform. It annoyed David that some other visitor could go straight in to visit her while he had to wait until six-thirty.

He decided there was no point in hanging around waiting when she might not even want to see him anyway, especially now she had someone else there. So he'd go in, give her the flowers and chocolates, say his bit about how it was him who found her, and how glad he was that she was recovering. Then if he picked up the vibes she didn't want him there, he'd clear off.

He marched along to the door, but glanced through the small glass panel before walking in. To his shock the other visitor was bending menacingly over the bed. David couldn't be certain it was Lotte in the bed, or for that matter what the man was doing to the patient, for his back was blocking the view. Yet David could see legs thrashing around under the covers and arms flailing about, which was enough for him to be absolutely certain the man was hurting whoever it was.

David charged in, tossing the flowers and chocolates on to a chair. 'What the hell do you think you're doing?' he yelled, catching the man by the collar of his jacket and throwing a punch at him.

Unfortunately David hadn't got a strong enough grip on the man's collar and he ducked the punch. Before David could catch hold of him again, he'd darted past him and out of the door.

David hit the bell push beside the bed. It was Lotte in the bed. She looked terrified and was rubbing at her throat, but there was no time to help her. 'Tell the nurse what happened, I'm going after him,' he said hurriedly.

By the time David got out of the room the double doors were swinging at the end of the corridor. He ran at full tilt after the man, nearly knocking down an elderly patient with a walking frame.

The reception area was full of people arriving for visiting and David could no longer see the man. But he made a mental note to tell the police he'd been of slim build and average height, with light brown hair and wearing a brown jacket.

He ran outside and along to the car park, but there were so many cars arriving and people getting out of them that it was impossible to tell who was just parking up, or about to leave. His heart was hammering, probably with shock at what he'd witnessed, but he realized that if the man had any sense he wouldn't draw attention to himself by attempting to leave straight away.

David positioned himself at the car park exit, so he could at least note the registration number if he saw the man again, and getting out his mobile phone he dialled 999 for help.

'You did well, sir,' the middle-aged, rather portly uniformed sergeant said some three hours later when practically all the cars in the car park had gone. David was disappointed he hadn't been able to identify Lotte's assailant in any of them. 'Of course there's every possibility he left his car elsewhere, or even had an accomplice waiting in a getaway car. But thanks to you that poor girl came to no further harm.'

'Could I just go and say goodnight to her?' David asked. He felt oddly exhausted: he supposed it was the trauma and being forced to explain what he'd seen to the police and give the man's description over and over again. He felt he'd done his bit helping to check each car leaving the car park, and he thought if he could just see Lotte smile, he might be able to wipe out the memory of the terror in her eyes earlier.

'Just five minutes,' the sergeant said with an understanding smile. 'Tell Boyce I said it was OK. The nurses might have other ideas, but you'll have to take your chances with them.'

PC Boyce was outside Lotte's door. It seemed her attacker must have been watching earlier in the day, and seized the moment when the policeman went off to get a snack from the cafeteria.

Boyce looked sheepish when David told him the sergeant had said it was OK for him to see Lotte. Clearly he'd been severely reprimanded for leaving his post earlier.

'Go on in,' he said. 'Thank heaven you came along

when you did – my life wouldn't have been worth living if he'd succeeded in killing her.'

David hesitated in the doorway. He hadn't thought of Lotte as a crime victim when he found her on the beach. He'd imagined she was a drunk or a depressive who'd attempted to take her own life, and while he was sorry for her, he felt no involvement. But then reading today about the mystery surrounding her, and finally coming in here to see someone attempting to kill her, suddenly made him feel ridiculously protective of her, as though she was one of his sisters.

She was wearing one of the standard white hospital gowns, and her face was almost as white as the gown. Her lips were cracked, and she had flaking skin all over her face. He could see now that he'd been right to think someone had hacked off her hair, for it stood out all around her head in clumps. But even if she was a mess, her blue eyes were lovely, and when she smiled at him he saw the same pretty girl who had been in the press photograph.

'Can I try again?' he asked. 'I don't know if anyone told you, but I'm David Mitchell, the one who found you on the beach.'

She smiled again. 'You seem to be making a habit of rescuing me,' she said, her voice a little husky. 'I had hoped you'd come in sometime so I could thank you for finding me on the beach, but you couldn't have picked a better night than tonight to do it. I owe you my life.'

David smiled with embarrassment. He didn't see himself as any kind of hero, it was just luck that he'd interrupted her attacker. 'Did you know him?' he asked. 'Or have you seen him before?'

'I don't know,' she shrugged, her eyes wide and scared. 'But I didn't get the feeling I had known him, not the way I have had with some other people. That makes losing my memory even scarier because I don't know who is good and who is bad. But thank you so much for the flowers and chocolates.' She pointed to the flowers which had been arranged in a vase and now stood on the locker. 'They are lovely.'

'Did he hurt you?' David asked, coming closer.

'A bit sore here.' She put her hand up to her neck. 'And scared witless, but don't let's talk about him and what happened, tell me about you.'

In just that one sentence David felt he knew all about her. A girl with no ego, and who cared more for others than herself.

'I'm thirty-two, single, recently split with my girl-friend, and I come from a village near Bristol. I'm one of eight children, and I'm the second to eldest,' he said, feeling as if someone had switched a spotlight on to him. 'I've recently started my own company; it's to do with telecommunications. But you don't want to know about that, it's boring.'

He liked the way her lips twitched with amusement at him rattling that out. 'One of eight, eh! Your mum had her work cut out. I was told you found me on the beach early in the morning. But why were you out at that time?'

David smiled at her directness. 'I go running. I take my neighbour's dog Toto, because Fred's got a broken leg and can't do more than hobble on his crutches. But Toto ran ahead and was sniffing at you. I thought you were a sack of rubbish or something until I got much closer. Can you remember being in the water?'

'Not really, only the very last bit as I felt the shingle scraping me. But I can remember you speaking to me and putting something warm around me. Even that's cloudy, like a dream. I think I only became really aware of what was going on around me once I got here.'

'Have you recovered any memories yet?' he asked. 'I read in the papers you were a hairdresser and you worked on a cruise ship. Did you have a boyfriend?'

'I have remembered some things, like the place I used to work in Brighton and the people I knew there. But everything since then is still all a blank.'

'I suppose if you had a boyfriend he would've claimed you by now,' David said.

Lotte smiled shyly. 'Not if I was mean to him! Or worse still, he may be responsible for me being in the sea!'

'I can't imagine any man even thinking about hurting you,' David said.

'Well, that one who came in here earlier hadn't come to bring me a bunch of grapes,' she said with a sigh. She looked at him hard, almost as if she was trying to decide if she could trust him with a confidence.

'I wish I knew what this is all about. It's been a horrible day. First the doctor told me I'd had a baby in the last couple of months. How can I not remember that?' she blurted out. 'I'm so worried about it being all alone and hurt, and now there is someone trying to kill me. Why? What can I have done?'

The baby added another even more horrifying dimension to her ordeal and David wished he dared scoop her up in his arms and hug her, but he was afraid that would frighten her further.

'I'm so sorry, it must be awful for you,' he said lamely, very aware that a missing baby was just about the most serious problem any mother could face, but unable to find the words to express that. 'But I'm sure the police will sort it all out, and the doctors here will get your memory back for you.'

A nurse opened the door and told him his visit was up.

'Can I come back again to see you?' he asked Lotte.

'Of course you can,' she said. 'I'd like that.'

'Can I bring you anything? Food, shampoo or anything?'

'No, I'm fine, I have a couple of friends from Brighton who have got that covered,' she said. 'Just bring yourself.'

As David left, he glanced back and she gave him a little wave of her hand. He knew right then that he'd be gutted if a boyfriend did turn up.

*

Lotte was violently sick during the night. She only just managed to get out of bed and into the bathroom attached to her room before the retching began.

Frightened by it, she pressed the bell to call a nurse.

'It'll be shock that's brought it on,' the nurse who answered said in sympathy, as she wiped Lotte's sweaty brow. 'You'd have to be made of steel not to react to someone trying to kill you. But you can rest assured it won't happen again. The policeman outside has been given orders he can't leave for any reason until he is replaced by someone else.'

Even after the sickness had stopped, Lotte was still shivering one minute, then overheating the next, and as she lay in the dark feeling wretched, tears rolled down her cheeks because she felt so terribly alone.

Almost everything she had remembered about her life so far had proved it to be a miserable one, and although Simon, Adam, Dale and Scott had all claimed she was liked and loved by many, she had still ended up half drowned on a beach. That suggested there must be something deeply repellent about her that had made her a target for hate.

Her parents didn't like her, there was no boyfriend. And someone wanted her dead.

But far, far worse to her was that she'd had a baby, yet until the doctor told her, she hadn't the faintest inkling about it. While she could accept without any guilt that she couldn't remember anything else in the past few years, she had a terrible sense of shame at not having some fine-tuned undeletable memory of her child.

She'd always been told that mothers had a sixth sense where their babies were concerned, so why wasn't hers working? Just a couple of months old but she'd already failed it.

Supposing it turned out she'd run away and left the baby alone? A baby couldn't live long without milk, and it could die before the police managed to find it. That would be murder, surely?

Not to know the sex of her baby, who the father was, or anything about it at all, was so frustrating that she felt like screaming and battering her head against a wall.

At ten the next morning one of the nurses popped in to tell Lotte they'd just had a phone call from Simon. 'He said he'd like to come over this afternoon and tidy up your hair. I said I thought you'd be fine about it. Was I right?'

Lotte nodded weakly. A couple of police had already been in to see her this morning, asking her more questions about the attack the previous evening. The attack and then the sickness during the night had left her feeling really rough, and she certainly didn't care what her hair looked like, but she desperately needed to talk to someone who knew her well. And Sundays were really the only time Simon was free to visit. When he'd come earlier in the week he'd had to cancel several of his clients' appointments.

While Lotte was having a bath earlier, she had noticed her stomach was flabby and there were some stretch marks too, which was proof she really had given birth. But who had hacked off her hair, and why? It didn't make any sense to do that if they had planned to kill her. Unless of course they just wanted to humiliate her.

'Are you OK?' the nurse asked, perhaps sensing her anxiety. 'I heard what happened yesterday – it must have been awful.'

'I'm fine now,' Lotte lied. 'I'll be even better with my hair cut properly.'

Simon arrived at two carrying a large red holdall. 'I've got all the stuff to make you gorgeous again,' he said, giving her a hug.

Putting the holdall on the bed, he got out a present wrapped in silver paper and trimmed with a purple bow. 'This is from everyone at the salon.'

Lotte opened it to find two pairs of silky pyjamas, one pink, one turquoise. 'That's wonderful,' she said with an appreciative smile. 'I feel hideous in this hospital gown.'

Simon dug further into the holdall and pulled out a small carrier bag. 'This is from Adam and me, just some things we knew you'd need.'

Lotte peeped in and saw a pair of slippers, a packet of three pairs of knickers, face cream and various cosmetics. Suddenly she couldn't hold back her tears.

'What on earth is it?' Simon asked in alarm. 'Was I overstepping the mark getting personal stuff? I'm sorry, I was just getting what I thought you'd need.'

'It was so very kind of you,' Lotte sobbed out. 'Just like you to be so thoughtful. You haven't overstepped the mark, it was just that after all the bad things that have happened, I didn't expect anything lovely ever again.'

Simon hugged her tightly to his chest and let her cry until she was ready to tell him what had been going on.

She began with the previous night's attempt on her life, telling the story baldly with hiccuping sobs. From there she went on to say that she felt whoever hacked off her hair was trying to humiliate her, and finally she told him that the doctor said she'd had a baby.

Simon's jaw dropped. 'Hell, babe! That's too much for anyone to take in all at once,' he gasped. 'I don't know what to say.'

He was silent for what seemed a very long time to Lotte, sitting on the bed looking blankly ahead. 'I'm OK, Simon,' she ventured. 'I remembered about you and Adam, so I'll remember everything else before long.'

'Your amnesia isn't as worrying as this man trying to hurt you,' he said. 'Have they caught him?'

Lotte shook her head and then explained about David Mitchell turning up in the nick of time and going after the man. 'Thank heavens for him! A few more minutes and I think he would've throttled me.'

'No wonder that policeman outside questioned me and searched my bag like I was a suspected Jack the Ripper!' Simon said.

'I'm so scared, Simon,' she admitted. 'Not so much of the man who tried to kill me, I believe the police will protect me, but about the baby. I can't bear the thought I don't remember the birth, who the father was, but most of all I'm terrified there's no one looking after the baby now.'

'But surely there's a record of his or her birth?' Simon exclaimed, dabbing at his forehead with a handkerchief.

'The police can't find any. The policeman who came in earlier today said they thought the birth may have been in France, and that I was coming back to England in the boat, and either I jumped or was pushed out. They've sent some men over there to investigate.'

'You poor love,' Simon said, and put his arms around her again and rocked her. 'This is nightmarish stuff, but the police will leave no stone unturned. Are they going to put it in the papers?'

'I think it may be in the Sunday papers already, and on the news tonight,' she said. 'Certainly all the nationals tomorrow.'

'People will respond to a missing baby,' he said firmly. 'I bet the police will be inundated with information. And you've recovered so much memory already, I'm sure the rest will come back pretty soon.'

'Dr Percival, the neurologist, will be coming round a bit later to see me again,' she said.

'Then I'd better finish making you gorgeous so he falls in love with you like everyone else does,' Simon said, but his smile didn't reach his eyes. 'Then he'll go the extra mile for you.'

Half an hour later, with her hair washed and conditioned, Simon had her sitting on a chair, a gown around her shoulders and another on the floor beneath her to catch the hair he was snipping off. He had been unusually silent while washing her hair and Lotte guessed he felt as helpless as she did.

'Why on earth would anyone hack off such lovely hair?' he said suddenly, proving that he had been mulling it over. 'It was half-way down your back when you left Kutz's, so sleek and shiny everyone admired it.'

'It seemed to me it might have been a punishment,' Lotte said.

'I can't imagine you doing anything bad enough to justify such a punishment,' he said as he ran a little hair gel through it with his fingers. 'But at least it will be easy to look after now, and it looks great.'

Lotte thought she looked like an elf with the feathery cut all around her face, but she liked it.

'It makes you look even younger,' Simon said, looking at her intently as he whipped the gown from her shoulders. 'Now, off into the bathroom and put on the new pjs and some face cream, and you'll feel like a new woman. I'll just collect up all this hair.'

Five minutes later Lotte came out of the bathroom wearing the pink pyjamas. Her face looked far less flaky as she'd rubbed cream into it. She'd added a little blusher, mascara and lipstick too.

'Wow, babe, that's more like the old Lotte!' Simon exclaimed.

'I feel much better,' she said shyly. 'The marks on my wrists and ankles are fading now, but look how bruised my neck is!' She held up her chin and Simon could see thumbprints on her windpipe and three finger imprints on each side of her neck.

'They'll fade very quickly,' Simon said. He was really shocked by the marks, but he'd purposely played it down as he didn't want her to sense his alarm. 'Now, hop back into bed because I've got some photos for you to look at. I thought they might help jog the old memory.'

Simon was a photography enthusiast. He took his camera to every party, to every major event, he even snapped his clients if he did a style he thought was really good. He was equally diligent in putting the pictures in albums, all dated with a caption under each one.

Lotte put aside her worries in the joy of seeing so many familiar faces and occasions she'd been part of. There were various staff parties – birthdays, Christmas, engagements and leaving ones. Some were just staff nights out, with everyone dressed to kill. She giggled at Simon in a white tuxedo, and another picture of Adam roller skating along the promenade wearing only Speedo swimming trunks and carrying an umbrella. She remembered he did it for charity.

There was the Space Age party when Adam was Spock from *Star Trek* and Simon was Captain Kirk. Lotte was dressed as Princess Leia from *Star Wars*. She was in so many of the pictures, and she was sure she'd never seen all of them before: at a dinner party, riding a carousel at the fair and lying on the sofa at Simon's flat.

'And what about this one?' Simon asked as he turned the page, and there she was again, this time in turquoise hot pants and a white camisole top. It looked as if she were in a night club or restaurant.

Lotte stared at it. She was very suntanned in the picture, and although she had no memory of seeing it before, all at once she remembered. It had been taken on her twentieth birthday in June 2000. She'd had a week's holiday and the weather had been so good she spent it all lying on the beach. She could almost feel the sultry heat in the club that night, hear Ricky Martin and Christina Aguilera's record 'Nobody Wants to Be Lonely'. She knew she looked good, and felt anything could happen that night.

'Well?' Simon asked, his expression fearful, but also determined. 'Do you remember?'

'Yes,' she sighed. She understood why he looked that way. That night was a major milestone in her life, but Simon was afraid that remembering it would prove too painful for her.

She remembered another song from that night, 'Whole Again' by Atomic Kitten. It had been 'their' song, and just as the events of that night had made her feel whole again, she knew she must recall everything again now to help the healing.

She could see Mark as she saw him for the very first time. Lean-faced with short-cropped dark hair, sleepy dark eyes looking right at her, deeply tanned skin that had a gloss as if he'd rubbed himself in cocoa butter. Slim and muscular in a black tee-shirt and jeans.

They smiled at each other, and then he was gone. Then suddenly he was right behind her. 'You're gorgeous,' he whispered right into her ear.

Every hair on her body jumped to attention and she felt a churning sensation in her stomach which was quite different from having too much to drink.

'I hope the memory isn't too painful,' Simon said, taking her hand and squeezing it. 'But I kinda thought if we got that one out, maybe others would follow. All of us in the salon who were there that night remember it so clearly. You and that guy just moved together like you were two magnets attracted to each other. I wish I'd taken a picture of him too.'

'I don't need one, I can remember everything about him,' Lotte said.

Simon went on turning pages of his albums. There were pictures taken at hair shows and exhibitions, many of the models sporting totally outrageous styles. One picture showed Lotte receiving the trophy for the best wedding style, and another coming third in the whole of the south of England for a cut she did. She remembered those evenings, the delight of knowing she was a really good hairdresser, the pleasure of hearing people's praise, the smells of the products heavy in the air, that chatter and laughter and the underlying tension as the competitors waited to be judged. Yet after Mark none of that touched her as deeply, it was never as important again. She really only entered the competitions for the sake of the salon, not for herself.

'You look tired now,' Simon said later, perhaps noticing she hadn't spoken for a while. 'I'd better go, I've been here longer than I intended. Are you OK?'

'It's been good to look at your pictures,' she said truthfully. 'But I could do with a snooze before the doctor comes.'

He gathered up his things, stuffed them into the red holdall and slung it over his shoulder. 'Bye, babe,' he said, bending to kiss her. 'I'm going to try and find the doctor before I go and see what he thinks about you coming to stay with Adam and me. I guess the police will be concerned about your safety, but we can make it really secure there, can't we?'

Lotte smiled up at him, touched by his kindness and desire to get her back on her feet. 'I'm sure we can. As long as I keep the door locked, who could get in?'

Lovely as it had been to have Simon visit, Lotte was glad to be alone again, for she could hear 'Whole Again' playing in her head, and she wanted to return to the memories of that night.

Mark led her out among the dancers but they didn't really dance, just held on to each other and smiled. There were coloured lights spinning, it was too noisy to hear each other speak and people kept jostling them, but none of that mattered. His hands were on her waist, hers were on his shoulders, and they moved together like one person.

She didn't care what he did for a job, where he lived or anything much else about him. For the first time in her life she knew what it was to want a man. And she knew just by the way he looked at her that he wanted her. That was enough.

Mark bought a bottle of Cava later and they went down on to the beach to drink it. It was a hot, sultry night with no wind and the moon cast a silver path on the sea. There were many other couples doing just the same as them, and as they sat on the shingle passing the bottle between them they could hear the noise of the town behind them. But none of this intruded on them; all they heard was the gentle sound of waves breaking on the beach.

Mark told her then that he was in the navy, home on leave for two weeks. He was twenty-four, and the street where his family lived was just a few away from her parents.

No one had ever kissed her like he did. Sensual, deep kisses that made her stomach churn and all sense of reality vanish. If he had tried to take her there on the beach surrounded by other couples, she doubted she would have stopped him. She just wanted him.

Later they went back to her flat. Fortunately Simon and Adam were out. There in her single bed they made love.

It was so hot they had no covers over them, and with the windows open wide the Saturday night sounds of Brighton – music, traffic and shouting drunks – wafted in.

She was embarrassed because he wanted her to put the condom on him and she didn't really know how to do it, and when he penetrated her it hurt more than she'd expected. But even if it wasn't quite as wonderful as all the petting and kissing before had been, Lotte felt she'd moved up a level in maturity.

The next morning she woke early and just lay curled up beside Mark, drinking in everything about him. He was every bit as handsome as she'd thought the previous night, even with a shadow of stubble on his chin. Such beautifully shaped lips, full and soft, turning up at the corners as if he were smiling. She liked his hair, it was cut like Tom Cruise's in *Top Gun*, sort of floppy on the top but very short at the back and sides. He had a rather long neck and a small, straight nose, and then that hunky muscular chest with just a sprinkling of dark hair.

He woke up as she was looking at him. 'Hello, gorgeous,' he said sleepily. 'I expected to find I'd dreamt you. But you are for real.'

In the ten days that followed Lotte was often tempted to play ill so she could be with Mark all day. As it was, they made love half the night, and she stumbled off to work almost asleep on her feet. Mark met her for lunch, just half an hour sitting in the sunshine holding hands, and then she had to wait all the way through till five to find him waiting for her again.

'He is a dreamboat,' Simon said thoughtfully, watching from the salon window as Mark crossed the road. 'What are you going to do when he goes back to sea?'

'Catch up on my sleep,' she said and laughed. She had pondered that same question many times already. She knew she loved Mark even if she didn't dare tell him so, and the thought of being without him filled her with panic. It was as though she'd only been firing on half her cylinders until he came along and made the other half work. He was on her mind from the moment she woke till she fell asleep. She could talk to him about anything – she'd even told him all about her parents one night. He'd been at primary school with Fleur, as it turned out, and though he didn't remember much about her, as she was a couple of years ahead of him, he did know she had died and recalled his parents saying how tragic it was.

The last night before he had to go back to Plymouth, Mark told her he loved her, and promised that on his next leave he'd take her to meet his parents. 'They are going to love you too,' he said, holding her face cupped in his hands and looking at her as if he was trying to imprint every detail of her face on to his mind.

Their lovemaking that night was slow and tender, both of them aware that the hours left together were ticking away. That Saturday morning was a beautiful one, promising to be very hot later, and he walked with her to Kutz before going home to collect his gear and then catch the train to Plymouth.

Lotte cried as he kissed her goodbye, but he promised he would phone and write as often as he could.

'My little Tinker Bell,' he murmured, stroking back her hair from her face. That was his nickname for her – he said she'd sprinkled magic dust on his life. 'We're together for the long haul now, a few weeks apart won't matter. You'll be in my heart every minute of each day. We were meant for one another.'

Around ten that morning a client came into the salon and said someone had been knocked down by a truck up near the railway station. At lunchtime on the local news they reported a man had died in the road accident but said the police were withholding his name until his family had been informed.

None of this even registered with Lotte. Her mind was stuck on wondering how she'd get through the next few weeks without Mark. But as she came out of the salon with Simon at six, dragging her feet with tiredness, they both spotted a news bulletin on a stand selling the evening paper.

It read, 'Leave ended with death for local sailor.'

Lotte blanched, her legs suddenly like jelly. 'It can't be him,' Simon gasped, and he went over to the newspaper stand to read the story. But just the way his shoulders slumped as he read the front page told Lotte that it was Mark who was dead.

People said things like, 'Well, you only knew him for such a short time.' As if that made it hurt less! When she called on Mark's family they looked at her oddly as if she was trying to elbow her way into their grief. Clearly to them she was just the girl he'd been knocking off during his leave. His mother even said if he hadn't been up half the night perhaps he might not have run across the road in front of the truck. Lotte had no standing at the funeral; her flowers weren't put on the coffin. She didn't even know any of his naval friends who came up from Plymouth to pay their last respects.

If it hadn't been for Simon and Adam she might have stepped in front of a truck herself. It crossed her mind many times that death by any means was preferable to living with such pain.

Lotte found herself crying as she recalled those terrible grief-filled weeks after Mark's death. She remembered that she refused to get out of bed, to eat, bathe or talk to anyone. It was only when Simon became ill that she stirred herself to take care of him.

'You will meet someone else one day that you can feel that way about again,' Simon assured her. 'You can get over it too. One day you'll suddenly realize you haven't thought of him for a day, a week, or even a month. It is curable.'

Lotte felt Simon was right. She didn't know whether she'd thought about Mark constantly for all of the time since then, but remembering him now didn't hurt the way she remembered it.

Had there been another boyfriend since? She would have to ask Dale.

Chapter Six

'What is your problem?' Marisa snapped at Dale. 'The guests who come into the spa come to give themselves a treat or to make themselves feel special. They certainly don't want to be greeted by someone sniffing and sobbing!'

'I'm not sniffing and sobbing,' Dale retorted.

'Your eyes are red and puffy,' Marisa said contemptuously. 'It looks like you've been crying all night.'

Dale had been crying most of the night.

Simon had rung her as he was leaving the hospital yesterday to tell her and Scott about Lotte being attacked on Saturday and that earlier the same day a doctor had informed her she'd had a baby recently.

It turned out that all the Sunday papers had covered the story about the baby, and reports of that and the attack had been on both radio and television that morning. But no one in the spa had read any Sunday papers or heard the radio or television bulletins, so Simon had to break the dreadful news. Dale was so shocked she could barely speak. Simon's voice kept cracking and it was clear he was in no fit state to discuss it further either.

After getting this news Dale somehow managed to

give both a massage and a manicure without breaking down. But the minute the last client had gone, she fled back to the cottage. Frankie, Scott, Michelle and Rosie were all there, and the minute Dale saw them all, she burst into tears.

They were all shocked rigid by the news. Scott was every bit as upset as Dale, and he pointed out that if this man was prepared to risk everything to try to kill Lotte in a public place, it put a whole different complexion on the mystery of her having been found washed up on the beach. The question they were all asking was what could be so bad that she had to be killed for it.

'This can't be right,' Dale kept repeating through her sobs. 'No one could have so many terrible things happen to her. Where is the baby? Who was the father? Who is this man who tried to kill her? And why did he want to do that?'

Scott was almost as distraught as Dale, and Frankie tried to make them feel better by going over to the kitchen and getting them some dinner on a tray. But it wasn't food they wanted, just answers no one could give them.

Frankie rang the hospital on their behalf to see how Lotte was. The Ward Sister said she was unhurt and recovering some memory, but advised them not to visit her for a couple of days as she needed complete rest.

Dale downed several glasses of brandy, hoping for

oblivion, but instead she lay awake crying, wondering how her friend was ever going to get over this.

Then the next morning she had Marisa on her back.

'Well, what is it about? A boyfriend dumped you?' she asked curtly.

Dale felt like slapping the woman. She could see both Scott and Frankie hovering by the door leading to the swimming pool, and could sense them willing her not to react to the woman's goading.

'Men don't dump me, I do the dumping,' Dale retorted. 'But I can cry when someone tries to kill my best friend, and it is discovered she had a baby recently, which the police haven't found. But I don't suppose you'd lose any sleep over a small baby left without its mother, would you? You haven't got a heart!'

'How dare you speak to me like that!' Marisa's dark eyes flashed dangerously. 'I shall be reporting your insolence. Now, cover those puffy eyes with makeup and get to work.'

'And I shall be reporting your lack of humanity,' Dale hissed back at her. 'You'd have made a great warder in a concentration camp.'

On Wednesday afternoon, eight days after Lotte was found on the beach, Dale and Simon were at St Richard's for an appointment with Dr Percival.

'The problem is,' he said, folding his hands together as if in prayer and holding them in front of his nose, 'Miss Wainwright has no injuries that require a hospital bed – physically she is in good shape. But I am very concerned about her mental health.'

Dale and Simon had requested this appointment in the hope that the doctor would support their wish to take Lotte home to Simon's flat in Brighton. But Dale had taken an instant dislike to Dr Percival because she thought was he was overbearing and lacking in sympathy.

Right from the moment she and Scott knew for certain that the girl on the beach was Lotte, they had been frightened for her. But now an attempt had been made on her life and she had learnt she'd given birth a couple of months earlier, they were terrified she'd turn in on herself and never recover.

When they had visited her the previous night they had tried very hard not to let her see that the possibility that her baby was out there somewhere hungry and unprotected was giving them sleepless nights too. Or that they didn't imagine every man coming along the hospital corridor could be her attacker returning. But they could see for themselves this was exactly what was on her mind.

Both Dale and Scott were overwhelmed by the enormity of it all and felt helpless because they were unable to stimulate her memory or protect her from further harm. Yet they could see how well Lotte reacted to Simon and Adam and they felt that these were the two people who could bring back her memory and defend her.

Dale had chosen to accompany Simon today because she wanted the doctor to know that she and Scott were one hundred per cent behind him and Adam.

'She's not mad, only lost her memory,' Dale said sharply, afraid Dr Percival wanted Lotte moved to a mental hospital. 'We both think she will recover quicker with her friends constantly jogging it. And Simon and Adam can keep her safe.'

'Madness, in the way many people perceive it, is a rare thing,' he retorted dismissively. 'Mental illness takes many forms and amnesia is just one of them. While sometimes it can be a fleeting problem brought on by anything from a blow to the head, trauma or surgery, it can also be permanent. But in Miss Wainwright's case it would appear to be caused by a deeply disturbing event which she has subconsciously suppressed.'

'We are aware of that,' Dale said, irritated by the way he was talking down to her. 'So how were you thinking of treating her, and where?'

'At the Vale,' he said.

'Surely not,' Dale gasped. One of the girls in the hairdresser's at Marchwood had said her grandfather had been put in the Vale when he became senile. She said it was an awful place.

'I think you have heard too many myths about the Vale,' Dr Percival said sharply. 'It is one of the top psychiatric hospitals in the South-East.'

'Lotte will just withdraw into herself there,' Simon said firmly. He wanted to add that he didn't think their friend should be in a place full of senile old people, depressives, bi-polars and drying-out alcoholics, but he was reluctant to say anything which might alienate the doctor.

'What makes a young man with no experience whatsoever in mental health imagine he knows better than someone who has spent twenty-five years at it?' Dr Percival sounded almost amused at Simon's impudence.

'I might not know anything about mental health, but I do know Lotte very well,' Simon said, leaning forward in his chair and putting his clenched fists on the doctor's desk. 'And I think as soon as she's settled in familiar surroundings, she'll begin to unravel whatever has happened to her.'

'And you don't imagine she will need professional help dealing with all the problems surrounding her baby? Firstly she's got to recover the memory of the birth, and how she felt about its conception, for we don't know if it was within a loving relationship. There's also the possibility the baby is dead.'

Simon was only too aware it was likely to be an emotional minefield for Lotte as she regained her memory. All four of her friends suspected that the baby's conception, the birth and the events afterwards had been the stuff of the worst nightmares. But they did believe she'd be able to deal with it better if she was surrounded by loving friends rather than just doctors and nurses.

'The little mite could have died in appalling circumstances,' the doctor went on. 'It's possible its body may never be found to give Lotte the answers she will need for recovery. I am not trying to alarm you, young man, only to point out that she might have to face huge, overwhelming problems.'

Simon gulped, suddenly unsure of himself. He cared deeply about Lotte, he wanted and needed to help her, but were Adam and he the right people for the job? Could he be sure that loving and caring for her was enough to heal her?

He paused, glancing at Dale's tense face. She took his hand and squeezed it as if silently assuring him he could do it.

'I admit we're taking on a lot,' he said when he'd steadied himself. 'But I think Lotte will be able to cope better with even the worst-case scenario if she's in a safe and loving environment. Adam and I may not be psychiatrists, but we are sensitive, caring and we love her. We'll have Dale and Scott too to help us. You try telling me that isn't a better basis for her recovery than the Vale!'

'So you want to tell me how to do my job now,' the doctor said, yet there was a softer expression in his eyes which suggested he was beginning to come round to the idea of a bunch of amateurs taking on his patient.

'No, sir,' Simon insisted. 'We will follow all your advice. But the hospital is overcrowded, and the other patients in the Vale will probably frighten Lotte. She has happy associations with my flat, and I can make it like Fort Knox to keep her safe. I doubt if you could do that at the Vale.'

'You are right there.' Percival sighed. 'So I am going to agree that you can take her home with you at the weekend, but only on the condition you call me on a regular basis and if you have any cause for alarm about her, you bring her back here.'

'I will,' Simon said, beaming at the doctor.

Simon and Dale had to wait half an hour until visiting time, so they went off to the coffee bar and Simon told her that DI Bryan had called round at his flat the previous evening.

'He had just broken off from the search for Lotte's attacker, but there was no good news. He said they hadn't got a single clear image of the man's face on CCTV, and no car either, which means he must have parked it away from the hospital. His knowledge of the hospital suggests a local man, so they've had David Mitchell, the guy that interrupted the attack, looking at mug shots and trying to create an identikit picture.' Simon sighed deeply, looking dejected. 'Sadly, he didn't get a real look at the attacker's face.'

'We owe David a lot,' Dale said. 'He's something of a hero. But it's eight days since he found her on the beach – surely the police should have found something concrete by now? Did Bryan say if they had any leads on her baby?'

The welfare and the whereabouts of the baby had become a concern for everyone in the locality since the press release about it. People were discussing it in the streets, shops and pubs, and back at Marchwood Manor it was virtually the only topic of conversation.

'I don't think so; he wanted to know about people Lotte used to hang around with in Brighton. And he was especially interested in her old boyfriends. He thought she might have contacted one of them when she left the cruise ship and that led to her getting pregnant.'

'Do you know of anyone?' Dale asked.

'No,' Simon responded, looking stricken. 'But as I told you before, Lotte would never have come to Brighton without contacting Adam and me. And if she had become pregnant, whether she was pleased about it or not, wherever she was in the world, she would have rung us or written. I told Bryan that's positive proof she's been held captive somewhere.'

'And what did he say to that?'

'He pointed out that she didn't ring or write about the rape in South America.'

'He's got a point there,' Dale agreed.

Simon tossed his head as he didn't see it that way. 'Bryan also suggested it was possible that her baby's father was someone she was protecting. He could be married or in the public eye. I told him she would at least have rung to say she couldn't explain who she was with. Then Bryan said she might have been afraid to tell me anything in case it got back to her parents! I ask you! How homophobic is that? I suppose he believes the old cliché that all gay men are gossips.'

'I don't think he is homophobic,' Dale said sooth-ingly. 'I think he would have said the same to anyone, man or woman, single or married. He's still looking for reasons why Lotte might have wanted to keep away from us. But since that chap stormed into the hospital and tried to kill her, it's fairly obvious this business is a whole lot more serious than her holing up with a mys-tery lover. I suppose they've got to explore every avenue, though. So did he say if they'd got any new evidence?'

'They've found out Lotte went to London after the cruise ended because she bought some new clothes in Oxford Street on her debit card,' Simon told her. 'She also withdrew some cash that same week. But she hasn't touched her account since, or notified her bank of her new address. Apparently they are still sending bank statements to the agency who got her the job on the cruise ship.'

Dale frowned. 'Well, that proves she was being held by someone, surely? No one can live on fresh air. What about her mobile phone?'

'They checked that out. It was last used to text you while you were still at sea,' Simon said.

'I can't remember now what that was about, prob-ably just to tell me what time she'd meet me in the bar, that's mostly what we texted each other about. Are you saying she didn't text or ring anyone after we docked at Southampton?'

'No one,' Simon said.

Dale looked bewildered. 'But I sent texts to about twenty people the moment we were ashore. What does that say about Lotte if she didn't send even one?'

'That she'd already decided she wasn't coming back to Brighton,' Simon said sadly. 'She wouldn't text her friends about where she was going because she knew we wouldn't approve.'

'Or whoever she was with took her phone away,' Dale said darkly.

By the time they got to Singleton Ward Dale was feeling tense. Earlier that afternoon she'd had another run-in with Marisa. This time it was about knocking off work early to come here. Then there was all the anxiety of talking to Dr Percival.

So when the nurse said they could only stay for ten minutes with Lotte as the police wanted to speak to her again, Dale felt really annoyed. She knew she wouldn't be able to visit her friend again before Saturday, and though she might have felt less irritated if Lotte had remembered something about her, she hadn't, and she directed most of her conversation to Simon.

While this was perfectly understandable if Lotte didn't have any idea how much Dale had been to her, it still stung. And Dale had always held such a dominant place in any group of friends that it was hard for her to accept her character wasn't forceful enough to blast her way through Lotte's amnesia.

It didn't help on the drive back to Brighton that Simon could talk about nothing else but Lotte coming home. He went on about how he and Adam were going to repaint her room and make it less clinical. That he was going to buy some new clothes for her, and perhaps go round to her parents and get some of her old personal belongings she'd left there. 'I'm going to try and motivate her folks into getting involved,' he said excitedly. 'There's a lot of water has flowed under that bridge. I think they might be ready now to make amends to her.'

Back in the staff bungalow at Marchwood, Scott, Frankie, Michelle and Rosie crowded round to hear about Lotte. Everyone working in the hotel was keenly interested in her case; they commented on the newspaper reports and watched out for anything on the news. But the spa staff felt even more involved because she was Dale and Scott's friend.

So Dale sat down in the lounge and told them all the details about the interview with Dr Percival. She said how great Simon had been and that he'd finally got permission to take Lotte home on Saturday. Then she moved on to the developments with the police about Lotte's bank account and buying clothes in Oxford Street.

Scott looked elated at that. 'It's only going to be a matter of time before they find out who she was in

London with,' he said. 'And it will be great once she's moved into Simon's place because we can go and see her anytime.'

'People everywhere are so upset at the thought of an abandoned baby that they'll be keeping their eyes and ears open,' Frankie chipped in. 'I wouldn't mind betting that in a week from now this will all be over, the attacker behind bars, the baby being cared for in hospital and the whole mystery solved.'

Frankie's remark, though well meant, sounded as though he was trivializing the seriousness of the situation and tears started to well up in Dale's eyes. It struck her that even if the baby was found fit and well, if it was the result of rape, Lotte might want nothing to do with it. But Dale couldn't bring herself to air that view. When Scott asked her what her tears were for, she said the first thing that came into her head.

'I'm afraid she'll never remember what I was to her,' she burst out.

'You're jealous of Simon!' Scott retorted and looked scathingly at her.

'No I'm not, don't be so ridiculous,' Dale snapped back. 'I like Simon and I'm glad that she's got someone kind and strong to take care of her.'

'I don't doubt that, but you're still feeling he's taking her away from you.'

Frankie, Rosie and Michelle were all ears. But to Dale this wasn't another episode of a soap opera, it was terrifyingly real.

She had seen Lotte in the aftermath of the rape in Ushuaia and felt her friend had been through enough horror to last her a lifetime. But this was far, far worse, especially as it was clear there was so much more to be uncovered. What if it was so terrible that when Lotte remembered it, she lost her mind permanently? And even if she managed to hang on to her sanity, she still was never going to be young and carefree again.

Dale was uncertain whether to pray for the baby's safety or hope that it had been stillborn. Yet she knew that whatever the circumstances of its birth, Lotte was still going to grieve for that lost child.

'I'm not jealous that Simon's taking her away from me,' Dale sobbed out. 'Don't you understand I feel helpless because I can't make anything better for her? I'm scared stiff for her. How can anyone come through all she has without cracking up?'

Michelle and Rosie rushed over to hug her. 'You've already done loads for her, after all it was you who recognized her in the paper and went to see her parents.'

'You went and found Simon and Adam too,' Frankie said. 'And you've risked your job by going over to visit her in hospital.'

Scott came over to her and put both arms around her, resting his forehead against hers. 'I'm sorry if it sounded like I was having a pop at you,' he said. 'I suppose I feel left out too. I'm miffed because I couldn't get out of here to go with you to see the neurologist today too. I think as well I resent that it was that chap

David who turned up to visit Lotte in the nick of time, when it should've been me. And I feel just as sad as you that Lotte hasn't remembered us yet, but it will be much easier to see her when she moves in with Simon and Adam and we won't have the stress of Marisa watching and checking up on us all the time.'

'I'm so scared, Scott,' Dale sobbed. 'I feel wound up like a spring.'

'Have a drink with us, then go to bed early,' he suggested. 'You must calm down or you won't be any good to Lotte.'

Dale did go off to bed early, but she didn't feel any happier. April from the hairdressing salon arrived at half past nine and it was quite obvious she was after Scott. He rallied to the situation, making the girl feel welcome and flirting with her, and if Dale had felt a little left out by Simon and Lotte, she felt even more so by Scott and April. She hoped he wouldn't let her stay with him tonight. Dale thought she just might scream if she heard sounds of lovemaking coming from Scott's room.

As she lay in bed listening to the sounds of laughter and chatter from the lounge, and feeling very alone, she was reminded that it was over a year since she'd last had a boyfriend. She'd thought that by coming to Brighton to work a whole new life would open up for her. But the reality was that she was always working, she had no friends aside from her work colleagues, and there never seemed to be any opportunity to meet potential new boyfriends. It had been much the same on the cruise ship, but at least there she was seeing new places.

She was missing her parents and her brothers and sister too. Her home in Chiswick was never silent, there was always something going on. But then her mother Kim and her father Clarke weren't exactly conventional people. Her father had been a printer back in the Eighties, but when he was made redundant, he and her mother took up what they liked to call 'scavenging'. That is, they bought and sold old stuff, sometimes antique, but mainly just interesting junk. All Dale's childhood she'd grown used to the basement of their big house in Chiswick being stuffed with pine chests, bedsteads, chairs, tables and weird bric-a-brac. It spilled over into the rest of the house, for her parents adored crazy objects. They had a 'Speak your Weight' weighing machine from a station in the hall, a collection of stuffed birds in glass cases in the sitting room, and the kitchen was stuffed with old china, old tin advertisements, china pigs which had once graced a butcher's shop, and a four-foot glittery pink flamingo her mother had bribed a windowdresser to part with.

Dale was one of four. Kyle, who was older by four years, was working in Japan now; Carrina, two years younger, was a dental nurse in London; and George at twenty-one had recently sat his finals in company law at Bristol University. At Christmas, when they'd all been home together, the house had rung with music and laughter, and Dale remembered at the time thinking how lucky she was to have such a great family. She thought that meant she'd finally grown up, as there had been a time when she'd been very embarrassed by her parents dressing like two old hippies, and turning the house into Steptoe's yard.

She wondered now if it would be healthier to back away from Lotte, to leave the police to discover what had happened and Simon and Adam to look after her. That way she wouldn't have Marisa on her back, and she'd have time to find new friends who would lift her up rather than bring her down and make her anxious.

David had told himself all week that he wouldn't go and see Lotte again, but on Friday evening he just couldn't help himself. There was something about her that made him crave her company.

He was amazed by how much better she looked now her hair had been sorted and her face was no longer scaly and peeling. She said she still felt weak, but the soreness in her limbs was fading now. She told him she was leaving for Brighton in the morning and he felt a pang of sadness looking at her, so adorable in pink pyjamas. He thought this might be the last time he would see her.

'So this is it! Last night in Chichester?' he said, trying to sound a great deal more pleased than he really was.

'Yes, I'm so happy to be going,' she said with a wide

smile. 'Everyone's been lovely to me in here, but I'm so bored being shut up in this room. At least at Simon's I can potter about cooking and cleaning.'

'Will you be having a policeman guarding you there too?' David asked.

'I don't think so. I spoke to Simon on the phone last night and he said he'd got a camera fitted so I can see who is at the door. If anyone suspicious does come around I can dial 999. Besides, he's taking the first week off to stay with me, and even after that he can be in and out all day between clients – his flat is only round the corner from his salon.'

David privately thought the police should watch the flat, at least while her attacker was still at large. But he didn't say anything for fear of making her nervous. 'Sounds like you'll be fine then,' he said. 'Any chance I could phone, or come to visit you?'

'Of course, I'd like that,' she said, sounding sincere. 'The best thing about you, David, is that I haven't got to try and remember anything about you. There's nothing missing.'

David nodded. He understood what she meant, even if it did stress the point that he was a Johnny-Come-Lately. 'Did the press release about the baby give the police any leads?'

Her face clouded over immediately. 'A few cranks, that's all,' she said sadly. 'They are in touch with the French police as they think whoever dumped me in the sea might have sailed over there, perhaps taking the baby with them. DI Bryan keeps popping in here to ask me stuff, but quite honestly I think the police are stumped.'

'You really need to get that memory back. Has anything new come up?'

'Nothing that's helpful to the police,' she shrugged. 'Almost every day there's something: a smell, a bit of music triggers off a little scene or a person from the past. Yesterday I remembered going to the pictures with a man whose hair I used to cut. That came back because one of the doctors wore the same aftershave as him.'

'And did this man figure in your life?' David asked.

Lotte smiled. 'No, he was nearly forty. I only agreed to go because the film was *Notting Hill* with Hugh Grant, and I'd been dying to see it. I don't think he approved of my choice of film and thought I was an airhead.'

'I liked *Notting Hill*,' David said. He was lying, he thought it was soppy, but he felt he could bear any amount of soppiness if he had Lotte sitting beside him.

'I would have thought you were the diehard, action kind of film man,' she said.

David smiled for she'd got him taped. 'I like those too,' he agreed. 'But it's good to have variety. What kind of food do you like best?'

Lotte looked thoughtful. 'I'm not sure. I like pasta dishes, Thai food and Chinese too. But there isn't much

I really don't like. I was brought up to eat everything that was put in front of me.'

As she made the last remark she suddenly had a scene flash into her head. She was sitting at a table and she felt nauseous at the sight and smell of the plate of food in front of her. It was kidneys.

She looked askance at David. 'That was weird! I suddenly got this memory, but I don't know when or where it was.'

She explained it to him.

'Eating kidneys sounds more like a nightmare,' he joked. 'But is there anyone else in the room with you? Does it feel like a recent memory?'

Lotte nodded. 'I feel I know the room really well, but I don't know who it belongs to, or where it is.'

'Can you get it back and kind of hold on to it? Then try to think what you did with the food that made you feel sick, or if the person who cooked it spoke to you.'

Lotte concentrated for a short while, her eyes closed. 'It's no good,' she said eventually. 'It's like a still frame: I can't leave the room, or even get up from the table, and no one else comes in.'

'What are you wearing?' David asked. 'That might give us the season. Is it an expensive trendy kitchen or just an average one?'

'I'm wearing a blue dress, it's got a full skirt. As for the kitchen, it's a bit stark, white cupboards, black granite work surface, long and thin, the table I'm sitting at is at the end, by a very small window.' Lotte frowned as she looked at David. 'How can something be so familiar, yet I don't know where it was?'

'You were wearing a blue dress when I found you on the beach,' David said. 'Did the police show it to you?'

'No, they didn't,' she said a little indignantly. 'Maybe that's my fault, I should have asked them to.'

'Not your fault at all,' David said, putting his hand over hers. 'They are paid to look into everything and anything, and I think checking out your clothes should be high priority, especially as that dress was pretty frumpy. You strike me as the kind of girl who was always fashionable.'

'I was once Simon and the others sorted me out,' she said with a little giggle and went on to tell him about the makeover she got when she joined Kutz.

'I'll ring Bryan when I leave,' David said. 'I'll tell him the dress is important. If it is the same one as you wore in the sea, that kitchen could be in the house you were staying in before you ended up on the beach, so it's really important. I think you should try and sketch the kitchen and the dress.'

'I'm useless at drawing.'

'So am I, but that doesn't matter. Just sitting with the pencil in your hand, thinking of what was there, might jog lots more. I'll go and ask one of the nurses if she can give me a sheet of paper.'

While he was gone Lotte concentrated really hard. The smell of the kidneys seemed to grow stronger, almost making her gag, yet nothing else became any clearer.

When David came back she drew a rough layout of the room, then did one of each of the four walls and what she remembered on each.

'Were the windows that small?' David asked. To him they looked hardly bigger than arrow slits in a castle wall. 'It must have been very dark in there?'

Lotte looked up at him, frowned, then smiled. 'No, it wasn't dark, but you've just reminded me that there was one of those Velux windows in the ceiling. The other windows were almost slits though.'

'Curious,' David said, then looked at her sketch again. He pointed to a small circle. 'Is that another window?'

'No, one of those brass ship's clocks.'

'And those?' He pointed to a collection of either shallow boxes or pictures.

'Oh, they were stuff like rope knots and other ship's stuff.'

'Like people have when they live at the seaside?'

Lotte thought hard. 'Yes, I suppose so.'

'So can you remember the smell of the sea? Hearing waves or anything else to bear that out?'

Lotte looked glum. 'No, I can only smell those kidneys. And they are making my stomach churn.'

'Does the clock have any significance?' he asked. 'Do you think you watched it a great deal? Did it show the right time? Is there any reason why you remember it?'

Lotte shook her head. 'I've no idea. I just remember it being there, that's all.'

David sighed. 'I would say it's a safe bet you were

somewhere close to the sea, and with boat people. Not just because of the things you remember, but because I can't imagine anyone planning to move someone, dead or alive, by boat, without owning one themselves.'

'That doesn't exactly narrow it down when we live on an island with hundreds of miles of coastline,' Lotte said.

'Well, I doubt anyone would go hundreds of miles to dump someone from their boat,' David said thoughtfully. 'If it was me, I'd go straight out into deep water and do the deed immediately.'

'We don't know that I was dumped. My hands and feet weren't tied – I could've just jumped over the side,' Lotte reminded him.

'Well, if you were going to do that you'd do it as soon as possible after setting off. You wouldn't wait till you were far out to sea.'

'I doubt I could swim more than eight to ten miles,' Lotte said. 'OK, maybe the current swept me along too, so we ought to think of harbours back along the coast from Selsey.'

'Chichester harbour is the obvious place,' David said. 'Unfortunately that's a vast area with thousands of boats, but maybe if you look at a map there might be a place name that jumps out at you.'

He looked at her hard. 'East and West Wittering, Bosham, Birdham, Itchenor. Any of them ring a bell?'

'They all sound kind of familiar,' she said, making a despairing gesture with her hands. 'But so do New

York, Sydney and Bali, and as far as I know I've never been to any of them.'

'But they are place names in common usage. The villages around Chichester harbour are only really known by people who live in the area.'

Lotte half smiled. 'I'm sure it will come back to me once I'm in Simon's place and feeling secure and relaxed. I can't wait. I've got an appointment with Percival tomorrow before I leave here. I don't like him much, so I won't be sorry not to have to see him again. But I do hope I'll see you!'

David grinned and picking up her small hand, held it between his two big ones. 'I shall be there as often as you can stand it.'

David didn't go straight home after saying goodbye to Lotte. Instead he went to the police station and demanded to speak to DI Bryan, determined to make him pull out all the stops on his investigations. To his surprise the detective appeared within minutes and ushered him through to an interview room.

David decided to hold back his rant about feeling the police weren't doing enough, at least for the time being. Instead he told Bryan what Lotte had remembered and showed him the sketch she had made.

'I've got this gut feeling this is where she was held,' he said, and talked the man through what Lotte had said about it. 'I was thinking about her being fed kidneys, and thought that's quite an odd dish for English people these days. But it's a common German dish. I think the house is by the sea, and when I named the villages around Chichester harbour, she said she thought they sounded familiar. Don't you think it would be a good place to start looking?'

'Anything else you might like to instruct us on?' Bryan said with heavy sarcasm.

'Yes, check out the dress she was wearing when I found her,' David suggested. 'It was a frumpy one, and from what I've gathered not her usual style. You haven't shown it to Dale or to Simon, have you?'

'No, but we have checked out the dress label. It's an American company.'

'That figures,' David said thoughtfully. 'It looked like a dress someone from the backwoods might wear.'

'Maybe it does, but she bought it in London – we checked it against clothes she bought there a couple of days after she left the cruise. She bought several items from the one shop. Unfortunately all the staff working there at the time of the purchase have now left; it's one of those shops that has a high turnover of staff. So there was no one who would remember Lotte buying the dress and if she was with anyone else.'

'Have you checked out the Americans on that cruise she worked on?'

'Yes, of course, that was one of our first lines of inquiry. They flew out of Heathrow the evening of the day the ship docked at Southampton. And they didn't return to England.'

'Oh,' said David, feeling disappointed.

'We've checked out everyone on the cruise, including the crew,' Bryan went on, 'paying particular attention to those living or owning property on the south coast, and those with boats. We've also made extensive inquiries at boat yards, marinas, and sailing clubs all around Chichester harbour. We've checked out every birth in that time period, both in hospital and at home, and drawn a blank because all the babies are accounted for. We've had lengthy dealings with the French police too. Now, if there's anything you think we haven't done or tried, do tell us, because believe you me, every police officer in southern England wants to find that baby.'

'I didn't mean to suggest you weren't doing your job,' David said. 'I guess Lotte's fears about the baby are washing over on to me. And I'm scared the person who attempted to kill her before isn't going to give up. I just hope Lotte's friends in Brighton really have made their place secure.'

'You can rest assured of that,' Bryan said. 'Two of the Brighton officers were there this morning to see the installation of CCTV and to check all locks on doors and windows.'

'I think that's a polite way of telling me to keep my nose out of your business,' David responded with a grin.

'Not exactly,' Bryan replied and smiled back. 'I can see it from your point of view. Lotte's a very pretty girl, it's an intriguing case, and as you found her it's understandable that you want to be involved. But you can help best by talking to her and prompting memories. That's the way we are going to solve this, and hopefully discover where her baby is. I just hope we aren't too late.'

Chapter Seven

Simon glanced at Lotte's set, white face and reached out across the back seat of Adam's car to take her hand. She hadn't said a word since they left the hospital.

'We've prettied up your room,' Adam said from the driver's seat. 'We thought the white paint was a bit harsh, so we got some wallpaper. Though I say it myself, I made a good job of hanging it.'

'But I chose it and got the curtains,' Simon said.

'You don't need to feel you are treading on eggshells with me,' Lotte said, her voice a little dull and slow. 'I'm fine, just quiet because I've been put on some pills.'

'You can be as silent as you like,' Adam said over his shoulder. 'We're just glad to have you home with us again. I was wondering if you'd like me to go round to your folks sometime this weekend and get the stuff you left there before you went on the cruise. You'll need some clothes and shoes and I think you took your personal things there too.'

Lotte felt the stiffness of her new jeans. Simon and Adam had brought them in this morning, along with a pale blue, long-sleeved tee-shirt, a bra, and a pair of sandals for her to wear to go home in. They said the girls at Kutz had clubbed together to buy them. It hadn't even occurred to her until then that she had nothing to wear other than pyjamas. She wondered where all the clothes and possessions she must have had while working on the cruise ship had gone.

'I don't remember taking anything to their house,' she said. 'Why did I? Couldn't I have left it with you?'

'You never mentioned it to us,' Simon replied. 'We certainly didn't tell you that you couldn't leave anything with us, but in the light of what we know about you and your parents now, we think you used your stuff as a way of testing the water with them.'

Lotte sniffed. 'Then they'll have chucked everything out by now.'

'They haven't,' Simon said. 'I rang them last night to say we were bringing you back today. Your dad told me they had a suitcase of yours and asked if you needed it.'

'He did?' Lotte was very surprised. 'You'll be telling me next they want to visit me!'

'I'd say that your dad does,' Simon said.

'Mum won't let him,' Lotte said bluntly. 'And anyway, I don't really want to see them.'

There was an awkward silence for a moment, ended by Simon asking what she fancied for her first meal. 'What about roast chicken?' he suggested.

'Umm,' Lotte said. 'With those fantastic roast potatoes you used to do!'

'Fresh runner beans, new carrots and my scrumptious gravy. It will be a first-night feast,' Simon said with laughter in his voice.

Lotte leant back and closed her eyes. It was true that the pills she'd been prescribed made her disinclined to talk. But even without them it would be hard to chat when her mind was stuck on the baby she'd had but couldn't remember.

She'd liked babies right back from when she was a small child herself. She'd been the sort of kid who was always asking if she could take neighbours' babies for a walk. As a teenager she rushed to cuddle any baby going; she used to imagine that when she got married she'd have at least four children.

While she'd never been present at a delivery, she knew from women who had talked about it that it was an unforgettable experience. But the birth itself wasn't everything, there was the nine months from conception to birth, the stomach growing daily, and the baby moving inside the mother. So how could something so momentous be wiped from her mind?

Dr Percival had said amnesia could act like nature's safety valve, holding back memory of terrible events or trauma until such time as the patient was strong enough to deal with it. That suggested that the baby's birth and indeed the conception and pregnancy was one long nightmare for her, something she wouldn't want to remember.

DI Bryan seemed to have the idea she was held by a group of people, but without any evidence of this Lotte was more inclined to think it was just one man. Maybe it was someone she met and fell for on the ship? Perhaps she didn't tell anyone about him because she knew they'd disapprove?

It could be that they were happy together in isolation at first, but maybe he was the jealous, unbalanced kind, and when after a while she had expressed the need to see old friends, he got frightened she'd leave him and imprisoned her?

On the other hand, her captor could've been a completely random psycho, perhaps a taxi driver at Southampton docks, who on the spur of the moment decided she was the girl he wanted and took her to some secret place.

She knew from the police that no hospital anywhere in the UK had admitted any woman in labour who fitted her description. So whether the baby was conceived lovingly or by force, it didn't bear dwelling on what it must have been like to deliver a first baby without medical assistance. Maybe her baby did die, perhaps that was the reason the father felt he had to kill her too, to cover up that he got her no medical help. She just wished she knew the truth, however awful it was. Surely nothing could be as bad as imagining a young baby dying of starvation and neglect; and those were the pictures which kept coming into her head.

'I expect Dale and Scott will be over tonight to see you,' Adam said over his shoulder, interrupting her reverie. 'We really like them both. But have you remembered anything at all about them and the cruise?'

'No, nothing,' Lotte replied. 'I've talked to them, laughed with them, but I still don't actually remember them. Sometimes I think someone must have opened my brain and cut out a chunk.'

'And what are your views on David Mitchell?' Adam asked with a hint of laughter in his voice. 'Aside from being your rescuer twice, and one of the nurses telling us he's smitten with you. Will you be pleased if he turns up to see you?'

'Yes, I like him,' she admitted. 'He said he was going to see DI Bryan and ask about the dress I was wearing when he found me. He seems to think it could be a good lead because it was old-fashioned and not a dress you'd find in any old high street.'

'I'd like to have seen it,' Simon said. 'I could've told the police right off whether it was something you'd normally wear. Did Bryan tell you I thought you'd been captured by some barmy religious sect?'

'What makes you think that?' she asked.

'Your mate Dale told me about the cranky Americans who –' Simon cut off abruptly before he let the cat out of the bag about her being raped while working on the cruise. This was something they had all agreed not to bring up until she remembered it herself.

'Who what?' Lotte asked.

'Oh, they just got attached to you. But they were religious.'

'I didn't used to be religious, did I?' Lotte asked. 'I don't even remember going to Sunday school.'

'Well, you weren't when you left us to join the cruise,' Adam said, taking his eyes off the road to grin round at her. 'You wanted to make loads of dosh, find a millionaire to marry and have a ball – all very ungodly!'

'My money!' Lotte exclaimed. 'I should have asked the police about that.'

'They did check it out. Haven't they told you that? You did some shopping in Oxford Street, and got some money out of a cash point during the week you left the cruise, but since then your account hasn't been touched,' Simon said. 'I seem to remember you said your wages would be paid into the bank here while you were away, and you hoped you'd make enough in tips never to draw any of it out.'

'Did I do that?' Lotte asked.

'The police won't tell us private stuff like that,' Adam said. 'But you can phone your bank and get your address changed to ours again. That way they'll send you a statement.'

Lotte began to feel much better as they drove into Brighton and she saw familiar sights again. It was an unusually hot day for so early in the year and the streets were full of people making the most of it. Simon began pointing out what he called 'crimes against humanity', which included bare-chested men with huge beer guts, fat women in boob tubes and shorts, and men wearing black socks with open-toed sandals. Lotte found herself laughing in a way she couldn't have imagined back in the hospital. It was as if she was becoming a different person.

From the moment Adam nosed his car into narrow Meeting House Lane, Lotte felt excited. She had always liked the way the flat was hidden away, even though in reality it was right in the centre of the North Lanes area with its many shops and restaurants. When she worked with Simon at Kutz it was great to get there in two minutes and to be able to pop home at lunchtime. She never understood why their landlord, who had an antiques shop beneath the flat, didn't choose to live there, but she supposed he had some grand house somewhere else.

'Who's the gardener?' Lotte asked as she looked up the metal spiral staircase and saw planters and tubs all along the balcony, most of them holding flowers or shrubs. The balcony had been completely bare when she'd lived here. 'It looks fabulous!'

'It's me,' Simon said a little sheepishly as he got out of the car and came round to open the door for her. 'I planted a few things early last year, just to get a bit of privacy when we were sitting on the balcony sunbathing. But it became addictive, I kept going to the garden centre for more, and now I even read gardening books. I really enjoy pottering about out here in the evenings watering them and stuff. Another week and I can put in all the summer bedding plants.'

'He's made it lovely,' Adam said, locking the car and starting on up the stairs to the front door. 'I'm really looking forward to sitting out here with a beer on warm nights, our own little paradise.'

Within an hour Lotte felt she was indeed in paradise. She had been very happy in the old white-painted, rather monastic spare room, but it had been transformed with pretty green and white Laura Ashley wallpaper, a white lacy blind and silky green curtains. It wasn't only the lovely room though, it was the security of being back with the two friends she knew she could always count on.

So many memories came flooding back as she went into the lounge and saw the big blue sofas, the vivid posters and paintings, mostly done by their artist friends, and the huge white shaggy rug on the floor. It wasn't as minimalist as she remembered. The shelves which once held a single bust, piece of sculpture or other ornament, were now stuffed with books, CDs and a thousand and one trinkets, ornaments and bits of bric-a-brac.

Yet all the extra stuff was a reminder of the huge circle of friends the boys had, and the raucous nights when everyone got together here. Lotte remembered many a wild night when she was too drunk to move from the sofa to her own bed, when the police called and asked them to turn the music down. She could almost hear *Fallin'*, that album by Alicia Keyes, playing; Simon had loved it and played it constantly for weeks.

It was in the early evening that Lotte had a major breakthrough in memory. All afternoon she had little, unimportant things from the past pop into her head – items of clothing she wore, records, and films – and Simon dated them all as belonging to the year 2000.

The three of them were still sitting at the kitchen table, eating cheese and biscuits after their meal, when Adam mentioned the attack on the Twin Towers in 2001. Lotte didn't know what he was talking about, but sensing from his serious tone it was a momentous, world-shattering event, she asked him to explain. Simon said he had recorded some of it on video tape and maybe watching would bring it all back.

It was the hysteria in the voice of the television newscaster as he described the scene of first one of the towers being hit by a plane, and then the other, which opened that locked door in her mind. She could hear other hysterical voices all around her, a hubbub of noise, confusion and distress as the truth of what was happening in New York got through.

Yet even more importantly, Lotte could see where she was at that crucial time. In a hairdressing salon on a ship!

She recalled an American woman bursting into the salon and screaming that she couldn't understand why the ship was still heading south, away from Miami where they'd been the previous day.

That day had been shocking and traumatic, but Lotte was overjoyed to find herself able to relive it, for it was proof that all her other locked memories could be unlocked too.

Detail about that period was there again in her head – she could see it, smell it, taste it. The memories might be grim, but she welcomed them.

When Dale had talked about the salon on the ship, Lotte had imagined it rather dark and cramped, but it wasn't; it was bright, light and airy, there was even a door open on to a balcony, and the sea beyond was turquoise and calm as a mill pond.

There were five or six hairdressers there that morning, including herself. They'd heard about the disaster some half an hour before the American woman burst in, and although they'd all been talking about it to their clients, and some women had cancelled appointments for that day, everything was still quite calm, perhaps because they hadn't as yet really assimilated just how bad things were.

'The captain should turn the ship around and sail back to New York,' the American woman yelled out, wild-eyed and beside herself with hysteria. 'And you should all be ashamed of yourselves for carrying on as though nothing has happened.'

'It would be irresponsible of the captain to even consider adding to the confusion in New York by going there,' Alice, the salon manager, said sharply, catching hold of the American woman's flailing arms and trying to push her into a chair. 'Now, if you feel you must go there, I'm sure that it can be arranged for you to be put ashore at the next port, but unless you have close family there that you need to be with, I suggest you stay away.'

Lotte remembered being as impressed by Alice's composure as she was horrified by the American woman's manic behaviour. From that moment, however, there was no attempt at behaving normally by anyone, for clients were cancelling and other passengers and staff kept bursting in to discuss the events as the full scale of the disaster unfolded.

As must have happened in shops and offices all around the world, the hairdressers and beauticians clustered around a television in the salon and watched the drama. Lotte was sure she must have seen recorded images of the planes' moments of impact with the towers at least a hundred times that day.

And at last she remembered Dale.

She had flitted between the hairdressing and beauty salons all day – it seemed some of her clients kept their appointments. Lotte remembered how she had her dark hair twisted up on to the top of her head and fastened with a white artificial rose. With her deep tan she looked very exotic.

It must have been around three in the afternoon when Dale came into the hairdressing salon and flopped down on to a chair, well away from the rest of the girls who were crowding around the television.

'It's morbid watching that over and over again,' she said in a loud, disapproving voice. 'It's not going to make it any better, and you can bet your life the Americans will keep harping on about it for centuries anyway.'

'Don't you care?' Amy, a South African girl, said.

'You think brooding on it shows you care?' Dale retorted with some sarcasm. 'I hate all this madness when there's a tragedy, it's like people get off on it. Any minute now they'll be making an appeal for money. Why do they need to do that? There's no one homeless, cold or hungry. Most will have insurance on anyone who is dead, and money won't stop them grieving.'

'The wives of the firemen who died should get something,' someone argued hotly.

'Why?' Dale asked. 'They get their widow's pension like any other woman who loses her husband. We don't go round with a collection for a woman whose husband has died of a heart attack or been run over going to work. OK, the firemen were brave, but then that's their job, like soldiers, policemen and all those other dangerous occupations.'

Lotte half smiled as she recalled how stroppy her friend had been that day. Yet that was perhaps the reason why she hadn't remembered Dale straight off at the hospital, for she'd been like a different person there, tearful, gentle and placid, certainly not opinionated or outspoken.

Dale on the cruise had put on a convincing display of being as hard as nails, self-centred, opinionated and just a bit of a bully, even if that was tempered by being beautiful, amusing and charm itself when it suited her. Yet she had actually meant what she said that day, and although it was hardly an appropriate time to speak out so forcefully, she made a lot of sense. She certainly kept her soft side well hidden, but Lotte already knew that she would give her last penny to anyone who really needed it.

And finally she recalled Scott too. The first memory to pop up was of him coming into the salon wearing only white shorts and a singlet, his skin golden-brown with the sheen of good health. He asked if someone could cut his hair immediately. It must have been on the first or second day, right at the start of the cruise, because she remembered the electric buzz that went around the other girls when they saw him. They were all whispering, asking who he was.

Lotte stepped forward to cut his hair and he gave her one of his heart-stopping smiles. 'OK, Barbie Girl,' he said. 'Make me less of Lenny the Lion and more Funky Fitness Man.'

'Well?' Simon said as he turned off the video. 'Did that do the trick?'

Lotte nodded. She was a little stunned by so much coming back all at once and needed time to sort through it. 'I remember Dale now, and what good friends we were. But that day was crazy, people were crying and going on and on about it. I know it was a terrible atrocity, but I didn't quite understand the depth of the shock and grief. It reminded me of when Lady Di was killed.'

'It was much the same here,' Adam said. 'In every pub, café, and shops too, people were glued to TVs.'

'I remember meeting Scott for the first time as well.' She told them a little about that and they both laughed because they could understand the impact he would have on a crowd of girls. As Simon pointed out, he'd have the same effect on some of their friends.

'So does your memory go beyond September the eleventh?' Simon asked a little later. 'Can you remember Christmas of that year?'

'Don't try to rush her,' Adam reproved his friend. 'Let her think about what she's recalled already today.'

Dale and Scott arrived at about eight that evening, and they were thrilled to find Lotte had remembered them. Memories came spilling out – a dive they'd got drunk in in Montevideo; the time Scott entered a limbo competition in Jamaica and was stunned to be beaten by a sixteen-stone woman. Dale reminded Lotte of the occasion when the three of them had been in a club in Cape Town, and when Dale couldn't find Lotte she assumed she'd gone back to the ship. With only ten minutes to go before the ship sailed and no sign of Lotte, Scott decided to run back to the club to check. Lotte had fallen asleep in the cloakroom, and but for Scott would've found herself stranded in Africa.

The stories kept coming, one after another, till Lotte said she had a stitch from laughing so much. Simon cut in then and said it was time Dale and Scott left as Lotte mustn't overdo it and it was time she went to bed. Dale

164

bristled at his bossiness and reminded Lotte how she had never liked to be told what to do.

'There'll be other times,' Lotte reassured her friend. 'Maybe when you get a day off we could spend it together and catch up?'

'Dale's very full of herself,' Simon said after she'd left with Scott. 'I like her, but she's one of those people who think the world revolves around them.'

'She might come across like that, but there's a lot more to her,' Lotte said in her defence. She had noticed Dale seemed a little resentful that Simon and Adam were friends of much longer standing than she was: every time one of them brought up an event in the past, Dale tried to top it with an anecdote from the cruise. 'I think she just feels a bit left out. I mean, it was she who recognized me in the paper and went to the police and my parents. She would have liked the opportunity to look after me.'

'Only to make herself feel more important,' Simon said cattily.

'No, because she cares about me,' Lotte said firmly. 'Now, don't be nasty about her, or we'll fall out.'

'So what about Scott?' Simon changed the subject. 'He's a good-looking bloke. Was there anything between you?'

Lotte grinned. 'I'd like to have had something,' she said. 'Both Dale and I fancied him, but so did all the girls, so we settled for being his friend, and he proved to be a very good one.'

'I'd say he likes you more than just a friend,' Simon said. 'I'd put money on it.'

Lotte just laughed. She didn't believe that. Simon had always been of the opinion that all men fancied her.

On Sunday David drove over from Chichester to see her, and Simon and Adam invited him to stay for lunch. He looked very handsome in a pale blue, open-necked shirt that matched his eyes and teamed perfectly with his cream chinos.

'How long will you have to stay cooped up indoors?' he asked as Lotte laid the table in the lounge.

She'd asked herself that same question earlier that morning when she saw the sun shining yet again and people taking a short cut through the alley down on to the promenade. She knew Simon didn't even think it was safe for her to sit out on the balcony, and while she didn't mind so much for herself, she felt sorry she couldn't go on out there now with David as his question suggested he'd rather be outside. 'I don't know. Until the police find whoever was responsible, I suppose,' she said with a sigh. 'But I don't expect anyone to stay in with me all the time.'

'It would be a pleasure to stay in with you,' David replied with a wide smile. 'But it would be even nicer to take you out for dinner, or a walk along the promenade.'

Lotte took a step nearer him and kissed him on the cheek. 'How very gallant,' she said teasingly.

He caught hold of her two arms and held her for a moment. 'I haven't been able to think of anything else but you since I found you on the beach,' he said, his eyes looking right into hers. 'I told myself at first that it was the mystery surrounding you, but I know it's not just that now.'

'David, I could've done all kinds of terrible things,' she said. She felt she had to warn him off even if she did really like him. 'We know I've had a baby, but I might be married, I could even have done something criminal. I wouldn't want you to become involved until we know about me.'

'I don't believe you've ever done anything bad,' he said, lifting one hand to caress her cheek. 'But even if you have, I want to be around to support you when it all comes out.'

It was Lotte who moved to kiss him. She couldn't stop herself because his mouth looked so soft and appealing and his hand on her face was making her heart race. It was the kind of sweet, gentle, lingering kiss that suggested passion was waiting in the wings.

'Ummm,' he said as she broke away, 'that was delicious. Any chance of seconds?'

Simon came into the room at that point and looked at them sharply as if he sensed something was going on. 'Lunch will be ready pretty soon. Would you like a beer, David?'

David followed Simon out into the kitchen and Lotte finished laying the table. As she went back to the kitchen to get some serving spoons, she overheard Simon talking about her.

'She needs to rest after lunch. The doctor told me it is as important that she regains her strength as it is to regain her memory. You are welcome to stay here while she has a snooze, but I doubt she'll go and lie down if you're here.'

Lotte knew Simon was right, she did tire easily, but she didn't like him telling David he should go. It was so disturbing having so much blank in her memory, and it felt good to be with David who she knew was not part of her past.

But she wasn't brave enough to challenge Simon's authority, so she said nothing.

Over lunch Lotte found herself warming still further to David. He was such easy company; she supposed that was coming from such a big family. There was real interest in his eyes as Adam talked about windowdressing and interior design. He asked questions, and there was none of that talking-down, homophobic angle many straight men tended to get into when they were speaking to gays. He had similar tastes in music to the boys, laughed at the same kind of jokes, and appreciated their cooking.

Adam had used a recipe for a pudding he'd never tried before and it had some very odd-sounding ingredients. He asked David whether he would like to try it, or go for the safer option of fresh fruit.

'I'll try anything once, except incest and Morris

dancing,' David responded, and Adam and Simon roared with laughter.

'I can't claim that as my own, it's an Oscar Wilde,' David admitted with an honesty which pleased the other two still more.

'He's great,' Adam whispered when David went off to the bathroom while they were having coffee. 'And we can see you really like him too, so at least one thing in your life has some promise.'

'More than one, I've got you two again,' she replied with a wide smile. 'And I've got a feeling everything's going to come back to me very soon, the baddies will be punished and I can get back to work and normality.'

On the Tuesday, Scott popped in to see Lotte on his day off.

'Dale was hoping she could get the day off too, but Marisa wouldn't wear it,' he explained. 'In fact she isn't getting any free day this week. Marisa is making her pay for other time she's had off.'

'When she came to the hospital?' Lotte asked.

Scott nodded. 'She's got it in for Dale,' he said glumly. 'I don't know what her grievance is but she's always picking on her. I tried to talk to Marisa about it once, but I got nowhere.'

'She probably fancies you,' Lotte suggested, 'and thinks you've got a thing for Dale.'

'She's a good friend, that's all,' Scott said.

'I don't suppose she believes that's all it is,' Lotte laughed. 'Besides, Dale's gorgeous, good at her job and probably capable of running Marchwood Spa. That's enough reason for the woman to resent her.'

'You were always good at seeing the whole picture,' Scott said thoughtfully. 'You are a great peacemaker too. When all this is over and you start thinking about working again, it would be fantastic if you'd come to Marchwood.'

'I doubt Marisa would welcome me,' Lotte laughed. 'She'd think I was another member of your harem, and that Dale would be even more threatening to her with an ally in tow.'

'Could you also be thinking you don't want to work long hours because of a new man on the horizon?' Scott raised one blond eyebrow quizzically.

Lotte giggled and blushed. 'Do you mean David? I hardly know him.'

'You've given the game away with that blush,' Scott teased her. 'My heart is broken now, I had such high hopes for us two.'

Lotte laughed. One of the best parts of regaining memories of both him and Dale was to find how much she loved them both. If she could pick her own brother and sister, they would be the ones she'd choose.

'That's her.' The older man at the wheel of the stationary blue transit van pointed to the dark-haired girl wearing white jeans and a red tee-shirt coming out of the drive of Marchwood Manor and going towards the bus stop. 'Nice tits and bum. Even better looking than the photo we've been given too.'

It was Wednesday morning, eleven days since Lotte had been released from hospital. 'How do we know she's going to visit the blonde one?' his younger companion asked.

'We don't, but the boss is sure she'll go there as it's her first day off since the blonde came out of hospital.'

The younger man chewed on his nails. 'I don't mind passing on the info where the girl is staying, but I don't like the idea of snatching her,' he admitted.

Bill glanced sideways at the younger man, a little surprised at his reluctance. He knew Alex had done worse things in the past than just bundling a girl into a van, and as he had an expensive drug habit he would be a fool to pass up earning a grand for something so easy.

Bill was thirty-eight. He'd been released from prison just six months ago and he needed some money to get over to Spain. He had a job lined up there as security officer in a night club and it was a chance to start out fresh. He neither knew nor cared what they wanted the blonde girl for, that wasn't his problem; all he had to do was deliver her. The first part of that was finding out where she was.

'It'll be a doddle,' Bill said, then, seeing the bus coming along behind him, he turned on the ignition and prepared to follow once the dark girl was on it. 'But don't you go yellow-bellied on me if we have a chance to get her later today. I need that money.'

'I won't back out, I can't afford to,' Alex said as he watched the girl get on to the bus. He was twenty-eight, his girl had left him, his family didn't want to know him any more, and he was in danger of being evicted from his flat. He wanted to go into rehab and try to get straight. His life was a wreck, but a grand would straighten it out.

Once on the bus, Dale busied herself sending texts to her sister, brothers and a few friends on the ride into Brighton. She wished her parents would join the twenty-first century and get a mobile phone, but they refused, saying they couldn't see the point when they had a perfectly good land line. This meant Dale had to phone them from the hotel call box on Sundays, a nuisance because she liked to go out to the pub on Sundays and they always got ratty if she forgot to ring. Texts were her favourite way of keeping in touch; in just a few words she could confirm she was alive and well and thinking about them without the need for small talk.

She was looking forward to spending the day with Lotte. Last Wednesday her day off had been cancelled by Marisa because a large group of ladies had booked into the spa for the day, and the other beauticians couldn't manage without Dale. Marisa pointed out that as she'd had such a lot of time off because of Lotte, it was about time she made it up.

She'd been over to see Lotte with Scott in the evening on three occasions. But Simon and Adam were always there, and they got on her nerves talking about people she didn't know. It was like they wanted Lotte all to themselves, and didn't think anyone else mattered to her. Then there was David. He hadn't visited while Dale had been there, but Lotte always mentioned him. That made her a bit jealous too, even though she knew she was being mean-spirited.

Poor Lotte still hadn't remembered the rape in Ushuaia, or anything about what happened when she left the cruise ship, and she was frantic about her baby, even though she remembered nothing of its birth.

DI Bryan had followed up hundreds of claims from the public that they'd seen Lotte in the last year, and even more from people who reported hearing a baby cry, or had seen a woman with a baby who they felt was acting suspiciously. But every such claim turned out to be a dead end. He had told Dale that he felt it was extremely unlikely the baby was alive.

All the boatyards and marinas right along the south coast had been checked out. There had been fingertip searches of several deserted premises Lotte could've been held in, and raids on houses following information received. But as time went on with no new evidence, or Lotte regaining her memory about where she'd been and with whom, Bryan feared that her captor must have slipped out of the country.

Dale wondered too how much longer Lotte would

have to stay holed up in the flat. She was surprised she wasn't going stir crazy, especially now the weather had turned so nice. But then, Lotte had always been much more patient than her.

Dale intended to try to make Lotte forget it all for today. In her basket she had a lasagne the chef at Marchwood had made for her, a bottle of wine from Frankie and some chocolates from Michelle and Rosie. Even Marisa had unbent enough to send some nice hand cream and her good wishes.

Bryan had asked Dale several times whether she thought Lotte had remembered being raped in South America but just hadn't said anything. Dale thought it extremely unlikely, for though Lotte had never been one to talk about her own problems, the rape had been such a serious event that she surely would have said something.

Dale got the idea Bryan hoped she'd prompt Lotte to remember it, and that way the rest of her memories might come back too. Dale couldn't decide whether it was less horrific to be told about it, or to have the memory come back all on its own.

'Quick! Get out here and follow her,' Bill said, pulling over to the kerb in the centre of Brighton. The dark girl had just got off the bus and now she was crossing the road. Bill felt she was heading for the Lanes and he couldn't follow her there in the van. 'Stay close by wherever she goes in, then ring me. I'll join you there.'

'I ain't got much credit on my phone,' Alex said.

'Text me then,' Bill said irritably. 'I'll follow you as best I can, I won't be far away.'

Alex loped off after Dale, six feet two and skinny as a rake, with lank brown hair in need of a cut and a grubby, worn denim jacket and even more worn jeans. Bill hoped he wouldn't make it so obvious he was following her that she'd sense it. He didn't appear to be the sharpest knife in the box; he had been begging on the streets until he was recruited for this.

Dale went through the routine of ringing the doorbell five times as Simon had insisted, then pulled a face at the CCTV camera for good measure.

She heard Lotte giggling as she came down the hall. 'Who goes there? Friend or foe?' she called out.

'Only me from over the sea, said Barnacle Bill the sailor,' Dale sang back through the letterbox.

'Scott used to sing that when he knocked on our cabin door!' Lotte said jubilantly as she opened the door. She flung her arms around Dale's neck. 'It's weird how memories come back just when you least expect them.'

Dale stepped inside, and Lotte shut the door and bolted it. 'The postman rang the bell this morning. I was fairly certain he was the real thing, I could see him clearly on the camera and his hands were full of mail. But I didn't dare open the door, just in case. I felt really silly when he left a card to say he had a parcel for

Adam, and now he'll have to go and collect it from the depot.'

'Better safe than sorry,' Dale said. 'Now, are you going to make me some coffee?'

She was so relieved to see Lotte looking much like her old self again. She wore jeans cut off just below the knee, and a turquoise tee-shirt. She'd put on a couple of pounds since leaving hospital, the bruises and all the flakiness had gone from her face, her new short haircut suited her, and if she could only go out in the sun to get some colour in her cheeks again, no one would guess what she'd been through.

'How are you doing? The true story,' Dale asked as they went into the kitchen together.

Lotte paused before putting the kettle on. 'I'm good, well, I'm not sick or cracking up. But I'm finding it hard to deal with this blank chunk of my life. Imagining stuff is probably worse than facing reality, especially about the baby. I keep expecting to feel something inside me, something that will convince me I really did have one. But I suppose that won't happen until I remember.'

Dale hugged her silently. She had no idea what to say. She couldn't even begin to imagine what it must be like to be in her friend's shoes.

It was so good to be back together again without anyone else butting in. They sat cross-legged, facing each other at either end of the sofa, just the way they used to sit on one of the bunks in their cabin, and talked about the first couple of weeks on the cruise.

'I thought you were a real airhead the first time I saw you,' Dale admitted.

'And I thought you were a conceited bully,' Lotte retorted.

'But I began to like you late on the first night when you handed me a glass of water as I got into the top bunk and said it would stop me having a hangover the next day. My mother used to do that and it felt really nice,' Dale admitted.

'And I began to like you when you said "Sweet dreams" in the dark. I didn't feel quite so alone,' Lotte said.

'We were an unlikely partnership,' Dale mused. 'Me so untidy, flinging clothes about round the cabin, and you liking everything in its place.'

'The other girls betted we wouldn't last a week without a cat fight,' Lotte laughed. 'Yet we never did fall out, did we?'

'Well, there was the time in Valparaiso when you fancied that sailor off another cruise ship,' Dale reminded her. 'You were legless and he was going to take you off to a hotel.'

'Yeah, you stopped me going,' Lotte said, putting on a mock wounded expression. 'I was savage. I was sure he was going to be the love of my life.'

'You slapped me round the face and said I was jealous,' Dale reminded her. 'If you'd met him when you were sober you wouldn't have even looked at him. He was a medallion man, all cock and no brains, and fancied himself rotten. He accused me of being a lesbian.'

Lotte giggled. 'I have to admit I saw him again the next morning and you were right – he was awful. He swaggered like Popeye, he'd done so much weight training he couldn't put his arms down to his sides, and he thought he was God's gift to womankind.'

Dale kept on reminding Lotte of different incidents, gradually working her way through the year towards Christmas. There were people and events Lotte didn't remember, but then there were others she recalled which Dale had forgotten.

They laughed so much, prompting each other with tales of difficult clients in the salon and some of their stranger workmates.

'Remember that girl on the housekeeping team who stripped off in the bar when she was drunk?' Lotte giggled. 'She was so fat and hairy we all wanted to die with embarrassment. She must've wanted to top herself the next day when her friends told her what she'd done.'

'She came to me for waxing a day or two after, but I didn't remind her,' Dale said with a smile. 'God knows I've done my share of cringe-worthy things when I've been drunk. I wouldn't want anyone reminding me of them.'

*

They heated up the lasagne later and opened the bottle of wine. 'I shall get sleepy,' Lotte warned Dale. 'It always makes me like that if I drink during the day.'

'Well, that's OK, I've got to get the bus back at four, there isn't a later one,' Dale said. 'You are supposed to have a rest in the afternoon anyway.'

Around half past two Lotte went off to the bathroom and came back a few minutes later looking worried. 'Don't suppose you've got any Tampax on you?' she asked Dale. 'I've just come on unexpectedly. I hadn't thought about that happening so I've got nothing.'

Dale looked in her bag and found one right at the bottom. 'But you'll need more,' she said. 'I'd better nip out and buy you some.'

'You're an angel,' Lotte said. 'I wouldn't like to have to ask Simon to get them.'

'It's nothing, I need some deodorant anyway.'

As soon as Dale was gone Lotte found she was a little unsteady on her feet, and realized she really shouldn't have drunk wine on top of the pills she was taking. But she felt good, much less anxious about everything. It was great to have Dale around and to look back on all the fun they'd had together.

When the five rings came at the door bell she went straight to the front door and opened it, forgetting to look first at the small CCTV screen.

The moment she saw the two tough-looking men on the balcony she sensed they meant her harm and she

179

tried to shut the door again. But she was too late – the older one had his hand on it, jamming it back.

'You're coming with us, sweetheart,' he said. His voice was as rough as sandpaper. 'We can do it the nice way or the nasty way, the choice is yours.'

Chapter Eight

The younger of the two men grabbed Lotte before she could even scream. He was holding her so tightly she couldn't free her arms to fight him and he pushed a wad of cloth into her mouth. Then he spun her around and fastened her hands behind her back with what felt like a noose of thick string.

'Right, down to the van now,' the older man said.

Lotte glanced up to where the camera was fixed on the wall above the door, and saw to her horror that they'd covered the lens with something. She wouldn't even have the security of knowing the police could identify the men.

'Hold her like she's drunk,' the older man ordered the younger one. 'Keep her face against your shoulder. I'll go ahead and open the van door.'

Realizing these instructions were to prevent anyone passing though the lane becoming aware she was being taken against her will, Lotte was determined to make it as obvious as possible. Unfortunately the lane was a backwater; few people came through and as luck would have it there was absolutely no one about as the men took her down the spiral staircase. But she struggled anyway, pulling back on each step, butting her head against the man's shoulder and kicking out at the banisters to make as much noise as she could.

'Stop that or I'll hurt you,' her captor hissed at her, holding her even closer to his side and pinching her cheek hard. 'I've got a knife and I'll use it if I have to.'

They reached the bottom of the stairs and the older man had the door of the blue van open in readiness. Just as Lotte was being bundled in, she heard Dale's voice.

'What are you doing? Let her go!' she yelled and although Lotte couldn't turn to see her, she could hear her friend running towards the van.

Lotte wished she could yell out for her to take down the van number plate and run to ring the police, but she couldn't speak with the cloth in her mouth. Sadly she realized that wouldn't be Dale's way anyway, she would fight to try to save her friend.

Lotte had been shoved into the van face down, and although she could hear Dale screaming loud enough to alert everyone in the surrounding buildings, suddenly it went quiet.

'Quick, Alex, gag her and tie her hands before she comes round,' the rough-voiced older man said, proving he'd knocked Dale out. 'And let's get the hell out of here.'

'But we can't take her too,' the younger one gasped out.

'We've no choice, she saw us.'

Lotte rolled over on to her side as the van door was

slammed shut. The engine turned over and revved up but it was plain the driver was rattled for the van kangarooed forward in the wrong gear. It was dark in the back for there was a solid partition behind the driving seat and no windows in the back door, but there was just enough light coming through a ventilator in the roof for her to see Dale motionless beside her.

Lotte's first thought was that Dale might not be able to breathe properly with a gag in her mouth, so she rolled herself over, then wriggled until her secured hands were by Dale's face and pulled the cloth out of her mouth.

A low moan came from her, and Lotte wished she could get her gag out of her own mouth as apart from preventing her from speaking, it was making her feel sick.

'Are you OK?' Dale asked, her voice quavering through either pain or fear.

Lotte made a grunting noise in her throat and drew up her knees to prod her friend with her feet, hoping that would make her realize she needed her gag taken out too. Dale didn't react, so Lotte turned over again and wriggled close enough so she could pinch her friend with her tied fingers, hoping that would give her the idea.

'I think he's broken my jaw, it hurts like hell and a back tooth is loose,' Dale whimpered. 'I shouldn't have gone out and left you.'

Lotte grunted furiously, turning yet again so Dale could see her face.

'Oh right, you're gagged so you can't answer me!' Dale said.

Lotte couldn't understand why Dale didn't seem to understand that she'd got to remove the gag. Lotte grunted again, shook her head and wriggled closer, and at last Dale caught on. But instead of turning over to remove it with her fingers, she put her face on Lotte's and pulled the cotton material out with her teeth. Lotte breathed a sigh of relief.

'That's the closest I'm ever getting to snogging you,' Dale whispered. She was terrified but she felt she'd got to try to lighten the mood.

The two girls lay face to face with their hands tied behind their backs.

'This van stinks of fish,' Dale whispered.

'Maybe it belongs to a fishmonger,' Lotte said. 'I wonder if it was these men who took me out to sea? Neither of them is the man who came to the hospital.'

Dale couldn't imagine what the men could possibly want Lotte for, but their desperate measures implied it was something very serious. 'That means there's quite a few people involved in this, so we should make a plan,' she urged. 'They thought they were only going to have you to cope with; two of us will make it harder. When they get to wherever it is we're going, I think we should play dumb and dazed, that way they won't be on their guard. I'll keep falling over and stuff, and that might give you the chance to leg it.'

'I'm not going without you!' Lotte said.

'Don't be a drip. It's unlikely we can both get away. But one stands a chance and can get help. It's best it's you that goes. That punch I got really hurt and the shock might make me useless at running.'

'But I've got bare feet,' Lotte said. 'I won't be able to run unless it's sand or grass, so it'll have to be you.'

Dale sighed.

'Besides, it's me they really want, so they aren't as likely to chase you,' Lotte added.

'Don't be thick,' Dale hissed. 'I can identify them. They aren't going to let either of us go easily. But you're right, you can't run with bare feet, so I guess it'll have to be me. Hell, this must be something very serious for them to risk snatching us in broad daylight. I wonder how they knew where you were.'

The van was tossing them about, and with their hands tied they couldn't prevent it. Lotte was so scared she was finding it hard to catch her breath.

'I'm sorry I got you into this,' she whispered, tears filling her eyes. 'Do you think they intend to kill us?'

Dale didn't answer immediately for she was weighing everything up. Although her heart was racing with fear, she felt the two men were just hired thugs, paid simply to capture Lotte. If that was the case they weren't likely to be willing to kill, not unless they were offered more money. And that would take time for them to negotiate.

Dale whispered what she was thinking to Lotte. The van was too noisy for the men to hear anything over it, but it was as well to be cautious. 'We've wrongfooted them, and we must make the most of it. We can play the girlie card, dumb and tearful, but we must keep our wits about us, take in everything about our surroundings.'

'Did you take your mobile with you when you left the flat?' Lotte asked, her heart leaping with hope.

'No, I left it there with you.'

'Oh.' Lotte sighed in disappointment. 'I suppose that would've been too much to hope for.'

'Just a bit,' Dale retorted. 'What did they do with my bag? Is it in here with us? There might be something useful to us in it.'

Lotte managed to sit up and looked around in the gloom. 'I think that's it,' she whispered, nodding towards the doors. She shuffled over on her bottom, then grasped the bag with her feet and shuffled back to Dale. 'Sit up, turn your back to me and rummage through it. You should know by the feel of the stuff what it is.'

'There's a pair of nail scissors,' Dale whispered as she thrust her tied hands into her bag behind her back.

'Great, lift them out,' Lotte said. 'We'll have to hide them on me, but feel for anything else first.'

A nail file was next, a pen, a small notepad and a lighter. Dale had a lot more things in there, including a bar of chocolate, the Tampax she'd gone to buy, even a condom, but none of this was stuff they felt the men would confiscate.

The girls almost saw the funny side of it as Dale with her hands tied behind her back attempted to slide the scissors into Lotte's bra. 'Shit!' she exclaimed. 'This is worse than Pin the Tail on the Donkey.'

The lighter went in her bra too, but the nail file, pen and notepad had to go in her jeans pocket for their shape made them impossible to hide anywhere else.

'If we keep our mouths shut and don't speak, they may not realize immediately that we've got the gags out,' Lotte said as they tried to make themselves more comfortable by sitting up with their backs against the wooden partition. 'Then if there's anyone around we can yell our heads off.'

'I wonder where we're going,' Dale mused. 'In films people can work it out by the turns in the road, the steepness of the hills, but I haven't got a clue.'

'I feel we've gone west out of Brighton,' Lotte said. 'But that's only because I was found near Chichester before. The fishy-smelling van suggests the coast, but that's a needle-in-a-haystack scenario.'

'Once the police see the men on the CCTV they'll track them down,' Dale said confidently.

'They'd put something over the camera,' Lotte recalled. 'They did five rings, you see, so I thought it was you and opened the door without looking at the screen. I'm so sorry.'

'Five rings?' Dale said thoughtfully. 'No one would do that just by chance. They must've been there this morning and heard me do it. That means they probably found you by following me.'

'How did they know about you?'

'Well, I was in the papers. I think the local one even said where I worked. But it's really creepy to think someone's been checking up on me, or hanging around to see where I go.'

'I wish I knew what these people want with me,' Lotte said fearfully. 'I'm so sorry you've been dragged into it too. And Simon and Adam are going to be frantic when they find me gone.'

'It's better I was with you than you being alone,' Dale said stoutly. 'Together we can outwit them.'

Neither of the girls could see their watches to find out what the time was, and in the darkness it seemed as if they were travelling for hours. When the van slowed right down and turned sharp left, they guessed that they had left the main road. While there were a lot of bends and junctions, it was obviously still a very busy road because they could hear many other vehicles. But all at once there was no other sound but the van's engine, and they concluded they were on a country lane.

'Get ready, it can't be far now,' Dale said, wriggling down on to her side. 'If I manage to make a break for it, try tripping up the one who goes to follow me – anything to give me a few extra seconds.'

They didn't speak again, just lay side by side, their tied hands behind them, both immersed in their own thoughts and private fears. The van made a sharp right-hand turn, then continued on much slower than before, and they heard branches scrape its sides.

'A remote place,' Dale said, her voice trembling. 'But if I can't get away, at least we'll have one another.'

The van turned right again and this time it practically had to squeeze between trees or hedges because these squeaked in protest on both sides of the van. Then it came to a stop.

'This is it,' Dale said when the ignition was turned off and they heard the men get out of the van. 'Don't forget, act dumb and dazed, stagger about like you don't know what day of the week it is.'

The girls strained their ears to hear what was going on when the van doors weren't opened immediately.

'I think they must have gone to speak to someone,' Dale said after a few minutes of complete silence. They could hear birdsong but nothing else, and it became hotter in the van as if it was standing in sunshine.

'I might not be able to get away if there's other people here,' Dale whispered.

Lotte sensed that Dale was terrified she'd fail her and for some reason that made her feel stronger. 'I'll try and make some kind of distraction so you can,' she said. 'But if you can't, then it doesn't matter.'

It was some twenty long, uncomfortable minutes before they heard the men again.

'What the fuck were we supposed to do?' they heard the older one with the rough voice grumbling. 'If we'd left her there that would be wrong too. He can sort this out, I've done my bit and I don't wanna go no further.'

The girls had to assume he was talking to the younger

man, but he didn't answer. Suddenly the van doors were opened and bright sunshine flooded in, blinding the girls momentarily.

'Come on out,' the older man said, grabbing Lotte's feet and pulling her towards the door.

Lotte didn't open her mouth or struggle, just allowed herself to be manhandled as if she were a rag doll, and when her feet touched the ground she slumped against the man.

'Is she OK?' the younger one asked, pausing in hauling Dale out.

Lotte didn't feel able to look around as that would confirm she was fit and well, but to her shock, some kind of thick cloth was suddenly slipped over her head, blotting out everything. Unable to see if Dale was now upright, or if she'd had her eyes covered too, all Lotte could do was scream and kick. Kicking with bare feet made little impression on her burly captor and he punched her in the stomach, which winded her and stopped her screaming.

She was lifted off her feet and slung across his shoulder and she knew the precise moment she was taken inside because it was suddenly much cooler. But the temperature where she was, and even her anxiety about how Dale was faring were for a moment or two less important than a familiar smell.

Lemon geranium. Her captor had brushed against it.

The smell brought with it a rush of memories. It could be sheer coincidence that this aromatic plant was here just inside the front door – it was after all a very common plant. But somehow she didn't think so.

Dazed, winded and unable to see anything, Lotte was only vaguely aware of being carried down some stairs and dumped unceremoniously on a bed.

'Just keep me and dump my friend somewhere out in the country,' she implored her captor, her voice muffled by the bag over her head. 'I don't know what I'm supposed to have done, but I know she's not involved and it isn't fair to keep her prisoner.'

'It's too late for that,' he said. 'And not my problem anyway. You just keep nice and quiet and do as you're told.'

At that she heard the other man coming in. 'I had to whack her again. She tried to run for it,' he said, and Lotte felt Dale being put down beside her.

The men left then, without another word, two pairs of feet going up stairs, the sound of a key being turned in a lock and the light clicking off.

'Dale,' Lotte said tentatively, 'are you conscious?' It was so frustrating having her hands tied, for she couldn't get the bag off her head or touch her friend.

'That bastard hit me again,' Dale groaned, her voice indistinct. 'What have I got over my eyes?'

'I think it's some kind of bag. I've got one too,' Lotte said. 'We need to get them off and undo our wrists. You keep still and I'll try and shuffle round till my hands are by your head.'

The smell of the lemon geranium had been like putting

a key into the locked box of Lotte's memory, and as she moved around on the iron bed and felt the rail, she knew she'd definitely been here before. Everything indicated this – the musty smell of the room, the feel of the quilt on the bed beneath her, the cool smoothness of the bed rail.

Once she was sitting with her back to Dale's face, a simple tug removed the bag over her head as there were no fastenings. She took hold of Dale's tied wrists, felt for the knot in the rope and quickly undid it.

'That feels good to be free,' Dale said. 'Two ticks and I'll get yours off too.'

'Thank heavens,' Lotte said as Dale pulled the bag off her head. The room was dark, but not totally, for a small beam of light was coming through a tiny window high up in the wall. Just one glance at that window and Lotte knew exactly where she was.

She looked down at the bags and saw they were thick cotton ones used for making cash deposits at banks.

'Ummm,' Dale moaned appreciatively and rubbed her wrists. 'Apart from the black eye that's coming and the loose teeth, I feel almost fine.'

Lotte felt a bit sick, but whether that was from the blow in her stomach or the fragments of memory returning, she didn't know. None of it was good.

Dale slumped back on the bed and Lotte lay beside her. They remained there silently side by side for some time, both considering their situation.

'We should explore every inch of this room, hide

those bits we got from my handbag, and then plan our escape,' Dale said at length.

'There's no need to explore,' Lotte said quietly. 'There's a bathroom over there, we can wash your face and put a cold compress on your eye, but there's no way out except through the door we came in by.'

'How do you know?' Dale asked.

It wasn't curiosity in her friend's voice, just fear, and Lotte turned over on to her stomach and began to cry.

'Don't, Lotte, we'll be OK, we'll blag our way out somehow,' Dale said.

But the plaintive tone in her friend's voice brought back yet another chunk of memory.

She was on the cruise ship and Dale was trying to comfort her, tears pouring down her own face.

Lotte felt she'd come up against a huge wall, like one holding back a dam. Only it wasn't water it was holding back but everything that had happened to her in the last couple of years. The sights, the sounds, the people, the places, the emotions, they were all there behind that wall.

It seemed incredible that the lemon geranium plant on the sill by the front door with its tangy, sweet smell could puncture a tiny hole in that wall, but it had, and now, as other memories like that small window and the feel of the quilt beneath them began to leak out, the hole was growing larger and larger.

She felt that any moment the whole structure would collapse, and she would be swept away on the flood of memory.

'You've remembered what it's all about?' Dale asked. She moved closer to her friend and leaning up on one elbow, smoothed Lotte's hair back from her face.

'Yes, it's all coming back,' Lotte sobbed. 'It's all my fault too for being so stupid and needy. Why was it that when I had good friends like you and Scott, and Simon and Adam, I couldn't have just admitted to one of you that I needed some help?

'They've stolen more than a year of my life, and my baby. They nearly stole my mind and my life too.' She paused to get her breath, for fear was bringing on a panic attack. 'There's no way to get any of that back and no way to get out of here alive either,' she finished up.

Chapter Nine

Dale felt an icy chill down her spine at Lotte's words. But she didn't ask for an explanation for she sensed Lotte was overwhelmed by returning memories and perhaps being a little paranoid. She thought it best to let her cry and get it out of her system.

Yet Dale herself was far from calm. She was terrified, bewildered and her face was sore, but above all she was furious with herself for rushing in mindlessly to try to rescue Lotte, when what she should have done was raise the alarm.

Her mother was always accusing her of rushing into things without engaging her brain first, and this was a first-class example of it. But rushing into love affairs, buying expensive clothes she couldn't afford or being too trusting wasn't dangerous. Whoever was behind this hadn't brought Lotte back here for a chat, they wanted her silenced for good, and Dale would be going with her.

'I must bathe your eye with cold water to bring the swelling down,' Lotte said a little while later.

Dale obediently followed her friend to the bathroom, touched that even under these circumstances Lotte was still thinking of someone other than herself.

Once the bright bathroom light was on, Dale saw

that the basement room they'd been locked into was done up like a guest room. Aside from the only daylight coming from a minute window up on ground level, and the musty odour of dampness, it was a comfortable room with pretty lilac-coloured wallpaper, a carpet in a slightly darker shade and white furniture including an iron bed. There were even prints of Edwardian children having a picnic on a beach.

The bathroom was small, just a shower, toilet and washbasin, but it was spotlessly clean, and there were thick, lilac-coloured towels on the rail.

'A five-star prison then!' Dale joked, forcing a grin and sitting down on the toilet to have her eye bathed. 'I just hope the hot water works.'

Lotte gave a weak smile, but didn't respond. She took some cottonwool balls from the cabinet, soaked them in cold water and pressed them to the swelling on her friend's right cheek.

'It looks bad,' she said, 'it's already very red and swollen. By tonight your eye will probably have closed up. But there's some painkillers in the cabinet. I think you should have a couple.'

The way she spoke was as if they were away in a bed and breakfast for the night, and it made Dale angry. She caught hold of Lotte's wrist. 'Never mind painkillers! Start explaining. Where is this place? Was it where you were held before?'

'Yes, it is. It's not far from Chichester,' Lotte said. 'A village on the harbour.'

Dale nodded. 'So it's all come back?'

'I don't know.' Lotte brushed her friend's hand off her arm and put her hands to her forehead as though it hurt, tears welling up in her eyes. 'There's too much to take in at once, and some of it so shocking.' She broke off, looking at Dale with stricken eyes. 'But you know that, don't you? Is that why you didn't try to remind me about being raped?'

Dale stood up and moved to embrace Lotte. 'I couldn't bring myself to,' she said softly. 'I even thought it was best you never remembered. Was it the men grabbing you that brought it all back?'

'No, just the scent of a plant.' Lotte sobbed against Dale's shoulder. 'Smells take us back to all kinds of places, don't they? The floor polish at school, the first perfume you ever wore, tar, bonfires, but the plant I smelled today when the man brushed against it, I bought it.'

Dale frowned, not understanding. 'Explain?'

Lotte backed away from her, looking around the room wildly. 'You must lie down.' She grabbed Dale's arm and led her back to the bed, pulling back the quilt so her friend could lie beneath it. 'You've had a really bad shock today.'

Dale did feel a bit wobbly with shock, but she wasn't prepared to let Lotte off the hook that easily. 'So have you. Don't try and stall,' she said a little harshly. 'Tell me about this place.'

'I have to go right back to Ushuaia,' Lotte said with a

desperate look on her face. 'That man stole a part of me and that led to everything else.'

Dale rolled her eyes with frustration. All she wanted to know now was who this place belonged to and why they were being held captive. But Lotte looked so demented she thought it best to humour her, so she lay down and pulled the quilt over her. 'OK, fire away!' she said.

'I couldn't talk to you about the rape on the ship,' Lotte began and her eyes filled with tears again. 'I wanted to, Dale, but it was too raw, too horrible, so I talked about it to Fern. I felt she and Howard were my saviours because they rescued me.

'For the first few nights, every time I closed my eyes I thought it was happening again. I'd feel him forcing his way into me, smell his body odour and bad breath. Fern would hold me tightly. She'd tell me I was safe and got me to pray with her.'

Dale snorted with derision.

'I know you thought she was a weird holy roller,' Lotte said, and she got up on the bed and sat with her back against the footboard looking at Dale. 'But I felt safe again with her, loved and cared for. She kind of made up for my cold mother, all the injustice when I was a kid. She told me that the only way I would keep that safe, loved and cared-for feeling was if I offered up my life to God.'

'So she's behind all this?' Dale asked incredulously. 'She captured you and kept you here? In the name of God!'

'It's far more complicated than that, so let me explain

it my way,' Lotte begged her. 'You need to understand how I was, to see the full picture. Remember when I went back to work on the ship? To all intents and purposes I was over the rape, a bit bruised, but recovering. Is that what you believed?'

Dale nodded.

'I wasn't, Dale, I was a mess inside. I wanted a mother, I was like a small child lost in a busy town, I was scared of everything and everyone. I forced myself to go ashore with you and Scott a few times and I might have acted as though I was enjoying it, but in fact it was an ordeal, a kind of terrible penance to have to be in a bar drinking and dancing. I began to see it, like Fern, as the Devil's way. I understood then why some women become nuns. I wanted to retreat from the world.'

'Why on earth didn't you tell me this?' Dale asked.

'I was afraid you'd think I was cracking up,' Lotte said simply. 'Maybe I was, I don't know. You are one smart and sassy girl, you don't suffer nutters or neurotics gladly, and I wanted to keep you as a friend, so I made out I was fine.'

'Oh, Lotte!' Dale sighed. 'I'd really like to say I would've understood, but if I'm honest I suppose I would've become impatient with you. But then I'm a selfish cow. I wanted you out whooping it up with me, not dwelling on something I could hardly get my head around.'

Lotte half smiled and reached forward to smooth her friend's hair from her face. 'I love your honesty,' she said. 'But you are a much nicer person than you realize.'

'Get on with the story,' Dale said. 'I couldn't bear it if they dragged us out of here to execute us and I hadn't heard it all.'

'Please don't joke about that,' Lotte reproved her. 'It's not so far from the truth, we certainly are in real danger. But you need to understand what happened to me, and about them, so that we can put our heads together and find a way to survive.'

'Shit, Lotte, that's a bit heavy!' Dale exclaimed.

'It is heavy,' Lotte said, reaching out for a pillow to put behind her back. 'Stop me if you lose the track or you don't understand something.'

Dale suddenly realized this was the real deal. It wasn't something exaggerated in the newspapers, not a bit of gossip or supposition. Lotte was ready to tell her what had really happened, and she had to pin her ears back and take it in. 'OK,' she said, wriggling down further under the quilt. 'Fire away.'

'You remember I told you I was going home to my parents in Brighton? I knew I could never do that and now you've met them you'll understand why. But I didn't think I could burden Simon and Adam with myself either, for they'd want me out partying with them, and I wasn't up for that.

'I didn't really have a plan as such, but I kind of thought I would go down to Dorset or Devon, somewhere rural and pretty, and hole up till I was strong again.'

Dale saw that her friend was leaning back, and it was clear that her mind was taking her back to the last full day on the ship, for as she started to talk it was as if she was there reliving it again.

'Do you remember how rough it was as we sailed through the Bay of Biscay? That bitingly cold March wind, and the sullen grey skies?'

Dale did remember. Many of the passengers were feeling queasy because the boat was pitching, and some of the girls in the hairdressing salon were finding it difficult to remain steady on their feet as they did their clients' hair.

'Fern came in at eleven for her hair appointment wearing an emerald-green jersey two-piece which looked stunning with her red hair,' Lotte went on.

Fern was astoundingly vain about her shoulder-length hair, and Lotte had realized she wanted it to be perfect every single day, as though she was a film star or royalty. She would never pull it back and put a band round it, as most women did. For formal evenings she had to have it put up; by day it had to be blowdried into a perfect coiffure. So even if it wasn't washed, it had to be dampened to style it.

'I don't know how I'll cope with my hair without you,' she said once Lotte had washed it and was combing it through. 'You are the best hairdresser I've ever had.'

Lotte felt warmed by that, and when Fern asked if she thought she'd stay working in Brighton after visiting her parents, she admitted she wasn't planning to go home at all. 'I can't face it,' she said. 'I've told you what my parents are like; going there is out of the question.

But it will be worse with my old friends. I can't go back to going out to clubs and pubs. So I thought I'd go down to the west of England, find a little flat in some pretty sleepy place, take long walks and read books until I feel brave enough to look for a new job.'

'I think that might be a mistake, honey,' Fern said, looking concerned. 'Being totally alone may sound good when you're on this ship with so much noise and clamour, but it's very different when there's absolutely no one to turn to. Why don't you come along to my stateroom later for a little chat about it?'

Lotte had no more clients by four o'clock as mostly everyone was packing to leave the ship the next day. As she walked along the passage to the Ramsdens' stateroom she saw suitcases standing outside many of the doors, waiting to be collected by a steward.

Fern hadn't even started her packing and Lotte offered to help her do it, and as she carefully laid out dresses and jackets on the bed, then folded them neatly with tissue paper so they wouldn't crease, Fern chatted.

'You're so good at that,' she said as she watched Lotte systematically empty the wardrobe, leaving only the clothes Fern needed for that evening and the following morning. 'I always make a real hash of it, so when I get back home everything needs ironing even if I haven't worn it.'

'I like doing this kind of thing,' Lotte admitted. 'In the old days I'd probably have made a very good lady's maid.'

'That's just what I need,' Fern said jokingly. 'Someone to pack, lay my clothes out, do my hair and maybe paint my nails too.'

They chatted all the while Lotte finished the packing, including Howard's too. Then suddenly Fern suggested Lotte came to London with them. 'We've booked a suite at the Dorchester and it has a small room in it which would be ideal for you.'

'I couldn't possibly do that.' Lotte wished she hadn't bleated about going off to the West Country on her own. She hadn't meant to make Fern feel sorry for her.

'But you can. We've got so many important functions to attend, it would help me greatly having you to help with my clothes and do my hair. But more importantly, honey, it'll give you breathing space, to decide what to do next when we go back to the States. You'd be in a safe environment with us, together we can do all the London sights, and we'll give you pocket money too. Do say you'll come with us. You know you've become the daughter we were never blessed with.'

Aside from the fact that Lotte had come to think of Fern as a mother figure, and it made her feel loved to be asked to go with her to London, Fern was only talking about two weeks. It seemed churlish to turn down such a generous offer when she could go down to the West Country afterwards if she wanted.

So she accepted gratefully, and when Howard returned a little later, he appeared delighted. Compared to his wife who had a big personality, plenty to say and mixed easily, Howard was very quiet. Lotte thought he was shy at first, but he wasn't, he was just a man who was happy to let others do the talking. He was of medium height and slender, with brown hair, fine aristocratic features and long, thin fingers: Lotte thought he looked like a pianist. She had told him this once and he laughed, saying he could play a few tunes on a calculator, but that was all. His main business was sports equipment, but Fern had told her they had many other business interests between them.

As Lotte went back to the cabin later, she decided she wouldn't tell Dale about this. Her friend didn't like the Ramsdens, so she would only pour cold water on the plan. Lotte felt she might end up having to admit that she'd never even rung her parents to confide in them about the rape, and that there was no question of going home to them.

But Dale was so excited about going home herself that she didn't ask any awkward questions, she just lay on the bunk talking about her family and let Lotte pack her case for her.

'Scott wants us to have a drink with him tomorrow before we go our separate ways,' Dale said later. 'I said we'd meet up with him and some of the others about one o'clock at the bar just the other side of Customs. Is that all right with you?'

Lotte gulped, afraid she was going to be found out, for the passengers on the ship would all have left by ten-thirty and she'd arranged to meet the Ramsdens in the luggage shed on the quay.

'I've already rung my mum to say I'll be on the eleven o'clock train,' she lied. 'She'll be really hurt if I ring again to say I want to have a drink first.'

That last evening was one of the best of the whole year, although it was after midnight before most of the staff were free to have a drink and let their hair down. Almost all the friends Lotte and Dale had made were leaving the ship for good, like them. It was really only officers and people in key jobs who would be signing on for another year. Everyone was feeling sentimental, remembering the good times, laughing about the calamities, and vowing they'd keep in touch for ever.

Like everyone else that night, Lotte passed out her mobile phone number and entered dozens of numbers into hers. When she went to bed later she felt so positive about everything that she believed within a couple of weeks she'd be ready to contact many of them again.

That positive feeling was still there the next morning, and she didn't feel ashamed she hadn't told Dale and Scott the truth about where she was going, because she intended to contact both of them again very soon.

She was shocked when Dale's dark eyes filled with tears as they said goodbye.

'You've been the best friend I've ever had,' she said, her lips wobbling all over the place. 'Don't you dare disappear out of my life.'

It was nearly as bad saying goodbye to Scott. He caught her up in the fiercest of bear hugs. 'Look after yourself, Barbie Girl,' he said gruffly. 'Come on down to Cornwall this summer. My mum and sisters will love you. It's an honour having you as a friend.'

Everything was frantic that morning: passengers flapping about where their luggage had been taken to, whether they would make their connecting train or plane, or whether the relative who was meeting them had got to Southampton. It was a chilly grey day, and although all the staff were doing their best to stay patient, helpful and caring for just another couple of hours, Lotte could see from their tight expressions that good humour was running out.

She slipped away just a few minutes after the Ramsdens left the ship, to join them as arranged down in the luggage shed.

Lotte didn't miss her mobile phone until they were in the suite at the Dorchester much later that afternoon.

Even the very best rooms at the Grand in Brighton weren't a patch on the suite the Ramsdens had been given. Their bedroom and the sitting room overlooked Park Lane with a glorious view of Hyde Park. It was decorated in pale blue and silver, with a fantastic chandelier, big squashy sofas, sumptuous curtains and carpets, and the bathroom was like something from a Hollywood film set. Even Lotte's small room was exquisite and she felt she'd made a really good decision to come with Fern and Howard.

'I'll ring the car hire company about your phone

while you unpack our cases,' Fern said. 'I expect it fell out of your bag in the car.'

Howard got a phone call soon after that and said he and Fern would have to make a lightning trip back to New York immediately to sort out some urgent business. Lotte said she couldn't possibly stay at the hotel without them, but they insisted, and Howard said they would only be gone two nights anyway, providing they could get the flights.

The next morning the car hire company rang to say they couldn't find Lotte's phone. She didn't see it as a calamity then as she had used it so rarely in the last year, just the odd text to Simon and to some of the others at the hairdresser's, and she only had about a pound's worth of credit left on it anyway.

She was very tired after the cruise, and with Fern and Howard gone she could doze when she liked, read, watch television and wander along nearby Oxford Street to look at the shops.

She spent two nights without Fern and Howard and when they returned they were anxious to take her to all the sights like Buckingham Palace, the Tower of London and Trafalgar Square. It was all so thrilling that she didn't give her phone another thought.

She had only been to London twice before, both times for hair competitions, and had never seen anything of the city. Fern and Howard had seen it all before, but they seemed to get a real kick out of showing it to her.

It was only on the fourth day, when they went on the

London Eye, that Lotte wished she could send Dale and Scott a text about it. Then it dawned on her that she hadn't got anyone's numbers written down anywhere. They were all in the missing phone. She didn't even know her own number so she could get it changed to a new phone.

Lotte was a bit down that evening, because she felt cut off, but Fern persuaded her to put on her one and only formal evening dress to go to dinner in the hotel. She had bought the dress to take on the cruise, but she'd only worn it once, at the staff Christmas party. It was black lace with a high neck and long sleeves. Dale had put her off it, saying it was something Morticia in the Addams family would wear. But Fern said it was classy and sophisticated.

'You are so beautiful,' she said, insisting that Lotte borrowed her diamond drop earrings for the night. 'Your hair, your skin, figure and face, all so perfect, along with the sweetest nature I've ever had the privilege to know. And I think losing your phone and all those contacts could be God's way of moving you on to the kind of life you deserve.'

They had lobster that night and vintage champagne. Fern said they should celebrate Lotte's liberation from reminders of the past, from people whispering behind their hands, and those who felt sorry for her. 'I never thought Dale was a suitable friend for you. She's what I call a "force fielder".'

Over the next day or two, while walking in Hyde Park

or strolling down Bond Street and other 'high end' streets, as Fern called them, she enlarged on her theory of 'force fielders'. These were people with dominant personalities, who drew people to them like iron filings to a magnet and caused them to become followers.

She did say that some of these people worked for good, citing Gandhi, Nelson Mandela and other well-known men and women who had an enraptured following. But she was far more voluble when she talked about those who used their gift for their own evil ends, and named Mugabe, Hitler and Stalin as the most notable.

While she didn't actually call Dale evil or even wicked, she pointed out that she had changed Lotte. This was of course true, at least to the extent that Dale had encouraged Lotte to be more assertive, outgoing and daring. But Fern went a stage further, hinting that Dale's influence had caused her to wear more provocative clothes and to risk going out alone in unknown territory, which was why she had been raped. She also said the reason Dale was angry about Fern taking care of her afterwards was because Dale wanted sole control over her.

Lotte didn't fall into believing this theory of Fern's right then, but it was like a slow leak dripping into a pail, and as time passed she found herself putting it forward as the truth. She even came round to believing she was better off without her old friends. Fern didn't approve of homosexuality of course, so Simon and Adam would be considered even worse than Dale.

But Lotte did agree right away that her mini skirts, tight jeans and strappy low-necked tops were provocative, even though Dale had never had any hand in choosing them. Ever since the rape she'd chosen to wear tracksuit bottoms and baggy tee-shirts because she wanted to be invisible. When Fern suggested she helped her buy some new clothes that would be demure yet still pretty, she was really pleased.

The print dresses, pastel cardigans, high-necked blouses and mid-calf skirts which Fern picked out would have made Dale scream with laughter, but they made Lotte feel safe. Sometimes when she glanced in a mirror she thought she looked like a wholesome extra from an American Fifties film, but she wanted to retreat into the background and her clothes helped her do that. Nobody looked at her twice.

She loved the two weeks at the Dorchester. When Fern and Howard were engaged in business meetings she could read, watch videos, or walk in Hyde Park. In the last year she'd rarely had any time to herself, just to be quiet and think about things. Sharing a cabin with Dale was like living in a train station, with people in and out all the time and incessant noise. Even in the salon there was always pressure: clients could be very difficult, the manager was always trying to squeeze extra people in each day, and the other girls could be catty.

All she had to do now was look after Fern's clothes, do her hair and nails and answer the phone for them while they were out. She had absolutely nothing to worry about and no decisions to make, because Fern and Howard arranged everything.

By the end of the first week she was wondering how she was going to cope alone when they went back to America. She could look after herself, but she felt panicky in crowds, and quite often froze completely when a stranger approached her. Going down to the West Country didn't seem quite so appealing any longer.

It was around the middle of the second week that Howard told her they were considering staying in England for a few more months to extend their business interests here.

'But that rather depends on us finding a suitable property to rent, and a housekeeper,' he said. 'Fern doesn't go for cooking, cleaning and laundry, but it's hard for us to find a suitable housekeeper as we need one who is loyal, totally discreet, and not only respects our beliefs but shares them.'

Lotte told him that housekeeper was her.

They tried to put her off, saying she might not like being alone all day, or having no friends nearby. But Lotte insisted that wouldn't worry her, that she still needed more quiet time and solitude before she went back to her old life. She was jubilant when they said they'd be delighted to have her with them. They even talked about taking her back to the States with them at the end of the year, or if she wanted to go back to hairdressing they would help her open her own salon in a place of her choosing.

Lotte was rather surprised that they found a house to rent so quickly. They went out on the Thursday morning and were back that evening with it all sewn up, and Howard had bought a new black Mercedes too.

'It's near that quaint place called Chichester,' Fern said. 'We're close enough to the sea to do some sailing, and the house is real cute.'

They left the Dorchester on Saturday morning, stopping for lunch on the way, and then at a supermarket just outside Chichester to stock up on food. They arrived at the village of Itchenor, which was around seven or eight miles beyond Chichester, just before four.

Lotte was feeling really good that day, excited, happy and optimistic about the future. She remembered feeling that she'd finally come out of the end of a dark tunnel into sunshine. It was a lovely day too, and there had been signs of spring all the way there – lambs in the fields, daffodils in gardens and blossom on trees. Fern had been saying on the way down that Lotte ought to learn to drive, for she'd be a bit cut off as there wasn't much of a bus service.

'I'll get a bike,' Lotte said and thought how good it would be to ride around country lanes or down to the beach on hot days. She didn't know that part of Sussex at all, but she'd heard it was good for cycling as it was quite flat.

Yet as Howard turned into a narrow drive between high hedges and overhanging trees, and Lotte saw the house beyond for the first time, the excitement vanished and she felt menaced.

Fern had described it as cute. Weird was the word which popped into Lotte's head, quickly followed by spooky.

The village was spread along a long, wide lane with grass verges and many beautiful old trees. Almost all the houses looked as if they belonged to wealthy people, and no two were the same. There were large, picture postcard thatched cottages, big mock Tudor places, and substantial family homes built during the Twenties and Thirties for the seriously rich. Most had large gardens, and even the smaller, older stone cottages which had probably once been home to farm labourers had been carefully and lovingly restored.

But 'Drummond', as the house Fern and Howard had rented was called, was built of ugly grey stone with slit-like windows, crenellations along the roof and a very heavy-looking front door as if it was trying to look like a castle.

Lotte made no comment, for if Fern thought it looked cute, she didn't want to put her off it.

It was clear that the owners of the houses on either side had sold a small portion of their land at the back for 'Drummond' to be built, with just a narrow access to the road between the two adjoining gardens. Lotte thought it was probably during the Thirties when times were hard and local councils didn't always check that a proposed building was going to suit the area it was planned for. There was no doubt in her mind that the owners of the neighbouring houses had grown thick hedges so they didn't have to look on to the ugliness of their neighbour.

Even the front garden was stark: no daffodils or trees in blossom, just the narrow, tunnel-like passage through the hedges to a wider paved area in front of the house. There were narrow flower beds on either side of the path to the front door but aside from a few clumps of weeds, they were just bare soil.

'Isn't it cute!' Fern exclaimed yet again as they went in with the suitcases and bags of groceries. 'So very English!'

Lotte wanted to say it wasn't English at all, that it had a nod towards Scottish Baronial perhaps, but she thought the architect needed locking up. She said nothing of course, even though it was gloomy inside as a result of the narrow windows. The kitchen was brighter because it had a window set in the ceiling, but the decor all over the house was in keeping with its style: dark reds, browns, blues and russets.

'Our office,' Fern said, indicating the room next to the front door. 'And the dining room,' she went on, opening the door beyond the office to a room painted dark blue, with several model sailing ships in cases on the walls and various other nautical items including a large compass. Even the table and chairs looked as if they'd come from a ward room, of dark reddish wood with seats of brown leather. The kitchen too had many nautical items, a brass ship's clock, sets of complicated knots in glass cases and the like. There was even a 'cookie' jar, as Fern called it, shaped like a lighthouse.

Upstairs the master bedroom took up the whole front of the house, and it was only here that the slit windows looked quite stylish, for there were four, right down to the floor with its dark red carpet. Lotte actually liked the dark Victorian-style wallpaper and matching curtains, and she supposed it was this room with its vast bed and whole wall of wardrobes that had sold the house to Fern.

She was glad her room was at the back and had slightly wider windows. The russet decor wasn't as oppressive as some of the other rooms, and over the hedged-in garden she could see fields and dozens of trees in blossom.

Even that very first night Lotte sensed something odd. As she and Fern put food away in the kitchen, it seemed strange that Fern already had a firm plan about where everything should go. People weren't usually like that in a strange house. When a light bulb fused in the hall, Howard went straight to a cupboard by the front door and got a new one out. It wouldn't have occurred to Lotte to look there. While she was glad they seemed so at home, it felt kind of supernatural that they were.

Lotte didn't realize that there was a room and another bathroom in the basement until a couple of days later. When she drew Fern's attention to the door leading to them, thinking she didn't know about it either, Fern seemed to find that very funny.

However, despite thinking the house was weird, and wishing she hadn't lost all her friends' addresses and telephone numbers, because she really would have liked to contact some of them, Lotte was happy. Fern and Howard were undemanding, easygoing people who ate whatever she cooked, didn't hold her to a rigid time-table and appreciated her looking after them.

They went out most days, sometimes just for a couple of hours, sometimes to sail down on the harbour, for they'd bought a little cabin cruiser and had it moored there. They got any shopping needed and brought it home with them.

Lotte would clean the house and do the laundry in the mornings, and in the afternoons she usually went for a walk. It was around a mile down to West Itchenor and the sea, but she loved it so much she went there most days. Chichester harbour was a vast natural one, with Hayling Island on one side, West Wittering with its lovely sandy beaches on the other, and little villages like Bosham, Birdham and West Itchenor scattered between.

There wasn't much at West Itchenor, just a pub, a boatyard and some pretty old cottages, but there was a little ferry boat from there across to Bosham, and Lotte loved seeing the sea and the sea birds and feeling the wind in her hair. Down there the events in Ushuaia seemed to fade away.

But hardly a day passed without Lotte thinking of Simon and Adam. She didn't have the excuse that she didn't know their address or phone number for not contacting them, for these were stamped firmly on her mind. It was fear of them turning up here to see her which prevented her. She knew only too well that Fern and Howard wouldn't welcome an openly gay couple. If she asked her friends not to call they would know that was the reason, and she could almost hear Simon asking how she could bear to work for anyone with such prejudices. But the longer she left it, the more difficult it became, for she knew they would be hurt and worried by her silence.

As the weather improved through April and May Lotte turned her attention to the two bare flower beds in the front garden. Her parents had been very fond of gardening, and although she'd never been allowed to do anything more than weeding and watering, she knew one flower from another and the conditions they liked.

There were several keen gardeners in the village who offered plants for sale that were surplus to their needs. They had them on a table by their gate with an honesty box for the money. Fern gave Lotte twenty pounds pocket money every week, and she had nothing to spend it on, as she hardly ever went into town, so she bought plants with it.

The lemon geranium was among the first batch of plants she bought, but she planted it up in a flowerpot and put it by the front door because she knew it wouldn't be hardy when winter came and it was so nice when its scent wafted out as you brushed by it.

She made the two flower beds in the front garden

look very pretty with penstemons, lavender and hardy geraniums, and once the summer really got underway they would billow out on to the path and soften the ugliness of the house.

One evening she asked Fern and Howard over dinner if they thought their landlord would mind her making a flower bed in the back garden as if would mean digging up a bit of the lawn.

'There's no point,' Howard said quite abruptly. 'We won't be here long enough.'

Fern looked flustered at his remark and passed it off by saying that they had always said they might be going back to the States.

'Yes, of course you did,' Lotte said, looking from one to the other in puzzlement because she knew there was something going on that they weren't telling her. 'Oh, don't feel bad about me,' she added, thinking they were afraid of leaving her in the lurch. 'I can go back to Brighton. I'm OK now.'

She felt she was fine too. She'd stopped getting heart palpitations every time a lone man walked towards her and sometimes she even fancied a night down at the pub, or would've done if she'd had anyone to go with. She missed Dale and Scott so much that she would have given anything to be able to ring them up and arrange to meet them again. And if she was really honest with herself, she was a little sick of all the praying she was expected to do.

Fern and Howard said prayers before they left the house in the morning, and again at night. On Sundays

Howard liked to read long passages from the Bible. It had been comforting at first, she'd even found that praying on her own worked like meditation and calmed her down. But she didn't find that necessary now and it was a bit irritating that she was expected to bend to their beliefs.

'We do feel bad about leaving you because we had hoped you would be with us when we had our baby,' Fern suddenly blurted out.

'You're having a baby?' Lotte exclaimed. She had imagined that at past forty Fern was too old for that. 'How wonderful!'

'Oh no, I'm not having one. I can't, I've never been able to bear a child,' Fern quickly replied. 'What we mean is that we've been trying to find someone here willing to give us a baby.'

'You mean you're going to adopt?' Lotte asked.

'No, it will be our baby, well, Howard's at least.'

Lotte frowned. 'You mean you're going to find a surrogate mother?'

'Yes, that's about the size of it.'

Over a couple of brandies Fern told Lotte the sad story of how she lost several babies when she first got married, and then eventually had to have her womb removed. She went on to say how much she and Howard had to offer a child, a lovely home in the States, money in the bank and so much love. She told her they wished they'd tried to adopt years ago, but now the societies said they were too old.

They had been to several different organizations in England who offered to arrange contact with young women willing to have a child by donor sperm, but when they looked into it they felt the women were either low life who used drugs, or slightly unbalanced people who might act irrationally when the baby was born.

'Now a woman in Romania has been put forward as being perfect for us. So that was where we were intending to go next, not straight back to America. But I've still got a heavy heart about it. This woman doesn't speak English, so we won't be able to be sure about anything.'

Fern looked so sad and troubled that Lotte hugged her. 'I never knew you wanted a baby so badly,' she said with real sympathy. 'I wish I could do something to help you.'

'You help us by just being around,' Fern said, patting Lotte's cheek affectionately.

Fern and Howard went to Romania, but returned after only two days. 'She was almost as old as me,' Fern said, looking really down and disappointed. 'We think she had been a prostitute; she looked raddled and grubby.'

'Just doing it for the money then?' Lotte said.

'Well, that's all any of them would do it for,' Howard said.

'I wouldn't, I'd do it for love,' Lotte said.

The words just slipped out without thought. What Lotte had meant was that having a baby for someone

220

else should only be an act of love. Like a woman having a baby for her infertile sister. But Fern's face lit up. 'You'd do it for us?' she said, her voice husky with emotion.

That was the pivotal moment when Lotte should have firmly explained she was speaking in general, idealistic terms, not actually offering to do it for them.

But Fern and Howard never gave her a chance to say that wasn't what she meant. They were so busy hugging each other, offering praise to the Lord for sending her to them, that Lotte found herself unable to say they had misunderstood.

Chapter Ten

'You agreed to have a baby for them?' Dale interrupted incredulously.

'No, I didn't,' Lotte retorted. 'I only agreed that it should be done for love. But Fern was like a bulldozer, she just brushed everything I said aside. I did get my courage up a day later to say she'd misunderstood me and that I couldn't possibly do it. But she laughed at me, said I just had a touch of the collywobbles and I'd be OK soon.

'Before I knew it she was making plans, drawing up ovulation charts and explaining how she'd have to take my temperature each morning so they knew when I was at my most fertile. I can't tell you how freaked out I was, and I knew that I was going to have to make a run for it.'

'Speaking of making a run for it,' Dale said, 'shouldn't we try battering down the door?'

'It's impossible, I tried it.' Lotte sighed. 'It's solid oak, only a chainsaw would get through it.'

'Who do you think is up there?' Dale cocked her head to listen.

'I doubt anyone is,' Lotte said. 'Howard probably was there, but I think he's gone away now. I can't hear anything. I don't think he'll come back until he's decided what to do with us. Even then he'll probably send someone else to do his dirty work.'

'Does that mean we won't get any food?' Dale asked, her voice faltering.

Lotte hesitated. 'I don't know,' she said weakly.

Realizing that was Lotte's gentle way of preparing her for starvation – after all, there was no point in feeding people you were planning to dispose of – Dale made a conscious effort to subdue the terror and panic rising within her.

'Right, so we'd better make plans for how we are going to overcome the men when they come to collect us,' she said, far more brightly than she felt.

'I thought about that a lot when I was down here before,' Lotte said. 'What I came up with was that I'd pretend to be out cold on the bed. That way, whoever came for me would have to pick me up. I planned to stick my nail file in his eye, and hopefully as he was screaming and carrying on, I could rush out.'

'But that didn't work?' Dale raised an eyebrow.

'That wasn't how I was taken. Do you want me to continue about what happened to me?'

Dale nodded. She needed something to take her mind off how serious their predicament really was.

'They went out a couple of days after this stuff about wanting a baby had come up,' Lotte said, sinking back against the bed rail as she recalled exactly what had happened.

She had woken to the sound of rain lashing against the window, and when she went to have a shower she was shivering despite it being the end of May. Later, as she put on one of the print dresses Fern had encouraged her to buy, all at once she saw how incredibly awful she looked. It was a defining moment, for suddenly she could cut through all the stuff which she'd seen as kindness and care, her own need to be loved, and realize that Fern and Howard had been playing a long game with her.

They had sucked her into their way of life by taking her to a luxurious hotel, giving her a wonderful time, and at the same time separating her from her old friends, under the guise of protecting her. They had even disposed of her old clothes and got her to buy new ones as a way of reinforcing her paranoia of men looking at her. Once down here she had the illusion of freedom – after all, she could walk out of the door whenever she chose. Yet they had actually been getting her into a state of mind where she was so indebted and dependent she had no will of her own.

But they hadn't quite got her to the point where she was prepared to have a baby for them. And now she understood that was their plan, she knew she must get away from them as quickly as possible.

'We're driving up to London today,' Fern said over breakfast. 'Would you like to come with us?'

Lotte's heart leapt. Not at being offered a trip to London, but the perfect opportunity to leave. They'd be gone for hours, and although it was cowardly not to tell them she was going, she couldn't face Fern doing the emotional blackmail bit about how good they'd been to her.

'I think I'd rather stay here, if you don't mind,' she said. 'It's such horrible weather, and if it's the same in London I won't be able to walk about and explore while you're busy.'

Neither of them looked concerned at her decision, and they left about half an hour later, saying they doubted they'd be back before eight that evening.

Lotte washed up the breakfast things, swept and tidied the kitchen, and on an impulse decided to have a look through all Fern and Howard's papers in the office before she left for good.

She wouldn't normally poke into anyone's private things. But she supposed that she'd feel less guilty about running off if she found something in the office which pointed to them not being quite the God-fearing, honourable people they purported to be.

There was nothing unusual in any of the desk drawers, just receipts for petrol and other expenses and a couple of invoice books for the sportswear company they owned in America.

The filing cabinet was locked though. Lotte had never seen it open, and for all she knew it could have stuff locked in it which belonged to the people who owned the house. But as she pulled down one of the box files on a shelf above the desk to see what was in there, a small key fell down.

The box file contained more correspondence, most

of it recent letters pertaining to a commercial property the Ramsdens were buying in Southampton. Lotte had heard them discussing this openly on many occasions. It was a semi-derelict warehouse which they were hoping to pull down and build an office block in its place, but strangely all the correspondence was addressed to Mr and Mrs Gullick, not Ramsden.

She didn't bother looking in any of the other box files for they'd all been here when they moved in – she supposed they all belonged to the landlord – and instead tried the small key in the filing cabinet. The key turned and she could open all three drawers.

There in the top drawer, sitting among several small boxes, was her old mobile phone.

It was unmistakable, for even though it was a common black Nokia Lotte had personalized it by sticking a row of crystals round the screen.

She felt as though someone had punched her in the stomach and winded her. Tears sprang into her eyes because they had lied when they claimed not to have seen it, called the car hire company to ask if they'd found it, and later, when she was upset at losing touch with all her friends, they'd suggested someone had picked her pocket at Southampton docks.

How easy it must have been for Fern to slip her hand into Lotte's bag while they were in the car and take it. The perfect way of cutting her off from everyone she knew!

Doing such a thing proved their intentions had never been honourable.

After all this time the battery was completely flat of course, and sadly she'd thrown the charger away back at the Dorchester, but she was delighted to have found it anyway, and she could buy another charger in Chichester and access all her numbers again.

The second drawer of the cabinet held many suspended cardboard files, all of them with single names which meant nothing to her, but one was labelled 'Drummond', the name of the house, so she pulled that one out.

The letter on the top of the file was a completion statement from a solicitor in London. It was dated September 2000 and related to the purchase of 'Drummond', by Mr and Mrs Gullick, for the sum of two hundred and fifty thousand pounds.

Lotte thought the file belonged to the landlord and was about to put it back in the cabinet when she noticed a handwritten note stapled to the card file. It was merely a list of items, a filing cabinet, desk and bookcase among them, but this was in Fern's writing.

Puzzled as to why Fern would be putting anything in this file if it didn't belong to her and Howard, Lotte flicked through it. There among the papers was a photocopied handwritten letter to a Mr J. C. Wetherall about items Mr and Mrs Gullick wished to have included in the purchase of the house. It was unmistakably Fern's writing, and even if it was signed by E. Gullick, there was no doubt of the writer's real identity.

Lotte was stunned. Not just by the different name,

for that could possibly be explained if Gullick was Fern's maiden name and for some reason she and Howard found it more convenient for business affairs. But why had they pretended they were renting the house? What possible reason could they have for that?

Unnerved, Lotte pulled out the file next to 'Drummond', which was labelled 'Farnley'.

This contained handwritten letters which were addressed to a Dr and Mrs Kent in Hartford, Connecticut, and sent from Marion Farnley from an address in Illinois. They appeared to have been sent on here by a third party, for there was a note to Fern attached to one, just saying, 'I thought you'd better see these', with an unreadable signature.

It seemed the writer of the letters, Marion Farnley, was pregnant, with her baby due in July, and indeed all the letters were about the progress of her pregnancy, her visits to the ante-natal clinic and how much weight she was putting on.

Lotte felt that the Kents were helping her financially, which suggested she could be a relative. The most recent letter, dated 12 May, seemed to confirm this, for Marion questioned whether everything was in place at the nursing home where the baby would be born.

There was a slightly curt tone to this latest letter. Marion wanted to know when the money would be transferred to her account. But a cold chill ran down Lotte's spine as she read: 'I expect this to happen before I hand my baby over to his new parents.'

Lotte stood there for a moment by the open drawer of the filing cabinet, her hand clasped to her mouth in shock. All at once she realized that Dr and Mrs Kent, like the Gullicks, were none other than Fern and Howard, and transferring funds in conjunction with a baby to new parents could only mean one thing.

They were selling babies!

Lotte went through all the other files one by one and to her horror she found she was right. Not just one isolated case, but dozens of mothers in almost every state in America, and most had handed over their child some time ago.

It was all there in black and white for there were records of payments to the mothers, most of whom received a thousand dollars for handing over their baby. Then there were itemized accounts for the new parents, not just the Ramsdens' fee of twenty-five thousand dollars, but also the costs for the mother at the nursing home.

From what Lotte could gather there was someone else involved in this too, staying at the address in Connecticut and presumably running it while the Ramsdens were away. Yet it seemed that both Fern and Howard were in the habit of going back there on a regular basis, for there were several references in the correspondence to the patients seeing Dr Kent, including the date in March when they'd left the Dorchester to return fleetingly to America.

There was nothing to tell Lotte how the Ramsdens

found these women in the first place. Some, Lotte felt, had been pregnant when they first met, but certain remarks in some of the handwritten letters, many written by women who clearly had had very little education, suggested some of them had agreed to become pregnant with donor sperm.

With all this appalling but riveting correspondence to go through, Lotte forgot the time. She wanted to read everything, and see the whole picture of how Fern and Howard had managed to keep this extremely lucrative business running for so long without detection. She guessed they had false passports to go with their aliases, but she wondered how they found couples desperate enough to pay thousands of dollars for a baby. It wasn't as if they could advertise such a service.

There was a thank-you letter from a couple in Dallas who had enclosed a photograph of a very pretty baby with dark curly hair. 'We bless the day Muriel at Birthright slipped us your number,' they wrote. 'We had been given the run-around by them for over two years, we felt they were never going to help us. You took us seriously immediately, you fulfilled all our dreams for us. Bless you.'

Lotte wondered if Birthright was a bona fide adoption society and this Muriel who worked there took kickbacks from the Ramsdens for every desperate couple she sent their way.

The more information Lotte turned up, the angrier and more horrified she became at what Fern and

Howard had been doing. She wondered how they had the nerve to pose as devout Christians when they were making a fortune out of childless couples. Lotte knew real adoption societies checked every last thing about the couples they gave babies to, but she guessed the only check Fern and Howard made was to be sure that the couples they intended to supply with a child could afford their charges. They wouldn't know or care if they were sick, mentally ill or sexual deviants.

And what of the natural birth mothers? Any woman who would agree to have a baby for money was suspect. They could have drink or drug addiction problems, sexually transmitted diseases, and possibly very low IQs. She wondered if any of the babies were given a thorough medical examination before they were passed over.

Lotte's heart was racing now, for she realized that what she had discovered was dynamite and she must get away quickly and inform the police. She went back to the files and removed a particularly incriminating letter from each folder which she tucked into a large manila envelope. Then, after shutting the drawers and locking the cabinet, she replaced the key where she'd found it, and ran upstairs to get her things together to leave.

Lotte came out of the front door carrying her red suitcase and put it down to turn and lock the door with the mortice key. She'd just taken the key from the door when she heard the car turning into the drive.

Her heart sank and a tremor of fear ran down her spine. It was too late to unlock the door and run in again and there was no escape. There was a gate to the side of the house but it was padlocked, and the fences and thick hedges on both sides of the house and drive ruled out escaping that way.

The black Mercedes glided to a halt and Howard got out, keeping the driver's door open, virtually barring the way to the narrow drive between the high hedges and overhanging trees. Fern got out on the passenger side and walked over to Lotte where she stood transfixed with fear on the doorstep.

'Going somewhere?' Fern asked.

Her face was as cold as a January day, her green eyes almost black now. She was as always beautifully dressed and groomed, with a leopard-print scarf at the neck of her cream trench-style raincoat and makeup as flawless as when she'd left the house earlier; even her hair, which Lotte had swept up into a French pleat that morning, was still perfect.

'Yes, I decided it was best if I left,' Lotte blurted out. 'I want to go home.'

Fern had always had a commanding presence, but now as she walked closer to Lotte she seemed even taller and utterly formidable. 'But you know you aren't welcome at home,' she said silkily. 'Come on inside and we'll talk about it over a cup of coffee. I'm so disappointed that you'd try and creep away like a thief in the night when we weren't here. But maybe you can explain that!'

Howard came up to stand behind his wife, and Lotte realized that if she was to try to dart by him, he'd catch her easily. She thought defence was the best line of attack.

'You shocked me by suggesting I should have a child for you,' she said. 'It changed everything. I just want to go now.'

'Oh, do grow up, Lotte,' Fern said scornfully as Howard unlocked the door. 'If you really hated the idea we wouldn't have pressed the issue.'

'You shouldn't have even suggested it,' Lotte said indignantly.

Fern took Lotte's arm firmly and led her inside. Howard picked up the suitcase and carried it in, shutting the door behind the three of them. He locked it, took the key out and put it in his pocket.

'I really don't want to stay for coffee and talk about anything,' Lotte said, feeling very awkward and scared. 'Just let me go!'

'Why the hurry?' Fern asked. 'You wouldn't have put anything in your case that doesn't belong to you, would you?'

'Of course not.' Lotte felt sick now, for Fern had put the suitcase down on a hall chair and was about to open it. The manila envelope was right on the top.

'Then you won't mind me looking,' Fern said and flicked the case open.

She bypassed the envelope first, rummaging around among the clothes, but then stood up straight with it in her hand. 'What's this?' she asked, giving Lotte a hard, cold look.

Lotte knew all was lost now. Fern was going to open the envelope, and once she saw the contents there was no way on earth she was going to let her go.

'I'd better look, for the cat seems to have got your tongue,' Fern said.

She pulled out the letters and blanched as she saw what they were. 'You ungrateful wretch!' she roared at Lotte, taking a step closer and slapping her hard around the face. 'We've done everything we could for you, but you throw it back in our faces by going though our private papers.'

'You've been selling babies!' Lotte retorted indignantly. 'There's no way you can justify that! Is that why you helped me after the rape? Did you hope I'd be pregnant and you could get a good price for it?'

Fern moved to slap her again but Lotte caught her hand and pushed her back against the wall. 'Don't you dare hit me again. You've spouted out all that religious claptrap at me, you've made out you cared,' she yelled. 'But all you are is a crook. The worst kind too, a lying, scheming swindler who preys on the weak and vulnerable.'

Howard, who had been just standing there until now, leapt forward, grabbed Lotte's arms and twisted them back behind her. 'You can cool off in the basement,' he said.

He bundled her down there so fast she was hardly aware what was happening. The door at the top of the stairs was slammed shut and she heard the key turn in the lock, then footsteps walking away into the kitchen.

Lotte was too angry with herself even to cry. She couldn't really believe she hadn't anticipated they might test her by coming back early. She might have known they would be extra vigilant since their suggestion she had a baby for them. Why did she spend so long reading everything? Why on earth hadn't she just grabbed some of it and made off to the police?

But the very worst thing of all was the knowledge that they would never let her go now. They couldn't, for if they did, they'd be stuck in prison for years.

It was forty-eight hours before they came to speak to her again.

During that time Lotte tried yelling and hammering on the door. She tried to gouge through to the hinges with a nail file she found in a drawer, and she tried moving the wardrobe over to the tiny window to see if she could climb out that way. But once balanced precariously on the dressing-table stool on top of the wardrobe, she found the window was so small she wouldn't be able to get her shoulders through it. She thought of breaking the glass and then shouting, but she knew the window was situated in a gully at the back of the house and it was unlikely her voice would reach either of the neighbouring houses. Besides, while Fern and Howard were in the house, they were likely to cover that window securely if they heard her, so she would use that as a last resort once they'd gone out.

When Howard finally opened the door the smell of roasting chicken which wafted in from the kitchen made her almost faint with hunger.

'Hungry?' he asked, grinning as if that was funny.

Lotte could only nod. She felt too weak for anything more.

'You can come up and eat with us as long as you behave,' he said. 'We want to talk to you.'

An hour later Lotte was staring speechlessly at Fern as she laid down what was going to happen.

She had wolfed down the chicken dinner, convinced that the change of heart in feeding her meant they were ready to bargain. She expected to be offered money to forget what she'd discovered, and after two days of being locked up without food, Lotte was prepared to erase everything from her mind in return for a good meal.

But that wasn't what they had in mind at all.

Fern said that Lotte had got to have a baby for them, with Howard as the father. When the baby was born she was to register its birth and apply for its passport, then the three of them and the baby would fly back to America. Lotte would then be free to return home and they would pay her five thousand dollars as long as she signed an agreement to say she'd consented to being impregnated with Howard's sperm and to give him their baby when it was born.

Howard said little, just sat at the table with his arms crossed, looking first at Fern and then at Lotte. It was

tempting because of his fine features and gentle manner to think he didn't really want any part in this, but it
had been he who had posed as Dr Kent and convinced
dozens of women he really was a doctor.

'Why would you want me to come to the States with
you?' Lotte asked.

'To keep an eye on you right till the end of course,'
Fern said. 'We know that if you did go rushing off to a
police precinct in New York, Philadelphia, or anywhere
in America for that matter, with such a story and nothing to back it up, you'd be laughed at. And of course
with your signature on the agreement you wouldn't
have a leg to stand on anyway. But we're just trying to
be fair, which is why we'd fly you home with enough
money to start a brand-new life.'

Howard escorted her back to the cellar then. He said
she needed to think over what they'd said to her.

Lotte had no real need to think it over, for they hadn't
offered her any kind of choice. Whatever they said, they
were not going to let her go free, not in America, here
or anywhere else, not now, not ever. They couldn't; she
knew too much.

She could bend over backwards to convince them
she was willing to go along with this baby thing, that she
wanted the money and she'd never blab to anyone, but
they were never going to trust her completely again.

The bottom line was they'd have to kill her. Either
now if she didn't agree to go along with their plans, or
later once they'd got what they wanted. A couple of

months ago she could never have thought it possible that they could even lie, let alone sell babies or kill. But she had no doubt about it now.

She wondered why she'd never noticed that fanatical look in Fern's green eyes before, or the slyness in Howard's. When he said prayers or read from the Bible he acted out the part of a preacher. Who knows what other parts he acted in different places? She knew about the doctor, but perhaps there were more. How could she have trusted either of them so implicitly for so long?

It was another twenty-four hours before Fern opened the basement door again.

'So what's it to be?' she asked, leaning back against the door post, her lips curved into a cruel smile. 'Are you going to be cooperative? Or do you want to stay down here for a few more days without food?'

Lotte felt sick with fear. 'How can you do this to me?' she asked tearfully. 'You were so kind and patient when I was raped. You said you thought of me as a daughter, and now this.'

'It's because of our feelings for you that we chose you to have Howard's seed planted within you,' Fern said, smiling broadly as if that made her terrible proposition quite ordinary. 'After all we've done for you I expected you to be glad to do this small thing.'

It struck Lotte then that Fern was truly deranged, for surely only a madwoman could think this was a small thing.

There was nothing to be gained by holding out. She

knew Fern would happily leave her to starve for days. If she played the game their way, maybe luck would smile on her and give her an opportunity to escape.

'OK, I'll have a baby for you,' Lotte said, forcing herself to sound, if not enthusiastic, then resigned.

'Good girl.' Fern beamed. 'I knew you'd come round in the end. Now you can come up for supper.'

Chapter Eleven

'I'm home!' Simon called out as he came in through the front door of the flat soon after five, carrying a bag of groceries.

When Lotte didn't respond he assumed she must be having a nap and went into the kitchen to put the shopping away in the fridge. He was surprised by the unwashed lunch dishes on the draining board; it wasn't like Lotte, who always cleared up immediately after meals.

He made himself a cup of coffee and crossed the hallway into the sitting room. He could see the indentations on the sofa where she and Dale had been sitting. Lotte's sandals were still there on the floor as well as glasses and an empty wine bottle.

Simon smiled. This was the explanation for the unwashed dishes – the wine must have gone straight to Lotte's head. He put down his coffee and picked up the glasses and bottle to take them to the kitchen. As he crossed the hallway he could see into Lotte's bedroom through the open door, but she wasn't lying on her bed.

In alarm he went right into her room. She wasn't there and nothing was out of place at all.

She wasn't in his room or the bathroom and although he wanted to believe she had just popped out to a shop with Dale, somehow he knew she wouldn't have done that.

With a hammering heart he grabbed the phone and rang the number DI Bryan had given him.

Adam came in a few minutes later while Simon was still waiting for the police to arrive. It was he who discovered putty had been put over the lens of the CCTV camera and that confirmed Lotte hadn't gone out shopping with Dale.

'But I don't understand why she would open the door if she couldn't see who was there,' Simon said wildly, beside himself with anxiety. 'I thought we'd made her as safe as could be.'

'Calm down, Si.' Adam hugged him. 'Someone's bound to have seen something; the police will find her.'

Within the hour Adam's confidence in both the police and their neighbours began to dwindle. No one living or working around the lane had seen anything. The police quickly brought in a forensics team to check the flat and the spiral staircase outside. But with no sightings of the men or the vehicle Lotte was taken away in, finding her would be like looking for the proverbial needle in a haystack.

Adam rang Marchwood Manor before the police arrived because he had found Dale's mobile phone on the sofa. She hadn't arrived back at the spa, and Scott said she had intended to catch the four-thirty bus from Brighton, which meant she should have arrived some ten minutes earlier.

Scott was deeply shocked and worried about Lotte, but at that point there was no sense in assuming Dale had been snatched with her. She could after all have missed the bus, and decided to go back later by taxi, though if that was the case it was odd she hadn't returned to Simon's for her mobile. Simon rang David then, feeling desperate to put everyone who cared about Lotte in the picture.

David arrived at the flat within the hour while the forensics team were still there. He had beads of perspiration on his forehead, his dark business suit was crumpled and there was fear in his eyes.

'I suppose she just forgot to look at the screen before opening the door,' he said as he stood in the hall with Simon and Adam watching the forensics men still out on the balcony. 'But that suggests to me she thought it was a friend. Maybe Dale running back to get her phone?'

'I suppose that could be the answer,' Simon said. 'But how did they know Lotte was here anyway?'

'The place Scott and Dale work at was mentioned in the newspapers. They could have followed Dale here in the morning,' David said.

'They'll kill her, won't they?' Simon's lips began to quiver.

'Not necessarily,' David replied but his voice lacked conviction.

'Come on! What other reason could they have for snatching her but to make sure she can never tell the police all she knows?' Adam butted in.

'But what can she know that is bad enough for any-one to take such risks?' Simon asked, shaking his head in bafflement.

One of the forensics team found a partial fingerprint on the hand rail of the staircase and some sand on the two lowest steps.

'I'd say there were two men and they both started off wearing gloves,' the tall, thin man with droopy eyelids said. 'There are several places on the banisters which are very clean, consistent with a gloved hand grabbing the rail. But the man holding the girl probably took his off on the way down because he'd got something fiddly to do. Tying her up maybe, unlocking the vehicle. The sand is interesting, I think it's been brought here on a shoe, from a beach rather than builder's sand.'

'Will you be able to pinpoint the area it came from?' David asked.

The forensics man shrugged. 'Only a fairly general area. But we'll do our best.'

DI Bryan came round a little later and looked grim when he heard Dale still hadn't arrived back at March-wood Manor.

'It looks as if she's been taken too,' he said, running his fingers through his hair distractedly. 'We'll check all CCTV footage around the town immediately and make inquiries at all the shops and flats around here. If these people followed Dale from Marchwood, they hung around here most of the day waiting, so someone must have seen them or the vehicle they were in. Dale received a text message on her phone at three-fifty, and replied to it, so we know she was still here then. Simon came back at five-fifteen. So that gives us a frame of one hour when the girls could've been snatched.'

'Most of the shops and offices are closed now,' Simon pointed out.

'We'll check them out first thing in the morning,' Bryan assured him and suggested Simon and Adam waited indoors, promising he'd let them know immediately if there were any developments.

'Have you thought any more about what I said the other day? You know, believing the boat Lotte was pushed out of, or escaped from, came from somewhere around Chichester harbour,' David asked, fully expecting Bryan to dismiss his opinion.

But to his surprise Bryan said he thought he could be right. 'Few people would take the chance of sailing in the dark in the open sea unless they were a very experienced sailor. But people who moor in the harbour and tend mostly to sail around there, might feel confident enough to go just outside the harbour in an emergency. Dumping someone in the sea amounts to that, I'd say, and maybe they did the same with the baby.'

David shuddered at that prospect. A young baby couldn't survive very long in a cold sea, and it could've been swept away from Lotte. Would any mother want to get the memory of that back?

'So why haven't you done a boat-to-boat search?' he asked.

'We have questioned hundreds of boat owners, but we're talking about an enormous area, David. Eleven square miles of water, over three and a half thousand moorings, fourteen sailing clubs and some twelve thousand craft visiting each year.'

'What about doing a house-to-house search?' David suggested. 'If this person moors his boat there, he could be living around there too. It's not such a formidable task. Itchenor, for instance, has only got two hundred and six dwellings. Some of the other villages are even smaller. So don't you think it's time you started on it?'

'There's no hard evidence she was there to justify a house-to-house search,' Bryan retorted, looking a little irritated now that David was telling him what to do.

'A baby is missing,' David pointed out forcefully. 'Doesn't that justify pulling out all the stops, regardless of evidence?'

'Lotte could have had her baby absolutely anywhere, it might not have even been in England,' Bryan said wearily. 'I've already told you we've checked all registered births around the time we believe it was born, and all of the babies are accounted for.'

'It could've been born in a garden shed, an outhouse or somewhere, without any medical attention. Maybe it was stillborn or died soon after the birth, and Lotte's abductors disposed of it,' David said wildly, his voice shaking with emotion. 'I haven't got any answers, but I have got a hunch Lotte was held in a seaside house.'

Bryan put his hand on David's shoulder in sympathy. 'Our best shot right now is with that partial print from the stairs, or her abductors' van being on a camera. We've already started checking that out. We were too late for an appeal for witnesses on the six o'clock news, but we'll make sure it's on at ten. First thing tomorrow we'll be stopping people on their way to work.'

'You have considered that they are going to kill her as soon as possible?' David said in desperation. 'They won't linger over it, they'll do it and then fuck off out of it.'

'I would agree with that if they only had Lotte, but it looks like they've got Dale too,' Bryan said, looking at his phone as if willing it to ring with good news. 'I don't believe they intended to take her, and that must have thrown a spanner in the works for them. And I think Dale and Lotte together could give anyone a run for their money.'

Bryan left soon after, and he'd no sooner gone than Scott turned up. He was pale and shaken. Dale had not arrived back at Marchwood, and he said everyone there was frantic. Simon made more coffee and the four men sat down in the sitting room to discuss what to do.

'I think we should do our own house-to-house,' David said. 'If we divided up the area into four, I reckon we could cover most of it in a couple of days.'

Simon and Adam weren't sure about that. They felt it might put the police's backs up.

'Well, I think it's a sound idea,' Scott said, supporting David eagerly. 'I can't go back to work while they are missing. And I'd get out there right now and start searching if I could.'

Simon and Adam looked at each other. 'OK,' Adam said. 'Si and I will do it too. To hell with upsetting the fuzz, the girls are far more important.'

Scott fished in his jacket pocket and brought out a photograph of the two girls together. 'Have you got a scanner so we could print up some of these to show round?'

Adam said he had and took the picture. It was one of the girls in a restaurant, looking very tanned and model-like. David looked at it and frowned.

'It's a lovely picture but I doubt Lotte looked like that while she was held captive. I'm pretty good with a computer; if you've got a picture of her looking more ordinary, without makeup and stuff, maybe with her hair tied back, I could probably superimpose more frumpy clothes on her, like that dress she was wearing when I found her.'

'If she was locked away no one would have seen her anyway,' Simon said, looking a bit bewildered.

'She might not have been locked away right at the start,' David replied, proving he'd spent a great deal of time thinking about this. 'The police know she was in London for a while because she bought new clothes with her bank card. What we don't know is whether she went there with this person, or people, or met them there. Either way she almost certainly went somewhere else with him, her, them, afterwards, and somehow I don't think that was against her will.'

'Why not?' Simon asked.

'It would be very hard to keep someone a prisoner for the best part of a year,' David said. 'And she got pregnant during that time too. So it could've been a love affair which went horribly wrong.'

'But we've got no way of knowing that she was brought down this way,' Adam said.

'No, we don't, but it's likely that she was. She could've been offered a job, lured into some crank religion, or just got hung up on some guy who offered her love and security. But whatever the reason, I'm betting she came down here willingly.'

'With all due respect, David,' Simon said politely, 'you've only known her for five minutes. How would you know that?'

David made a kind of expansive shrug with both shoulders and hands. 'She struck me as a cautious girl, not a madcap who could be lured off on a promise of something exotic or exciting. I don't think she'd even move away to an area she wasn't familiar with. But Chichester would seem safe. It's not far from her home town, she knew what it was like.'

'David's right about her being cautious. It took for ever to persuade her to sign up for the cruise,' Simon said, as if he'd suddenly remembered that. 'Right up till the day before she left I half expected her to back down.'

'What made her want to do it in the first place?' David asked.

'Mainly money,' Simon said. 'She wanted to get enough for a deposit on a flat of her own. The reason she didn't back out was because we all kept teasing her and saying she would. I think she felt she had to do it to save face.'

'David hit the nail right on the head,' Scott said. 'Lotte isn't what you'd call bold. Unless she was thumped over the head and locked up somewhere, she would have only agreed to go with people she trusted and to a place she felt was safe. So that in itself suggests she wasn't under lock and key, at least not at first. There is a strong chance, then, that people may have seen her around.'

'OK, so we're in agreement. We know from the dress she was wearing when I found her on the beach, and from purchases of other clothes while in London, that she was unlikely to have looked like a fashion plate.' David paused and stabbed his finger at the photo. 'So no one would connect this glamour puss with the frumpy little mouse they might have seen. I reckon one of the biggest mistakes the police have made was releasing that picture of her looking gorgeous.'

'We've got lots of pictures of her on the computer.' Simon got to his feet. 'Let's go and look for suitable ones.'

'Are you really all up for going out tomorrow to look?' David asked. 'What about your jobs?'

'Lotte is worth more than a poxy job,' Adam said, and Simon grinned at him affectionately.

'I daresay Marisa will have me hung, drawn and quartered,' Scott said. 'But Dale and Lotte are like my sisters, and my two best mates. I can't let them down, so I don't give a toss about the job.'

At eight the following morning David met up with Scott in the car park by the café at Chichester marina as they'd agreed to do the night before. Scott was wearing jeans and a red sweatshirt; David felt a bit overdressed in chinos and a checked jacket.

'Any trouble getting the day off?' he asked Scott as they walked into the café.

Scott wrinkled his nose. 'It didn't go down too well with the manageress – she's never liked Dale. But I think she might have a strike on her hands if she sacks me; all the other spa staff are right behind me. What about you?'

'Well, I more or less choose my own hours,' David said. 'I'll just have to work a bit harder when this is over.' He was about to order coffee for himself and Scott when Simon and Adam walked in. 'Make that four coffees,' he said to the girl behind the counter.

The previous evening Simon had found the perfect photograph of Lotte. Adam had taken it without her realizing, while she was gazing reflectively into space. She had no makeup on, her hair was in two plaits and she was wearing a pale blue round-necked sweater. She looked quaintly old-fashioned, shy, vulnerable and just a little troubled.

With the headline 'Have you seen her?' above the picture and a brief reminder that she was the girl found on Selsey beach, but that she'd been kidnapped again and it was thought her life was in danger, it sent out a powerful and emotional message that anyone who had seen her, however briefly, should ring the police immediately.

Simon had printed off hundreds of copies, and the boys' plan was to show it to people and talk to them about Lotte, and to leave the picture in places where people congregated, like this café.

'I suggest we start by each taking one of the jetties,' David said. 'Show the picture to anyone aboard each of the boats, ask them about owners of neighbouring boats too, if they were down here when Lotte was washed up on the beach on the sixth of May. Take the name and telephone number of anyone who was here then, or anyone who thinks they've seen Lotte before.'

'We'll be here all day,' Adam said, glancing out of the window at the huge number of yachts moored in the marina.

'Just don't get into pointless chatting,' David said. 'We've got to cover as much ground as possible.'

Simon and Adam walked along to one end of the moorings to start there, and David and Scott took the other, so they would meet in the middle. It was a dull morning and there was a stiff breeze which made it seem quite cold, and most of the people aboard the boats were having breakfast.

David found on his jetty that people were interested and helpful, at times a bit too much so, and he had a job to get away from them. No one recognized Lotte, though, and some of the people who weren't local didn't even know the story of her being discovered on the beach. In two hours David had found only one person who had been here around the time she was washed up at Selsey, and he hadn't sailed out of the marina.

Scott reported much the same when they conferred around mid-morning.

'They were all too keen to gossip about other boat owners,' he said gloomily. 'One guy kept rabbiting on about a man who brings a new girl down with him every weekend. I asked him how the man killed them, and he said, "Oh, he don't kill them, only shags them." He was so thick he didn't even realize I was being sarcastic!'

David smiled, but he was beginning to feel daunted by the formidable task they'd set themselves. With over 3,500 moorings around the harbour, it could take weeks to check them all. But maybe they could do this whole marina today, and start knocking on house doors tomorrow.

It was almost six-thirty when the boys joined up, having spoken to every boat owner aboard. They'd only grabbed coffee and a sandwich for lunch and kept on with the questions. Not one person had seen Lotte, but between them they had the names of five people who had been here around the time Lotte was found at Selsey.

'Shall I hand the names over to Bryan?' David asked the others as they walked back to the car park. They had planned to go and have an Indian meal together, and Scott was going to stay over with David in Selsey.

'Good idea,' Simon said. 'It might make him sit up and take notice. God only knows what his men are doing!'

Scott and David arrived back at David's house from the Indian meal around ten. Simon and Adam had just left them to drive back to Brighton. David got them both a beer from the fridge and talked a little about Simon and Adam. He admitted he'd never spent any time before in the company of gay men.

'I'll never be homophobic again,' Scott said with a little chuckle. 'I never even thought about them being gay all evening, they were such good company. They care so much for Lotte, like she's their sister. To be honest, I'd sooner be with them than half the straight guys I know. They can talk about something other than football, they are sensitive and have a cracking sense of humour. I used to get that good buzz being with Dale and Lotte too. We'd laugh and laugh till our sides ached.'

'Weren't you ever tempted to go for something more than friendship?' David asked. 'I mean, they are both lovely girls.'

'I was in the beginning,' Scott admitted. 'But getting involved with anyone when you work on a cruise ship can be a minefield. Besides, they never so much as hinted that they wanted to be anything more than just friends, and that suited me. I could pretend one of them was my girlfriend if some other bird started coming on to me. But if I wanted to flit off they didn't mind that either. I could confide in them, lark around with them, it was great. I'd give anything to have them both here again now.'

David nodded. He'd had a few revelations about friendship today too. He didn't know any other gay men, and Scott was the kind of muscle-bound hero who normally made him feel inadequate. Yet he'd felt bound to these three men today. He'd even been able to admit over dinner that he thought he had fallen in love with Lotte. He'd seen nothing but understanding in their eyes either, no resentment that he was taking the lead in their search, not even any irritation that he'd known her such a short time. In fact, they acted as though his feelings for her were even stronger than theirs.

'What will we do if the girls are found dead?' David said in little more than a whisper.

'I don't know, mate,' Scott said, shaking his head. 'It's all been like a weird dream so far. Unreal, sort of removed from me. But the police will have informed Dale's parents today, and they are bound to come down here tomorrow. That will make it very real and I can hardly bear the thought of having to face them.'

David saw Scott's eyes glinting with unshed tears and

he reached out and put a companionable hand on his shoulder. 'Yeah, that's going to be tough,' he agreed.

'I wonder what the girls are doing now,' Scott said. 'Will Lotte have remembered stuff now that more bad shit is happening?'

Chapter Twelve

As the boys were eating in the Indian restaurant, Lotte was lying on the bed next to Dale, relieved that her friend had finally stopped freaking out and fallen asleep.

Although Dale had been calm enough when they were first shoved into the basement, she had woken this morning like a woman possessed. It didn't help that her eye was closed up and looked terrible, and she couldn't seem to accept that there would be no morning cup of tea or breakfast. A little later she began raging that she hadn't been able to sleep for hunger, and how was she going to be able to stand that hunger growing ever greater as the day progressed?

Lotte had tried to convince her that raging against their imprisonment wouldn't help her. There was no one upstairs to hear, and the neighbours were too far away. But Dale still dragged the wardrobe under the tiny window, put the stool on top of it, then climbed up to try to reach the window which was too small to get out of.

'I was in here for months,' Lotte told her again and again. 'There isn't a spot on the wall or a stain on the carpet I don't know. Listen to me! The thing to do is rest up and plan what we're going to do when they come for us. Rushing about will only deplete your strength.'

Oddly enough, the only way Lotte could get Dale to lie down on the bed beside her and rest was by telling her more about what Fern and Howard had done to her. But it was so hard to tell, for looking back it was like a surreal art house film where the only explanation for the bizarre events is that the leading characters were insane.

And Lotte thought she must have been insane too because she hadn't recognized Fern and Howard's madness right from the start. Surely any normal person would've run a mile from a couple who insisted on kneeling down to pray on a cruise ship? And if the couple really were that holy, why weren't they giving some of their wealth to the poor and sick, instead of frittering it away on hedonistic pleasures?

But now Dale had fallen asleep the silence was total. While sleeping in the bedroom upstairs Lotte had heard owls at night and the occasional scurry of small creatures pushing their way through the hedges. By day there was birdsong, the sound of lorries going down the road, horses' hooves and dogs barking. Down here there was no sound. Even when it rained she couldn't hear it.

She had told Dale the bare bones of what had happened to her after she tried to escape, and no doubt in the days ahead she'd give her more detail, because as she'd been telling it, more and more other memories kept coming back.

It would be easy to dissolve into tears now, to feel

again the terror and helplessness she'd battled with before in this room. But she wasn't going to give way to fear again. She was going to go calmly over what happened before, the mistakes she made and the ones the Ramsdens made, and prepare for when the men came back for her and Dale.

Looking back on her previous incarceration in this basement room, Lotte was fairly certain they had been drugging her most of the time. Although she was terrified the first couple of days when they were starving her, her mind had been very sharp. But it didn't remain that way, not after she began to have regular meals; in fact she could remember spending a great deal of time lying on the bed in a kind of trance.

But whether she was drugged or not, Lotte was very aware that once Fern had what she considered to be Lotte's agreement, she wasted no time in her plans for the baby. She drew up an ovulation chart and took Lotte's temperature every morning before she allowed her a cup of tea, to discover when she was at her most fertile.

On the sixth day of her captivity Fern beamed at her. 'Tonight's the night,' she said as she slid her thermometer back into its case. 'You'd better do it in our room as the bed is bigger.'

Until that moment Lotte had thought Fern was going to use the turkey baster method of impregnation, but suddenly she realized this was not so.

'Oh no.' She backed away from Fern in shock. 'We're not doing it like that!'

'Don't be ridiculous,' Fern snapped. 'It's a far more efficient way, the sperm is kept at the right temperature.'

'I can't bear the idea of Howard doing that to me,' Lotte burst out. 'And how could you stand it either? He's your husband, for God's sake!'

'I want his child,' Fern said, and once again she had that scary glint in her eyes. 'So I can bear it. And don't you even think of making it difficult for him, he's finding it hard enough coming to terms with it as it is.'

Lotte remembered observing that day that Howard was a nothing man. He was reasonably attractive, with his slender build and fine features, but he had no personality. He never voiced an opinion about anything, and he wasn't a conversationalist either. Even when he was alone with Fern it was probably mainly she who did the talking. He gave nothing of himself away, his likes and dislikes, or his taste in music, books or sport.

Therefore it was hard to imagine him being passionate about anything, certainly not in a carnal way or about being a father. Lotte thought he had given up his free will to his wife long ago, and just did what she told him. Yet he seemed perfectly content that way. All the time they were in London together she never heard them have a cross word.

They had dinner at seven-thirty that evening, and Fern plied Lotte with wine. 'It will help you relax,' she said by way of an explanation and gave her a small blue tablet too.

By the time Lotte had taken a bath she felt decidedly

woozy, in fact she staggered as she came out of the bath-room and had to steady herself against the wall. Fern was standing at the bedroom door and came forward to take her arm. 'Into bed with you,' she said in a very busi-nesslike manner. 'Howard will be up in a minute.'

Lotte's last clear thought before Howard appeared in the doorway, wearing only a pair of pale blue boxer shorts, was that her best chance of escape might be immediately after the sex. Howard wouldn't be on his guard, he'd left his trousers somewhere downstairs, and the front-door key was probably in his pocket. Fern was likely to fuss round him, and if Lotte said she was going to her own bed, she doubted they'd stop her.

It was the weirdest thing Lotte had ever experienced as Howard stood looking down at her. The pill and the wine made her feel she was floating, but she was aware of Fern sitting beside her on the bed, and it looked as if she intended to stay there.

'Come on, honey,' Fern said to Howard, patting the bed beside Lotte. 'There's nothing to be scared of.'

Her remark made Lotte feel as if they were three children playing at being grown-ups. That feeling grew even stronger as Howard finally lay down beside her and put his arm over her as if to cuddle her.

Fern pulled the bedcovers off Lotte, then rolled her cotton nightdress up to expose her body. Lotte imme-diately closed her eyes tightly as she didn't want to see Howard looking at her, or what he looked like without his shorts. She was too dopey now to care much what was going to be done to her; all she wanted was for it to be over quickly so she could go to sleep.

He tentatively cupped her breast in his hand, and then stroked her belly, but at least he was gentle and he smelled of lavender soap. His hand moved down to her pubic hair and he began to probe into her with his finger, and it was only then that she felt he was getting a bit excited as his breath was coming faster.

She felt nothing, neither disgust nor pleasure. He muttered something about her being dry, and almost instantaneously she felt him put some kind of cool jelly on her and his fingers slid inside her more easily.

His heavy breathing and wondering where Fern was made her open her eyes just a crack. Howard was lying on his side facing her, but to Lotte's shock Fern was right up against his back and she had her arm around his middle, her hand caressing his erect penis as she kissed his shoulders.

'Put it in her now,' she ordered him.

Lotte felt as if she was watching a blue movie, for although Howard had parted her legs and knelt between them to push himself into her, Fern appeared to be orchestrating everything. She was undulating against her husband's back in simulated intercourse, and although Lotte couldn't and didn't want to see, she was fairly certain the woman was masturbating at the same time.

They were both murmuring swear words, their excitement rising to fever pitch. Howard was trying to kiss Lotte now, but she turned her face away into the pillow and tried to block out the way his fingers were digging into her buttocks, forcing her to move with him. She willed it to be over quickly and that the couple's passion would make them sleep so soundly she could escape.

It seemed to go on for ever, his fingers kneading her buttocks, his breath hot on her shoulder, and the continual pounding into her. But even more unnerving was the knowledge that Fern was getting some depraved kick from it all, for she could hear her moaning and murmuring things Lotte didn't want to hear.

Suddenly Howard yelled out that he was coming, and Fern thrust her face closer to him so she could kiss him at the moment he ejaculated.

That was the worst part of all, for Lotte was lying there with Howard still inside her, and he was kissing his wife as if he thought he was in her. She had never felt so used and shamed and that was the moment when she truly began to hate them.

'I'll go to my bed now,' she said, wriggling away from Howard, who was still kissing Fern passionately.

'No, you must lie still for a while,' Fern broke off to say. But Howard was making love to Fern, Lotte could hear the sound of his fingers penetrating her and his lips on her body, and it disgusted her so much she felt she might retch.

It grew more obscene, for although the curtains had been pulled it was still light outside, and enough light was coming through the curtains for Lotte to see that

Howard had moved down the bed to satisfy Fern with his tongue. She could hear the slurping sound, feel the bed moving with them, and Fern's heavy breathing and moaning.

Lotte couldn't stand another minute of it and felt too that they wouldn't notice her leave the bed while they were glued to each other. She moved inch by inch to the edge of the bed, then slid her legs over it, and dropping to her knees so they wouldn't see her, she made for the door.

She was holding her breath as she opened it, afraid that the light would come flooding in and surely alert them, but they didn't appear to notice as she slipped through it.

There was no time to dress, not even to find shoes. They could leap up at any minute and she only had to run to a neighbour for assistance. She was aware of sperm running down her legs as she crept silently down the stairs, and that sickened her even more.

She had expected to find Howard's trousers in the sitting room, but they weren't there, nor in the kitchen or his study. Fern appearing to be reaching a climax for she was practically shouting now, and Lotte guessed that once it was over for her she would immediately realize her prisoner was trying to escape. There just wasn't time to find those keys now.

The one chance she had of escape was to go and get into the bed in her old room. If she pretended to be fast asleep when they found where she was, they might leave her there if they were feeling mellow. Later, when they'd gone back to their bed and were in a deep sleep, she would climb out of the bedroom window on to the roof of the kitchen extension. From there she could more or less jump to the grass, climb over the side gate and then creep down the drive to the road.

She hadn't been in her bed that long, perhaps only five or ten minutes, when Fern came in. Lotte sensed her coming right up to her and peering closely at her, but she must have been convinced she really was sleeping because she went back to bed with Howard.

Howard went downstairs to make them hot drinks, and Lotte felt so sleepy she was in danger of dropping off.

'Leave the door open just in case she does wake up and thinks of trying to get out,' Fern said as Howard came back upstairs with their drinks. 'I know we've got all the keys up here with us, but I'd rather head her off before that.'

Lotte waited and waited, forcing herself to stay awake. They had turned off the bedside light but they were talking to each other very quietly for a long time.

Finally there was silence, but still she had to wait until she was absolutely certain they were asleep. Finally she heard a faint snoring, and a deeper one too. She crept out of bed, pulled on a pair of pyjamas which were the only clothes left in the room, and closing the bedroom door very softly, opened the window.

The roof of the kitchen extension was further down than she had imagined, and the window very narrow and awkward, but her desperation to escape cancelled out her fear. First she threw down a blanket to protect herself from the barbed wire on the top of the side gate. Then, getting out on to the window sill, she turned over on to her stomach and gradually wriggled herself backwards and downwards while holding on to the window frame, her toes stretching out for the roof beneath. But her fingers couldn't hold her weight with such a small ledge to hold on to, and she fell. It wasn't far, no more than two feet, but it hurt her bare feet and made a loud clatter.

It was harder still to climb from the kitchen roof to the ground. She was afraid the guttering would snap off if she pulled on it; even the down pipe seemed to be coming loose from the wall as she attempted to use that to climb down. But the light hadn't come on in the bedroom above, so they obviously hadn't heard her. Somehow she managed to get over the guttering, and hanging on for grim death with hands and knees on the down pipe, she gradually managed to let her hands slide down it, then jumped the last few feet.

Creeping cautiously across the patio area outside the kitchen, with the blanket in her hands, she made for the side gate. It was about six foot six high, with a frame above the gate which had the barbed wire nailed on to it.

Lotte tossed the blanket up over the barbed wire and climbed the gate. It was easy enough as in the hedge to the side of it were many places where she could put her feet. She was over and down the other side in just a minute; all there was left now to contend with was the gravel drive.

She had never been good at walking barefoot on stones and she crept forward along the side of the house wincing at every step. But however painful it was, it was so good to be free, and she planned to run first to the phone box and call the police, then hide in someone's front garden until they arrived.

But as she got to the end of the side wall of the house Fern stepped out in front of her, quickly followed by Howard.

'Where do you think you're going?' Fern asked, her voice dripping with sarcasm.

They were both in dressing gowns and slippers. But they had the studied calmness of a couple who had taken their time to come and stop her. They'd probably heard her getting out of the window, but let her strain herself trying to get away.

It was a crushing defeat. Lotte had prepared herself for the possibility they might hear her on the gravel and come out of the house after her, but she hadn't expected them to be lying in wait for her. And there was no chance of being able to push past them for they stood blocking her path and they were poised to restrain her forcibly.

Lotte screamed then, as loud and for as long as she could. Howard caught hold of her and slapped her face to shut her up, but she fought him and kept screaming until he bundled her inside the door.

'That's a fine way to thank us for our kindness to you,' Fern said once the door was closed and locked. 'Trying to slip out of here like a thief in the night!'

Lotte shouted abuse at them then. She no longer cared if they hit her, starved her or even tortured her. It all came out, how they'd fooled her into thinking they cared about her, that they were cruel, calculating and depraved people. But she saw how mad they really were then for they just looked at her in wide-eyed astonishment, not understanding why she saw them in such a way.

'You hide behind all that religious claptrap,' she screamed at them. 'You've been selling babies! That's the lowest, worst kind of crime imaginable. And now you're forcing me to have one for you. But even if that perverted act does make me pregnant, you'll never get the baby, I'll make sure of that. I'd sooner see it go into care than be brought up by a couple of maniacs like you.'

Fern slapped her around the face then, knocking her back against the wall in the hall. 'You ungrateful little bitch,' she yelled, and yanked at Lotte's hair, making her scream again with pain. 'I saved you from that man in Ushuaia and nursed you back to health.'

Howard manhandled Lotte back into the basement room, pushing her down the stairs. 'We're disappointed in you,' he said before he locked the door on her. 'Now you've lost all your privileges.'

Looking back on that night when she was incandescent with rage at what Howard and Fern had done to her, Lotte now knew that it was impossible to stay at that level of anger for very long, especially when food was withheld. She held out for three days, spitting at them, shouting abuse and hurling things when they came in, but hunger, fear and loneliness finally got to her, and she caved in.

It seemed incredible to her now, but when Fern said she would 'forgive' her, Lotte actually began to believe she was the one at fault. She didn't even lash out when Fern said they had to try again that night for the baby before her fertile period passed.

Howard came down to the basement room in his pyjamas without Fern, carrying a large vodka and orange juice for Lotte. The following morning when she woke she was certain the drink had been laced with a drug. She remembered Howard sitting on the bed talking about how he loved sailing, the first time she'd ever heard him talk about anything with some passion, then it all became hazy. She had a faint recollection of being cuddled and of responding slightly to his caresses but she couldn't remember anything more.

She woke later, fumbled for the light switch and found it was half past three in the morning. Howard was gone and she had the telltale stickiness between her legs. She got up at once to wash herself but she was so wobbly on her feet she went back to bed without even climbing the stairs to see if he'd locked the door.

On one or other of those two attempts, Lotte got pregnant, and she didn't know whether she was relieved or horrified. It was a relief not to have to submit to

Howard any more, and to know they wouldn't hit her again, but then it was terrifying to know she had a baby growing within her which had been forced upon her.

Fern was beside herself with joy from the moment the first test was positive, and there were moments when that joy washed over on to Lotte because Fern was so kind and loving towards her. But even with whatever it was they slipped her daily to keep her docile, from time to time outrage bubbled to the surface and Lotte would plot her escape.

It made sense to pretend she had accepted the situation fully and even felt pleasure at giving Fern and Howard their baby, for that would mean they'd relax their vigilance. But in fact they watched her more closely than ever. On warm, sunny days they'd allow her into the garden, but they stayed with her constantly. She had her meals in the kitchen, she could watch television in the lounge, but they kept the doors and all the windows except the small fanlights locked all the time. Even the telephone was locked into the study and they carried the keys for everything on their person. If they went out she was put back in the basement room.

They had said originally that they were intending to take her to the States for the birth, but they appeared to have abandoned that plan. Lotte guessed they realized she would make a scene the very minute she was in a public place, and they couldn't take the risk she might expose their racket.

Lotte had fully expected that Fern would take her for

a medical check-up before long. But the weeks slipped slowly by and Fern still didn't seek a doctor's advice. Lotte began to fear that she never would, perhaps for the very same reasons they didn't dare try to take her to America.

'Shouldn't I go to a clinic?' Lotte asked one morning, trying very hard to look as if she had no motive other than checking the baby was healthy and a good size. 'I mean, I could have high blood pressure or one of those other problems women get.'

'You are doing just fine,' Fern said. 'I know a great deal about childbirth. I used to be a nurse.'

Lotte would tell herself that all she had to do was to keep chatting, laugh, smile and make happy jokes and lull them both into security so they would slip up. But it didn't happen. They still kept the front door locked, the phone safely in the locked study, and when they went out she had to go down to the basement room.

Dale stirred on the bed beside Lotte and opened her eyes. 'Have you heard anyone up there while I've been asleep?' she asked.

'No,' Lotte sighed. 'I would've woken you up if I had. Go back to sleep – I'm sure they'll come tomorrow.'

'What will we do then?' Dale asked, her voice cracking with fear.

'We'll have to play that by ear,' Lotte said.

'Have you remembered having the baby?' Dale asked in little more than a whisper.

Lotte sighed deeply. 'Oh yes, Dale. That came back as soon as I was in here again.'

'Can you tell me about it?' Dale asked, her dark eyes deeply troubled.

Lotte lay down beside her friend. Remembering what she'd been through had been bad enough, and she really didn't want to have Dale asking her questions, but now that Dale's life was in danger she owed it to her to explain what it was all about. 'I guess I'll have to,' she said reluctantly, then, taking a deep breath, blurted out the story of her two nights with Howard.

'The absolute bastard!' Dale exclaimed. 'But you were in here all the time you were pregnant? And where did you have the baby?'

'Right here,' Lotte said. 'On this bed!'

Chapter Thirteen

Lotte remembered that her pregnancy seemed interminable; just long dreary days with little to do and nothing to look forward to. As the months dragged on she felt so apathetic that she eventually even lost the energy to try to outwit Howard and Fern.

Back in September, once the summer tourists had gone home, they would take her out for walks. Howard would drive them somewhere isolated where they weren't likely to run into anyone. But he had bought a child's restraint, a piece of webbing with a wrist band round each end. One went round his wrist, the other round hers.

After the first two outings, Lotte realized this could be the opportunity she'd been waiting for to get help. So she wrote a letter explaining her plight, asking the recipient to contact the police and come and rescue her. On the next outing she had it tucked into the pocket of her dress and she looked eagerly for someone to pass it to, or somewhere to leave it where it would be found.

Unfortunately Fern and Howard made sure they didn't walk near other people. Lotte guessed that even if she said she needed to go to the toilet Fern would check first to see there was no one else in there and check again once she'd come out.

That day they went to the beach at West Wittering, and as it was grey and chilly there were few other cars parked up. But while they were walking on the beach, the sun came out, and by the time they got back to the car park, there were a lot more cars. Fern and Howard seemed quite relaxed after the bracing walk, and in a moment when they were talking together and not looking at her, Lotte managed to stick her letter against a car's windscreen.

Fate was not on Lotte's side, however. Fern glanced back, saw the envelope she hadn't noticed earlier and suspected it was Lotte's work. After she'd retrieved it and read the contents she was absolutely furious, and that evening she ranted and raved at Lotte, demanding to know how she could be so selfish as to run away from them and steal Howard's baby.

'Me selfish!' Lotte exclaimed incredulously. 'It is you who have stolen everything from me. My liberty, and my womb to grow a child I don't want! You are cold-blooded monsters! If you and Howard wanted a baby to love, you should have gone through legal channels to do so, not hijack someone and keep them prisoner. But what makes me angriest of all about you is that I believed you were kind, decent people. How could I have been that stupid?'

Fern slapped her hard around the face, and as further punishment Lotte was pushed back into the basement again. They kept her there for a whole week. Her meals were brought to her, she was given books to read, even some embroidery to do, but she wasn't allowed upstairs or out into the fresh air at all.

A week of isolation was enough to make Lotte realize she must pretend to be contrite to get through this. She had no chance of escape from the basement, and she needed fresh air and some company to keep her health and sanity too. She cried a bit and told them she was sorry for what she'd done and that it was just because she felt frightened and terribly alone.

Fern's attitude would have been laughable under any other circumstances for she seemed to believe that offering money was the cure-all for absolutely everything. She said that as soon as the baby was born they would be taking it back with them to the States and they were going to give Lotte a thousand pounds to start a new life.

Lotte didn't want a thousand pounds. She didn't want to be pregnant either, and steadfastly refused even to consider that the baby growing within her was any part of her. All she wanted was her freedom. But as she got to around the fifth month and she felt the first tiny movements, like holding a butterfly in her hand, all at once she didn't feel quite so detached.

She realized that however repugnant its conception had been, the baby was just a helpless innocent who had to be protected from maniacs like Fern and Howard. Lotte didn't for one moment envisage keeping the baby herself; she hated its father far too much for that. But if it was humanly possible she intended to see it was placed with the right adoptive parents, and that Fern and Howard went to prison for the crimes they had committed.

As the pregnancy advanced Lotte would put her hands on her swelling belly, feel the strong movements within and pray silently for divine intervention.

It was ironic that she chose to find faith at the time Fern and Howard had dropped all pretence of being religious. They no longer had prayers and Howard didn't read from the Bible. But Lotte had found comfort in praying after the rape, and even if her captors' recent treatment of her should have made her feel prayer was futile and God a myth, she needed something to hang on to. And in the absence of worried parents looking for her, God was the only being she could call on.

She asked Him for a miracle, that Fern or Howard would leave the front door keys somewhere where she could grab them; that the police would turn up with a search warrant, or that her captors would suddenly be shocked by the enormity of what they had already done, and intended to do, and just let her go.

Sadly, Lotte knew she couldn't count on a miracle. She was terribly afraid of what lay ahead, both the pain of the birth and the rush of natural maternal emotions she guessed would come with it. She suspected too that once the baby was born, she would actually be in mortal danger. Fern might say that if Lotte went to the police with her story, no one would believe her, but she was too intelligent to truly believe that. The only way she and Howard could be sure the true story would never come out was by killing her.

Somehow Lotte had got to escape.

Christmas passed like any other day, except Fern made a little more effort with the dinner and drank a lot more than she usually did. Lotte pointedly asked them in the morning if they were going to church – she rarely missed an opportunity to taunt them about their beliefs.

When they first moved down here Lotte had asked if they were going to attend the local church, but they said the Church of England wasn't to their liking and that they preferred an Evangelical form of worship. That, as it turned out, was just an excuse not to go to any church, and all that endless praying they'd done on the cruise ship, in London and then here was a facade they hid behind to create a holy, trustworthy image. They didn't bother to hide behind it now, and it was clear their faith was as non-existent as their morals.

That was the day Lotte took the kitchen knife. Fern wandered off a little drunkenly as they were washing up, and Lotte seized the moment to grab the newly sharpened knife, wrap it in a tea towel and slide it down the side of her jogging pants. She made the excuse that she needed a lie-down to go down to the basement, then quickly wove the knife into the bottom of the wicker laundry basket.

They missed the knife on Boxing Day when Howard went to cut up some vegetables, and immediately made a search of the basement. When they failed to find it Lotte felt she'd won her first battle.

From mid-January until almost the end of February, Lotte only rarely got out of the basement. Howard went away on business for days at a time, and perhaps because Fern was worried by the missing knife, Lotte had to remain locked up. Fern brought meals on a tray, opened the door, dumped the tray on the top step, then quickly locked the door again. Lotte was so big and slow she couldn't have run up the stairs to overpower Fern even if she'd wanted to, but it did make her worry about what would happen if she went into labour and Howard was still away.

She woke on 20 February to a nagging ache in her back. As Howard had come home the night before, Fern let her come up to the kitchen for breakfast.

'It could be labour starting,' Fern said, exchanging glances with Howard. 'I know you're not due for a couple more weeks but it often does start with backache.'

Lotte had some toast and a couple of cups of tea, then went into the lounge to watch television. She was certain she was in labour but she was less certain that Fern knew as much about birthing as she'd claimed. What would happen if there were complications?

The backache turned to clearly defined and regular contractions around midday. They were five minutes apart and quite mild until two o'clock, when all at once they became far stronger. It was at that point that Fern insisted Lotte went back down to the basement and put on the cotton gown she'd bought for the birth.

Lotte remembered looking up at the tiny window as she walked around the room trying to ease the contractions, and seeing snowflakes falling. Somehow that seemed like a kind of omen that she was never going to get out of this room, and she became even more scared.

Fern gave her something to drink a bit later, saying it would help the pain. In fact all it did was make Lotte feel woozy in between contractions; it didn't dull the pain at all.

She lost all track of time. It seemed to her that it was now one continuous pain which came in waves of severity from excruciating to so unbearable she thought she would die, and for much of it she was alone. She clung to the bed rail, arching her back up from the mattress to try to alleviate the agony, and felt sweat pouring from her.

'Get me help, you bitch!' Lotte demanded at one point when Fern did come down the stairs and laid a cool and ineffectual hand on her forehead.

'Now, now,' Fern said, as if she had nothing worse than a cold. 'You'll be fine, just breathe away the pain.'

A spurt of water coming from Lotte soaked the sheet beneath her.

'Nothing to worry about, that's just your waters breaking. Things will move on faster now,' Fern said, stripping off the wet sheet and sliding a clean one beneath her. 'Soon you'll get the urge to bear down.'

Lotte had moments of utter clarity between the terrible pains; she saw Fern's indifference to her pain and her irritation that it was taking so long. She had tied her normally carefully arranged hair back into a ponytail, and she wore a white linen apron over her tee-shirt and jogging pants. She spoke in a practised tone as she trotted out her insincere little platitudes, but then she would disappear up the stairs for what was probably only minutes, yet seemed like hours because Lotte was so afraid.

She swore to herself then that she would make Fern suffer once this was over. The hidden knife might not be as useful now as effective pain control, but it would be if she survived this.

'You should eat something, honey,' Howard called down the stairs to his wife. 'It's after seven and you haven't had a thing since breakfast.'

'Make me a ham sandwich,' Fern called back. 'I'll be up soon.'

'You go up there again and leave me and I'll strangle you the first chance I get,' Lotte snarled at the woman.

It was at that moment that the need to bear down began, and Fern finally stayed at her post. She had fastened a towel around the bed rail and put the end in Lotte's hands to pull on as she bore down.

'Push with the contraction,' she ordered Lotte. 'Use every bit of the pain and we'll get the baby out quickly.'

Lotte was only too anxious for the ordeal to be over, and she pushed with all her might. She was vaguely aware that Howard had come down to the basement and was preparing the Moses basket ready to receive the baby, but he didn't speak to her.

She made one long hard push after another, her legs bent, feet pressing hard into the mattress as she gripped the towel with her hands.

'I can see his head,' Fern announced. 'He won't be long now.'

It was only in those final moments that Lotte saw Fern did have some real experience of midwifery, for she told Lotte when to stop pushing, just to pant as the baby's head was born. With the next contraction, which was suddenly much milder, Lotte felt the baby's body slither out of her into Fern's hands.

'It's a little girl,' Fern said. 'And honey, she's a real beauty, just as I knew she'd be.'

For a short while Lotte forgot all the wrongs this couple had done her, and those that they intended to do in the future. She felt euphoric at delivering her baby safely, that the pain was over, and at the baby's first lusty cry, tears rolled down her cheeks too.

She was beautiful, with well-rounded limbs, plump cheeks and the blonde fuzz on her head. Fern wrapped her tightly in a cotton blanket and passed her to Howard who tucked her into her basket with evident pride.

'Can I hold her?' Lotte asked.

'Later, when I've got you all cleaned up and you've had a drink and something to eat,' Fern agreed. 'But Howard's going to take her upstairs now. She needs to be kept really warm – it's a bitter cold night tonight.'

Lotte was in a kind of warm bubble for the few hours left of the day. Fern washed her, changed the bed, brought her tea, sandwiches and cake, and praised her for her courage. Lotte was exhausted and soon dropped off to sleep.

The next morning she woke to the sound of the baby crying and instinct made her get out of bed. It was only when she found the door locked that the full implications hit her. She'd given birth and they'd taken the baby away, just as they intended, but somehow being told what would happen hadn't prepared her in any way for the reality.

She was bleeding heavily, her insides felt as if they might fall out, and she could hear her baby crying. That wail of distress was touching a nerve in her brain and jangling it but she couldn't get to her. But she had to, even if she had to break down the door.

Lotte hammered on the door with all the force she could muster, then went down the stairs to pick up a shoe to make even more noise.

'For God's sake stop that racket!' she heard Howard shout. 'What on earth's the matter?'

'Open the door,' she yelled out. 'My baby's crying.'

'It's our baby,' he corrected her. 'And Fern has just

281

picked her up to feed her. Go back to bed, it's only six in the morning. I'll bring you a cup of tea in a minute.'

Lotte felt deflated. The crying had stopped, evidence she supposed that her baby was being fed, but somehow that didn't quite stop the jangling of her nerves.

Howard did bring her tea.

'I want to see my baby,' Lotte demanded.

Howard put the tea down and went straight back to the stairs. 'I told you, she's our baby,' he said over his shoulder. 'This was what we agreed, and as soon as you've recovered from the birth we'll be making plans to take her Stateside. Don't make trouble, Lotte. You'll only regret it.'

During the following two days Lotte heard the baby crying a great deal and each time she felt agitated and worried that Fern wasn't taking proper care of her. Howard brought food and drinks down to her but his replies when she asked for information were noncommittal and vague.

'Babies do cry!' he said in answer to her question about what was wrong. 'Fern knows what she's doing.'

'Just let me come up and see her,' Lotte begged him. 'I'll be satisfied if I can see her being looked after properly.'

Howard refused. His excuse was that Fern had to bond with the baby and she didn't need any distracting influences.

*

Howard didn't come back that evening with a hot drink as he normally did. Lotte had a feeling it was to remind her that they could stop feeding her altogether if she made a nuisance of herself.

That night seemed endless. She was sore from the birth, bleeding profusely, and she wondered if she'd been torn in the delivery. She must have slept eventually because she woke from a dream where her body was swelling up like a balloon and she couldn't turn over.

She switched on the bedside light because she was scared and sweaty. It took a few moments to realize she really was swelling up; her breasts were twice their normal size, as hard as rocks, and she was feverish.

When she heard the baby crying and Howard's footsteps up in the kitchen, she called to him and said she wasn't well.

He told her to go back to bed and he'd come and see her later.

Lotte must have cried hundreds of times since she'd been brought here as she realized Howard and Fern weren't the kind, loving, very special people she'd believed them to be. But she had never cried the way she did then. She saw that she had no bargaining tools left; they'd got the baby, they had all the power. She was just a fool who had been so desperate to be loved that she'd fallen into their hands like a ripe apple.

She hadn't told anyone on the cruise where she was going when she left because she didn't want their disapproval. That was so pathetic. If she was honest, even she knew that she was doing the wrong thing, so why did she do it? Masochism or lunacy?

Fern came down just after ten, bringing a mug of tea for her. 'Now, what is all this about not feeling well?' she asked sharply. She was wearing a dressing gown, with no makeup and her hair just scragged back in a rough pony-tail. There were dark circles beneath her eyes and her complexion looked muddy. It was the first time Lotte had ever seen her looking frayed, old and tired.

Lotte told her about her throbbing, swollen breasts and that she was sore down below and losing blood heavily.

'Well, what do you expect?' Fern said irritably. 'Child-birth is a messy business. As for your breasts, that's just the milk coming in, I'll give you something to dry it up. All women feel upset on the fourth day, it's connected with the milk. But you've got nothing to be upset about, just be glad you can rest. At least you haven't got to feed and change the baby constantly.'

'Let me come up and I'll help you,' Lotte offered eagerly.

'I don't want you near her,' Fern said. 'She's mine now.'

She left then, rushing up the stairs as if she couldn't bear to breathe the same air a moment longer. Howard came down later with a box of Epsom salts and some painkillers. He said Lotte had to stir a couple of spoons of the salts into a glass of water and drink it down to get rid of the milk. The painkillers would take down her temperature.

By ten that night her breasts were softer and she no longer felt feverish but she couldn't stop crying. Strangely, she kept thinking about her mother, and wondering what sort of a delivery she'd had. Maybe it was a difficult one, and that was the reason she'd preferred Fleur? Yet Lotte hadn't been aware Fleur was the favourite, not until she died.

She thought then that if she did get out of this alive, she would try to make peace with her parents. But thinking about them only made her cry more, for they had never tried to contact her after she left home to go and work at the hotel and they hadn't even written while she was working on the ship, so they wouldn't care what she'd been through here.

March came in with sunshine, but Lotte only knew that because late in the afternoon it hit the tiny window for about half an hour or so. But a shaft of sunshine was very welcome when she hadn't seen more than a little square of grey sky for weeks. She found herself reaching out to touch the particles of dust in the beam. As a child she'd thought they were fairies and if you caught one you could make a wish.

Her wish was just to know what was going on upstairs, for Howard always brought the meals now and they were growing sketchier by the day – sandwiches instead of a cooked meal, tinned soup in a mug, no fresh fruit or vegetables. She had to suppose this was because Fern was busy with the baby, but when she asked Howard how she was getting on he told her it was none of her business.

But it was her business. Each time she heard her baby crying she still felt a jangling within her. She wanted to know when this ordeal was going to end for her, and when they were going back to the States. She wondered too if Fern had become disenchanted with having a baby of her own, and whether she and Howard might change their original plan to be parents and sell the baby to a desperate couple. She couldn't work out whether that would be a lesser evil or a greater one.

Lotte had recovered well from the birth. By the time the baby was four weeks old she'd stopped bleeding and was no longer sore. She spent an hour every day doing gentle exercises to make up for not being allowed out for walks or even upstairs.

Listening at the door was the thing she spent most of her time doing. Fern had always kept her voice down before the baby was born, sounding calm and measured almost the whole time. But Lotte thought that maybe this was just for her benefit, to create an image of someone who never lost control, for she didn't sound like that now.

She screamed at Howard, about food, cleaning the baby's bottles, that the house looked like a pig sty and there was washing needing to be done.

In one respect it pleased Lotte that everything was unravelling for them, for maybe if Fern was having second thoughts about having a baby of her own, she might just hand her back to her real mother, or at least let her out to help. But even as she hoped for that miracle, she knew it was in vain. Fern wasn't the kind to back down about anything.

Lotte didn't just listen at the door when they were rowing, she kept her ears pinned back constantly, hoping to find out what they were planning. Unfortunately she mostly only heard snippets of information because they would walk into the lounge or office out of earshot during their conversation. One such snippet was about registering the baby's birth.

'It's normal for the hospital or a midwife present at a home birth to pass on details of the birth to the Registrar,' Howard said. 'If we say the baby was born at home without anyone present, they might be suspicious.'

They moved away then and about five minutes passed before she heard Fern speak, her voice raised in anger.

'Why didn't you find out before that we only get forty-two days to do it?

Lotte had often lost track of the date and even which day of the week it was during her pregnancy, but she usually got her sense of time back when they gave her a newspaper to read, or let her watch television. She knew the date the baby was born was 20 February because Howard had a newspaper that morning, and from the day after she'd kept a kind of diary in a notebook. She jotted down how she was feeling each day, and anything else which happened, in the hope that if she ever got free it might be evidence against Fern and Howard.

It was the end of March when Fern charged Howard with not finding out they had only forty-two days. Lotte did a quick calculation on her fingers and found it meant the birth must be registered by 9 April.

Howard said something in reply but his voice was muffled. Then Fern yelled at him, 'You should've worked all this out – what are we going to do now?'

'Get a forged one, but that's going to take longer,' Howard snarled back at her. 'Now get off my back, this is all your doing anyway.'

Lotte gathered from this that Howard was nervous both about registering the birth and getting a passport for the baby. She knew from applying for her own passport to go on the cruise that they checked and double-checked every last thing. They were probably even more vigilant with parents who weren't from the UK, what with people making fraudulent claims they had children just to get financial benefits.

Yet Lotte felt no glee that the Ramsdens' plans were falling apart, for angry, worried people didn't make good parents. What she did feel was white-hot hatred for the couple, and every time the baby cried she was afraid they were hurting her.

It was during one of their many rows, when Lotte

could hear the baby crying in the background, that she made up her mind to fight her way out of the basement.

Ever since she got the knife she'd imagined many different ways of attacking them with it, but before the baby was born she hadn't felt physically strong enough to overpower either Fern or Howard.

Things were changing now, however. By the end of March and through April, Howard often went off leaving Fern alone with the baby, and Lotte knew she must be very tired, and probably not as sharp as she used to be. Besides, Lotte felt so angry and desperate now she thought she could take on anyone.

'So did you attack one of them with the knife?' Dale asked.

Her friend's voice so close to her startled Lotte. She'd been so immersed in what happened to her a few weeks earlier that she'd lost touch with the present, and it was a shock to find Dale lying there next to her and realize she'd been relating it all.

'I stood up on the top step and waited for one of them to come,' she said. 'I must have stood there for over two hours, and during that time I could hear my baby crying. But the house was so quiet, too quiet. I realized they'd gone out and left the baby alone. Can you imagine how I felt about that? I was powerless and unable to comfort her. I imagined her choking, or suffocating under covers she'd pulled over her face. I was scared for myself too, because if they'd leave a baby alone, they'd be capable of leaving me down here to die of starvation as well.'

Dale was horrified by how deeply disturbed her friend was by that memory: she was shaking and wild-eyed, her voice rasping with emotion. She took Lotte's hand in hers and rubbed it between her hands, murmuring a reminder that she wasn't alone now.

'I went back down the stairs later,' Lotte went on. 'I was stiff with cold because they'd turned off the heating, so I had to get under the bedcovers to warm up. The hours went by so slowly, but still there was no sound of them upstairs. Six o'clock came and I'd had nothing to eat since a cup of tea and slice of toast at eight. I wasn't concerned about my hunger, but I was about the baby's – she was only ten weeks old and she needed a feed every four hours. But she wasn't crying any more.

'Then just as I thought all was lost I heard them come in the front door. So I was right, they had left the baby, and that made me savage, but I stayed quiet to listen, and I heard them say something about London.'

Lotte turned her head towards Dale. 'Can you believe anyone would go to London for the day and leave a small baby alone?

'They were making coffee in the kitchen and I heard Fern laughing about something, and then she said, "God in heaven, the baby's not crying!" I was just about to scream out, "Get up there, you bitch, and check if she's OK," but Howard said he would go. He even made a joke about how she'd be so hungry she'd need two bottles.'

'You must have been beside yourself,' Dale said in sympathy. 'Was the baby all right?'

'Well, that was just it,' Lotte began and her eyes filled with tears. 'I heard Howard walking up the stairs. You can hear that clearly in here. He seemed to be up there for ages, and I was standing up by the door holding my breath because I sensed something was seriously wrong. Then he came down, really slowly. He went into the kitchen and Fern asked why he hadn't brought the baby down. He said, "I don't know how to tell you this, honey, but she's dead. I think it's a crib death."'

'She died! Oh my God no,' Dale exclaimed in horror.

'I'd had a sort of foreboding all day,' Lotte sobbed. 'Even when she was crying it was kind of weak, not the way she cried when she was born. It was very cold without the heating on, she could have pushed her covers off, and a new baby can't wriggle back under them when it's cold the way a puppy or kitten would do.'

'So what did you do when you heard this?' Dale asked.

'I banged on the door and yelled at the top of my voice. Howard shouted back at me to shut up or else. He sounded like he'd enjoy an opportunity to beat the shit out of someone. So in the end I thought it would be better to just shut up and wait.'

'How long did you wait, Lotte?' Dale looked fearfully at her.

'Five days, without food and just cold water to drink.'

Chapter Fourteen

Scott woke as David put a mug of tea for him on the floor beside the sofa. He rubbed his eyes, stretched out his legs and felt rather surprised he'd slept so well when the sofa was a foot too short for him.

He glanced at his watch. It was just after seven, and raining heavily, yet David was already washed, shaved and dressed. But dark circles beneath his eyes suggested he hadn't slept much. 'So where to today?' Scott asked, guessing David had spent much of the night planning the day ahead.

'I think we should start a house-to-house,' David replied, sitting down on the other sofa. 'The shops, garages and the pubs too. If Simon and Adam will take Bosham and Fishbourne on the far side of the harbour, we could check out Birdham and Itchenor on this side.'

Scott sat up to drink his tea. The rain was lashing against the window and it wasn't an inviting proposition to be out in it. 'I didn't think to bring a coat,' he said.

'I've got a spare one you can borrow. But I doubt the rain will last all day.'

They drank their tea in companionable silence. Scott hadn't noticed much about the house the previous evening, but he saw now that the lounge was quite spartan, with two brown leather sofas, a TV and sound system on a low sideboard, no ornaments or feminine touches. But that seemed odd as the walls were painted a pale peach and the patterned curtains toned perfectly.

'Did you used to live here with a girl?' he asked curiously.

'Yes, a while back,' David said with a sigh, perching on a footstool. 'It was a big mistake – she was a high-flying career girl.'

'What was wrong with that?' Scott asked.

'I didn't want to spend the rest of my life with a woman who cared more about sales projections and profit margins than having a family.'

'I can't say I've ever given having a family much thought,' Scott said with a grin. 'Or getting married for that matter. Just happy to pootle along having a good time, I guess.'

'It was only living with someone dynamic like Rose that made me realize I'm quite an old-fashioned kind of guy,' David smiled. 'I actually want to be a hunter-gatherer.'

Scott threw off his blanket. 'Well, I'd better get up then so we can go out hunting for the girls.'

They met up with Simon and Adam for breakfast, as arranged, in a café on the A27 near Apuldram. Scott noticed that Simon looked as if he hadn't slept much either, but then he thought of Lotte as a sister and he felt he'd let her down by not making the flat more secure.

No one had spoken about how it would be if the girls were found dead, yet Scott knew it was foremost in all their minds. He supposed they were all afraid to voice that fear, in case to speak of death was to invite it in.

It was interesting that they had all accepted David as their leader even though he'd only known Lotte for such a short time. He certainly hadn't pushed for it; he just naturally had that quality to take the helm. The man was direct, quietly confident, with no pomposity at all. Scott thought that perhaps that came from being one of eight; after all, you must have to learn from an early age to hold your own or lose your identity, yet also be flexible. But however he got how he was, Scott liked him.

'So what d'you want us to do today, boss?' Adam asked.

David half smiled at the title, but made no comment. 'Go to as many houses as possible, do the shops, pubs, garages, anywhere where people go regularly. Try to stimulate their memories.'

'How?' Simon asked.

'Use your imagination!' David exclaimed, as if Simon's question was a daft one. 'First show them the snap of the girls looking like models, and stress we fear they might be killed if they aren't found soon. That will get their interest, and then you can show them the snap of Lotte where she looks sad and frumpy. Remind them about her being found on the beach and that there was evidence she'd had a baby recently. A lost baby touches everyone and they might remember seeing Lotte while she was pregnant. The more impression you make on each person you speak to, the more you stir their emotions, the more likely they are to remember something which could be useful.'

The men split up after they'd finished their breakfast and arranged to meet at six that evening to compare notes. David said if one of them got lucky, to ring and tell the other group, and to phone the police immediately for their help.

'Remember, a lead can come from just the tiniest little bit of information,' David said emphatically. 'Make the people you talk to consider whether they've noticed anything unusual or out of place in a neighbouring house: maybe the sound of a baby crying, shouting, extra food carried in, lights left on, or coming and going at strange times. Stress that they might be saving the girls' lives!'

Tears welled up in Simon's eyes, Adam looked grimly determined, and Scott thought it was astounding that he could feel so close to and involved with men he'd known for such a short time.

Scott bought a newspaper before he and David set off and felt gratified to find another full page about the girls' disappearance. Ever since David found Lotte on the beach, they'd all felt the press had failed to maximize on the drama of the story. It might have alerted Scott and Dale that the girl was Lotte, but it hadn't had a huge impact on the general public. Likewise, the police had appeared less than dynamic in their investigation. Yet now the paper reported that they were conducting a house-to-house search in the Selsey area.

'Why there?' Scott asked David, as they sat in the car reading the report. 'Have we got it wrong? Or is it them?'

'Maybe they've got some new evidence,' David suggested. 'But they told me that day I found Lotte that she'd been washed along the coast from the direction of Bracklesham Bay. If she'd fallen from a boat sailing out of Selsey, or was pushed, she would've ended up around Pagham harbour or even further along the coast towards Bognor.'

'Should we ring Simon and Adam and tell them about this, then?' Scott asked, thinking it was pointless them searching on the other side of the harbour if the police thought the girls were in Selsey.

David shrugged. 'I don't believe they are there,' he said. 'People don't launch boats in Selsey and there's certainly no moorings there that I know of.'

'But Lotte could've been kept there and then taken by car to wherever the boat was moored? Maybe the police have had a tip-off?'

David frowned, looking a lot less certain. 'Maybe I should ring and ask DI Bryan?'

'Worth a try.' Scott grinned. 'He can only tell you to keep your nose out.'

David got his phone out of his pocket and rang the number.

'It's David Mitchell,' he said when Bryan answered.

'Just read in the paper that you are doing a house-to-house at Selsey. We wondered why there? Have you got a new lead?'

Scott watched David as he listened to the lengthy reply, but there was no discernible excitement, or disappointment. Scott thought he ought to take up playing poker.

'Yes, we did, and we're checking out Birdham and Itchenor today,' David said eventually, his tone defensive.

'Of course we'll ring you if we turn anything up,' he said a few moments later. 'As long as you do the same for us,' he added cheekily.

David put his phone back in his pocket. 'He'd been told we were asking questions in the marina yesterday. I think he was dying to tell us to bugger off home and leave this to professionals, but he didn't quite have the brass neck to. Instead he gave me a lecture about not harassing people.'

'So what did he say was going on in Selsey?' Scott asked.

'The night before last, several people heard banging and screaming. But none of them was able to pinpoint exactly where the noise was coming from, and each one lived in a different part of the town. This has led Bryan to think the noise might have been coming from a van which was moved several times.'

Scott looked puzzled. 'Surely no one with any sense would risk taking two people they'd abducted into a built-up area unless they'd bound and gagged them?'

David grimaced. 'It might just be a few kids bombing around the town in a van winding people up for a laugh. That's the kind of thing I would have thought hilarious when I was seventeen or eighteen.'

'So we carry on with the original plan then?' Scott asked.

'Sure thing!' David grinned. 'Let's go!'

They had almost finished in Birdham at two o'clock when Scott struck lucky.

Birdham was a small, pretty village, just a lovely old church and a primary school, but not much else. There were a few old cottages, but in the main the houses and bungalows were modern and expensive-looking. Fortunately the people who were at home were keenly interested in what the boys had to say, so much so that they had sometimes found it difficult to get away.

David had signalled to Scott when he had finished his side of Cherry Lane that he was going to walk back to the car to wait for him, when the door Scott was knocking on was opened by a stout, elderly woman with hairs sprouting on her chin.

'I don't buy anything at the door,' she growled at him. 'So be off with you!'

It had rained hard all morning and Scott was wet through despite the cagoule David had lent him, so he was tempted just to turn on his heel and walk away from the cantankerous old woman.

'I'm not selling anything,' he snapped. 'I'm conducting

a house-to-house inquiry to see if anyone has seen this girl.' He handed the woman Lotte's picture. 'I expect you've seen pictures of her in the paper,' he added.

'I never read newspapers, they only print lies,' she said abruptly.

Scott couldn't bring himself to be as rude as she was. So he explained how Lotte had disappeared for a year and was then found washed up on the beach. All at once the woman took the photo and peered closely at it.

'I've seen her at Pagham Nature Reserve,' she said.

'You have?' Scott exclaimed incredulously, not really believing her.

'Yes, once, last autumn. I often go birdwatching there when the tourists have all gone home. The reason I remember this girl was because she stared at me, almost as if she wanted to say something to me.'

'Was she alone, or with someone?'

'With a man and a woman, much older than her. The woman was bossy, she took hold of the girl by the arm and almost dragged her back to the car park.'

'I don't suppose you can remember what the couple looked like?' Scott could feel his pulse quickening with excitement.

'The woman looked like Rita Hayworth,' she replied without hesitation. 'Of course you're too young to remember her, but she was a famous Hollywood film star with red hair and very shapely. This woman was taller though, might have been five foot eight.'

A mental picture of Fern Ramsden from the cruise popped into Scott's head. 'Did you hear her speak?' he asked, his pulse beginning to race. 'The red-headed woman, I mean?'

'She spoke sharply to the girl, but I couldn't hear exactly what she said.'

'So you wouldn't know if she was an American?'

'No, son, she was too far away from me. But I'm sure the girl in your picture is the one I saw. I was a bit worried about her afterwards, she had the look of a frightened deer. Do you know what I mean?'

Scott did know, he'd seen Lotte look that way on several occasions, all big blue eyes and quivering lips. He'd even teasingly called her Bambi at times. He felt like hugging this odd woman, who liked to pretend she was a miserable old dragon but was in fact an observant and caring person.

'Yes, I do know. You've been a tremendous help, and if you don't mind I'll pass your details on to the police because they'll want to speak to you and show you pictures to identify this couple. May I have your name and phone number?' he asked.

She said her name was Miss Margaret Foster and told him she was a retired schoolteacher. Now she'd got over her resentment at him knocking on her door, it was as if she wanted to keep him there. She said she couldn't remember what the man looked like, she only noticed the two women, and she was sure they weren't mother and daughter.

'Will you let me know if you find the girls?' she said after he'd written down her phone number.

Scott smiled at her. 'If we find them I'll bring them round to meet you because you've given us a great lead and they would certainly like to thank you.'

He could hardly wait to get back to the car to tell David and get him to ring Bryan too.

The policeman was disappointingly cool and was not convinced the couple could be the Ramsdens. 'They went back to the States, we checked with the airline,' he said. 'They haven't come back either.'

'Maybe not as Ramsden, but they could have with a different identity,' David pointed out.

Scott took the phone from David to say his bit. 'I'm telling you Miss Foster's description of the woman she saw was spot on for Fern Ramsden. Dale used to nickname her Rita and she once showed me a picture of Rita Hayworth to explain. It was incredible how much she looked like the actress. Why don't you get some pictures of the Ramsdens from the cruise ship and go round and show them to Miss Foster?'

David took the phone back. 'What do you think then?' he asked.

'A day's house-to-house qualifies you two as detectives, does it?' Bryan asked sarcastically.

David pulled a face at Scott who was listening to what was being said. 'Sorry, sir, I didn't mean to tell you how to do your job,' he said, making a gesture to Scott that implied he knew he was being smarmy.

'That's OK.' Bryan chuckled. 'I really appreciate your help, thanks for this. We'll keep in touch.'

They rang Simon and Adam to give them the news, and as they hadn't had so much as a sniff of a lead, Simon said they would come back to join up with Scott and David and blitz Itchenor.

The Ship Inn down by Itchenor harbour was where they arranged to meet up. David, who had been to the pub many times before, said the landlord was a great character and he felt sure he would give them any assistance he could.

As they turned into the road which led to the harbour Scott was surprised by the many different kinds of houses, everything from mock Tudor mansions and stone cottages to palatial, colonial-style bungalows. Many were tucked away behind high hedges, only glimpsed through wrought-iron gates, and the gardens were beautiful.

'There's obviously some seriously wealthy people live here,' he said. 'And I bet most of them have got boats.'

David agreed. He said he often came to the pub during the summer and the talk was always about sailing.

'I wish we had a picture of the Ramsdens to show around,' Scott said as they drove into the pub car park.

'I think saying she looks like Rita Hayworth will be enough,' David said with a smile. 'People are a bit older here, they will know what the actress looked like. And somehow I think women who fit that description in a sailing community must be rather thin on the ground.'

*

As the boys were in the pub ready to begin asking more questions, Kim and Clarke Moore, Dale's parents, along with her younger sister Carrina were knocking on the Wainwrights' front door in Brighton.

At home in Chiswick, no one would look twice at the couple's unconventional appearance, for there were hundreds of people trapped in a Sixties time warp in their neighbourhood. Kim had flowing, henna-dyed hair, and she favoured vintage clothes in silks and velvets, usually jazzed up with brightly coloured scarves, fur or feather trims, and chunky, ostentatious jewellery. Today she was more soberly dressed because of the seriousness of the situation, in a mid-calf-length black linen dress and a checked jacket, yet with Clarke in a buckskin fringed jacket and his grey hair tied back in a pony-tail, they still stood out as middle-aged hippies.

Carrina was twenty-three, and so frightened for her older sister that her pretty face was pale and drawn. She didn't share Dale's exotic appearance; she had light brown hair, blue eyes and a delicate pink and white complexion. But she had a curvy, womanly body like Dale.

They had driven down to Brighton the previous morning and spent most of the day at the police station hoping to hear that Dale and Lotte had been found. When it became clear to them this wasn't likely to be imminent, they had contacted the press and offered a substantial reward for information about where the girls were being held.

During the late afternoon they had driven out to Marchwood Spa to talk to some of the staff there, hoping Dale might have revealed something useful to one of the other girls. While Quentin Sellers, the general manager of the hotel, was very sympathetic, and all the staff were deeply concerned about Dale, the Moores couldn't fail to notice that Marisa the spa manageress was barely civil to them.

Frankie, one of the hairdressers, urged them to ignore her. He said Marisa had been irritated by the way Dale reacted when Lotte was found on the beach; she felt it was hysterical. But Frankie also pointed out that Marisa might have felt her role at the spa threatened by Dale because she was not only very efficient, but popular with the other staff and clients. Now Scott had disappeared to help find the girls and Marisa couldn't get anyone qualified to take over his duties, she was blaming Dale for that too.

After a night in a hotel, Kim and Clarke had gone straight to the police again to see if there had been any developments. It seemed the house-to-house search in Selsey they were undertaking had not as yet revealed anything, so Kim thought they should call on the Wainwrights.

'Why?' Clarke asked his wife. 'We've been told they don't care much about Lotte, so we can't hope they'll be any different about Dale. It's only going to upset you.'

'I daresay it will,' Kim agreed, her eyes filling with tears once more because she was so afraid she was never going to see her daughter again. 'But our girls became close friends on that cruise and I feel I need to do this for their sakes.'

Kim knew her daughter had never connected with anyone before as she had with Lotte. When she came home after the cruise Kim saw how this friend had influenced her for the good, for she was more thoughtful with people, kinder and far less bumptious. Kim felt she was prepared to love Lotte just on the strength of that, and when Dale told her how she was raped, she took the girl she'd never met to her heart.

But this feeling changed when Dale told her over the phone about Lotte being found on a beach suffering from memory loss. While she felt sorry for her, it was all too mysterious, and Kim felt her daughter might get sucked into something which would pull her down too. She warned Dale that some people were natural victims, and went through life attracting trouble, even going as far as to say she thought Dale shouldn't involve herself.

But now Kim had talked to DI Bryan and discovered a little more about Lotte and her family background, she felt ashamed she'd taken such a line. Dale was to be admired for caring for her friend, and even though that meant she was now in danger, Kim felt proud of her.

'You'd better come in,' Mr Wainwright said as he opened the door. 'The missus don't think there's any point in us getting together. But I'm glad to see you.'

Kim looked hard at Lotte's father, with his thin, deeply lined face and faded, sad blue eyes. She guessed that he was no more than fifty-five, but he looked much older. From what Dale had said about him, and that wasn't much, it sounded as if he'd spent his entire adult life going along with whatever his wife wanted. She was already pitying him.

'Our girls have been abducted, surely that is enough of a point to us meeting,' Kim said crisply. 'I'm Kim, this is Clarke and our other daughter Carrina.'

'Ted,' he said, shaking their hands. 'I'm pleased to meet you. Do come through, we're in the kitchen.'

He led them down the passageway and as he walked into the kitchen his wife got up from her seat at the table. 'I'm Peggy,' she said. Kim got the idea that it had taken a great effort on her part to hold out her hand and smile as her husband introduced them all.

'Tea or coffee?' she asked.

Kim and Clarke often came up against difficult people in buying and selling second-hand goods, but Kim was famous for winning over even the most frosty and cantankerous. Undeterred by the strained atmosphere, she said they'd like tea, and admired the garden she could see through the window.

'You must have green fingers,' she said. 'Look how much colour you've got there! All those lovely delphiniums and lupins. My garden is always dreary after the spring bulbs until I get the summer bedding in.'

'I spend a lot of time on it,' Peggy admitted, but she

307

looked pleased at having her efforts admired. 'It's a shame it's raining today, it would be nice to sit outside.'

Kim kept up her charm offensive while the tea was being made. She admired the pot plants on the window sill and some old jugs hanging under the wall cupboards, and discussed the pros and cons of dishwashers. It was only once the tea was on the table and a plate of biscuits had been passed round, that she spoke of Dale and Lotte.

'Lotte's two male friends have joined Scott from Marchwood Manor and David, the guy who found her at Selsey, to do a house-to-house search around Chichester harbour,' she said. 'It's my suggestion that we go there and help. What do you think?'

'Oh no.' Peggy shook her head. 'I couldn't do that!'

'Why on earth not?' Kim asked. 'I'm sure if you were being held captive you'd expect Lotte to come looking for you.'

'She hasn't been near nor by me for years,' Peggy replied.

'Whose fault is that?' Kim said bluntly. 'As I understand it, you didn't welcome her. This is your chance to change things between you now. Get out there and be a real mother.'

'I'd expect Mum and Dad to come looking for me if I was in Lotte's position,' Carrina spoke up. 'We've had our ups and downs but when something serious like this happens you just have to forget all that.'

'You don't know anything that's gone on between

us,' Peggy snapped. She looked to her husband for support but he turned his head away.

'But we do,' Kim said pointedly. 'We know you turned against Lotte when her older sister died. How could you take that out on Lotte? It wasn't her fault. I bet she wished she'd never regained some of her memory when she recalled that! But now's your chance to put that right.'

'How dare you come in here and judge me?' Peggy said angrily, her face growing very flushed.

'I dare because at any moment we could get the worst news in the whole world. That is, that our daughters are dead,' Kim said, looking hard at the other woman. 'I could bet that you would've sold your own soul if it would've saved your other daughter. Am I right?'

Peggy nodded.

'Right then, I want you to get up off your arse now, to remember that Lotte is a gift from God, just as your Fleur was, and that a mother's role is to protect and nurture.'

'But . . .' Peggy began.

Kim waved her hands to interrupt her. 'What went on between you and Lotte can end here right now if you want it to. Just come with us and join the search.'

'But it's nearly two. By the time we get to Chichester the day will be almost over.'

Kim looked exasperated. 'If your husband was to keel over with a heart attack, would you say, "He's close on sixty so it isn't worth getting help"?'

'Of course not,' Peggy said indignantly.

'Well, we can be in Chichester in forty minutes, and it doesn't get dark till late. Evenings are a good time to knock on doors, people are home from work. And there's those four young men who've taken time off from work to hunt for the girls. Don't you think they'd expect us to help?'

Clarke smiled at Ted. He was proud of his wife for bullying Lotte's mother. Maybe if someone had spoken to her like that when she lost her other daughter, she wouldn't have turned against the second child. But then, Kim had always been hot-headed and pushy, and Dale was just like her.

'I don't like the way you speak to me,' Peggy said, folding her arms across her chest in a way that reminded him of Les Dawson the comedian, who used to impersonate gossiping women. 'You've got some nerve coming in here throwing your weight around and telling us what we should do.'

'Yes, I know,' Kim said blithely. 'My Dale is just like me too. But do you know what? Your Lotte made her a nicer person. She made her care for other people, she made her gentler, more thoughtful. As she's my daughter I'd still have laid my life on the line for her, even if she'd remained selfish, opinionated and careless. But I've got a huge debt of gratitude to your Lotte, even though I've never met her, so I believe that entitles me to make her parents do the right thing by her.'

Clarke saw Peggy was wavering now. He guessed Ted had wanted to do the right thing from when they first arrived, but he was too weak to speak out. Kim obviously thought this too for she was now looking straight at the man.

'Come on, Ted, are you a man or a mouse?' she asked. 'We've had no opinion from you yet. Do you think we should all join the search in Chichester?'

Ted opened his mouth but no words came out. Perhaps he was afraid of upsetting his wife. But Carrina moved over to him and slipped her hand into his, looking up at him.

'Of course you want to look for her,' she said softly. 'You've been dying to go since she was first captured, haven't you?'

Carrina had always been the most sensitive of their children, and Clarke saw that her instinct was sound. Putting her small hand in his was a masterstroke, for with all the old memories of both his daughters that would evoke, he'd be unable to say no.

'Yes,' he mumbled. But then his head came up and he looked at his wife. 'Yes, I've been wanting to search for her,' he said firmly.

Clarke looked back at Peggy. Clearly stunned that her husband had defied her, she was staring at him as if waiting for an explanation.

'So we're all going now?' Kim said, perhaps wishing to move things on a bit. 'Better get some comfy shoes on.'

Peggy's eyes suddenly filled with tears. 'I should have had help when Fleur died,' she blurted out. 'Nowadays they give people counselling, but I got nothing. I didn't understand what I was feeling and I had nobody to talk to about it.'

Kim took a couple of steps towards her. 'It must have been hideous. Losing a child is the worst thing that can happen to a mother. I'm sure if it happened to me I'd have gone right off the rails. But it isn't too late to talk about it and get it out of your system, Peggy.'

'It might be too late to explain to Lotte,' Peggy said brokenly. 'The police told me she'd had a baby. That's our grandchild! But where is it? What happened, and what's going to happen now?'

Chapter Fifteen

Lotte lay back on the bed, watching Dale struggling hopelessly as she tried to get through the tiny window.

They had pushed the wardrobe beneath it, climbed up and smashed all the glass out with a shoe on their first day here, and took turns to shout out in the hope that someone nearby would hear them. Unfortunately the window was right down at ground level outside and tucked away in a kind of alcove, so the sound probably didn't carry very well from there. Lotte had also tried to climb out in the last few days of her previous imprisonment in the basement room, but failed. Dale wouldn't listen, though.

'They say if you can get your head through a hole the rest of your body can go through it too,' she kept saying to Lotte. But each time she stuck her head through and then tried to get her shoulders after it, she became stuck and had to withdraw, tears of frustration running down her cheeks. She had tried to push Lotte through too, for she was smaller, but it didn't work.

Lotte had given up on trying to stop Dale wearing herself out fruitlessly because she remembered that during her last five days here without food, she hadn't been rational either.

When she wasn't doing exactly what Dale was doing, she had been crouched at the top of the stairs, kitchen knife in hand, waiting for either Fern or Howard to come in so she could stab them. She had been frozen with cold and weak with hunger, yet that was nowhere near as important to her as the loss of her baby and desire for revenge.

Fern and Howard went out a great deal during those five days, but when they were in they were strangely silent. There was no more shouting from Fern, no banging around, no cooking smells, not even the sound of the radio or television. Lotte would have seen this silence as grief if it had been their own baby, or they'd been devoted foster parents, but she knew they had no hearts and therefore they were just quiet because they were considering their next move.

At first she thought their intention was to leave her here to starve to death, but after a while it occurred to her that the house was far too valuable to them for that. They wouldn't just walk away and leave it; apart from losing the money, eventually their crime would be discovered. So it seemed most likely that their plan was to weaken her sufficiently so that they could move her to kill her and dispose of her body elsewhere, perhaps along with the baby's.

Back then Lotte had no real hope of rescue. Instead, she told herself that they would have to come down to get her at some stage, and that would give her a slim chance of escape.

But this time round, she really did believe rescue was

likely. For one thing, the minute she and Dale were reported missing the police would have gone into overdrive to find them. Dale's parents, along with Scott, Adam and Simon, would all be making waves around Brighton and that might prompt someone who had seen something to come forward. Maybe the two men who brought them here were local, and perhaps they had no idea what they were getting into, not until they read about the abduction in the papers. So they just might feel bad about what they'd done and go to the police.

But even if no one came forward, by now the police must have discovered the American Ramsdens were here in England as Mr and Mrs Gullick, and that would surely lead on to finding this house.

Lotte looked up at Dale and saw she was yet again attempting to get her shoulders through the window. 'Please come down now, Dale, you'll just wear yourself out,' she pleaded. 'Shout by all means, but by now you should've accepted it isn't possible to climb out. Save your strength for when they come back to get us.'

'They aren't coming back, they've left us here to die,' Dale sobbed, kneeling down on the top of the wardrobe. She suddenly slumped forward till her head met her knees, and made a horrible wailing sound. 'How long can we last without food?'

'For weeks, as long as you drink water,' Lotte replied. 'But it won't come to that. They'll do something about us long before. And we'll be ready for them.'

'How can we fight them?' Dale wailed. 'They were

big hefty guys, we haven't even got anything to use as a weapon.'

'We have. Just get down off that wardrobe and I'll show you,' Lotte said.

Dale turned to look at her friend with bleak eyes. She wiped them with the back of her hand, then carefully lowered herself to the chair by the wardrobe. 'Go on then,' she said, once she was down on the floor again.

Lotte got off the bed and went over to the wardrobe, lifting one end of it. 'Hold it for me,' she ordered, and once Dale had a firm grip on it, she fished beneath it and appeared to be scratching at something with her nails.

'What is it?' Dale asked in bewilderment. 'Be quick, this is heavy!'

'You can put it down now,' Lotte said as she withdrew her hand from beneath the wardrobe. 'I stuck this up there with elastoplast when I was in here before.' She held out a Stanley knife.

Dale's eyes widened. 'Christ almighty!' she exclaimed.

'I got it just before I had the baby. Howard had been doing some little job in the kitchen and I saw this at the top of his tool box. I nicked it when he turned away. I really wanted a chisel to dig out the screws on the door, but this was better than nothing. And we could do those men a real injury with it.'

'Maybe one of them,' Dale said, squirming at the thought of attacking anyone with a Stanley knife. 'But not both of them!'

'We can work on that,' Lotte said. 'One idea I've had is that I could pretend to be out cold on the bed when they come for us, while you hide in the bathroom. When the man bends over me, I stab him, then leap up to get the other one, and you come running out of the bathroom to help too.'

Dale shook her head doubtfully. 'You might be able to slash his face with the knife, but I can't see that stopping him, not with another man there to help him. They'd soon overpower us. Tell me what happened when they came for you before. Maybe that will give us another idea!'

'I was groggy. I guess once you get beyond the hunger pains, you become apathetic, because I hadn't even attempted to get out of bed that day. Anyway, suddenly Howard and Fern were coming down the stairs and telling me to get dressed because we were going out.'

Looking back at that period of her captivity, Lotte found it very odd that on that particular day as Fern and Howard came bursting into the basement, she was huddled under the bedcovers and didn't want to move. Yet right up till the day before, her sole motivation had been to get out of that room, whatever it took, and to wreak revenge on Fern and Howard.

'I said, get up and get dressed,' Fern repeated more sharply, and Lotte noticed then that she was wearing jeans and a thick Arran sweater. The only time she'd ever seen Fern in jeans was when she went sailing, and although

Lotte's mind was fuzzy with hunger, it registered that they were intending to take her out to sea to drown her.

Terror cleared her mind enough to realize that by acting like she was sick, unsteady on her feet and a little vacant, they just might be lured into complacency.

'I don't feel very well,' she said, speaking very slowly and lifting her head from the pillow even slower. 'Can't I just stay here?'

'No, you can't,' Fern snapped at her.

'How is the baby?' Lotte asked, spinning out the question as if she could barely speak.

She saw the couple exchange glances and felt their unease. 'Come on, get up,' Fern said curtly.

It wasn't difficult to play dopey and stagger around the floor like a badly coordinated six-year-old. She wanted them to feel unable to leave to let her dress in case she fell back into bed, yet irritated enough not to watch her very closely.

'Naughty! You mustn't watch me dress,' she said, shaking a finger at Howard as she dropped her pyjamas trousers to the floor. She had knickers beneath them, but the jacket was so long he wouldn't know that.

He turned his back on her, and Lotte could feel Fern's growing exasperation as she took for ever to put on her dress and button it up.

'Must clean my teeth,' Lotte said once she'd added a cardigan. She disappeared into the bathroom, ran the tap to hide any suspicious sounds, then retrieved the kitchen knife from its hiding place tucked into the willow stems beneath the laundry basket. She wrapped a tissue round it and slipped it into the pocket of her dress, then noisily cleaned her teeth.

By the time she was ready to leave the basement, Lotte's earlier grogginess had gone completely. She knew it was a certainty that the couple intended to kill her, and that they would succeed if she didn't find the courage and strength to fight them. She felt so weak from being starved, and her arms and legs ached as if she had a bad dose of flu, so all she could hope for was that if she continued to act dopey and unsuspecting, they would relax their usual vigilance.

Until she got to the top of the basement stairs she had imagined it was mid-morning, but the murky light coming through the hall window told her it was early evening and dusk outside. That made her even more frightened because it sort of confirmed they really were intending to dispose of her that night.

'Can I have a cup of tea?' she asked, anxious to act untroubled. 'And a sandwich?'

'You can have some milk and a couple of biscuits, just to tide you over,' Fern said. She sounded almost kindly, and when Lotte turned to look at her, the woman's expression was relaxed, even affectionate towards her.

Such insincerity when she'd taken her child and allowed it to die, and was now intending to kill Lotte too, was almost too much to bear. 'That would be nice,' she replied, forcing an innocent, trusting smile as her hand ran over the lump of the knife against her hip.

It was odd to see Fern without her usual perfect makeup and not a hair out of place. Her face looked grey and careworn, her hair decidedly ratty. But the dirt and mess in the kitchen was far more shocking. The work surfaces were strewn with takeaway food cartons, unwashed dishes, cups and glasses, and the tiled floor was filthy. It was proof that all their plans had fallen apart, and maybe they were even unravelling mentally too, for she'd never seen the kitchen looking anything less than gleaming before.

Fern took a clean glass from one of the wall cupboards, then went over to the fridge to get the milk. Lotte moved closer to her, at the same time glancing back at Howard.

He was just outside the kitchen, looking intently at a little booklet with a blue cover. He wasn't watching her or his wife at all.

The fridge was a tall one, the bottom half a freezer, and Fern was reaching for a bottle of milk just above shoulder height. All at once Lotte saw a chance. It wasn't the kind of moment she'd hoped for, but it might be the only one she'd get, so she slid her hand into her pocket, scraping the knife blade free of the tissue paper against her hip as she drew it out.

Fern still had her back to Lotte, filling the glass from the bottle with the fridge door still open. She put the bottle back on the shelf and as she began to turn to give the glass of milk to Lotte she gave the fridge door a little push with her shoulder to shut it.

'Just what I wanted,' Lotte said. Bringing her left hand up as if to take the milk, she held the knife in her right hand, and as Fern turned her body fully to pass over the glass, Lotte leapt forward, plunging the knife into her chest with all the force she could muster.

The knife did not go in smoothly. There was resistance, as if she'd struck bone, and an odd sort of scraping noise before Fern's surprised shriek drowned it and the glass of milk clattered to the floor. Fern staggered backwards towards the sink under the window, the knife embedded in her chest. Blood was seeping out, staining her cream sweater.

Howard rushed to his wife. 'What have you done?' he yelled at Lotte.

Lotte was unable to move, transfixed with horror that she'd actually stabbed another human being. It was only when Fern's voice rasped out, demanding that Howard must get Lotte, that she came to her senses.

The table was between her and them, and Lotte looked around wildly for another weapon, but there was nothing suitable within reach. Howard was coming round the table, his thin face grim with determination and hatred. Lotte dodged the other way, picked up a used coffee pot and threw it at him. It caught him on the forehead, making him lurch back, and the still-warm coffee ran down his face.

'You bitch,' he yelled as he wiped away coffee grounds from his face, and came after her looking even more savage now.

She dodged him several more times, going to the right when he went to the left, then to the left when he went right. She was trying to give herself thinking time, for Fern had pulled the knife out of her chest and was holding on to the wound, with blood coming through her fingers. She was swaying, and maybe in a few minutes she'd pass out or even die.

'See to her, you bastard,' Lotte hissed at him, willing him to obey her and give her the chance to get out through the front door.

'You won't get away,' Howard threw back at her. 'I've got the keys.'

Fern didn't just keel over as Lotte had always imagined anyone mortally wounded would do. She just slowly sank down on to a chair. 'Help me, honey,' she bleated out, her face drained of all colour. 'Help me!'

'Help you?' Lotte roared back at her. 'You've put me through hell, stolen my baby and let it die, and intended to kill me too! I want you to die!'

Howard stopped trying to catch Lotte and ran to his wife, helping her down on to the kitchen floor. Lotte ran for the front door, but as expected it was locked and the key missing. She ran to the back door but that was the same, then into the lounge to try the windows. They too were locked as they always were. She picked up a heavy candlestick on the mantelpiece and struck the window with it, but amazingly, the glass didn't break.

She was just backing up to take a run at the window

when Howard came in behind her and caught hold of the candlestick in her hand.

'That'll do,' he said. 'You've done enough damage for one night.'

His cheeks were wet with tears and he was shaking, and she surmised that Fern had died.

'Is she dead?' She had to have it confirmed.

He nodded and looked so utterly devastated that Lotte felt unable to say anything spiteful.

'Let me go now,' she said. 'If you lock me up again you'll just be getting in deeper and deeper. I killed her after all, and we can tell the police everything else was Fern's doing.'

He looked at her long and hard for some time. Lotte could see he was really scared, and that he didn't know what to do any more. Fern had always been the strong one, the organizer and the boss; Howard's role had been mainly supportive.

'I can help you,' Lotte wheedled. 'This is awful but we can get out of it if we keep our heads and work together. We have to do something: either ring the police and tell them what happened, or get rid of her body. You can't leave her lying in the kitchen. And what did you do with the baby's body?'

He didn't answer, he couldn't even look directly at her, and Lotte sensed she was right in thinking that he and Fern had intended to dispose of both her and the baby together tonight.

Just the thought of that made Lotte want to reach

out for something heavy and dash his brains out, but even though he was thin he was wiry and much stronger than she was and it could end up with her brains being spilled out.

'You aren't a bad man, Howard,' she said, putting her hands on his arm. 'I know it was all Fern pushing for this – she was crazy! If you ring the police now I'll tell them that. We could even say you were away on business for much of the time and didn't know what was going on.'

All at once his eyes flashed dangerously. 'It was you who made all this happen,' he snarled at her. 'You cast a spell over my Fern and you did your best to drive a wedge between us.'

'I didn't,' Lotte said, her stomach churning with fear because he looked so savage.

'Oh, but you did,' he said. 'You fooled Fern into believing you'd willingly have a baby for us, but you just wanted me, didn't you?'

'Want you?' Lotte couldn't help but look and sound scornful as the idea was so preposterous. 'I had to be drugged, starved and kept prisoner before I submitted to you.'

All at once he grabbed her hands and yanked them behind her back. She screamed out and tried to fight him off but his hands were like steel vices. He dragged her by both her hands back to the hall, snatched up a length of rope hanging on a peg by the door, and secured her hands behind her back.

'Stop screaming or I'll gag you,' he said, and pushing her forcefully on to the hall chair, he used another length of rope to tie her ankles.

He left her for just a couple of seconds and came back with a pair of kitchen scissors in his hands. He caught hold of a clump of her hair and cut it, then another and another, going all over her head until her blonde hair lay thick on the floor all around the chair. His breath was rasping as he did so, and it seemed to her that there was some kind of symbolism in this act, though she didn't understand what.

Lotte was too scared to say anything. She knew by the two ready prepared lengths of rope that he and Fern had planned what they were going to do with her well in advance. But Howard hadn't expected to have to do it alone; he was clearly completely unbalanced by Fern's death and the knowledge that now he'd have to get rid of her body too. Lotte decided to remain silent so he didn't gag her. She might need her voice later.

Once she was secured, Howard went into the kitchen, and although Lotte couldn't see more than a few feet into the room she heard him pour himself a drink. She guessed it was brandy to calm his nerves – he gulped it down like a man dying of thirst. A little later she heard him open the cupboard by the back door. She guessed by the crackling sound that he was getting out the picnic blanket with a waterproof backing, intending to wrap Fern's body in it.

In the next ten minutes she heard the glugging of

drink, sobbing, sniffing and rustling as he wrapped his wife up. But Lotte's mind was on how she could undo her hands. She'd seen hundreds of films where rope was cut by a shard of glass, even a rusty nail, but such things didn't lie around waiting to be discovered. If she tried to shuffle or hop along the passage to find something, Howard would hear her.

She fumbled with the rope and found it wasn't very tight; she thought with a bit of wriggling she might be able to get free. But it seemed wiser to leave her hands tied until he put her in the car.

When he came back into the hall his eyes were red and puffy from crying. She could smell brandy on his breath and he had blood all over his trousers and shirt.

He looked down at her and his lip curled back like a savage dog's. 'We had it all until you came along,' he snarled at her. 'I always knew you'd be trouble, but you bewitched her with your wide blue eyes and your little girl looks. I hate you!'

She wanted to hurl abuse back at him, to tell him he was a weak pervert, dominated by a ruthless, cruel woman, but she knew it wasn't advisable to antagonize him any further.

He gagged her before unlocking the front door and hauled her outside. To her surprise his car wasn't there, only a big, dark-coloured van. She supposed he must have bought or hired it in the last couple of days because she hadn't seen it before. It was too dark now to tell the exact colour, or what make of van it was, and when he opened the back doors to shove her in, she could see nothing, but there was a faint smell of fish.

He bundled her in roughly, and slammed the doors. Once he had returned to the house, Lotte tried loosening her hands. But it wasn't as easy as she'd expected; as she moved one hand the rope just tightened round the other, and now she felt sick with terror because she couldn't get free.

As her eyes grew used to the darkness she could see a small bundle, around fifteen inches long and six or seven inches thick, near her. Tears sprang up for she knew it was her baby. She'd never been allowed to hold her in her arms and now they were going to share the same grave.

Howard came back then, carrying Fern wrapped up and secured with rope. He put her in a great deal more carefully than he had Lotte and she saw he was still crying.

Just a few minutes after leaving the house the van bumped over rough ground and Lotte realized they must be on the hard, the area above the waterline at West Itchenor where Howard's boat was moored. Clearly he was planning to load her and Fern on to the boat, then park his van elsewhere. Once the tide had come right in, he would sail out into the harbour and on out to the open sea. She realized then that the little blue book he'd been looking at so intently earlier was the tide times. She was glad then that she'd stabbed the woman he loved, and she hoped he would have a miserable, lonely life and a terrible, painful death. Someone so cold-blooded deserved to suffer. And even if the thought of that didn't make her any less terrified, it justified her killing Fern.

As she lay there waiting for the moment when he'd come and haul her out on to the boat, it struck her that he was taking a very big risk. It might be dark but it was only about nine in the evening, and people must be about and would see him. But then, she'd never been down here at this time of night, so for all she knew there could be many men loading up their boats for fishing trips and suchlike, and what Howard was doing wouldn't look suspicious.

The back door of the van was flung open and Lotte was hauled out by her feet and slung over his shoulder, quickly followed by a blanket to hide her and cut off her view. He walked only a few steps over stones, wheezing with the effort, then climbed up four or five steps on to a jetty. Dangling down his back, Lotte could see water between the gaps in the planks, but within a few yards he jumped on to his boat, which rocked beneath them.

She was thrown into the tiny cabin. It was a small drop, no more than three feet, but she banged her head, jarred her whole back, and a pain shot through her elbow.

By the time Howard returned, grunting and wheezing under the weight of Fern who was perhaps three stone heavier than Lotte, she was beside herself with terror, for she'd again attempted to get her hands untied and failed.

Howard eased his wife's body in with care, stopping to rest and get his breath back. Lotte was so close to Fern on the floor of the cabin that she could smell her blood, mingled with Opium, the perfume she always wore, and it made her feel sick.

Howard went off and briefly came back on board once more, presumably with the baby's body, but he didn't put it in the cabin with them. Lotte felt the boat lurch as he jumped off again, and then heard the sound of the van being driven away.

Desperation made her go all out to get free, but even though she almost stripped the skin from the back of her hands pulling them against the rope, she couldn't release them. She tried to bang her tied feet on the cabin floor in the hope that someone would hear the sound, and she grunted against the gag too, but it was to no avail. The tide was coming in fast, she could hear the slap of waves against the hull, and now she understood the phrase 'staring death in the face', for she could see absolutely no way of escape.

It was some time before Howard returned, perhaps an hour, during which Lotte had endured cramp in her legs and pins and needles in her arms and she felt she might suffocate with the gag. He took no more than a cursory look into the cabin, but even so she got a strong whiff of drink and wondered if he'd been into the pub in his bloodstained clothes, or had gone home. He slammed the cabin door and started up the engine.

Lotte's cotton dress and cardigan wouldn't have been

warm enough at night on land. But once they were out on open water she was freezing. Lying there shivering, she strained her ears, hoping to hear other craft, but there was nothing close by.

She knew when they'd left the harbour for the swell increased dramatically. All she could see was a square of night sky though the glass panel on the cabin door, and now and again spray flicking up over the stern too. Howard was there, steering the boat, but he was to the right of her line of vision. She wondered how far he was going to go before he threw her overboard.

Time had ceased to have any meaning. It felt as though she'd been in the boat for hours, but she guessed it was probably little more than two, when he cut the engine.

The cabin door opened and in he came to drag her out by the shoulders.

'Calm down,' he snapped at her as she bucked and struggled. 'There's nothing to gain by doing that.'

He hoisted her up to sit her on the side of the boat, and to her amazement cut the rope at her ankles with a penknife.

'I'm not going to drop you in tied up,' he said, blasting brandy fumes in her face. 'They'll think you took your own life when they find your body. I'm putting the baby in with you too.'

Then he cut the rope on her wrists, and finally removed the gag.

'I regret the day we rescued you from that man in South America,' he said, grabbing hold of her chin and yanking it so she had to look at him. Dark as it was, she could see a maniacal gleam in his eyes, and his face was contorted with hatred. 'We should have stood and watched him kill you. You destroyed everything I had with my Fern. We were sweethearts right from kids, there was never anyone else for either of us. Now you've killed her, and I'm all alone. I can't even give her a Christian burial – I'll have to weigh her down so she's never found. You did that to me!'

'I'm sorry she's gone, but don't do this, please,' Lotte whimpered.

He didn't answer, just let go of her chin, pushed her in the chest and suddenly she was in the sea. It was such a shock, and so cold she felt her heart might stop. But she managed to tread water and rub the water from her eyes, and she saw him standing on the boat grinning down at her, holding something in his hands.

'You said you wanted to hold it!' he said, and with a chilling laugh he pulled the covers from the bundle to reveal her baby, dressed in white. 'Here you are, catch!' he shouted, and hurled her at Lotte.

Lotte was too horrified to react for a minute. It was only when Howard started up the boat again and headed on further out to sea that she realized the baby was right in front of her. She looked perfect, just very pale, stiff and cold, dressed in a white babygro. Lotte caught her up in her arms as she trod water and held her tightly. She was so icy cold Fern must have put her in the freezer.

'I'm so sorry, little one,' she whispered, almost choking

on her tears. 'Forgive my part in this. I wish I could've protected you.'

The wash from the boat went right over her head and swept the baby from her arms. By the time she'd righted herself and spat out the salt water she'd swallowed, she could no longer see her. 'God bless!' she cried out into the inky darkness.

Chapter Sixteen

'How far were you from the shore?' Dale asked in awed tones. She was absolutely stunned by Lotte's story. While she knew from the facts that Lotte had either been thrown into the sea, or had jumped of her own accord, she hadn't actually considered what that might entail, or even how it had come about. But even more disturbing was that Lotte had killed Fern.

Dale couldn't imagine anyone less likely than Lotte to stab another human being, she was far too docile and kind, and rarely moved to anger. It kind of proved that anyone could do anything if pushed hard enough. Yet awful as it was to think she had been forced to kill Fern, the image of her baby being thrown into the sea with her was heartbreaking and sickening. Dale thought she would be capable of killing Howard with her own bare hands for that appalling deed.

'How far from the shore? I don't know, distances are deceptive at night, especially at sea,' Lotte replied. 'I could see lights very clearly, I thought it was just a quick swim away, but the shore never seemed to get closer. I suppose I was being swept along sideways with the current.'

'But you must've been in there for hours! How did you survive?'

'Sheer determination, I presume.' Lotte shrugged. 'I can remember at the start I was so furious at Howard's evilness that I felt I had to reach someone to tell them about it. But I couldn't really swim, it was too rough. I was just bobbing around like a cork in the water, letting it take me where it pleased. But I think that anger kept me from giving up.'

'You must have been terrified,' Dale said in a small voice.

'Not exactly. I was terrified in the house, the van and the boat, but that was because I didn't know what was going to happen to me. But out there in the sea I felt I was in control. I made myself forget how cold I was, and keep moving towards the lights. I knew if I did start to think I was too tired to move then I would drown. So I kept my mind on what Howard and Fern had done to me and vowed I would expose them.'

Lotte shuddered as she recalled that cold which struck right through to her innards, making it hard to move her arms and legs. She wasn't going to tell Dale, but much of the time she couldn't see the lights on the shore because the waves were too big. As they kept rolling over her, she had to force herself to make a concerted effort to ride with them. The sea and the sky were both black as ink, there was no moon and scarcely any stars either. It was the loneliest she'd ever been, as though she was the only surviving person on the planet. Yet even worse was the knowledge that her baby was being sucked down into the depths. That was like a physical pain which was stronger even than the intense cold.

'Do you remember getting to the beach?' Dale asked.

Lotte shook her head. 'I do remember seeing the first lights of dawn in the sky, which gave me hope that someone would spot me and rescue me. But I think I must have been slipping in and out of consciousness then, and the waves just washed me along. I do remember the scrape of shingle beneath me, but that was only fleeting.'

The two girls sat in silence on the bed for some time.

'It will be different this time when the men come for us,' Dale said at length, her voice shaking with fear. 'They aren't going to make us drinks like Fern did for you, and you can't stab anyone with a Stanley knife, the blade isn't long enough to do more than cut skin.'

'But then they won't want to kill us,' Lotte said soothingly, putting her arms around her friend because she sensed she was about to go into a panic attack. She didn't truly believe the men wouldn't kill them, but she felt she had to be positive for Dale's sake. 'They might even refuse Howard if he tells them that's what he wants. So he'll have to come here himself. Between us we can handle him.'

'You think so?' Dale asked. 'I wonder where he is right now? And what he did with Fern's body.'

'I've got a feeling he's somewhere close by,' Lotte replied. 'Looking back, I think it was him who tried to strangle me in hospital. Funny that seeing him didn't immediately jog my memory, but then I was still pretty out of it during those first few days in hospital.'

'You seemed to rally round after meeting your rescuer,' Dale pointed out.

'Mmmm,' Lotte murmured.

'Do you like him?'

'Yes, very much, in fact David's a very good reason to get out of here alive,' Lotte said. 'But will he be put off me when he finds out I killed Fern?'

'I think it will make him have more respect for you, babe,' Dale said with a watery smile, the first one of the day. 'I know I won't be pushing you around any more, not now I know what you're capable of!'

'You never did push me around, just the odd nudge,' Lotte laughed. 'Now, shall we both do some shouting out the window?'

The sea and sky had turned a sullen grey in the rain and the footpath along the edge of the shore from Itchenor towards West Wittering was getting very muddy.

'I don't know why he sent us this way, there's no one about,' Peggy Wainwright said testily to Kim Moore. 'And in this rain too!'

When the two sets of parents met up with the boys at Itchenor, David suggested the two women took the footpath, and talked to any dog walkers or hikers they met. It hadn't been raining then, though it was overcast, but they both had raincoats and sturdy shoes. Carrina went with her father and Ted Wainwright.

336

'A drop of rain won't hurt us, and the whole point of sending us along here is because it's a regular route for dog walkers and hikers,' Kim pointed out. 'They are the sort of people who would probably remember anything out of the ordinary.'

At that moment, a middle-aged couple walking their golden Labrador came along the path. Kim stopped them to show pictures of Lotte and Dale and explained what danger they were in.

Five minutes later the couple walked on. They hadn't seen or heard anything unusual.

'They didn't even know what day of the week it was, much less remember anything they'd seen in the past,' Peggy said waspishly. 'And my feet are beginning to hurt.'

Kim stopped dead, put her hands on her hips and turned to Peggy. 'You are a truly remarkable woman,' she said, her voice dripping with sarcasm. 'I doubt there's another mother in the whole of England with as little concern for her daughter. I would walk with bare feet on red-hot coals to find Dale, but you don't even want to walk along a pleasant footpath.'

'I think this kind of thing is better left to the police,' Peggy responded, clutching her big navy-blue plastic handbag to her chest. 'Why would anyone tell us anything?'

'Because they feel for us?' Kim suggested. 'Because most people actually want to help with something like this? Has it even occurred to you that your daughter may already be dead? Do you care one way or the other?'

'Now, look here!' Peggy replied with indignation. 'Of course I care.'

'Well, damn well show you do then,' Kim snapped. 'And keep on walking till your feet bleed, without complaining.'

Kim knew David had put her with Peggy in the hope that she might defrost the woman, but she didn't have an iced-up heart, it was made of granite. Everything Peggy had said today proved she actually felt she was right to have no time for Lotte. Kim might have understood such an attitude if Lotte had been responsible in some way for Fleur's death, or indeed done something terrible later on, but there was absolutely no excuse for the woman's behaviour. The most surprising thing in all this was that by all accounts Lotte had turned out to be such a good, kind person despite the lack of love shown to her. Kim thought she could very well have turned to drink or drugs or had children and ill-treated them the way she had been.

David and the other boys had been elated when they met up with them because at last the police really were pulling out all the stops to find the girls. On the drive from Brighton they'd been astounded by the huge number of police cars around, and it seemed reinforcements had been called in from all over Sussex and Hampshire. Right now they were crawling all over Selsey, Chichester and on both sides of the harbour. There had been another appeal for information on the television last night and today the story was front-page news in all the nationals. As David had pointed out, there couldn't be anyone left in England who didn't know about Lotte and Dale.

David had received a call from DI Bryan that morning to say the American police had drawn a blank in finding the Mr and Mrs Ramsden who had flown back to New York on 16 March 2002, immediately after the cruise ship docked at Southampton. The cruise company had given them the couple's home address in Long Island, but it was a false one. A banker had lived there for twelve years with his wife and children. It seemed the Ramsdens had booked and paid for the cruise while in London some six months before embarking, and they had picked up their tickets from the cruise offices too, so no correspondence had to be sent to Long Island. Howard had settled his bar bill on the ship with cash, so they were unable to track him with his credit card either.

Bryan was now waiting on details of all passengers flying from New York to London during the week after 16 March, as it seemed likely the Ramsdens returned to England almost immediately under another name. Meanwhile, police officers with photographs of the Ramsdens were calling on sailing clubs, ship's chandlers, supermarkets, chemists and even estate agents in the area in the hope that someone would recognize them and know the name they were using here and where they were living.

A police officer had brought some of these leaflets with pictures of the Ramsdens over to David for him and his party to show around. David just wished they could have had them with them on the previous day, as they might have had a better response from people they called on.

'There is something far bigger behind this than just abducting Lotte,' Bryan told David in a very grave manner. 'I think we'll find the identity of Ramsden is just a throwaway one for holidays and the like as they don't appear to have a credit card in that name. In my experience people who live with dual and treble identities are almost always serial criminals. The identity they used to fly back here from the States is probably their main one, and we should be able to track them better once we know it. They might have bought property here in that name, maybe even run some sort of legitimate business. But I'll ring you when I have more news.'

By seven that evening, when the group met back at the pub in Itchenor to compare notes, they were all disheartened and damp with the rain. Between them, including Peggy Wainwright who was grumbling about her sore feet, they had called at every house in the village and the surrounding area down to West Wittering, and every single person out walking had been spoken to. All without producing one lead.

Of course, there were dozens of houses where no

one answered the door, and possibly some of the people they did talk to would remember something later. Five people thought they had seen Fern before, but couldn't remember where. No one remembered Howard at all.

'It was just a wild goose chase,' Peggy said dismissively as she downed a large gin and tonic. 'The girls obviously aren't around here. I didn't expect they would be. It's far too upmarket an area for such carrying-on!'

Scott and David exchanged glances – they were both looking forward to the moment when Peggy and her husband went home. Ted was OK, he'd gone off with Clarke and Carrina and willingly walked miles without complaint as they knocked on doors. But both Scott and David felt he ought to be a real man and stick up for his daughter.

Kim looked as if she was going to dissolve into tears at any minute. Clarke was sitting next to her, holding her hand and talking to her in a low voice, no doubt trying to comfort her by saying that any minute the police could have some new evidence. Carrina looked desperately sad and troubled, and kept looking to her parents as if willing them to find a happy solution to all this. Simon and Adam looked worn down too. It had been a long and fruitless day for everyone.

'I think you should all go home now,' David said. 'We can't do any more tonight, and to be honest I'm not sure if there is *anything* more we can do.'

A little buzz of conversation went around the table, Simon suggesting other villages, Adam asking if they should look as far away as Southsea. Once again, Peggy said they should leave the police to find the girls and looked accusingly at Kim and Clarke as if they'd dragged her into something which had nothing to do with her.

Clarke got up first. 'I think today has been very hard for Kim and Carrina. I'm taking them back to the hotel now.' He looked across at Ted and Peggy. 'Are you ready? I'll drop you off.'

Kim stood up, her face pale and drawn. 'Can I just thank you all,' she said in a low voice. 'Clarke and I appreciate so much that you are all trying so hard to find the girls. Maybe tomorrow there will be good news!'

They left the bar just a few moments later, Peggy and Ted behind them, with Peggy still wittering on about her sore feet.

'I don't envy Kim having to put up with that harridan in the car with her all the way to Brighton,' Adam said.

'Kim admitted to me she nearly decked the woman,' Simon said. 'I don't actually believe Lotte is Peggy's daughter.'

Adam laughed mirthlessly. 'Surely no one would be cruel enough to leave a baby on her doorstep?'

Simon smiled. 'Oh, she belongs to Ted all right; his eyes are the same as Lotte's and he's got her gentle way. I think he got two women pregnant at the same time and switched the babies at birth.'

Adam grinned. 'I'd forgive any man for screwing around with a wife like that.'

David and Scott smiled at this exchange between Simon and Adam. They were all overwrought and Kim and Clarke's presence today had made them all even more tense and afraid. It was good to see some of that tension disperse with a joke.

'I don't think there's much to be gained by coming out again tomorrow,' David said with a sigh. 'Maybe you'd better both get back to work. And you too, Scott,' he added.

David knew all three were willing to go on searching for as long as it took, but their jobs would be at risk if they didn't get back, and now the police were investigating fully, they weren't really needed and might even be in the way. As he glanced at their faces he sensed a faint suggestion of relief, though Adam was quick to suggest that if the girls hadn't been found by Sunday, perhaps they could widen their search.

'What about you then, David?' Scott asked.

'Well, I'm going to go back to the houses we got no reply at earlier in the day,' he said. 'And anywhere there's still no answer, I'm going to get the police to check up on who lives there.'

'You want us to help?' Simon asked.

David shook his head. 'No, I can do this alone, and you've got a long drive home. Just drop Scott at my house on the way so he can pick up his car.'

After they had said goodbye and driven off, David set off up the road, away from the harbour, to knock on doors. With some dismay he suddenly realized that he could very well have called at the place the girls were being held, or had been held, already today.

He didn't know why this hadn't occurred to him before, but the fact of the matter was, if the person who answered the door was pleasant and tried to be helpful, he and the others would immediately assume they were good guys. So basically all they had done in the last few days was a kind of canvassing job, letting people know about the case. They hadn't really done anything to find the girls.

'You could go crazy thinking that way,' he murmured to himself, remembering that he had after all been asking neighbours to keep an eye on one another, and report anything suspicious. Then there was Margaret Foster in Birdham; it was she who described the woman with Lotte, and that led the investigation to Fern Ramsden. But he could see he'd been somewhat naive to imagine guilt showed up in people's faces.

He looked at his watch. It was half past seven, which meant he had just two hours at most to knock on doors without disturbing people. He thought too that he ought to try to get into the mindset of the people holding the girls, for that would help him to know what to look for.

'They'll be jittery with so many police around,' he murmured to himself.

He thought that it was very likely they intended to dispose of the girls at sea. Lotte might have survived before, but that was a real fluke, and provided the victim was killed first and weighted down, it did appear to be the easiest way to dispose of a body. Once out at sea in the dark there was little chance of being observed; the only danger period would be getting the girls on to the boat.

At four of the houses he was making return calls to, the owners were in this time. Each of them knew the story of the girls who'd been abducted, though none of them believed they could be held here in their village.

When shown pictures of the girls and then Fern and Howard, all of them took a second, much closer look at Fern, as if she initially looked familiar, but then said they didn't think they'd seen her.

This had happened a few times during the day too, and as David walked on up the road to the next house he mused on this, wondering if it could be that Fern's hairstyle or even the colour was different now. She was a striking-looking woman, but the picture from the cruise company was a particularly glamorous shot of her in evening dress, with titian wavy hair loose on her bare shoulders, and wearing a diamond necklace. If she'd had her hair tied back, or she'd even worn a hat, she'd be much less memorable.

He felt very flat and disheartened, and now he wished he'd gone back with Scott and had a couple of pints. He wondered too if he was a fool getting hung up on a girl he hardly knew. When he'd phoned home and told his parents about her they'd been a bit chilly, as though they thought he shouldn't get involved.

But how could he not get involved? He'd found her on the beach, stopped that guy from throttling her, and when he'd kissed her at Simon's flat he'd felt there were fireworks going off in his head. It was like she was meant for him.

Just as he was on the point of turning round and walking back to where he'd parked his car by the pub, around a hundred yards ahead of him, on the other side of the road, he saw a blue van coming out of a drive. His heart quickened, for it was the first blue one he'd spotted since being told one was seen waiting in the alleyway by Simon's flat. Only today he had pointed out to Scott the comparative rarity of them.

The van was turning his way, going down towards the harbour, and David stood at the kerb as if waiting to cross the road. As the car passed he got a fleeting look at the driver, and to his astonishment he thought it was the same man he'd chased at the hospital.

A white-hot flush of excitement washed over him. He couldn't be certain of course, after all he'd only seen that man's face for the briefest of moments when he'd turned from throttling Lotte as David came into the room. It could just be wishful thinking.

But put this man in a blue van near the harbour and it suddenly seemed very likely.

He pulled the photograph of Howard Ramsden from his folder and studied it closely. Howard was clean-shaven, elegant, polished, wearing a dinner jacket and bow-tie, and with very well-cut hair. At first glance he had nothing in common with the man David had just seen, except they were both slender with thin faces, but if he was to add longer hair to the man in the picture, some stubble on the chin and ordinary clothes, it could be the same man.

David got out his phone to ring Bryan, but had second thoughts and decided to check out the house the man had come from first.

He was confused when he saw the narrow drive with ten-foot-high hedges on both sides. He thought the van was coming from the grounds of the huge, half-timbered cottage on his left where he'd called that morning. But the drive didn't belong to that house or to the house on the right; it clearly led to another house altogether which he hadn't realized was there earlier.

He felt strangely nervous walking up the gravelled drive. It felt like trespassing, because it was so enclosed by hedges, but as he walked and saw the house at the end of it, he stopped short in surprise.

It was one of the ugliest houses he'd ever seen, and he wondered if the neighbours had purposely grown their hedges so high to hide it. It reminded him of the house in *Hatter's Castle*, a creaky old film based on the book by A. J. Cronin. The crenellations around the top, the narrow windows and the awful grey stone gave it a bizarre appearance, like a mock castle. It might have looked at home in Scotland, but certainly not in a pretty Sussex village.

He rang the bell several times but no one answered. He peered in through the front windows. There were vertical blinds but they hadn't been shut completely and he could see one room was a study or office with filing cabinets and a desk, the other was a lounge. There was nothing very remarkable about either room, except that the decor was sombre and dark.

David stood with his back to the front door for a moment, looking at the narrow driveway which led into the property. It was barely seven feet wide and about twenty yards long before it opened up to an oblong plot of land perhaps twenty-two yards wide on which the house was built. The high hedges continued right around the plot. It was apparent that the owner of the house on his left had sold some of his land for this house to be built, though it beggared belief that the buyer had managed to get planning permission for such a monstrosity. But it was probably built in the late Thirties when planning laws were very lax.

Both houses on either side were so far away that David could only see the top of their roofs above the hedges. This ought to have given the house a comfortingly private feel, and if the architect had had any imagination it could have been a deliciously secret hideaway. But instead, austere was the word which sprang to David's mind. No money had been wasted on frivolity, just a gravel drive and then a stone-built raised flower bed to separate the drive from the rest of the front garden which was just concrete slabs.

There were plants in the raised bed, but it looked uncared for and full of weeds. He walked to the left-hand side of the house and saw there was a side gate to the back garden set in a wall. The gate was wood, some seven feet high, with a great deal of barbed wire fastened to the door frame and across the wall. This seemed a case of security over-egging as the house looked forbidding enough on its own.

For a minute or two he considered braving the barbed wire just to take a look at the back of the house, but it was nearly dark, and if he got caught he might be charged with breaking and entering. He would ring Bryan and tell him about it as he walked back to his car.

Howard Ramsden was severely rattled as he drove away from his house. Ever since that little bitch stabbed Fern he hadn't had a moment's peace of mind and things were getting worse every day. He so much regretted not chucking her in the sea tied up and heavily weighted. No one had missed her in a year and no one cared about her, and if she hadn't been found alive by now she would have been entirely forgotten by everyone who ever knew her. But Fern had felt very strongly that her death should look like a simple suicide by drowning and that her body would be found with that of the baby. Even though Fern was dead, he had felt compelled to honour her wishes.

Of course, he had never imagined that Lotte would have a chance of surviving. She was so small, thin and weak, a wisp of a girl that he hadn't even expected could swim. But even a really strong swimmer in robust health would be unlikely to get to the shore from where he pushed her in for the water was icy so early in the year.

Yet somehow she managed to survive, and her face was splashed across the papers and on the television news. He couldn't take the chance that she might recover her memory, there was too much at stake, so instead he took the risk of going to the hospital to throttle her.

Again he was thwarted, by some young man bringing flowers for her. It was fortunate he'd had the presence of mind to park his car outside the hospital grounds and knew of a short cut through a hole in the fence to get out unseen. But it was a close shave.

From then on his life had been a living nightmare, on edge, unable to sleep at night, just waiting for the police to come knocking on the door. Fern had always said he didn't think things through, though how could she claim that when if it hadn't been for her getting all wound up in Lotte, he wouldn't have got into this mess?

Jarvis, an old friend and business partner, put him in touch with the two men who found out where Lotte was and grabbed her. Jarvis had been his and Fern's distributor fifteen years before when they had been smuggling heroin from South America into Holland. Cruise ships were a good cover; everyone knew that only middle-aged people who wanted to see the world in safe, sanitized, bite-sized pieces went on them, and he and Fern fitted in perfectly, playing up the Born Again Christian act, which was an excellent way of keeping other people at a distance. They chose a South American-bound ship which sailed out of Rotterdam.

Most of the passengers would join an organized bus tour when they got to any port, particularly in Colombia, for they found the dirt, noise, overcrowding and higher than average quota of beggars, ruffians and pickpockets too intimidating. They'd be gone for some six hours seeing mountains, forests, waterfalls and pretty touristy villages, returning to the ship laden with handmade souvenirs, believing they'd experienced Colombia.

But he and Fern would cry off, saying they wanted to visit the churches. They would slip away to meet their contact and exchange American dollars for the goods, often concealed in some kind of artefact.

Jarvis had been based near Rotterdam then, and it had been a breeze going through Customs with bags stuffed with crummy trophies from every port of call. The Customs men were looking out for young, poor smugglers, not wealthy cruisers wearing designer clothes and carrying bags of stuff guaranteed to grace the windows of a charity shop within a month. They certainly weren't interested in checking every last tacky hand-carved monkey, parrot or stationery box that passed by them.

Jarvis had given up the heroin business after a close shave with the law and moved to Southampton to open a bar. He was part of the reason Howard and Fern had bought a house near Chichester harbour, for they liked and trusted him and intended to carry on working with him on some project or other.

As it turned out, they never did work together again, for Jarvis had his own interests, namely providing muscle for anyone who needed it, and they were doing just fine with the lucrative adoption business.

But they carried on cruising a couple of times a year, for the ships were full of promiscuous girls who'd signed on as waitresses and stewardesses so they could see the world. These girls often became pregnant and were usually very unhappy about it. Fern didn't need to do anything more than act sympathetic and give the girls a number for them to call her for a 'chat' when their contract was up. Two out of every five girls did ring her, and one could usually be counted on to go for the service they were offering.

Much as Howard trusted Jarvis, when he contacted him and asked for help, he didn't tell him that Fern was dead. Somehow he doubted the man would help him without her around. He just told him the girl found on the beach had enough information on him, Fern, and Jarvis too, to get them all put away for life and she had to be captured.

The men wouldn't use their own transport so he had to buy this van and lend it to them, but he hadn't for one moment expected them to snatch the other girl too. Once they'd dumped the girls in his house they took their fee and said they wanted nothing more to do with it, however much money he offered. Even Jarvis said he thought Howard had only wanted to scare the girl, and if he'd known killing was the plan he wouldn't have got involved.

So Howard was well and truly up shit creek. He was fairly sure Jarvis wouldn't grass him up, but he wouldn't lift a finger to help. He couldn't let the girls go because they would expose him. He couldn't just let them starve to death in the house either because he wanted to sell it and get the hell out of England. And now, before he'd been able to come up with a foolproof plan, the police were crawling over the entire area.

He had gone to the house this evening to check the little window. Lotte had broken it the time before, and he'd had to board it up from the outside in case someone heard her yelling.

He'd put the house on the market after he'd dumped Lotte and Fern at sea. It had taken a whole day to clean the kitchen and get rid of every trace of Fern's blood, and another to put new glass in the basement window and make sure the room was spotless.

But he had to postpone viewings of the house once he'd got the two girls in the basement. When Lotte was there alone it was doubtful her voice would be heard from that window because of where it was situated. But with two of them yelling out of it they might very well be heard.

As expected, they had smashed it out, and his ears were still ringing with all the abuse the girls had flung at him. He'd had to kneel in the rain to fix the boards back on and they hadn't let up for even one minute.

He didn't actually mind being called a pervert or a cold-blooded killer, it was the things Lotte said about Fern which got to him. She said he'd been Fern's puppet and asked if he knew that she was having it off with two of the officers on the cruise ship. She implied Fern was bisexual too and that was why she wanted Lotte with them. She even said Fern had told her he was useless in bed, and that she'd had dozens of affairs because he couldn't satisfy her. Then Lotte suggested he came inside and went to bed with both her and Dale and found out what real women were like.

It had been tempting, for they were both so fresh, young and pretty, even though he knew it was just a ploy to get him down there in the room with them so they could overpower him and escape. He was both shocked and stimulated by some of the things meek little Lotte had said she'd do to him. A big part of him wanted to believe she meant it.

But the stuff she said about Fern hurt, for he couldn't be certain she was lying. Fern had been a remarkably beautiful woman with a voluptuous body and any man would want her. He knew there had been two officers on the last cruise who flirted with her, and she admitted to having fantasies about making love to women. He had often felt, too, that he didn't fully satisfy her.

Had Fern confided in Lotte? Was this whole thing about having the baby some plan of Fern's to oust him and have Lotte as her partner?

The first time he had sex with Lotte, with Fern right there watching and getting turned on, was the most thrilling experience of his life. He had wanted it again and again, but Lotte got pregnant almost immediately and that ended it. He had the idea that Fern was jealous because she was afraid he preferred Lotte to her, but maybe she was jealous that he got to make love to Lotte?

She needn't have worried. To him, Lotte was just another common tart, even if she was pretty. Fern was his whole world, without her he felt lost, scared and worthless. He kept telling himself that he would be OK once he got back to the States – today he'd even been tempted to jump on the next plane immediately and forget everything that had happened here.

But the house was worth at least two hundred thousand, and he owned it free and clear. People said it was ugly, and while he and Fern had never agreed with that – they loved its quaintness – a new owner could tear it down and rebuild it. Howard couldn't bear to walk away and lose so much money. So he had to get the girls out of there. It would have to be real quick, for the police were everywhere and people in the village had been alerted so they were all looking for anything suspicious.

He parked his van some distance from the harbour and walked the rest of the way past the pub to the shore to see if there were any police down there. He was getting nervous about the van now it had been mentioned in the press that the police were looking for a blue van; he wished he'd got a white one, they were really common.

The sun was setting and it had turned the water a beautiful pink and mauve. It had stopped raining at last, and as he looked across the harbour towards Bosham with its pretty old cottages and the square tower of the church, the beauty of the scene made Howard feel quite emotional.

It had been this view which made Fern and him look for a house here. They had seen this place as a sanctuary, a place where they would always be safe, no matter how hot it got for them back in the States. They had their boat, each other and enough money never to have to worry again. They didn't socialize with anyone, they didn't need anyone, or so he had thought until Fern got this idea about having a baby of their own.

There were many people around, including four policemen stopping to question them. In fact Howard could sense a kind of buzz in the air as if everyone was expecting some kind of drama very soon. His boat was bobbing temptingly on its mooring, but as much as he wished he could just go out on it and forget everything, he knew he couldn't.

He realized he couldn't possibly use the boat to get

rid of the girls now, not in the middle of the night or anytime in the near future. He'd be stopped the moment he drove anywhere near the water's edge. So it would have to be plan B. And he needed to implement it now before the police found him and his house.

Chapter Seventeen

'He's come back!' Lotte hissed when she heard footsteps up in the hall above them.

Dale was on top of the wardrobe, trying to push the boards off the outside of the window. 'What do we do?' she whispered.

'Get down off there.' Lotte beckoned with her hands. 'You go into the bathroom and if he comes down here you pretend to be unconscious. I need to get him to relax his guard for a moment, so I'll get all hysterical about you. As he starts to walk towards the bathroom to see you, I'll jump on him with the Stanley knife.'

'Wouldn't it be better if you ran for help?' Dale suggested. 'I know you haven't got any shoes and running will be hard, but I don't think you'll be able to stop him with that knife.'

'I doubt he'll leave the door unlocked when he comes down anyway,' Lotte said. 'He probably won't believe you're sick either. Not when we were screaming at him less than an hour ago. We'll just have to play it by ear.'

Dale climbed down from the wardrobe and they both listened intently. 'Where is he now?' Dale asked.

'In the office,' Lotte whispered back. 'I'd say he's

collecting up papers. Maybe that means he's scared the police are on his tail?'

They could hear drawers being opened, the odd dull thump of stuff being dropped into a box. Then he went out of the front door and they heard the sound of a car door being opened.

'He's running scared,' Lotte said gleefully. 'Taking anything incriminating from here. Time to make him more scared.'

She ran up the flight of stairs and began screaming 'Help!' at the top of her voice. She was making so much noise she couldn't tell whether he'd come in and shut the door or not. Dale scuttled away to the bathroom.

'Howard! If that's you, come quick,' Lotte yelled. 'Dale's had a kind of turn, she's not breathing.'

Even as the words came out of her mouth it occurred to her that one of them not breathing would solve at least half his problem, but she was banking on him reacting as any normal person would.

'I'm busy,' he called back. 'Now shut that row.'

'I'm scared, I don't know what to do,' she shouted back. 'Please come and look at her.'

She hammered on the door with Dale's shoe, guessing the constant banging would annoy him enough to act. She kept yelling and pretending to sob. He took something else outside, she could feel a draught coming from the open front door, and she yelled still louder.

'Shut the fuck up or it'll be the worse for you,' he snarled as he came indoors.

Somehow she knew he was bracing himself to come down and get them and that had been his intention all along. She guessed the men who snatched her had let him down, probably because the police were pulling out all the stops to find them. She'd observed Howard for long enough to know organization didn't come naturally to him. He was too used to being told what to do by Fern. He had never struck her as a violent man either, but a frightened animal was a dangerous one, and she knew she mustn't underestimate him.

All at once she heard the key in the door and he opened it just a crack to see where she was. 'Please, please help Dale,' Lotte whimpered from her position at the bottom of the stairs. 'She's out cold.'

When he was boarding up the window she had been surprised to see how rough he looked: several days' worth of stubble on his chin, his eyes bloodshot and his hair badly in need of a cut. Now as he slunk round the door, quickly locking it behind him, she thought he must have been sleeping on his boat, or in his car, for his trousers were crumpled and very stained and his shoes were white with salt water. The pockets in his old brown waxed jacket were bulging and a piece of rope was dangling ominously out of one of them.

'Shut up, for God's sake!' he said as he came down the stairs and she continued to wail about Dale. 'Where is she anyway?'

Lotte had the Stanley knife in her hand with the sleeve of her tee-shirt covering it. 'She's in the bathroom,' she sobbed out. 'Get a doctor for her, please. I don't want her to die!'

He gave her one of his withering looks. 'Get in the bathroom ahead of me so I can see what you're doing,' he said.

That foiled her plan. She'd intended to jump him from behind. Dale was doing a fine acting job, lying just inside the door, legs and arms sprawled out. Lotte had no choice but to step over her, and now she couldn't see how she could attack Howard.

He kicked Dale in the side, and she winced involuntarily. 'Just as I expected,' he snarled. 'I didn't believe you for a moment. But I've gotta take you to a new place, so you just stay where you are while I secure you.'

He pulled the rope from his pocket, and before Lotte could even gather herself to speak he had bent down, flipped Dale over on to her front and was starting to tie her hands together behind her back. Lotte grabbed the towel rail and kicked out with her bare foot, catching him on the shoulder. She hadn't got the strength to really hurt him, he merely swayed back, but as his head came up to look at her, she leapt forward, knife in hand, and slashed him across the face, screaming manically.

Dale leapt to her feet, shedding the rope from her hands which hadn't yet been secured, and brought her knee up into Howard's groin.

He was cut right across his cheek and it looked like a deep cut for it wasn't bleeding much. Lotte thought they'd got the better of him then, for he began to lurch back into the bedroom. Dale went after him, her shoe in her hand, intending to inflict some further damage. But suddenly he had another length of rope in his hands which he whipped over Dale's head, drawing her backwards towards him with it tight against her windpipe.

Lotte's stomach lurched. Howard's eyes were burning like a crazy person's, and Dale looked frozen with terror. 'A knee in the small of her back as I pull on the rope and she'll be dead in four seconds,' he said. 'I learned that trick in the army.'

Lotte had no idea if that was true, but Dale's eyes were already beginning to bulge with the pressure on her throat. Lotte still had the knife in her hand but she couldn't use it, not while he held Dale that way.

'Let her go,' Lotte said, her voice cracking in fright. 'She doesn't know anything, she can't hurt you. You've got me, do what you like to me.'

'If you don't want me to strangle her, you come and tie her up,' he said, a wolfish grin on his face. 'And put that fucking knife down.'

Lotte hesitated.

Dale made a strangled kind of moan, and Lotte saw he was tightening his grip on her neck. 'OK,' she said, placing the knife on a chest of drawers close to Howard. 'Just don't hurt her.'

Howard continued to hold the rope tightly while Lotte secured first Dale's wrists and then her ankles.

When she didn't tie the ankles tightly enough for his liking, he kicked out at her. Blood was running down his cheek now, making him look fearsome.

Dale's face was chalk white and she was trembling with fear. It was clear that Howard was going to kill them both, if not here, wherever he planned to take them, and in desperation Lotte played the only card she had left.

'Wouldn't you like to fuck me one more time?' she asked, looking right into his eyes and forcing herself to smile at him as if that was what she wanted. 'Or if not a fuck, how about a blow job?'

She saw Dale's eyes widen even more, for close as they'd been as friends Lotte had always maintained a kind of purity, never speaking of such things.

'You're just playing for time, hoping rescue will come,' he said dismissively. 'Help won't come though. It's dark now and anyone who was out there searching will have gone home.'

To Lotte that sounded as if police had been around today in the village and that was why he needed to move them.

'You've got me wrong. I hoped if I pleased you that you'd let us go,' she replied, doing her very best wide-eyed dumb blonde look. 'Don't you want to find out if I'm good at pleasing you?'

A quick glance at Dale and she saw something in her expression that said her friend was doing her best to get the rope untied on her wrists. If she could get them free she was close enough to grab the knife again.

'Come on, Howard,' Lotte said teasingly. 'Don't tell me you've never dreamt about me sucking your cock?'

She knew she was winning because he licked his lips and the look in his eyes was excited rather than vicious. She stepped closer to him and ran her hands over the front of his trousers. He was rock hard and she nudged him back towards the bed, silently willing Dale to undo her ties and come to her rescue.

Howard sat on the edge of the bed. Unfortunately he had Dale right in his line of vision, but Lotte could only hope he might close his eyes before long.

'What have we got here?' she said as she slowly unzipped his trousers. She felt quite sick at the thought of what she had to do; all she could hope for was that Dale would get loose quickly.

She reached into his trousers and rubbed his cock through his boxer shorts, but he stuck his hand in and pulled it out for her.

At the sight of his long, thin penis with its purple helmet, the memory of that night with him and Fern came back sharply. A surge of anger at what he and his wife had done to her rushed through her and as she tentatively reached out her hand to hold it, she felt her stomach heave again.

Taking a deep breath, she bent over to take it in her mouth, trying very hard not to think about what she was doing, but she gagged involuntarily just as her lips touched it.

All at once his penis sagged and virtually disappeared.

If she hadn't been in such a perilous position she might have laughed.

'I don't want you touching me,' he said, and before she could move away he'd got hold of her arm and was twisting it up behind her back, at the same time getting off the bed.

She struggled to get free, but he had her in a vice-like grip. From his pocket came another piece of rope, and he was soon securing her wrists.

Ten minutes later both she and Dale were tied up and gagged. He'd fixed their ankles with a short length of rope so they could still hobble along but not run away, presumably because he wanted them to walk to wherever he was taking them.

Lotte felt too utterly demoralized and humiliated even to try to think of any further escape. She wished she hadn't lowered herself by offering oral sex, even if she hadn't intended to go through with it; somehow just touching him had made her feel dirty. Dale was looking at her strangely – she must have shocked her rigid too.

'We're going now,' Howard said, grabbing Lotte by the arm and pushing her towards the stairs.

She had no shoes and the prospect of being dragged across rough ground with bare feet was not inviting, but compared with his intention of killing them, that was nothing. And Lotte knew he would do it this time, he couldn't afford to fail again.

As the girls were bundled roughly into the back of the van waiting outside, Lotte recognized it as the same one they'd been abducted in by the faint smell of fish. In there too were the boxes Howard had been packing earlier. Lotte offered up a prayer that he wouldn't kill them tonight, for the longer he took to deal with them, the more chance there was the police would find them.

Lotte tried to work out where they were going by the right- and left-hand turns. Before she had the baby she used to pore over a map of this area in an attempt to cement where everything was in her head, just in case she managed to escape. She knew they'd gone towards Selsey but veered off before they got there; sadly she couldn't remember what lay in that direction.

Dale was making funny noises, wriggling and thumping with her feet. It was obvious she wanted Lotte's attention but she couldn't work out what her friend was trying to tell her and it was too dark to read any facial expressions.

The van turned on to a bumpy, rutted lane. It was very narrow as branches of trees were brushing against both sides of the van. Lotte was in a cold sweat now; this was fear beyond anything she'd ever experienced.

The van continued along the lane for another five or ten minutes, then stopped and the lights were turned off. Lotte heard Howard get out of the van and walk away, but he had only gone some ten feet when she heard the clicking sound of a lock and the rattle of a chain.

Dale wriggled closer to Lotte and pressed herself up

hard against her. Lotte assumed this was a reminder they were in this together, and pressed back.

The back doors opened and Howard reached in, caught hold of Lotte's foot and dragged her out roughly. He had a torch in his hand but that was only illuminating the ground beneath them, and it was too dark all around to see anything. But as he caught hold of her arm and lifted the torch, she saw what looked like a garden shed in front of them. She thought they might be on an allotment.

He shoved her into the shed with such force that she fell flat on her face on the floor. By the time she'd rolled over and got into a sitting position he was back at the door with Dale. He pushed her in equally brutally, but instead of falling over she bumped into the side wall and knocked over a huge stack of plastic flower pots.

Then Howard came right into the shed, put his torch down on the floor and caught hold of the girls by their shoulders, swinging them together back to back. Pulling out yet another length of rope, which Lotte saw had been already made into a noose with a slip knot, he put it over both their shoulders, down to their waists, and pulled it tight, securing them together. He then tied the other end of it to what, in the darkness, looked like a heavy-duty workbench.

He was breathing really heavily, and mumbling too. Lotte caught the words 'Get it over with', but nothing else. She got the impression he was every bit as frightened as they were, and the speed at which he was trying to do everything suggested he was terrified of getting caught.

Once they were secured, he ran back to the van again. But as soon as Lotte heard a sloshing sound and his slower step as though carrying something heavy, she knew he was carrying a can of petrol.

Dale must have heard it too for they both struggled and gave muffled shouts against their gags, but he was already pouring it all around outside for they could smell it. Suddenly, through her fear, Lotte felt a prick on her wrist, and Dale's fingers snaking into hers behind their back. In a flash she realized her friend had managed to get the Stanley knife before they left the house and that was what she'd been trying to convey to her in the van. Dale's hands were already free and now she was cutting through Lotte's bonds. But there was the big rope round them both too and their ankles were tied, and the moment Howard struck the match the place would go up.

Howard had come inside now, and his face looked fiendish in the light of the torch as he continued to slosh the petrol around. 'Dry as a tinder box,' he muttered gleefully. 'Nothing left behind but a few bones.'

The rope on Lotte's hands fell away just as he came over and poured the last of the petrol over them. It stank and stung their eyes, but Lotte made herself resist the desire to rub them with her freed hands. She could feel Dale sawing on the bigger rope holding them together, but suddenly Howard walked out of the door and shut it behind him, and then they heard him putting the padlock on the chain and locking it.

Dale wrenched off her gag. 'Shit, I thought we'd have time. He was working so fast,' she whispered. 'What can we do now?'

Lotte pulled her gag off too. 'Just finish cutting the rope,' she said, trying to think logically, but fear was making everything freeze up.

Dale hacked through the last couple of strands, but she was crying in terror now. They could hear Howard striking matches outside and they were both braced for the whole place to suddenly go up.

'His matches aren't working,' Lotte said, after hearing him swear softly. Her eyes swept in desperation around the dark shed. It stood to reason that if there were flower pots in here there had to be gardening tools too. 'You take that side, I'll take this,' she whispered to her friend. 'Find something to smash our way out of here.'

They heard him swear again and for a second or two a chink of light came on around the door which suggested he'd gone back to the van to look for more matches. Just that little bit of light let Lotte see a row of spades, forks, hoes and other tools hanging on a bracket. She lifted down the spade, and as the light went out, continued to feel with her hands. And they came upon the familiar shape of an axe.

She grabbed Dale, put a spade in her hands, and still with their feet tied, they hobbled to the back of the shed.

They were just lifting their tools to whack them against the wall when they heard the whoosh of the petrol catching fire. It acted like a spur to Lotte, and heaving the heavy axe behind her head she smashed it down on to the planks, splintering them immediately. Dale's spade followed suit, and a small hole appeared.

Lotte heaved again, using even more force now because the flames were already licking inside the shed. This time a whole plank split and she hacked away all around it as though possessed, with Dale using her spade to prise the loose pieces of wood away.

'Out now,' Lotte rasped, catching hold of Dale around the middle and thrusting her through the hole.

The flames were licking across the floor towards Lotte now and as they reached her feet and ran up her legs, she leapt head-first into the hole after her friend. She felt Dale hauling her through, and as her feet came through the hole, she rolled Lotte on the wet grass to put out the flames on her jeans.

'Is he still there?' Lotte asked. She was shaken up, but aware enough to know they must have made a lot of noise getting out.

'I thought I heard the van start up just after the shed caught fire,' Dale said as she dragged her friend further back from the shed which was now completely ablaze. 'But he may just have moved it back a few yards. Either way, we'd better stay here for a while just in case he's somewhere near watching.'

Dale had got her ankles untied and she gave the knife

to Lotte to do hers. 'I'll just creep over a bit and see if the van's gone,' she said.

Lotte's heart was still racing from the very close shave. It was very hot so near to the blaze and her eyes stung from the petrol, but she still managed to smile as Dale slunk away on her belly and forearms like a Marine.

She was only gone a few minutes. 'The van's gone,' she said as she returned.

'We can't be certain he's gone right away,' Lotte reminded her. 'Any sensible person would go, but he's not exactly normal.'

'Well, we can't spend the night here,' Dale said softly. 'Your legs and feet need medical attention. I think we should find our way to the nearest house to ring the police.'

It was only then that Lotte felt the pain of the burns. She was wearing cut-off jeans, and she had smelled the denim singeing, but now she saw there were not only burn holes in the material by her knees and on her thighs, but her lower legs and feet were burnt too. She hadn't felt anything before, but now her attention had been drawn to them, they stung and throbbed.

Dale stripped off her tee-shirt, leaving herself in just her bra. 'I'll use this to bind your feet up,' she said, ripping it into two pieces. 'We don't want any dirt getting into those burns.'

She knelt down and made a kind of rough bootee on either foot, securing them around Lotte's ankles with the piece of rope Howard had used. Then she pulled

Lotte to her feet. 'I'll keep the trusty Stanley knife as a souvenir,' she said, putting it in her jeans pocket.

'How did you get it?' Lotte asked.

'When he bundled you up the stairs I walked backwards and grabbed it. I managed to shove it in the waist of my jeans. I cut the rope while we were in the van, though I nicked my wrists a few times. I bet when we get to the light I'll find I look like one of those self-harm people.'

'We'll dine out on this story for the rest of our lives,' Lotte said with a hysterical giggle. Now the worst was over she felt very strange, all wobbly, tearful but giggly too.

'Don't speak about dining yet, just lean on me and hobble,' Dale said.

Lotte leaned over and picked up the axe.

'You don't need that now,' Dale reproved her.

'I do. Just in case. It pays to have insurance,' Lotte insisted.

They skirted round the still-burning shed, and paused for a moment to look back at it. All around them was velvety darkness, a mild night with a clear sky studded with stars, yet the fire was very bright orange, with a red core at the heart of it. Only the four corner posts of the shed remained whole now; the roof had caved in along with all four sides. But there must have been cans of paint or turpentine in there for every now and then there was a bang and another flare-up.

'It would've been a horrible death,' Dale said in a

small, shaky voice. 'I owe you my life, I was so busy panicking I didn't think to look for tools to get out.'

'You had the presence of mind to get the knife,' Lotte reminded her. 'If we'd still been tied we couldn't have done anything.'

They could see no lights anywhere. While they knew they couldn't possibly be more than a mile or two from a house with a phone, it felt like being in a wilderness.

'We're free at last,' Lotte said with a smile in her voice. 'We can have fish and chips, or bacon and egg. I could even murder a McDonald's or three.'

'Then we'd better get moving,' Dale said.

'I doubt that place belonged to him,' Lotte said as they walked on, Dale supporting her. 'Just think, he must've driven around looking for somewhere to kill us. Fancy anyone being as wicked as that!'

Dale chuckled. 'Fancy you being wicked enough to offer him a blow job!'

'I suppose that's proof that we'd all do anything to save our own skin,' Lotte said. 'Mind you, I was banking on you walloping him or something. If I'd had to do it I might have bit it off.'

They walked down the narrow lane for some fifteen minutes in silence, both locked in their own thoughts. Lotte was thinking about Simon and Adam and how worried they must be, and she wondered if David had been to see them throughout all this. She felt utterly exhausted now, for fear and hunger had kept her awake ever since they were first captured. Her burnt feet were hurting too, the thin material covering them no protection from the stones on the lane.

There was a kind of dog-leg turn in the lane, and as they came out of it back on to a straight stretch, to their horror they saw Howard's van parked up by a farm gate.

Both girls froze, shrinking back into the bushes which lined the lane. It was unlikely he'd seen them as the van was turned in to face the gate. He'd clearly stopped there to watch the fire.

'He could have seen us silhouetted against the flames,' Dale whispered.

'I don't think he'd be sitting there so calmly if he had,' Lotte said.

'He might not be in there!' Dale whispered back fearfully. 'He could be anywhere. Even right behind us.'

Lotte looked at Dale in shocked surprise, realizing that she was falling apart. She was shaking like a leaf, her eyes were full of terror, and when Lotte took her hand to comfort her, her pulse was racing far too fast.

All at once Lotte felt a whole new surge of red-hot anger run through her. She'd been tormented, abused, starved and terrified by this man for far too long. He and his wife had already stripped her of everything, but to turn her brave and confident friend into a basket case was the last straw, and she knew she had to put a stop to him now, for good.

'Stay here,' she said to Dale, pushing her firmly further back into the bushes. 'I'm going to check out the van.'

Dale let out a kind of frightened mew, but Lotte was

not going to allow herself to be sidetracked. Holding the axe in her right hand and supporting it with her left, she ran lightly towards the van, not even feeling her burnt foot or the rough ground digging into it. When she was nearly in view of the van mirrors, she ducked down so he wouldn't see her and crawled the rest of the way.

His head was lolling back against the seat head-rest. He had fallen asleep!

For a few seconds Lotte crouched on the ground, just looking at him. To her it was outrageous that he could be so soothed by watching two people burn alive that he fell asleep. That was like adding petrol to the fire already burning inside her.

With the axe in her right hand she lifted it high above her head. With her left hand she opened the van door. He stirred but she was already swinging the axe down on him, and as the blade sliced into his thighs he woke, and the look of utter disbelief on his face when he saw her was laughable.

'My turn to terrify you now,' she said, pulling the axe back and swinging it sideways so that it not only broke the windscreen but sliced into his chest. He screamed as though he was being burned alive, but she was fairly sure his waxed jacket had prevented the blade from doing him any serious damage.

He screamed for mercy as she lifted the axe a third time and whacked it down with force across his lap. Blood came spurting out fiercely enough to splatter Lotte too.

'You showed no mercy with me,' she roared at him. 'You and your wife treated me worse than some kind of farm animal, and what did I ever do to you? You stole my life, my baby, my everything. You sat here believing you were watching us die in those flames! You aren't a man, you're a monster!'

She hit him again and again, tears streaming down her face until she finally backed away, too exhausted to hit him again. She was soaked in his blood, and she could hear no sound from him, yet in those moments as she stumbled back to find Dale, she understood why Indians used to take their enemies' scalps, for his blood soaking into her clothes had finally released her from her hatred and anger.

Chapter Eighteen

'You've found them?' David had been woken from a deep sleep by the telephone ringing, but the moment he was told it was the police and the girls were found, he was wide awake.

'Are they hurt?' he asked, his heart pounding.

'I can't tell you that. I wasn't there. I was just asked to ring you and let you know they've been taken to St Richard's,' the officer replied.

Five minutes later, fully dressed, David was in his car on the way to the hospital.

It was too early for the roads to be busy, and the clear sky and already warm sun promised a good day ahead. But he knew that even if he were stuck in a traffic jam with it raining cats and dogs, he'd still be happy because Lotte was alive.

David assumed the officer who rang him must have phoned Dale and Lotte's parents too; he thought he would give Simon and Adam a ring later just in case they hadn't been told.

He was in such a hurry to park his car at the hospital and get in to see the girls that he almost clipped an estate Volvo driven by an elderly man in a flat cap, who was just pulling out.

'Slow down, son,' the man shouted out of the window. 'You're a long time dead!'

Something about that remark made David laugh. 'Point taken, Pops,' he called back as he drove on into a parking space more sedately.

The girls were in Singleton Ward where Lotte had been before, but in a shared room.

'I'm afraid I can't let you disturb them now,' a dark-skinned Ward Sister told him when he inquired about the girls. 'They are fast asleep, and after what they've been through they need sleep.'

'What happened to them? Are they badly hurt?' he asked in alarm.

'I don't know the details about what happened, but I do know their injuries aren't too serious,' she said, smiling and showing very white teeth. 'But there's a policeman waiting to talk to them, so why don't you have a little chat with him?'

PC Andrew Duggan was dozing in the chair in the waiting room. He'd been on the night shift and had been one of eight officers who rushed out to Moor Lane when the call came in that the girls had taken refuge at a house there, and that Howard Ramsden, the man they'd been searching for, was in his van, injured, nearby.

Duggan had been part of the team headed by DI Bryan working on the girls' abduction, so like all the team, he was overjoyed to hear they were alive. However, when they got to the isolated house where the girls were, his first impression on seeing Lotte completely drenched in blood was that she must have a life-threatening injury.

As David Mitchell came into the waiting room, Duggan woke and rubbed his eyes.

'You found them then?' David said after quickly introducing himself. 'I rang DI Bryan yesterday about a house called "Drummond" in Itchenor. Is that where they were? With the Ramsdens?'

'We haven't got the complete story yet,' Duggan said. 'But basically, Howard Ramsden took the girls out to Moor Lane, tied them up in a shed on an allotment and set fire to it. Their escape was down to using their wits and sheer determination, I'd say.'

'And Ramsden?'

'He's in intensive care,' Duggan said. 'It's touch and go if he'll make it. Your Lotte gave him his comeuppance with an axe.'

'An axe!' David exclaimed.

Duggan nodded and grinned. 'Yes, really! An axe. She gave it some welly too! Nearly amputated his legs. Fair play to her, that's all I can say. She was a very brave girl.'

'How bad are her injuries?' David's head was spinning at the thought of anyone almost amputating legs with an axe.

'She got some burns on her legs and feet while escaping from the shed,' Duggan said. 'The other girl has only minor cuts, but both of them were traumatized when they were brought in here. Lack of food and sleep has all played its part too. But I'm told they will recover quickly.'

'Thank God for that.' David sighed with relief. There was so much he wanted to ask, whether Fern had been caught too, and if they'd found the baby, but all he managed to ask was whether the girls' parents had been told, and Scott, Simon and Adam.

'Yes, they've all been notified, but advised not to come till this evening. We didn't bother to tell you that. We knew you're sweet on Lotte so you'd have ignored it.'

David smiled, but the smile faded quickly as he considered what he'd been told. 'If this guy dies, where does that leave Lotte?'

Duggan grimaced. 'Well, she could be facing a murder charge!'

David's eyes widened. 'No! After what she's been through?'

'There has to be due process in law. Even when someone's an utter bastard and really deserved it,' Duggan said apologetically. 'But she'll be able to plead self-defence and it would be a travesty of justice if she wasn't acquitted. It's early days anyhow, and we've still got a helluva lot of investigating to do. We only found out late yesterday that the Ramsdens reside here under a false name. We also found papers in Ramsden's van which link him and his wife to an illegal business in the States. We still haven't found Fern, or Lotte's baby. But once she wakes up maybe she can tell us more.'

David had to go out for some fresh air after talking to the policeman because he suddenly felt quite faint. On the way here he'd believed Lotte's nightmare was finally over. He'd expected there to be some hiccups – no one could go through so much without some cost to their health or sanity – but he'd hoped that he could be there beside her, helping her with that, and rebuilding her life.

Now she might be charged with murder!

He could hardly credit that the law could be so idiotic, for although he didn't actually know any details about what this couple had put her through the previous time they imprisoned her, she had ended up in the sea. After that there was another attempt on her life, and the abduction, and finally they had tried to burn her alive, so surely she was entitled to defend herself?

Meanwhile, back in the waiting room, Duggan rested his elbows on his knees and held his head in his hands, contemplating what he had seen last night.

He was only thirty, but he'd been with the force five years and seen many acts of extreme violence during that time. But he had never seen injuries as bad as those Lotte Wainwright had inflicted on the American. He had spoken of it quite lightly to David, almost as if he approved wholeheartedly, but in fact he had been shocked to the core by such a young, dainty girl being so brutal.

It wasn't one or two swipes with an axe, it was a

frenzied, vicious assault that had turned the man's lower limbs to pulp. In homicide cases it was the state of mind of the accused which was all important in deciding whether the charge was manslaughter or murder. There was no doubt in Duggan's mind that Lotte had attacked this man with absolute desire for his death, rather than in self-defence, and that she'd relished every blow of that axe. But then, the man had tried to incinerate her and her friend in that shed, so maybe that was justification?

When David realized it wasn't reasonable to expect to see Lotte before early evening, he went to work instead, buying some newspapers on the way. All the nationals had something about the girls being found, but no detail of how it came about, except for the *Sun*, which appeared to have got its information from the emergency service log. The paper ran a dramatic headline saying 'Saved from the Jaws of Death', with an old picture of the girls taken on the cruise. They had padded out their lack of new information with the full back story of how Lotte had been found half drowned on the beach, that she'd had a baby which had still not been discovered, and how she and her friend had been abducted later. But it was the only paper to state that one of the girls had rung 999 and said the man who had held them captive had tried to burn them alive in a shed. It also reported that a man who had been badly injured was taken to hospital in Chichester for emergency surgery, and the police were waiting to question him about his involvement.

David had found it very hard to concentrate at work for his mind was exclusively on Lotte. It wasn't so much the possibility of her being charged with murder if Howard died, for there was no point in worrying about that at the moment. What really concerned him was whether or not he had unwittingly overdramatized his feelings for her, because she'd appeared so vulnerable.

His mother rang to say she was glad to hear Lotte had been found, but advised him not to rush into anything. Just the tone of her voice suggested that what she really meant was, 'Keep well away, son, that one's trouble.'

Just as one swallow didn't make a summer, he thought one kiss might not make a love affair. But he told himself she was a friend anyway, and there was still so much to learn about what had happened to her.

'I know you've been through hell, Lotte, but try and tell me a bit more about what happened, both this time and the time before, if you remember that now,' DI Bryan said gently.

It was late afternoon and the girls had only just woken when he got to the hospital. While he was waiting, Kim and Clarke Moore arrived, so he suggested they spoke to their daughter in Sister's office, while he talked to Lotte. He was anxious to reassure her that this wasn't a formal police interview, just a little chat to put him in the picture about what had taken place.

Considering the terrible events of the previous night, and the starvation of the past few days, Lotte looked surprisingly good. Bryan knew she had burns on her legs and feet, but they were beneath the covers. Aside from a few lacerations on her hands, no doubt incurred while trying to get out of the shed, she looked unharmed, except for the haunted look in her eyes.

'All my memory has returned,' she said, and half smiled at him, which made the haunted look vanish. Once again she was just a very pretty small blonde with speedwell-blue eyes and a soft, sweet mouth. 'Well, at least as far as I know. How would you know for certain?'

'You've got a point there,' Bryan agreed. 'I forget what I did ten minutes ago, and who knows what I've forgotten about the past!'

'Well, it's all come back, in as much as I can recall what happened in each month, each year,' she said thoughtfully. 'When you last interviewed me we were concerned about the baby I'd had and where it was . . .' She broke off, the haunted look came back and she picked at a scab on her hand.

'She's dead, I'm afraid,' she blurted out, and her eyes dropped. 'Howard threw her body into the sea with me.'

'What did she die from?' Bryan asked cautiously.

Lotte gave a dramatic sigh and waved her arms in a way which suggested she hardly knew where to start. 'Neglect! Well, that's my opinion. They left her crying for hours.'

Bryan must have looked puzzled as to why she wasn't looking after the baby.

'I'll explain all that when I get to that part,' she said quickly. 'But you'll be able to find her cause of death when you find her body, won't you? It's bound to wash up on a beach somewhere before long.'

Bryan frowned, suddenly remembering a message that had been sent to the station that morning. 'A baby's body was found yesterday on the beach beneath the Seven Sisters,' he said. 'That's near Eastbourne.'

'She was wearing a white babygro,' Lotte said, then, barely stopping to draw breath, she launched into the story of how Fern and Howard had invited her to stay with them at the Dorchester, when she left the cruise.

'I supposed it turned my head to be somewhere so grand, and so I jumped at the chance of moving with them to Sussex as their housekeeper/PA,' she said.

'Mind you, I must have been pretty thick not to cotton on there was a hidden agenda,' she added with a wry smile. 'But people go and act as nannies, housekeepers and PAs all the time, don't they? You see adverts in *The Lady* magazine. Not all those people who advertise can be weird.'

'Of course not,' he reassured her. 'And we know now they were a pair of practised deceivers. Anyone could've fallen for it.'

She carried on telling him about her life with them quite calmly. It was only when she got to the part about where Fern and Howard suggested that she had a baby for them that she began to get distressed.

Bryan found it distressing too, for it was only the previous night, when police officers had found papers in Howard's van relating to a babies for sale business, that he understood what had been behind all this.

Yet even so, he hadn't imagined that Howard Ramsden had fathered Lotte's baby. He'd had the idea that was the work of another man, and the couple had induced her to stay with them until they found adoptive parents.

Bryan could understand why Lotte was faltering now. He too was stunned by the enormity of what this couple had done to her, and he moved to perch on the bed beside her and hug her. 'You've been through so much, so bravely,' he said gently. 'I wish I didn't have to bring it all back with questions.'

She went on then to outline briefly how she was locked up and subjected to threats and emotional blackmail. She was too embarrassed to say anything much about the actual baby-making, and he didn't press her. But she did describe how she tried to escape after the first time, and said she knew that was what sealed her fate because the couple never trusted her again.

She tried to shorten the details about her pregnancy and the birth which took place on 20 February, so Bryan frequently had to stop her and ask for more detail, for it was vitally important he understood fully how she'd been treated.

It was very telling that she said nothing about how she was after the birth, only that the Ramsdens kept going out, and must have often left the baby behind because she heard it crying. She might not have wanted a baby, and hated Howard and Fern, but her instinct was to protect her child and it must have been torment to be unable to. She said she sensed the baby was growing weaker and needed medical help but this was not forthcoming, and eventually she died.

'I know I never got to hold her when she was born, and that I hated the way they forced me to have her, but she was still mine, and I felt so much pain when I knew she was dead,' she sobbed out. 'I'm quite certain she died from neglect. She was plump and healthy when she was born, but two and a half months later she was dead, and that's really why I killed Fern. God, I hated her with all my being for that!'

Bryan could only stare at Lotte in shock, unable to believe what he'd just heard.

'You killed Fern?' he asked incredulously. He had imagined the woman to be in hiding somewhere, it hadn't crossed his mind she was dead. He certainly would never have imagined Lotte killing her.

Had Bryan got Lotte's story second-hand, he had no doubt he would have pooh-poohed her being unable to escape. If truth be told, he thought he would have believed much of the story to be too far-fetched. But aside from the honesty in those clear blue eyes, and Lotte's obvious distress, Bryan had been at the house in

Itchenor the previous evening following the call from David Mitchell. What Mitchell had said, about the man he had seen and the blue van, was enough for Bryan to obtain a search warrant.

There was absolutely no doubt Lotte and Dale had been kept there in the basement room. He found dark and blonde hairs on the crumpled sheets, saw the heavy lock on the outside of the door, and the way the wardrobe had been pushed under the window and the glass smashed out was all evidence of imprisonment.

There were fresh bloodstains on the basement room carpet, so he'd called in forensics immediately to go over the entire house. The kitchen had been cleaned thoroughly but they found further splatters of blood on the plinth below the kitchen cupboards.

Last night, before they had test results, Bryan had thought the blood belonged to the girls. It was only this morning, when they were able to take samples of Howard's blood and compare them, that they discovered it was his blood in the basement. But they were still none the wiser who the blood in the kitchen belonged to, until Lotte admitted she had stabbed Fern there.

Bryan was still reeling from the shock of Lotte attacking Howard with the axe, and then to hear she had dispatched Fern well before that took some getting his head around. Lotte was the kind of girl he wouldn't expect even to steal a sweet from Woolworth's Pick and Mix. He would expect her to run from a spider, to cry at old movies. He would have staked his reputation on her being incapable of any violence.

Because of that he took her very carefully through the evening prior to her being taken out to sea, when they brought her up to the kitchen and she had the knife in her pocket.

Lotte told the story clearly and dispassionately, from the moment she asked for a glass of milk to the stabbing. Then she described the subsequent moments when Howard chased her round the table while his wife grew weaker, to when she was sitting in the hall bound hand and foot, waiting for him to finish tying Fern into the picnic rug.

'I told him to ring the police,' she said calmly. 'I told him I would admit it was me. But he wouldn't listen.'

Finally there was only the ride to the boat, to be loaded aboard with Fern and the baby, to tell him about.

'We sailed for quite some time; it felt like hours. Then he got me out of the cabin, sat me on the side of the boat and untied me. Then he suddenly pushed me in and threw the baby after me,' she stated.

She stopped short, her lips quivering, and took a moment or two to compose herself. 'I had to make it to the shore to make sure he was punished. If only my memory hadn't gone then, I'd have been able to tell you where he was and everything.'

Bryan was afraid that in a court case, the prosecution would tear her story about amnesia apart, suggesting she invented it because she wanted to hide the stabbing.

They were likely to suggest that she entered into this *ménage à trois* of her own volition, and killed Fern to have Howard all to herself.

But Bryan did not harbour such thoughts. He felt that Lotte was actually incapable of lying or any kind of deception.

'I don't think I fully understood exactly what damage Howard had done to me until the moment I saw him sleeping in that van, after we escaped from the fire,' she said a little later. 'I knew exactly what he'd done of course, after all I remembered all the details, and I'd talked about it to Dale and mulled it over in my head. So I wasn't under any illusions about him, I knew him to be a very nasty piece of work. I just didn't see the effect it had had on me.

'But it was different when I saw him sleeping. He thought he'd burnt us alive, yet he could fall asleep watching it! What sort of a man did that make him?'

'A very, very evil one,' Bryan said. 'He had it coming to him; no one could feel any sympathy for him after what he did to you.'

'But why did I go so far?' she asked in a small voice, her blue eyes brimming with tears. 'One whack with the axe would've stopped him coming after us. It would have shown him I wasn't quite the mouse he took me for. But I kept on and on.'

Bryan's sympathy for her brought a lump to his throat. He knew exactly why she couldn't stop. Each whack was for all the injustices which had been piled on her, from her parents, the sweetheart who was run over, the rapist, to all that the Ramsdens had done to her. He felt nothing but understanding and empathy for her. Furthermore, he fervently hoped that Howard Ramsden would survive, so that he would never walk again, never father another child, and would have to stand trial for all his crimes either here or in the States.

'He deserved all those whacks,' he said, his voice cracking with emotion. 'You had so much courage to confront him, and I promise you will get through this and have a good life again.' He paused, cleared his throat and smiled at her.

'Now, I happen to know there's a man dying to see you. He's walked miles, talked to hundreds of people on your behalf, did everything in his power to find you. So I'm going to get out of the way and give him a chance to spend some time with this very special lady.'

'Do you mean David?' she asked in a small voice.

Bryan laughed. 'We ought to call him Chief Inspector Mitchell,' he joked. 'If it hadn't been for his questions around the villages, coming up with someone who had seen Fern Ramsden, and most importantly spotting the blue van at the house in Itchenor, we'd still be searching fruitlessly around Selsey.'

David stood in the doorway of the room just looking at Lotte for what seemed like ten minutes, though she knew it couldn't have actually been more than twenty seconds. He looked more handsome and rugged than she remembered, wearing a dark business suit and striped shirt and with his light brown hair just a little tousled.

'I'm sorry to stare,' he said eventually. 'But there've been times when I thought I'd never see you again.'

'I'm surprised you want to,' she said with a shy smile. 'I'm nothing but trouble.'

'I saw Dale outside in the corridor,' he said, walking over to the locker and putting down a large bar of Cadbury's chocolate and a bunch of freesias.

'I thought she was with her parents?'

'She was. They've gone to check in to a hotel near here and they are coming back later. She said she was going for a walk because she had cabin fever.'

'We're both suffering from that,' Lotte said with a smile. 'But I suspect she was just being diplomatic and getting out of the way. And thank you for the flowers and chocolate. Freesias are my favourite, they are so delicate and smell heavenly. And I'm a real pig with chocolate. I'll probably stuff myself with that tonight.'

'Then I'd better get you started,' he said with a grin and broke off a couple of pieces, giving one to her.

'Has anyone told you what happened?' she asked, her mouth full of chocolate.

He knew without asking that she meant the axe business and he nodded.

'I'll have to stand trial for it, and killing Fern.'

David hadn't been told about Fern, but he swallowed hard and pretended he knew.

'You'll be acquitted,' he said staunchly. 'No one will blame you; they both deserved all they got.'

'Back away now, David,' she said softly. 'I'm not what you need.'

David looked at her for a moment or two without answering. She looked so young and vulnerable, yet he already knew from Dale that she had not only kept her head in the fire, but pushed her friend out first. She was brave and resourceful, but he suspected she wanted him out of her life because she was afraid she was too damaged ever to be able to form a full sexual relationship with any man.

'I think that's up to me to decide,' he said. 'Besides, just now all I am is your friend. If you don't want me to be anything else, then that's fine.'

She turned her head on to the pillow, and he saw a tear rolling down her cheek. He moved closer and gently wiped it away with one finger.

'You've had such a raw deal it must be difficult to believe it will ever be any different,' he said softly, bending to kiss her cheek. 'But it will, Lotte. Just don't push away your friends; they are the ones who will help make it all come right for you.'

She looked at him with tear-filled eyes. 'I remembered everything while we were stuck in the basement,' she said in a croaky voice. 'I told it all to Dale, and back there it was like I was watching some strange film I'd acted in, scene by scene. But talking to DI Bryan just now and repeating the whole miserable tale brought

393

it home to me that it wasn't a film I'd acted in, but for real.'

'I can understand that,' David said, taking one of her hands and holding it between both of his. 'It must be the most surreal, weirdest thing to lose your memory, then have bits popping back, perhaps without the explanation as to why they happened, or why you felt as you did.'

'I don't think you're quite getting what I'm trying to tell you,' she said with a sigh. 'You remember I said to you before that it was nice being with you because I knew there wasn't any past with us?'

'Yes, I remember that.'

'But we are all the sum of our past experiences,' she said. 'When I first met you I didn't know what had gone before, at least not all of it. So to all intents and purposes I was still the person I had been before all that shit happened. But that shit altered me, and in a way that can never be put back. I have been a rape victim, I've had a child who died. I've killed, and attacked someone else with such savagery he'll probably die too. Now, you tell me, David, how I can have a "normal" life again.'

There was still so much that David didn't know about all this, but he realized it really was terrible by the pain in her eyes.

It probably would be wise to do as she'd said, and what his mother advised, to walk away and forget her. But wise didn't come into it, not when he'd found her on the beach and felt sure that wasn't just chance. His heart swelled up as he looked at her, and that wasn't sympathy, he knew it was love.

'You can have a normal life again if you just take it a day at a time,' he said eventually. 'It's not going to be easy, babe, you'll have nightmares, I expect, you'll find yourself dwelling on it all, and yes, you will have to face a trial. But while all that stuff is going on, there will be other things too.'

'Like what?' she asked, her eyes filling with tears.

'Good things,' he said. 'There'll be days on the beach when it's hot. There'll be picnics, dinner parties, going to the pictures and getting very drunk. I'd like to take you to a fun fair and ride a rollercoaster, paddle by moonlight in the sea, and hold you in my arms and kiss you till you forget everything but that.'

'Would you?' she asked.

'Well, I didn't tramp round the whole of Chichester harbour asking questions and showing your photo just because I'm a do-gooder,' he said with a smile. 'I did it because I was desperate to find you, and to do all those things I've already mentioned with you.'

'Including kissing me?' she asked shyly.

'Most of all kissing you,' he replied. He had been perched on the edge of the bed as he held her hand, but now he leaned towards her and kissed her lips. Just a gentle but lingering kiss, his hand on her cheek. 'I do have a variety of different kisses,' he said, taking his mouth just a few inches away from hers. 'That was the "maybe-the-nurse-will-come-in" one. Tomorrow, if the burns on your feet don't hurt too much and you can stand up, we could repeat the variety we tried in Simon's flat.'

'What's that one called?' she whispered.

'The "I've-been-dying-to-hold-you-in-my-arms" one,' he said as he kissed her nose.

She laughed. 'How long will I have to stay here for?'

'Not long I wouldn't think, just until they are sure the burns are healing. Dale told me she can leave tomorrow. Her parents want to take her home for a few days. You could come and stay at mine.'

'That's very sweet of you, David, but it's too soon for that,' she said. 'Besides, if they charge me with murder won't I have to go to prison until the trial?'

'Is that the worry lurking at the back of your mind?'

Lotte nodded.

David knew very little about criminal law, only odd things he'd picked up in pubs. 'I shouldn't think so, babe,' he said. 'You'll get bail as long as the police don't oppose it, and I can't see Bryan doing that. But going back to stay with Simon and Adam will be the best thing for you. All your friends are in Brighton, and though I'd love to take care of you, I do have to go to work so you'd be alone a lot.'

'You would come and see me though?' she asked anxiously.

'Of course, so often you'll get bored with me. Now, can I have the "here's-one-for-the-road" kiss?'

'You've got to go?

'Yes, because Dale is lurking outside the door wanting to come in, and I think when her parents come back they'll want to talk to you. You might get a visit from yours too!'

'I doubt that,' she said, and caught hold of his face with both her hands and pulled him closer to kiss him.

It was a delicious kiss, sweet enough for Lotte to want to say, hold-on-I'm-coming-home-with-you. Instead when it ended she just smiled. 'I guess that was the "now-don't-you-go-forgetting-me" kiss?'

'As if.' He laughed and turned to go. 'It was the "now-eat-up-that-chocolate-before-Dale-gets-back-or-she'll-want-some" kiss,' he said at the door, and then left, blowing her another one.

Kim and Clarke Moore came into the room with Dale about five minutes after David had left. Lotte had seen lots of pictures of them, and Dale described them as 'wacky' when she was being affectionate, 'mad' when she was irritated by them. But Lotte would have described them as 'colourful'.

Kim was wearing a vintage lilac and green patterned crêpe dress, with lilac-coloured tights which made her look as though she'd got some weird skin disease. Her red hair was held back with a green silky band which had a kind of silky pompom resting just above her right ear. And she had a complete rainbow of eye shadow.

Clarke wore jeans and a red, fringed cowboy shirt,

his long greying hair held back in a pony-tail. They were as warm as a thirteen-tog duvet, hugging Lotte spontaneously as though they'd met her dozens of times before.

Kim talked fast, and flitted from subject to subject like a butterfly. One minute she was talking about the awful food in the hospital café, the next about the antiques shops in Brighton, and then with another leap describing the hotel they'd booked into in Chichester.

But Lotte was fairly certain it was just a nervous reaction to the last few days of terrible anxiety.

'It was such a relief to get the call from the police,' Kim said eventually, perhaps suddenly remembering that Lotte hadn't witnessed the reunion between her and her daughter and therefore didn't know there had been buckets of tears. She went on to relate how thrilled and excited she'd been all day, her eyes shining with delight as she constantly patted Dale's cheek.

Each time Kim turned away from Dale, Dale pulled a rude face at Lotte because she'd doubtlessly heard all this several times already.

Lotte lay back on her pillows, only too happy to listen to the woman's joy, even if her daughter was getting bored with it.

'Dale tells me that it was you, Lotte, who got you both out of the shed. She said she was frozen with fear.'

Lotte looked across at her friend and wagged a reproving finger at her. 'If she hadn't had the presence of mind to hold on to the Stanley knife when Howard dragged us out of the house, we would've burned to death.'

Kim rounded on Dale. 'You didn't tell me that!' she said accusingly.

'Oh Mum, enough,' Dale said impatiently. 'What happened was horrible, and just about the most scary thing I can imagine. But it's over now, and we both want to move on.'

'I hate that expression "move on",' Kim said, looking sullen. 'I heard someone say it to a woman who had only been widowed for a few weeks. Why should she move on? To what? Surely it's better to stay put until you've figured out where you want to go?'

Lotte wanted to laugh. She could see now where Dale got that belligerent streak. 'I think I agree with you there, Mrs Moore,' Lotte said. 'Moving on could also be called running away.'

'So how was it with Lover Boy?' Dale asked, making a ridiculous pouty mouth.

'Lovely to see him,' Lotte said guardedly, wishing her friend could be more tactful.

'What a nice young man he is,' Kim said. 'We really liked him, didn't we, Clarke? He organized us all, and motivated some of us who really didn't want to do anything.' She stopped short when her husband shot her a warning look. Lotte realized she had been talking about her parents.

It had been a surprise when David told her that her parents had joined the house-to-house; she just couldn't imagine them doing such a thing. But it was no surprise to hear that her mother hadn't really got the heart for it.

'How come my parents joined you?' she asked.

'Well, we called on them,' Kim said. 'I mean, when we arrived in Brighton we were so frantic about you both. We thought if we saw them we could help one another.'

'You wouldn't get much help from my mum,' Lotte said dourly.

There was an embarrassed silence. Lotte had to break it. 'It's OK, don't feel bad because of it. She's been that way for a long time, I'm used to it. But how did you get on with Simon, Adam and Scott? I understand they were with you too?'

Kim was very enthusiastic about them, and asked Lotte if there wasn't something going on between Dale and Scott. Dale said she was far too nosy and told a funny tale about how Kim had tried to play Cupid when Dale had a crush on a boy in their street.

'She kept making suggestions as to how she could get him to come to our house. I was terrified that she'd go and kidnap him.'

'I got him to come round in the end though,' Kim said silkily.

'Yes, and how cringeworthy was that!' Dale said indignantly. 'She found out he was a bit of a maths genius and asked if he'd come and coach me! I ask you! I was fifteen, and I didn't even know my tables.'

'How did it end?' Lotte asked, thinking how wonderful it must be to have parents like Kim and Clarke.

'Very badly,' Clarke spoke up. 'He got very serious about Dale, and of course her being so contrary, it put her off. He became almost a stalker and eventually I had to threaten to knock his block off if I found him hanging around on our doorstep any more.'

Lotte laughed, and suddenly she couldn't stop; everything Dale or Kim or Clarke said was funny to her. Dale joined in, and before long they both had tears running down their cheeks.

'You're getting hysterical now,' Clarke said after a bit, but he was grinning too. 'I think it's time we left, and you two went to sleep.'

'We'll pick you up in the morning, and come with you to the police station when you make your statement,' Kim said to her daughter. 'We can go straight home after that.'

Kim turned to Lotte and went to hug her. 'Why don't you come home with us too?' she asked. 'Let me feed you up and look after those burned feet for a bit? We could bring you back when Dale has to return to Marchwood.'

'That's really kind of you, Mrs Moore,' Lotte said, touched by the kindness. 'But I'll be here for another day at least, and anyway I think Dale has seen enough of me for a while.'

'Too right I have,' Dale said, and then began to laugh again.

'If you change your mind you could always ask David to bring you up,' Kim said, and bent to kiss Lotte on the forehead. 'I just wish I'd insisted Dale brought you home with her after the cruise. If I had, none of this would've happened.'

Chapter Nineteen

DI Bryan could see by the Ward Sister's expression that she had little real sympathy for her patient even though she was trying to insist that Howard Ramsden should be left in peace. Once the newspapers had got a sniff of the nature of his crime, they had gone into a feeding frenzy, including lying in wait outside the hospital. They were only allowed to print basic facts about him until after his trial, should he make it to one, but they'd still managed to divulge enough information about Lotte's ordeal at his hands to make people hate him.

'He really isn't up to questioning,' she insisted. 'He is conscious of course, but traumatized by his injuries.'

The Sister was an attractive brunette in her thirties with a curvaceous figure and doleful dark eyes. She was Bryan's type and he was determined to charm her.

'And his victims are traumatized by what he did to them,' he said pointedly. 'I have the unenviable job of arresting young Lotte because she's admitted killing his wife, but with a statement from him that shows she had just cause to act in self-defence, and that he disposed of his wife's body, I could at least get Lotte bail until the trial.'

The nurse's attractive face softened in sympathy. 'It's

terrible that she has to be charged with anything. And awful that she might be put in prison, after all she's been through. Is it true her baby died through his and his wife's neglect and that he threw her into the sea after Lotte?'

Her dark eyes were deep, mysterious pools, and her lips were very plump and kissable. Bryan wanted to prolong this conversation. 'So it is alleged,' he said cautiously. 'He hasn't been charged with anything yet because it was touch and go whether he would make it. Plus the American police want him back over there too, they've got a whole book on him, it seems. I could tell you more over a drink if you'd let me talk to him.'

She laughed, a deep, throaty laugh. 'Go on then, and come and have a cup of tea with me afterwards in the canteen. I'm due a break.'

'I was thinking more of a glass of wine in the evening,' he said.

'I'm sure you were,' she said with a knowing look. 'But a cup of tea comes first.'

'That will be good, Sister Miranda Cole,' he said, reading her badge.

'Mind you don't bully him, Detective Inspector Bryan.'

'Tony to you,' he said. 'Is he in pain by the way?'

'Some of the time. We had to amputate his right leg the day before yesterday, and he's on strong medication. But the pain will get easier in time.'

'Shame,' Bryan said, and smiled as she waved a reproving finger at him.

The man lying in the hospital bed with a cradle holding the blankets away from his injuries bore little resemblance to the suave, dinner-jacketed man in the photograph that Bryan had seen. It was to be expected that he'd be a bit haggard, but it was far worse than that. He looked as if he was only hours from death, for his thin face was as grey as his hair, his eyes were hollow and his neck scraggier than a turkey's.

Bryan introduced himself and explained this was an informal interview about the events of the evening of 5 May which led to him taking Lotte out to sea and pushing her in.

To Bryan's surprise the man seemed very eager to talk. 'She killed Fern in cold blood,' he said in a faint, croaky voice. 'She was nothing but trouble from the moment we helped her in Ushuaia, and I was a fool to let her get her claws into me.'

Bryan listened in absolute amazement as the man croaked his way through a complete fairy story. He began by saying he and Fern felt sorry for Lotte at the end of the cruise because her parents wouldn't welcome her home. Fern was afraid she might take her own life if she was left on her own, so they asked if she'd like to come down to Itchenor. But he claimed she was never intended to be an employee, only a guest until she got back on her feet. However, she proceeded to come on sexually to Howard.

'I ignored her at first, I thought she was just being affectionate. But then she got in my bed one night while

405

Fern was away, and to my shame I gave in to her,' he claimed.

He said he tried to make her leave, but she refused and said she'd tell Fern if he forced her to go. But later she told him she was pregnant, showing him a testing kit with a positive result, so he felt he had to tell Fern.

Bryan was staggered by how devious the man was. He told lies and distortions of truth so smoothly and with such conviction that it was hardly surprising he and his wife had got away with so much for so long.

'And how did Fern take your infidelity?' he asked.

'She understood that Lotte was a little Jezebel, put on this earth to tempt men, but she felt it was her Christian duty to forgive, and to take the child when it was born and bring it up as our own. My Fern was a big-hearted woman, and mostly she had people's full measure. But I knew in this case she was blind to the girl's true nature, and we'd have more trouble with the little slut.'

Bryan thought that anyone who had come as close to death as this man had, and who was as God-fearing as he claimed to be, would be afraid to tell such thundering lies. He insisted Lotte was never a prisoner and could have walked out of the house whenever she chose.

'She set her sights on me,' he said, as if that explained why she had her baby without any medical attention. 'She thought that as soon as the baby was born I'd leave Fern. But when she saw that wasn't how it was going to be, she turned real nasty. That's why she smothered the baby.'

'What!' Bryan exclaimed. He really couldn't believe the man had said that.

'Surely you didn't think the baby died of natural causes?' Ramsden exclaimed, his eyes wide and incredulous. 'The little bitch smothered her own baby! She went upstairs while we were having supper, and Fern followed a bit later to see if everything was OK, and the baby was dead in the little cradle. She'd smothered her with a pillow.'

A little tremor of excitement ran down Bryan's spine at that preposterous claim. At the autopsy on the baby it was proved that Lotte was the mother and Howard the father. The baby had been slightly underweight, but there was no evidence of anything else which could account for a natural death. Yet in cases of Sudden Infant Death Syndrome this was almost always the case too.

The length of time her body had been in the sea clouded the picture still further, but a couple of tiny feathers, like those from a pillow, had been found lodged in her trachea. The pathologist said there was no absolute proof that the baby had been suffocated with a pillow, but he thought it likely as these feathers were probably inhaled as the smothering began.

If Lotte had done this, she would have anticipated that someone might discover later that was how the baby died, so in preparation for this would have been likely to say that was how she thought Fern or Howard killed her. Yet she hadn't; she'd said she thought the baby died from neglect.

Even if Lotte had smothered her, Howard couldn't have known just by looking at the baby that was how she died. He knew only because it was he who killed her.

Bryan didn't pull Howard up with this, but let him go on to say that Fern was going to call the police, and that was when Lotte stabbed her.

'You wouldn't credit a little thing like her could be so strong or savage,' he said. 'She did it afore I could stop her.'

'And this was on the evening of the fifth of May?'

'Yes, I already told you that,' Ramsden said, as if irritated at being pulled up on a detail again.

Bryan smiled to himself for this time he had some real proof the man was lying. The pathologist had put the baby's death three or four days earlier than 5 May which was when Lotte said she overheard the couple talking about the baby's death.

'Lotte was too strong for you to restrain then?' Bryan asked sarcastically. 'And what reason did you have for not calling the police?'

'I wanted to, but Lotte said she would tell them I'd raped her and kept her prisoner,' Howard said. 'Anyways, I was so upset at Fern and the baby being dead, I just went along with her plan to take them out to sea. I hardly knew what I was doing.'

Bryan tried to imagine how a man distraught at having his wife and child murdered would then go along with the instructions of a slip of a girl and cart their bodies off to his boat.

That defied belief.

'Flinging herself in the water with the baby after we'd weighted Fern and dropped her in was her way of making sure I got blamed,' he said. 'She sure must've been some actress to fool you all into believing she'd lost her memory.'

Bryan had heard enough. He got up from his chair and putting his hands on the bed, he leaned forward towards Howard. 'Even if I was to buy all that crap,' he hissed at him, 'how do you explain away why you had Lotte abducted from Brighton and her friend too? What was the purpose of keeping them prisoner?'

'Just to teach her a lesson,' he said.

'And the fire at the shed? More lessons to learn?'

That was the only time Howard looked unsure of himself. 'I was going to let them go. But she killed my wife and baby,' he said, his lips trembling and tears coming into his eyes. 'She'd pushed me too far with her evilness, I just snapped.'

'Just snapping is when you push someone into the path of a bus or hit them with a broken bottle. Someone who goes to buy a chain and padlock, plus a couple of gallons of petrol, two days before he uses them is making preparations. And tying the girls up and driving them to a place you must have found days earlier is definitely the action of a cold-blooded killer. The truth is, it was the only option left to you. You knew there were

409

police all around the harbour and the net was closing in. You thought burning their bodies would get rid of any forensic evidence to prove it was you. You planned to jump on a plane the next day and go back to the States.'

Howard seemed to shrink back into his pillow.

Bryan bent over, pushing his face up to within inches of the other man's. 'You are going to die, you know that, don't you?' he whispered. 'Everyone here knows it. Though they'll never admit it to you. They are running a book on how much longer you can survive. I put a tenner on you lasting a week. Aren't you scared about your Judgment Day up there at the Pearly Gates?'

Howard's eyes grew wider and his lips trembled more.

'I know mostly you only use your religion to con people,' Bryan went on. 'But you used to be a preacher, as was your father too, and I think you're still a believer deep down. You've preached about the Fires of Hell and Everlasting Damnation, you know that's what's to come for sinners like you.'

Howard's pale, haggard face seemed to grow even paler.

'Just think on that, an eternity of pain worse than you've got now. If you decide it might be more expedient to tell the truth before you die, for you will be forgiven if you tell the truth, then just get Sister to call me.'

*

Bryan walked down to the canteen with Miranda.

'Was it a fruitful interview?' she asked.

'No, he lied through his teeth,' Bryan said with a grin. 'But I've got a feeling he might have a few nasty night-mares in the coming days. He might tell you he needs to speak to me. Ring me straight away, won't you?'

'What did you tell him?' Her voice was suspicious but her eyes were smiling.

'Just that he hadn't got much longer, and it might be a good idea to tell the truth before he pops off.'

'But there's no real reason why he would die, not now,' Miranda frowned. 'He's over the danger period.'

'He doesn't have to know that, does he? I actually want him to live so he can stand trial, whether that's here or in the States if they decide to repatriate him. Personally I'd rather he was sent home, the prisons are grimmer there and it will save our taxpayers the expense of keeping him. But I'll tell him he will live after he's told the truth.'

She looked at Bryan reflectively. 'I wouldn't want to get on the wrong side of you!'

'The right side is excellent though,' he grinned. 'To prove it I'll treat you to whatever delights the canteen stocks.'

It was with a very heavy heart that DI Bryan got out of the squad car with WPC Rington in Meeting House Lane at eight-thirty in the morning. Lotte had been back living with her two friends for almost a week now, and when he'd seen her on Saturday, two days earlier, she had looked so much better, with colour in her cheeks and her eyes brighter and less fearful.

But that improvement was going to disappear in a matter of minutes for he'd come to arrest her for the murder of Fern Ramsden. She would have to spend the rest of the day giving her statement at the police station, with her solicitor present, spend the night in the cells, then tomorrow she would appear in court for a preliminary hearing.

Last night, in desperation, he'd gone to see her parents to ask if they would stand bail for her, and have her home if the court stipulated that was to be a bail condition. As they hadn't visited her in hospital, he half expected they would refuse, and they did. Her mother said it was 'all too shameful' and Lotte would have to fend for herself.

He knew that Simon and Adam would willingly stand bail, but as they owned no property or other valuable assets they wouldn't be considered. So unless a miracle occurred, by tomorrow night Lotte would be in prison, on remand. And he had a sinking feeling it would break her.

Simon answered the door, and his initial bright smile vanished as he saw the uniformed constable accompanying Bryan.

'This isn't just a chat, is it?' he said.

'No, I'm sorry,' Bryan replied. 'We've come to arrest her.'

As they walked into the flat, Lotte called out to ask who it was at the door. When Simon didn't reply she came out into the hall from the kitchen to see. She was wearing pale pink jeans and a tee-shirt of the same colour, her hair loose on her shoulders, and she looked very pretty.

'Oh,' she said, putting her hand over her mouth as she sensed this was not a social call. 'This is it then?'

'I'm afraid so, Lotte,' Bryan said, wishing he was anywhere but here, about to take her into custody. 'I am arresting you, Lotte Wainwright, for the murder of Fern Ramsden on the fifth of May 2003.'

Her eyes above the hand over her mouth seemed to grow larger and more fearful with each word of the caution. As he finished, she sagged against the wall, the colour draining from her cheeks.

'Are you OK, Lotte?' Simon asked. 'Can I get you a drink of water? You look like you're going to pass out.'

She straightened up. 'I'm fine, Simon, you go off to work. Don't worry.'

'Shall I phone Mr Harding for you?' he asked, his voice trembling.

Bryan had given her the solicitor's number when she first came out of hospital. Harding was one of the best solicitors in Brighton, and if anyone could pull a rabbit out of the hat, it would be him.

'Yes, please,' she said. 'But I don't suppose he'll be there till nine. Could you ring David too for me?'

Most of the time Bryan loved his job. But as the

constable drove out of Meeting House Lane, with Lotte slumped in the back, he wished he was a truck driver, a plumber or a shop assistant, any job where he didn't have to see a young woman who had already gone through so much suffering get another whole lot piled on to her.

'Now, this is how we're going to do this,' Frank Harding said to Lotte, looking intently at her across the small table in the interview room.

The room was impregnated with stale cigarette smoke. Even the walls had turned the dirty brown of nicotine and the one small window, which overlooked another wall, was fixed so it opened less than an inch.

'You have the right to refuse to answer their questions,' Harding explained. 'But most times it is counterproductive. And I know that you've already told DI Bryan the whole nine yards informally. So my advice is to tell it how you told him before, this time for the tape. The complete truth, nothing hidden or held back.'

Lotte nodded. She felt comfortable with Harding; he had a nice face with a wide smile, there was sincerity in his pale blue eyes and the creases around them were laughter lines. He was a bit tubby, with thinning hair, and probably getting on for sixty, but there was something very youthful about him.

'I'll be with you all the time. If you want a break, just ask,' he said.

'OK,' Lotte said.

'Then I'll tell them you are ready.'

As the tape recorder was being switched on in the interview room, and one of the two police officers stated the time and date and the names of everyone present, about a mile out to sea near Bognor Regis a suspicious-looking bundle had surfaced.

Brothers Reg and Norman Dooley were both firemen in Littlehampton. They were thirty-eight and forty respectively, married with five children between them. They were stocky men with good physiques from sport and weight training, both almost bald, with very similar round, jovial faces.

Although they were on different watches, every so often their time off coincided and they would borrow a friend's small motor boat and go fishing together. It was a beautiful day, calm, warm and sunny, and they'd both stripped off their shirts and were enjoying the sun and sea more than concerning themselves with catching fish. They'd already caught nine or ten good-sized mackerel, enough really to take home and clean and gut, but Reg suggested they baited one more line, and then call it a day.

They were sitting on the floor of the boat, the engine turned off and the boat bobbing around in the waves. Reg asked Norman if he wanted a sandwich and got up to get them from their cool-box. While he was up he looked over the side to see if they'd caught anything, and he spotted the bundle floating a few yards away from the boat.

'Take a look at this, Norm,' he said. 'What d'you reckon it is?'

Norman got up and looked. The wrapping was a dark green plaid with several rubber bungees holding it together. 'The bedding of someone sleeping rough?' he suggested. 'They always tie their stuff up with those bungees, don't they?'

Reg said he'd start up the boat and go a bit nearer and they could get it with the boat hook.

Norman stood by with the hook as Reg steered the boat nearer. 'Got it,' Norman shouted above the engine noise. 'Turn off!'

Reg switched off the engine and went to help his brother. Once they'd pulled it to the side of the boat, Norman leaned over and ran his hands down the entire length of the bundle.

'Holy shit!' he exclaimed. 'I think it might be a body!'

Bryan was just going to get some lunch when a call came in from the Bognor Regis police that a body had been found in the sea. The fishermen who found it had towed it to the shore.

When the bundle was unwrapped it was found to be a tall, red-headed woman aged about forty-five. There was no doubt it was Fern Ramsden. Air inside her body had brought her bobbing up to the surface like a cork.

The body had been taken to the mortuary where it would be examined. Bryan decided to take a ride down to Bognor and see if the corpse had any secrets to give up.

'Nurse, nurse!'

Sister Miranda Cole sighed and got up from the desk where she was writing up her notes. Howard Ramsden was fast becoming one of her least favourite patients; he whinged about everything and everyone, always stating before he started, 'I'm not including you in this because you're a honey.'

His pain was the worst in the world, the food was appalling, this nurse or that nurse was rude or offhand, there was too much noise in the corridor, no one tried to make him comfortable. The complaints were endless.

He had had nightmares for the past two nights. The nurses on duty said he was screaming at the top of his lungs and he had to be given a stronger sedative. Miranda smiled when she was told this, and hoped he was so badly frightened he would confess what he'd done. But she couldn't hope for that just now, it was only two in the afternoon, no time for nightmares or confessions.

'Yes, Mr Ramsden?' she said starchily as she got to his bed.

'My leg sure is throbbing,' he bleated out.

'I've told you several times already that this happens sometimes after a limb is amputated.'

'But it's agony.'

'I hardly think it's that,' she said crisply. 'And you are already on the highest dose allowed of painkilling drugs.'

'How am I to bear it?' he asked.

'Maybe you should make your peace with your Maker,' she said sharply. The moment the words came out she regretted it. She knew only too well it wasn't right for a nurse to sit in judgment on a patient. She blamed Tony Bryan for that.

'You are very hard on me, Sister,' he whined.

Miranda only heard the self-pity and looked down at him with contempt. Tony had telephoned her the previous evening and expressed his anxiety for Lotte now that he had no choice but to arrest and charge her.

'You have done unspeakable things to a vulnerable young woman,' she spat out. 'I might find it possible to be kind to you if you'd just be man enough to admit what you've done. What difference can it make to you anyway? Your punishment is assured, whatever you do or say.'

She walked away from his bed then, too angry to care what he made of that.

Bryan, dressed in scrubs, stood well back from the pathologist and his assistant as they examined Fern Ramsden. He loathed autopsies, especially on those who'd been dead for some time. The smell was sickening and the sound of scalpels and other implements cutting through flesh sent a creeping feeling down the back of his legs.

'You say your young lady only stabbed her once with a narrow-bladed kitchen knife?' the pathologist asked.

'That's right,' Bryan said. 'We recovered a knife from the house which was shown to her today and she confirmed it was the one she used. Six inches long, no serration, the kind you might use for slicing vegetables.'

'I see that wound,' the man said. 'But there is another one lower down – the knife that inflicted this was much larger. I'd say a French cook's knife. That was the one which killed her; the first was well above the victim's heart and didn't go far enough in to damage anything vital.'

Bryan overcame his squeamishness and stepped forward. It was difficult to believe that the woman on the slab, looking so grotesque and atrophied from immersion in salt water for so long, was the same glamorous, sexy redhead he'd seen photographs of.

'But the cuts are at different angles,' he said.

'The blows came from different directions, and the larger one was from someone left-handed. They were not from the same person.' The pathologist poked around the torso for a few moments. 'I'd say the second, larger one was inflicted by a man, judging by the force required to get such depth of penetration, and the victim would have been lying down when he did it.'

'Hallelujah,' Bryan exclaimed and punched the air in delight. 'So after all that sanctimonious bastard has said about how much he loved her, he killed her! Let him get out of that one!'

'Anything else you need to know?' The pathologist's eyes were smiling above his mask at Bryan's glee.

'No, just fax the report through as soon as you're done. I think I'll do a spot of hospital visiting before I go back to the station.'

Bryan felt as if he was walking on air as he made his way up to the high-dependency ward where Ramsden was being cared for. It would be good to see Miranda too, but absolutely superb to shatter that man's supreme confidence by telling him his wife's body had been found.

Miranda was busy in the main ward. Bryan waved to her and indicated where he was going.

Ramsden appeared even more haggard than he'd been on the last visit. He was propped up on pillows but he looked very sick.

'Just come to tell you the good tidings,' Bryan said jovially. 'We found your wife's body today!'

'You did?' Ramsden said, and Bryan could almost see the cogs in his brain whirling as he tried to decide how he should react to this news.

He put his left hand up to his eyes and partially covered them, as if hiding his tears. 'At least now I'll be able to bury her and have closure,' he said at length.

Bryan poured the man a glass of water and held it

out to him. The left hand came away from his dry eyes and took the glass.

'Left-handed?' Bryant asked. 'The second fatal stab wound in your wife's chest was struck by a left-handed man. It had to be you, there was no other man there.'

Ramsden stared at him, his eyes wide like those of a rabbit caught in a car's headlights.

'You killed your wife,' Bryan said quietly. 'You killed the baby too and but for Lotte's smartness you would've killed her and Dale. I can prove all this, but somehow I doubt you'll still be with us for a trial. So I'm giving you the chance to redeem yourself and admit it all.'

'I told you the truth the other day,' the man said, his voice shaking.

Bryan shook his head slowly. 'You told me a heap of shit. I'm going away now to get another officer, a solicitor for you and a tape recorder. By the time I get back I want you ready to tell me about Fern and the baby. The true story this time.'

Bryan wheeled round and walked towards the door, then stopping and turning back with his hand still on the door, looked hard at Ramsden. 'Just so you'll know the score, I don't give a toss whether you get repatriated to stand trial in the States, whether you get tried here, or even if you die before any decision is made about you. All I care about is that lovely young girl you've so badly wronged.

'I'll tell you now, before I get back with witnesses, that if you give me a full and frank confession tonight,

421

I'll see you get treated fairly. If you don't, you might find me leaning on that stump of yours, getting your pain relief delayed, and a dozen other nasty little tricks I know.'

He walked away then, whistling 'Dixie'.

Chapter Twenty

'But I must see her, please!' David begged the desk sergeant at Brighton police station.

'I'm sorry, sir, but it's not allowed,' the man repeated. He had the look of a bloodhound with saggy jowls and bags under his eyes. 'If you want to write her a note I'll make sure she gets it. If you want to leave her cigarettes or chocolate, I'll pass then on to her. But you can't see her.'

'Can I speak to DI Bryan then?'

'He's out on a case,' the sergeant said. 'I don't think he'll be back here this evening.'

It was just after seven in the evening. David had been working out of the office all day and he didn't get Simon's message about Lotte being arrested until he got home at five-thirty and checked his voice mail. He jumped in the car immediately and drove over to Brighton, and now it seemed he'd just been wasting his time.

'David!' A familiar voice made him turn round to see that Simon had just come in.

'Am I glad to see you – they won't let me see her,' David explained.

'Nor me neither,' Simon said. 'I just brought her some smarter clothes for court tomorrow morning and her makeup and stuff. I can't believe they are doing this to her.'

Simon put the small suitcase on to the counter and the desk sergeant said he would send it down to Lotte. David quickly wrote her a note explaining why he couldn't see her and that he'd be at the court in the morning. He ended it with a dozen kisses saying they were all 'good-luck-and-just-until-we-get-the-chance-for-real' ones. He hoped that might make her smile.

'How is she?' David asked as he handed over the note. 'She must be terrified.'

'The officer down in the cells is a good sort, we don't whack prisoners with truncheons like on the films,' the sergeant said dryly. 'I haven't seen her personally but I know there is a great deal of sympathy for her, so stop worrying.'

As the two men left the police station Simon suggested David came back with him and stayed the night in Lotte's room rather than drive back to Chichester and return in the morning. 'We could get a pizza or something and have a few drinks. We all need something to calm us down.'

David was glad of the offer; he didn't fancy being alone.

Down in the cells, Lotte sat on the bunk looking through a magazine one of the policewomen had sent down for her. She was looking at it, but not taking it in, for she knew that by this time tomorrow night she would be in Holloway Prison. Just the very name of the place sent cold shudders down her spine. She remembered watching the TV series *Bad Girls*, which was set in the prison, and thinking how scary it would be to be in there. While she knew the writers of the programme would exaggerate how awful it was, it was still the prison where some of the most dangerous and wicked women served their sentences, so it wasn't going to be like a boarding school.

She opened the note from David and read it once again. She guessed he'd written it hurriedly in front of the desk sergeant, and couldn't say much for that reason. His note, and the clothes and makeup so carefully picked out and packed by Simon, meant so much. It was comforting to know they were out there thinking and worrying about her. She had been disappointed that DI Bryan hadn't come to see her before going off duty, but she supposed she was after all just another case to him.

She had never, ever imagined herself being in a police cell, and now she was here, with the sound of a drunk shouting out abuse down the corridor, she felt the full weight of everything that had happened to her in the last year or so.

It was strange that she hadn't felt it before today. But as the memories had come back to her it was almost as if she was looking down watching someone else's life. It hadn't seemed like it had all really happened to her.

The rape in Ushuaia had been an appalling and

terrifying incident, yet now it didn't seem as hideous as being in that bed with Howard and Fern. She wondered how she managed to cope with Howard's baby growing in her belly. Yet she didn't remember ever hating the baby, only him.

How could they have left her locked in the basement for such long periods? Surely they must have known how frightened and lonely she was, especially when she went into labour? There were times during the birth when she thought she was going to die, the pain was so intense. She'd never known pain like that. Didn't they realize how terrifying it was for her knowing there was no doctor on call and no operating theatre should that be needed?

It really was unbelievable that anyone could be so casual about human life as Fern and Howard were. She wondered if they had treated all the mothers whose babies they sold as callously.

And she recalled all those hours after the birth when she had stood poised on the stairs with that knife in her hand waiting for Fern or Howard to come down. She must have been half out of her mind! Would she really have been able to kill them if the opportunity had arisen? She doubted it somehow. It was only once she knew the baby was dead and they were going to kill her too that she got desperate enough to find that extra toughness.

When she thought back on all she had endured, be that pain, loneliness, shame, hunger or fear, the worst thing of all was not getting to hold her baby. How could they snatch her away as if she was nothing to her?

Even now, nearly four months later, she still felt the raw pain of separation. She thought she could've borne it better had she held her, fed and changed her, and studied every detail about her. At least then she would have her little face imprinted on her very soul, and her smell in her nostrils and the touch of her skin would be for ever there in her mind. But she'd had all that stolen from her.

A policewoman told her earlier that she mustn't worry too much about going to Holloway, because when it got about that she'd stabbed someone in self-defence, she would be admired. Did that mean she'd have to pretend to be a hard case? Somehow she didn't think she could fool anyone for very long.

'I'd like to go over that part just one more time to clarify it,' DI Bryan said to Ramsden.

He had come back to the hospital, as he said he would, with another officer and a tape recorder. Waiting for them was Mike Branning, the duty solicitor on call that evening, to make certain Ramsden had legal representation.

It was of course very unusual to have such an interview in a hospital, but because of the special circumstances – the possibility Ramsden might die, or be repatriated to the States if he survived, and because Lotte Wainwright had been charged with killing his wife, while it now appeared that it was he who did the killing – the top brass had given the go-ahead.

Bryan hadn't expected for one moment that Ramsden would cooperate and tell the truth. He thought the man was such a practised liar and confidence trickster that he probably wouldn't know the truth if it stared him in the face. All Bryan was really hoping for was that the overall tone of the statement would reveal the man's character, that he would be at a loss to explain certain things, and that would be enough to get Lotte off the hook.

But maybe the prospect of meeting his Maker shortly had clarified Howard's mind, for right from the start of the interview he abandoned the structure of lies he'd told earlier.

He said it was pure chance that they had come upon Lotte being raped in Ushuaia and that taking her back to their suite on the cruise ship was nothing more than common kindness. But he went on to say that Fern quickly became very attached to her, as if she was a daughter. That was why Fern asked her to join them at the Dorchester and then offered her a job as their housekeeper/PA.

Bryan didn't think that was absolutely true – he was fairly certain the couple had earmarked her for something more lucrative for them almost as soon as they rescued her in Ushuaia – but he let it pass.

Howard said he thought Fern's initial idea for Lotte to have a baby for her was to create a kind of idealistic perfect family unit where all three adults would live in harmony and bring up the baby together.

'So you would in fact have had two wives?' Bryan remarked.

'Fern didn't see it that way,' Ramsden said indignantly.

Bryan was fairly certain that to Ramsden this was the sole attraction for as they got further into the interview it was patently clear he had never wanted a child of his own.

It was equally clear that the couple were breathtakingly arrogant, for they believed that they were offering Lotte the opportunity of a lifetime. Just the incredulous way Ramsden spoke of her refusal showed how egotistical they were and how used to getting their own way.

He said they offered her a compromise in that if she wanted out after the baby was born, they would give her a lump sum of money and keep the baby themselves.

Up to this point it didn't sound as if they were actually imprisoning Lotte, only using a kind of moral blackmail on her to have a baby for them. But it was apparent that Lotte lost the chance and even the will to escape when they began drugging her. Howard claimed it was only a mild sedative which removed anxiety. Fern stepped up the dose several days before the night they were to try for a baby. She said this was to make Lotte 'more receptive'.

Howard skirted around the events of the first night they tried for a baby. All he said was that Lotte seemed quite amenable. But she obviously wasn't, as Howard admitted she tried to escape the same night, and he and Fern were so scared she might succeed next time and try to make trouble for them that they kept her locked in after that.

While Fern was overjoyed when Lotte became pregnant, Howard said he was already regretting the whole idea. He didn't actually admit to the tape that he was disappointed he wasn't going to get a pretty young woman in his bed on a regular basis after all, or that he didn't fancy having a squalling baby around either. But that was probably the size of it because he said that when Fern saw he was drawing back on the whole thing, she became angry and moody.

He did admit that as Lotte's pregnancy progressed both he and Fern became aware they'd got themselves into an impossible situation. He mentioned taking her out for walks in remote places but they were always nervous that she would appeal to someone for help. They also knew that however much money they offered the girl, they still couldn't trust her not to go to the police. They couldn't arrange a private adoption in England, and they didn't have any contacts here for getting a false passport for the baby. He blamed Fern, she blamed him, and all the while they knew Lotte was constantly vigilant for a chance to escape which put them under even greater strain.

Finally the little girl was born. Howard said absolutely nothing about the birth. Perhaps, like so many men, he believed that childbirth was as natural as breathing and involved no pain or risks.

But he said plenty about Fern being like a child with a new dolly. He said she refused even to discuss their future because she was 'bonding' with their baby.

So while Lotte was crying down in the basement, Howard was left to try to plan some way out of the mess. He had made inquiries about registering the baby's birth, and that appeared quite simple, with no proof needed that he and Fern were the parents. But to get a passport for the baby would be much more difficult, for they would have to submit their own passports, and it would soon be discovered that they were forged ones.

Their original plan, made some time before the baby was born, had been to get Lotte to register the birth and apply for the passport. She was to travel with them to America, and then she would go along with the adoption there. But it became clear that whatever inducements they offered her, she was never going to agree to their plans.

By the time the baby was born they knew she would snatch any opportunity to seek help and get them arrested. No bribe, however large, was going to ensure she got quietly on a flight back to the States with them and the baby. That was when Howard decided both she and the baby had to be killed.

It was the story from this point on that Bryan wanted repeated, so he could be sure it was absolutely clear on the tape.

'You want me to tell you again about when I smothered the baby?' Howard asked. He actually smirked as he spoke, as if he was proud of the way he'd got out of the no-win situation.

'That's right,' Bryan agreed, trying very hard to hide how much he despised him. 'You said it was the first of May, is that correct?'

'Yes, we went up to London that day to see someone about a passport for the baby. We didn't have any luck because they couldn't do one for a child born to American parents. We were both really tired and blue when we got back, and the baby wasn't crying. Fern was afraid to go and look in case she had died, so I went up. She wasn't dead, just lying there quietly. I just thought, this is the way out! Pillow over the face, over and out. Problem solved.'

Bryan's stomach churned at such callousness.

'Go on,' he prompted.

'I took one of the pillows off our bed and did it, pressed it hard against her face. I felt bad, she was after all my daughter. But we couldn't take her to the States and we couldn't stay here for ever. It took about five minutes, she struggled a bit, then I put the pillow back on our bed and went down to tell Fern I thought it was a crib death.'

Mike Manning, the solicitor, looked shell-shocked and blinked furiously.

'So were you and Fern OK together after this?' Bryan went on.

'Hell, no!' he exclaimed. 'She was like a bear with a sore arse, I've never known nothing like it, shouting, crying, going on and on about how I screwed up. Me! It was never my idea to keep the girl against her will, or to force her to have a baby for us. That was hers, the crazy broad. Then she came up with the idea of putting the girl in the sea with the baby; she said they'd get washed up and everyone would think Lotte threw herself in because her baby died.'

'And what was your view of that plan?'

Howard was silent for a little while. He looked exhausted and Bryan thought the solicitor would say the interview had to be halted till the morning, but he didn't.

'I thought it was a good one. It wasn't messy, it would be easy, and we could get a flight back to America the next day if we wanted.'

'Can you confirm what day this was?'

'May fifth,' Ramsden replied. 'About seven in the evening I got Lotte up from the basement. She seemed real calm, asked for a sandwich and a glass of milk. Then, just as Fern was about to pass her the glass, she produces a knife out of nowhere and sticks it in Fern's chest.'

'What did you do?'

'Well, I tried to catch the little bitch, but she kept dodging round the table. She even threw a coffee pot at me. Fern was staggering about with blood coming out of her chest.'

'Were you aware that Fern's wound wasn't a fatal one?'

'Well, it wasn't very deep but she was losing a lot of

blood and I knew she needed a doctor. But I couldn't get a doctor, could I? Not with a dead baby in the house and Lotte creating a rumpus.'

'So what did you do?'

'Well, I guess I kinda freaked out because Lotte had run into the lounge and was throwing stuff at the windows to try and break them. I was scared someone would hear her, and Fern was begging me for help. All at once I had the knife out of a drawer and I was sticking it in her.'

'What kind of knife was it?' Bryan asked.

'One of those big ones you chop stuff with. It had a triangular blade.'

'So you are admitting you stabbed your wife?'

'You know I did, you've seen the other wound on her!'

'I want you to say what you did.'

'I stabbed her, right here in the heart.' He touched his chest with his left hand.

'And tell me again where Lotte was while you were doing this?'

'She was in the lounge screaming and throwing stuff at the windows to try and get out that way. Soon as I finished Fern off I went after her to tie her up.'

'Did she know Fern was dead?'

'Yes, I told her, but she thought she'd killed her. She started on saying I should ring the police and she'd tell them it was her fault. But I wasn't going to do that.'

'So what did you do?'

'I wrapped Fern up in a picnic blanket and tied those

434

elastic tie things with hooks on either end round her. I'd already put the baby in the van. I took Lotte out next, then Fern, and drove down to my boat.'

The rest was just like Lotte had already told Bryan, except Howard admitted that after casting Lotte over the side and throwing the baby in too, he found it really hard to get Fern up over the side of the boat on his own because she was heavy with the big stones he'd put inside the blanket. He said as he finally got her half-way over, some of the stones fell out of the blanket into the water.

'I thought she'd sink anyway, and she did, disappeared right under the water. I said a few prayers and then I turned the boat around and went home.'

'You said a few prayers?' Bryan was so incredulous he couldn't resist commenting.

'Sure, I said I was sorry, but she got me into all this and it was the only way out for me.'

'I think we should stop the tape now and let my client have some rest,' Mike Branning said.

The interview was formally ended and the tape recorder turned off. Bryan walked away from Ramsden's bed without even saying goodbye for he was sickened by the man's final remark. He had claimed to have loved Fern; according to Lotte they had been together for almost thirty years and before things got out of hand they were very happy together. Yet he had killed her and his own baby to save his own neck.

*

A nurse came into the room after the police had gone. She offered Howard a bedpan, gave him some further medication, plumped up his pillows to make him more comfortable, then left, leaving just a dim night light on above his bed.

But although Howard shut his eyes he could not drop off to sleep. He felt as if Fern was in the room with him, vengeful and angry because he'd betrayed her.

He wished it was possible to go back and do things differently. He had loved Fern for his whole life, and he knew how awful it was going to be without her. Since the night he put her in the sea, he hadn't had one moment's peace of mind.

If he closed his eyes he could see her so clearly, her beautiful red hair waving on her bare shoulders. He'd always loved the way a sprinkling of freckles came out on her shoulders and arms in the sun, just as he'd loved her shape – full breasts, small waist and a backside that wiggled in such a sexy way when she walked.

Fern Swann was sixteen years old when he met her in 1974. He, Howard Barnes, was seventeen. Her folks came to live in the same trailer park he lived in, just a few miles outside Kansas City. It was called Merry-wood, but the only merriment there ever was, was the first couple of hours' drinking on a Friday night; later it would be the same old cursing and fighting that went on all week.

There was no wood either. The trailer park was situated between two highways, with only a chain-link fence to stop the many dogs and small children getting killed on the roads. In summer the dust was so thick you could clean a window at nine in the morning, and by noon you wouldn't see through it.

It was the last-chance trailer park. If you got thrown off there, there was nowhere else would have you. By the time a child was nine or ten they knew their place was right at the bottom of the heap.

Fern was the eldest of four, he was the eldest of five. All either of them had ever known was being dirt poor. They both had weak, messed-up mothers, and dads who hardly ever worked and liked to drink all day. They both knew more than was good for them about the adult world. They'd seen their mothers with black eyes, tried to soothe their younger siblings when they were hungry or when they were ridiculed at school for being dirty or smelly. Fern had helped her mother when she had a primitive abortion and Howard was weary of putting up 'welcome home' banners when his father got out of prison.

Fern was waiting on tables, Howard working in a gas station, and most of the money they earned had to be handed over to their mothers for the whole family. They had no decent clothes or any real friends, and they both had the burden of caring for their younger siblings. Maybe if they had met and fallen in love with someone who lived the same sort of life and didn't dream of a better one, things might have turned out differently. But from the first time they sat out together

437

one night on a couple of old car seats someone had dumped at the trailer park, and aired their little dreams to each other, they both sensed they'd found the one person who could make them come true.

The East and West Coasts of America may have been infected by the Peace and Love Movement of the late Sixties, but it had virtually bypassed Kansas. The thousands of well-attended churches, chapels and meeting houses right across the State were testament to Kansas being a God-fearing State. If not for this, Fern and Howard might well have drifted off on a completely different path, perhaps even straight to a criminal one, but instead they chose to join the Christ The Redeemer Evangelical Church.

The love of God or piety had little to do with it. Fern heard churchy folk handed out clothes to the needy, and she reckoned that she and Howard could move up a notch or two with some better ones.

They were given clothes, not only for themselves but their siblings too, but what really influenced them to keep going to that church was the preacher. He talked with such passion about God washing away men's sins and raising them up to the heavens that the people in the congregation couldn't wait to open their wallets, purses and pockets and fill the collection plate as it was passed around.

'I'm going to be a preacher,' Howard said with utter conviction to Fern one night after a service. 'We'll get married and travel all over America in a bus preaching the Word.'

It was the showmanship of preaching that Howard was drawn to, along with all that money in the collection plate. He would've preferred listening to poems than verses from the Bible, for there were times when he barely understood them. But he loved it when people stood up around him and bore witness to God calling them away from drink or a life of crime. It was high drama, exciting, moving, and both he and Fern were quick to notice it was a great way to induce people to put even more in the collection plate.

Doubtless sexual frustration boosted their religious fervour too. They were both virgins when they met, and they were both only too aware that an unwanted pregnancy would mean they would be trapped in Merrywood for ever. But they were a passionate couple, and the frantic petting they did nightly behind bushes and in back alleys did nothing to satisfy their needs. Throwing themselves into the Evangelical Church with its spirited music, extravagant witnessing and exaggerated claims of brother- and sisterhood, made them feel part of something bigger.

The preacher must have seen a kindred spirit in Howard as he took him on as his aide, giving him room and board at his house, and Fern trained to be a nurse so that she too could leave the trailer park.

Three years later they got married when Fern landed a job at a nursing home. The owners of the home liked the idea of having a 'man of the cloth' around to talk to the patients, so they let the couple have a small apartment on the premises.

Both Howard and Fern had always looked back on that time as being the happiest of their lives. They were together as man and wife at last and unable to get enough of each other. But it was also their lucky break. The lonely old patients were so grateful to the couple for all their kindnesses that many of them left them money in their wills. Had anyone cared to take a little more notice, they might have observed it was the richest of the patients and the ones with the fewest relatives the couple made a fuss of. But the people who owned the nursing home were too busy cutting corners and planning their own get-rich-quick schemes to notice what anyone else was doing.

By the time Fern and Howard were in their late twenties they had amassed a tidy sum between them and Howard had become a formidable preacher. They moved to Alabama to start their own church, but Fern also did private nursing in people's homes, invariably the old and frail. Sometimes, too, she was hired to care for a new mother and her baby, sometimes she was called in by a midwife to assist her, and this was where she learned the rudiments of midwifery.

Howard felt that this period in his life was when he was at his very best. Preacher Barnes became renowned for his fiery sermons that kept the congregation enthralled. He took witnessing a stage further than any other preacher, creating the best show in town as he urged sinners to come forward and testify to their sins and let Jesus into their hearts.

Folk often marvelled how so many broken people, the damaged, drunks and ex-criminals, found their way to him, but it was more to do with him giving them a few dollars to bare their souls than a call from God.

It wasn't all trickery, though, for he and Fern fed these people a hot meal and gave them sympathy and hope when they told them they had been saved by Jesus. Most soon slipped back to their old habits, but as Fern always pointed out, the flood of life's rejects, the dispossessed, mentally ill and the inadequate, would never dry up, and if they genuinely saved just one in a hundred, that was God's work. And as long as Howard continued to put on a show at the church, his real congregation would continue to put money in the collection box.

It was in Alabama that they arranged the first adoption. No money changed hands; the young girl had come to Howard and Fern distraught because her family would disown her if they were to discover she was having a baby. The Barneses also knew a couple desperate for a child. The girl had her baby in Howard and Fern's small home, with Fern assisting the midwife, and soon after the birth the baby was handed to its new parents. The papers were signed later, and the adoption became a legal one.

That arranged adoption and helping the young mother was an act of pure altruism. But it led to others where they asked for a small fee to cover expenses. There were real expenses too, for the midwife, the laundry and the mother's food while she was with them. Howard was satisfied with just the gratitude from the couples who had waited so long for a child of their own. But Fern pointed out that gratitude wouldn't keep her and Howard when they were old.

It was around that time that Howard realized Fern wanted far more than he did. He was entirely happy and contented with his life as a preacher. The role gave him dignity, poise and importance, and it pleased him to see his wife nursing in the same community, for that proved they were totally dedicated to helping others.

But Fern was growing tired of sitting people on bed-pans, of changing dressings and bed linen, of bathing, monitoring and handing out medicine. She wanted to wear beautiful clothes, see foreign places, have her nails painted scarlet and be admired as a woman, not just for her nursing skills.

She often teased Howard by saying she led him around by his penis, and it was very true that she used sex to get what she wanted. They were both highly sexed, but Fern could hold out, and frequently did until he agreed to whatever she was asking.

That was how she got him to go along with the plan for the adoption agency. Hartford in Connecticut was the place she picked; close enough to New York and Boston to make it practical for prospective adoptive parents, but distant enough for the mothers to feel secure in the knowledge that their relatives wouldn't drop in.

There in a large house on the outskirts of town, Howard and Fern became Dr and Mrs Kent and set up their business, with an associate who had fingers in various pies and would direct would-be adoptive parents to them for a fee.

White babies were at a premium in the early years, and Howard often donned a dog collar again to go down to New York. It wasn't just in the hope of finding frightened pregnant girls a long way from home who might be tempted by the offer of free room and board in return for giving their baby away. He also looked for girls who for a sum of money would agree to have a baby for someone else. Sometimes the girls were impregnated with the sperm of the would-be adoptive father. But mostly Howard used his own, telling the parents it came from a sportsman, scientist or mathematician, whichever he thought they'd prefer.

It was soon a thriving business which they ran efficiently between them, outwardly as a charitable trust which helped unmarried mothers estranged from their parents through their confinement. Not even their closest neighbours or those who came in to clean, cook or garden, suspected they were in fact selling the babies. This was partly because they made sure they displayed no signs of wealth, and they had an office elsewhere in town where they handled the business side of things.

But when they went away on cruises or to New York, Boston or England, sometimes as Gullick, sometimes as Ramsden, Fern wore the kind of clothes and jewellery she had always craved.

The drug smuggling was born out of this. They had met Jarvis in a hotel in the Bahamas and when they told him they often went on cruise ships, he put the proposition to them about booking on a Dutch cruise line to South America and picking up a package for him in Colombia.

The danger element in the drug smuggling worked like an aphrodisiac on them both. They became more and more sexually charged as the ship neared Colombia and the pick-up point, and again as they approached Rotterdam at the other end. Once they'd delivered their package and picked up the money, they invariably went straight to a hotel and had wild sex which lasted for hours.

When Jarvis retired from drug trafficking, they did too, for they felt their run of good luck couldn't last much longer. They took cruises to places other than South America, and concentrated their energies on their adoption business.

It was rather ironic that they were back in South America when they got involved with Lotte. They had never been to Chile before and thought it would be wonderful to see the fiords. In truth they were a little disappointed; the ports along the way were dull, and the scenery wasn't as spectacular as they'd expected.

If it hadn't been for meeting Lotte, they might have given up the adoption business, sold the house in

Hartford and probably the one in Itchenor, and moved to Florida. They could have been sitting out by a pool now, watching the sunset with a drink in their hands. Now she was gone, and he was dying. It had all been for nothing.

Chapter Twenty-One

Lotte was awake at dawn. The window in the cell was frosted glass, and even if it had been clear she couldn't have seen out of it because it was too high up on the wall, but she lay on the narrow hard bunk looking at it and observed daylight gradually brightening it.

It reminded her of the window in the basement, and it seemed to her that although she had viewed that room as a prison, the real thing was a great deal worse. She'd had a shower there, but there were no such luxuries in a police station. She supposed there might be a sink with hot water further down the corridor which they'd let her use for a wash, but she doubted she'd get any privacy.

All night long there had been noise from the other cells. A couple of drunks were singing and shouting, and another rough male voice with a Liverpool accent kept shouting for them to shut up. She guessed it would be noisy in Holloway too. She was so scared she felt sick.

'Ready, Lotte?' The fresh-faced WPC who had brought her breakfast earlier and let her use the sink at the end of the corridor to wash her face and clean her teeth, was now ready to take her upstairs to the van which would take her to the court.

This same WPC had brought her a bar of chocolate late last night, perhaps because she'd noted Lotte hadn't eaten the cheese sandwich she'd been given. That little kindness had meant a lot.

'As ready as I'll ever be,' Lotte replied, her voice cracking because she was so afraid. Simon must have borrowed the navy and white pin-striped trouser suit she was wearing from one of the girls at the salon. It fitted as if it had been made for her, and she was very grateful to the owner for she had had very few clothes back at his flat and nothing suitable for a court appearance. Luckily she'd only recently washed her hair, so it looked OK, and on the WPC's advice she left it loose. Her hands were shaking so badly she hadn't put on much makeup, just some mascara, blusher and lipstick.

'You look really nice,' the WPC said, putting her hand on Lotte's arm. 'We'll all be thinking about you today. All of us feel for you.'

Lotte tried to smile and thank the woman, but the little kindness made the tears well up and she knew if she started to cry she would never stop.

The cell at the police station was swapped for another under the court. But this time the door was just bars, so she could see people coming and going. She was the only female prisoner as far as she could tell, and although

447

some of the men called out to her and asked what she was in for, she didn't reply.

She had been there nearly two hours, her heart thumping and her palms sticky with nervousness, when at eleven, a court official came and unlocked the door and led her up a different staircase to the one she'd come in by. As she got to the top she found herself in the courtroom and was asked to sit in the dock.

There were perhaps twenty people already there in the court. Mr Harding, her solicitor, was talking animatedly to DI Bryan. Both men glanced round and on seeing her, smiled, but then continued their conversation, which she found unnerving.

Simon, Adam, David and Scott were all sitting together. Their smiles and little waves and gestures of solidarity were all stiff, as if they were struggling to hold their emotions in check. She thought that the row of rather untidy-looking people by the door must be press, because they looked as though they were on a mission and all seemed to know one another. There were a few other older people too, some of whom she recognized as neighbours of her parents, but her mother and father hadn't come.

Lotte wasn't sure whether she was disappointed by that, or relieved, but all at once the Clerk of the Court was asking everyone to rise for the magistrate.

Mr Harding had explained that this court appearance would be a very brief one, where he would tell the magistrate the general details about her alleged crime and personal circumstances, and would then ask for bail.

448

He'd already explained to Lotte how unlikely it was that the magistrate would agree to that, and she assumed that meant that within about ten minutes she'd be back in the cell beneath the courts, waiting for the transport which would take her to Holloway Prison to be remanded in custody.

As Lotte had never been in a court before, she had no real idea what to expect, but she had thought it would all be very formal and serious, especially as she was charged with murder. But Bryan and the solicitor were smiling, and when Bryan went forward to speak to the magistrate, she saw David and Simon look round at her with puzzled expressions.

The conversation between the Detective Inspector and the magistrate seemed to go on and on. All around the courtroom people began talking to one another in whispers. Lotte didn't know whether this sort of thing happened often in courts, but it seemed very strange and disorganized.

All at once the magistrate banged his gavel on his desk for silence. He looked directly at Lotte.

'It has been decided, Miss Wainwright, that there are no charges for you to answer today, or in the future. You may leave the court.'

Lotte was so stunned she didn't attempt to move. She opened her mouth to ask why, but the magistrate had already got up and was leaving. She heard someone give a whoop of joy, and although she wasn't sure who it was, she thought it must be David.

Mr Harding came over to her, his smile so wide it almost reached either ear. 'It's all over for you,' he said. 'Come on, you can leave. Ramsden made a full confession.'

'Why? How? I mean, confession to what? I stabbed Fern,' she stuttered out, her words falling over one another.

'You might have stabbed her, but you didn't kill her,' he said, taking her hand and squeezing it between both of his. 'Ramsden stabbed her after you.'

They were asked to clear the courtroom then and Lotte walked out with Mr Harding still explaining how it all came about.

DI Bryan was waiting outside the court. Like Harding, he had a wide, wide smile.

'This is the man you have to thank for it all,' Harding said. 'I doubt he'll admit it, Lotte, but he's gone more than the extra mile for you. I'd say he ran a marathon.'

'You go home and try to forget any of this ever happened.' Bryan stepped forward to hug her and kiss her cheek. 'I'll come round in a day or two to tie up any loose ends and answer any questions you may have. But all charges against you have been dropped. You are completely free.'

It was more than an hour before Lotte could really take in exactly what had happened. She had been so terrified, and so sure she was going to prison, that to be told it was all over and she was free, seemed like a bad joke.

She was sure someone would come along and say they'd got it wrong and she would be arrested again.

She and the boys, who were just as confused as she was, had let Mr Harding lead them into a café for some coffee. There the solicitor explained about Fern's body being washed up, the results of the autopsy, and how Bryan had gone to Ramsden's hospital bed and wrung a full confession out of him.

'He smothered my baby?' Lotte said in horror. That seemed a million times worse than everything that had been done to her, or Howard stabbing Fern.

Harding nodded and patted her hand in sympathy. 'You could sue Ramsden for compensation for what he did to you,' he said. 'My practice could handle that for you. I doubt whether you'll ever feel money will give you back what he took from you, but he is a wealthy man and it would enable you to open your own hairdressing salon or buy a nice house.'

'I'll think about it,' she said.

Scott mentioned telephoning Dale, who hadn't been too well since getting home with her parents; her mother felt it was delayed shock. Because of this Scott had decided not to tell her Lotte had been arrested, as it might only have made her worse. 'But now I've got some good news, I really want to speak to her,' he said. 'I'd better find out when she's coming back to work. Marisa has been making some very pointed remarks.'

Mr Harding said he had to go then, and Scott, Simon and Adam all agreed they had to get back to work too, but suggested they held a small celebratory party at the flat tonight. 'David will look after you today,' Simon said, grinning from ear to ear.

'Where to?' David asked when all the others had dispersed. 'I bet you didn't sleep at all last night. Would you like to go home and have a sleep now?'

'Certainly not,' she laughed. 'I want to be out in the sunshine, I've spent too long in the past year inside and sleeping. And I'm starving!'

'So how about I take you to lunch somewhere where we can sit outside?' he suggested.

'That sounds wonderful,' Lotte said. 'But can I go home and change first? This suit is a bit formal and too warm.'

He explained that he'd stayed in her room the previous night and he'd left jeans and a casual jacket there. 'I hope I don't seem like I'm pushing things,' he said as they walked towards the flat. 'I mean, staying in your bed, leaving stuff there, even being the one left with you today. I didn't ask the guys to disappear. They just did that.'

Lotte glanced sideways at him, amused by the anxiety in his voice. She guessed that Simon had engineered the others to say they had to go, because he knew she would like to be alone with David.

'I don't think anything like that,' she said quite truthfully. 'And after all you did for Dale and me while we were locked up, you are welcome to sleep in my bed.'

'With you in it too?' he said with a boyish grin.

'That's the only bit which is scary,' she admitted,

dropping her eyes from his. 'I mean, embarking on something like that after everything that's happened.'

He just took her hand and held it, not saying a word, and she knew he understood.

As they got into Meeting House Lane, Lotte saw her father standing there, looking up at the flat. At the sound of their footsteps he turned and saw them. He looked worried and embarrassed.

'I got to the court late because I couldn't find a parking space,' he said. 'I was told what had happened and I'm so relieved and glad for you.'

'Thank you, Dad.' She gave him a tight little smile.

'Are you going to ask me in?'

Lotte looked at him hard for a few moments without replying. She had always cast her mother as the hard, cruel one, and believed her father was a good, kind man who was bullied too. But if she'd learned just one thing from everything that had happened to her, it was that you couldn't call yourself an adult until you'd learned to stand up for yourself and never blame other people for your own mistakes.

'No, I'm not going to ask you in, Dad,' she said. 'You've been too late all my life.'

'But I couldn't help not finding a parking space.'

Lotte shrugged. 'You could have walked or taken the bus; you could have left home earlier.'

'I was trying to make amends,' he said, a whine in his voice.

'How does being late make amends? If I'd been sent

to prison I wouldn't have seen you. It's just like all the other times when you should've been there to defend me, but you let me down. At least Mum is consistent. She doesn't even pretend to care.'

'She would've come, she's got one of her heads,' he said.

Lotte gave a wry smile. 'Oh yes, the famous heads that stopped her doing anything connected with me, like parents' evening, sports day or prize-giving.'

'You've grown very hard,' he said, his voice shaking.

'You and Mum can take all the credit for that,' Lotte said, and she walked on then, up the spiral staircase, without looking back.

Ted looked at David, who was still standing there because he couldn't bring himself to leave the older man like that. 'Well, that's a fine turnout! I took the morning off work to go to court for her.'

'You weren't there all those other times when she needed you,' David said, a little embarrassed to be put on the spot. 'You should be proud she learned to manage so well without you.'

The older man's eyes were swimming, and David felt a pang of sympathy for him. But he felt far more for Lotte because she deserved better parents. He turned away and went up the stairs, leaving Ted Wainwright standing there.

David took Lotte to a pub he knew on the bank of the river at Arundel.

They'd had fish and chips, and sticky toffee pudding, and now they were sitting back in their seats enjoying the sun and the scenery. Lotte said she couldn't think of a better view, with Arundel Castle as a grey and rather forbidding backdrop, the many trees, and the swans gliding by on the river which meandered through lush meadows full of fluffy white meadowsweet and buttercups.

'So what now?' David asked.

'Do you mean "what now", as in "right now"? Or did you mean what do I do now for a job, or, with the rest of my life?'

'I'd like to know about both when you are ready.' David reached across the table and took her hand. 'But I didn't mean you to think about a job or the rest of your life right now. I just want you to have a lovely day, doing whatever you like. To me it's wonderful just to have you with me.'

She patted his cheek as if amused by that. 'It all feels a bit surreal,' she admitted. 'I'm going to need time to work out who I am now. How did I get savage enough to stick a knife in anyone? Or be that cruel to my dad this morning?'

'I guess no one knows what they are capable of until they are tested,' he said thoughtfully, kissing the tips of her fingers. 'In my opinion the things that you've done were the right reactions to exceptional circumstances; you found hidden strengths when you needed to. But your basic nature hasn't changed. As for your dad, I think that was long overdue. If you'd invited him in and given him tea nothing would change. He'd creep round to see you sometimes on his own, and never give your mum a bollocking for being such a lousy mother. Maybe he'll do that now.'

'Pigs might fly,' Lotte said gloomily, then laughed. 'Let's go to West Wittering and paddle in the sea.'

An hour later as they walked hand in hand in the sea carrying their shoes, Lotte felt as if the past was fading away. They had both rolled their jeans up to their knees, and the sensation of the cold water and sand squiggling up between her toes was a good one. She had put on a skimpy little turquoise camisole top, and the sun was hot on the back of her neck and the tops of her arms, but she didn't care if she was burning. It was so good to be outside, to feel all this space around her.

She'd walked on this beach with Fern and Howard last December, a raw, bitterly cold day when not even dog walkers were about. But oddly, the thought of them and what they did to her couldn't impinge on today and spoil it.

David was telling her about his seven brothers and sisters, and how their parents ran a very successful fish and chip shop in Weston-Super-Mare. He spoke of them all with such affection and humour that Lotte wanted to meet them, but she wondered what he would tell them about her. That reminded her that he didn't actually know her entire story, just as Adam, Simon and

Scott didn't either. All they'd had so far in the days since she'd left hospital was edited highlights.

'There's an awful lot more I've got to tell you, David,' she said a little later as they walked back to his car. 'And until I do it's going to be hanging between us like dirty washing.'

He didn't answer, just walked to his car, unlocked it and then came round to open the passenger door for her.

'Sit on the seat and let me clean the sand off your feet,' he said. He opened the boot of the car and got out a big bottle of water and an old towel. 'My mum always did this when we were small,' he said as he poured water over her feet and then dried them.

There was something about him washing sand off her feet which suddenly made her cry, and all at once it was as if the floodgates had opened.

'Oh, Lotte!' he said, kneeling down outside the car and trying to comfort her. 'Was it because I didn't respond to you saying you wanted to tell me everything? I only didn't answer because I couldn't think of the right thing to say.'

'It isn't that,' she sobbed. 'It's you washing my feet. It was so thoughtful and lovely.'

He put his hand under her chin and lifted her face up, mopping away the tears with the towel. 'Your feet were burned a little while ago. I didn't want the sand to make them sore again.'

Lotte's tears turned to a strangled giggle. 'I thought

457

the Ramsdens had stolen everything from me, but now you're stealing my heart.'

David sat back on his haunches by the car and laughed. 'You stole mine the day I found you on the beach,' he said. 'Only we men are slow and I didn't realize it was missing for a while.'

Lotte smiled and reached out to caress his cheek. 'You, David Mitchell, are gorgeous.'

'And so are you, Lotte Wainwright,' he said, leaning forward to kiss her.

It wasn't just a casual kiss, even though he was kneeling in a car park and she was sitting in the car. It had the sweetness of an exploratory first kiss, but with undertones of passion and the desire to possess. Lotte lost herself in it, savouring the sensuality of his lips and tongue and not wanting it to end.

David broke away first, nuzzling his nose gently against her. 'We'd better get back now,' he said with a sigh. 'You can't have a party to celebrate you being free if you don't show up.'

'Surprise, surprise,' Simon called out from the hall. 'Come and see, Lotte!'

It was just after nine and most of their friends and all the staff from Kutz were already in the flat.

Lotte had had a bath earlier, washed her hair and put on a pink sequined top and white jeans. She was a bit burnt on her neck and arms, but her face had a becoming pink glow. When Simon called out she went into the hall, expecting it was someone who used to work in Kutz when she was there.

But to her amazement it was Dale.

Lotte shrieked with delight and flung her arms round her friend. 'What a fantastic surprise,' she said. 'What made you come and are you feeling better now?'

'I felt instantly better when Scott rang me to tell me what happened in court today. I had to come right away.'

'I am so glad you did,' Lotte said, hugging her again. 'I couldn't really celebrate without you, or have the full post mortem. You are staying, aren't you? I can make you up a bed in my room; Simon's got one of those inflatable mattresses.'

'Glad you asked,' Dale laughed. 'I didn't even stop to think where I'd sleep.'

It was a very happy, noisy party, but by one in the morning Lotte had retreated on to one of the sofas and was just watching everyone else. Dale and Scott were dancing together, and there was no doubt they were about to become more than just good friends. He was smiling right into her eyes, his hands were running over her curves, and Dale was stroking his ears and neck and looking like she'd fallen in love.

She had said drunkenly a little earlier that her parents had told her she'd changed for the better, and if they'd known locking her up for a few days would have such an effect, they would have done it years ago.

Lotte could laugh at that now because she knew it wasn't just the days in the basement, or even working on the cruise ship which had changed Dale from a selfish prima donna to a person who was sensitive to others. It was friendship which had made the difference. She'd learned to care for someone more than she cared for herself, she'd discovered the magic of having someone to share good times and bad with, someone to lean on and to be leant on. To laugh at herself and to share it with another.

And it hadn't been one-way traffic. Dale had made Lotte braver, tougher and less hung up about what people thought of her. Together they'd rounded each other out and discovered new strengths.

'You look tired.'

Lotte looked up at the sound of David's voice. He'd been engrossed in talking to Simon when she last looked to see where he was. That was another thing she liked about him; apart from being kind, generous, sexy and gorgeous, he didn't need looking after – he could mingle with people and chat.

'I suppose I must be, but it's such a good party I wouldn't want to be the one to break it up,' she smiled. 'Come and sit here with me.'

He sat down beside her and put his arm around her, drawing her close. 'That's better,' he sighed. 'I've been itching to cuddle you all evening.'

She tucked her feet up on the sofa and snuggled right

into his arms. She didn't think she could remember ever feeling so safe or happy before.

'What are you thinking about?' David asked her after a minute or two. He was running the tips of his fingers up and down her neck by her ear in a way that was making her wish Dale had somewhere else to sleep tonight.

'Wondering how I can have you all to myself,' she said, turning her face up to his to kiss him.

Simon had said earlier today that she might need counselling to deal with what she'd been through, and perhaps she would once it all began to sink in properly. But right now there was nothing on her mind but David.

His kiss made her tingle all over and everyone in the room disappear, and she pressed closer to him for more.

'That is the "we-stay-here-snogging-till-first-light-then-I-whisk-you-back-to-my-place" kiss,' he whispered. 'Or is that too presumptuous?'

'When you kiss the way you do you are allowed to be presumptuous,' she said with a smile. Suddenly she realized that what she'd said to David that night in St Richard's when he'd saved her from Howard still applied. It was good that he was not from her past. She didn't know yet whether they had a future together, but it felt as if they did right now. 'But I've already told Dale I'd go out to Marchwood with her tomorrow morning,' she said. 'She needs to talk to the boss there about coming back and she knows all her and Scott's friends in the spa are burning to meet me. But you could come with us too! They are all just as intrigued by you as by me, and then we could go on somewhere afterwards.'

'If that's OK with you,' he smiled.

On her way to the bathroom a little later Lotte saw Scott kissing Dale goodbye out on the balcony by the front door. Lotte knew it wasn't a drunken mistake on Scott's part; he hadn't been drinking because he had to drive back to Marchwood and be up early in the morning.

She slipped into the bathroom without alerting them she'd seen them, smiling to herself. She thought they'd make the most perfect couple.

On the way out to Marchwood Manor the next morning in David's car, Dale suggested Lotte ask if they had any vacancies for hairdressers. 'It would be great,' she said excitedly. 'We'd all be together again.'

'I think I want to stay with Simon and Adam for the rest of the summer,' Lotte said. 'They'll take me back at Kutz too, and besides, after last night you and Scott don't need anyone playing gooseberry.'

Dale blushed. 'I might've known you'd pick up on that. You never miss anything!'

As David parked the car in the hotel car park, Lotte suggested she and he should get a cup of coffee while Dale went into the spa and saw her boss first.

'There's no need for that,' Dale said. 'Come on in with me now.'

Lotte had her misgivings about this. She didn't work there, David looked a bit crumpled after a night on the sofa, and from what Dale had told her before about Marisa De Vere it was clear she wasn't the most genial of people. But assuming Dale knew she was going to get a warm welcome, she allowed her friend to lead the way.

As they walked in through the doors into the tranquillity of the spa reception area, a slender, dark-haired woman by the desk spun round to Dale.

'To what do we owe the pleasure of this visit?' she said, her tone pure poison.

Lotte had rarely known her friend lost for a quick, pithy retort, but clearly the frosty greeting was so unexpected that Dale was momentarily stunned. 'I came to tell you I'm ready to come back,' she said in a small voice.

'The spa doesn't need someone as unreliable as you,' Marisa replied. 'And who are these people you've dragged in with you?'

Had Lotte seen Dale ready to fight her own corner, she would've apologized for intruding and backed away. But the colour had drained from Dale's face and she was staring open-mouthed in disbelief at Marisa.

Lotte stepped closer to the woman. 'I'm Lotte Wainwright, the friend who inadvertently prevented Dale from working,' she snapped. 'She couldn't help what happened to her, and how dare you speak to her in such an unpleasant manner!'

'This is nothing to do with you.' Marisa's voice rose a little. 'Kindly leave the spa immediately. You, Dale, can collect your belongings and we'll send on your cards and any money due to you.'

Lotte's blood was up. No one was going to treat her friend like that.

'Oh no you don't,' she said warningly to the woman. 'I think you'll find some of the other staff will walk out if you sack Dale. I know Scott will, and possibly the hairdressers too.'

As she spoke, she saw the door to the hairdressing salon open and guessed the man with highlighted hair, eyes almost popping out of his head as he looked in, was Frankie. Dale had talked about him a lot while they were imprisoned. 'Frankie!' She beckoned to him to come out. 'This woman intends to sack Dale for being so careless as to let herself be abducted and have her life threatened. I've already told her Scott will walk out in sympathy if she does. How about you?'

'She wants to sack you, babe?' Frankie asked incredulously, coming forward to hug Dale. 'No way. She can't do that. We'll all walk out if she does.'

He let go of Dale and walked swiftly back to the salon, yelled for everyone to come out, then did the same in the beauty salon. Hearing the noise he was making, Scott appeared too from the swimming pool.

Lotte glanced at David. He raised one eyebrow and

smiled. 'See what you can do if you put your mind to it?' he said quietly as the reception area began to fill up with people.

There was nothing for it but for Lotte to explain to everyone.

'Dale came back this morning hoping to return to work,' she began. 'She brought myself and David out here too because she believed as you'd all been so interested and supportive since I was found by David on the beach, that you'd like to meet us. Maybe she shouldn't have brought us in here without checking with the manager first, but did she deserve to be sacked for unreliability?

'How has she been unreliable? She was only away from work because she was abducted with me. That happened because she tried to save me. That was brave. Not unreliable.'

Lotte paused to look from one face to another. Most of the staff were nodding their heads in agreement with what she'd said. 'I don't believe so either,' she went on. 'In fact, I think Marisa is being not only unfair, but vindictive for some reason. So I'm going to ask who will support Dale by stepping forward and refusing to work until she receives a full apology.'

Scott leapt forward and Dale shot him a look of gratitude. Frankie was almost as quick off the mark, in fact he accused Marisa of having always been unpleasant to Dale. Then the other male hairdresser joined them, quickly followed by all the girls.

'Oh dear! You've got no one left to finish off the clients' treatments and haircuts,' Lotte said mischievously as she saw a couple of women in towelling robes peeping out of the beauty salon door. 'What is to be done, Marisa? I know, I'll go and get the general manager. Could someone tell me his name?'

Frankie called out that it was Mr Sellers and offered to get him for her.

The expression on Marisa's face was laughable. Shock that someone had dared stand up to her, panic that she could now be in trouble, mingled with jealousy and hatred. Lotte half expected her to start stamping her dainty little feet in rage.

In the midst of this, Quentin Sellers walked in and asked what was going on.

Scott took over then, no doubt aware that the hotel manager wouldn't wish to speak to Lotte as she didn't work there. He took him out of the spa back into the hotel to explain.

The five minutes the two men were gone seemed much longer, with Dale looking at the floor, Marisa glowering at Lotte and everyone else speaking in whispers. David caught hold of Lotte's hand and whispered that he was proud of her.

Then Scott came back.

'Mr Sellers would like to see you immediately in his office,' he said curtly to Marisa. 'He asked the rest of you if you would please return to your clients and he will address us all later. As for you, Dale, he regrets he wasn't around earlier to welcome you back personally after your ordeal and asks that you and your friends go into the lounge for coffee and he'll join you very shortly.'

Marisa had a face like thunder now, for clearly it was she who was in trouble. She flounced off, her high heels tapping out a staccato message on the hardwood floor. The rest of the staff tittered, then disappeared back into their respective salons.

'It's OK, Dale,' Scott said, coming over and running his hands affectionately down the sides of her head and shoulders. 'He was appalled at what Marisa said today. It won't be you being sacked. But I'll have to go, I've got to do a fitness appraisal for someone in the gym. Come in the pool for a swim later and we'll talk.'

Two hours later Lotte and David said goodbye to Dale in the car park. It seemed Mr Sellers had already been aware that Marisa was something of a bully to all the staff in the spa. She'd also been rude to quite a few guests and had been on a warning. Today's incident had clarified Mr Sellers' mind and he had decided she was the one to be fired. To save any further unpleasantness, he'd asked that she leave immediately.

When he came out to speak to Dale, Lotte and David he was charming, asking the girls about their ordeal, offering his congratulations to Lotte that all charges against her had been dropped. He asked if she'd like to work at his salon, but Lotte thanked him warmly and declined.

As for Dale, Mr Sellers asked if she would manage the spa on a trial basis. He said while she'd been absent he'd become aware that the rest of the staff liked and respected her, but was afraid that after what she'd been through it might be too much for her.

Dale said she wasn't sure she could manage it, but she'd give it her best shot.

Once the three of them were on their own again, Dale hugged Lotte tightly. 'You were so great this morning,' she said, her eyes full of tears. 'I couldn't believe you could be so confident, so strong. I ought to have, of course, after all it was you who held me together in the basement. Don't you think she's amazing, David?' she asked.

'Totally,' he said, looking at Lotte tenderly.

Lotte sniggered. 'What are you two like?' she said. 'Is this Boost Lotte's Morale Day?'

Dale reached out and took Lotte's hand. She couldn't say what she wanted to, for it was all mixed up in her head: gratitude, love, admiration, pride, along with a degree of fear that her friend would never entirely recover from what she'd been through. Dale might be excited about her budding romance with Scott, and her new job here at the spa, but she was happiest of all to see her friend with David, for she really felt he was going to heal all Lotte's wounds.

'Be happy with David,' she said simply, and turned and walked away from them. It was a glorious day and she was going for a swim now before she started looking around the spa and finding out what had been going on in her absence.

She glanced over her shoulder and saw that David was kissing Lotte. She smiled. Everything seemed to be going right for both of them at last.

Lesley Pearse

ABOUT LESLEY

Lesley Pearse is one of the UK's best-loved novelists, with fans across the globe and book sales of over two million copies to date.

A true storyteller and a master of gripping storylines that keep the reader hooked from beginning to end, Lesley introduces readers to unforgettable characters who it is impossible not to care about. There is no easily defined genre or formula; her books, whether crime, as in *Till We Meet Again*, historical adventure like *Never Look Back*, or the passionately emotive *Trust Me*, based on the true-life scandal of British child migrants sent to Australia in the post-war period, engage the reader completely.

'Lesley's life has been as packed with drama as her books'

Truth is often stranger than fiction and Lesley's life has been as packed with drama as her books. She was three when her mother died under tragic circumstances. Her father was away at sea and it was only when a neighbour saw Lesley and her brother playing outside without coats that suspicion was aroused – their mother had been dead for some time. With her father in the Royal Marines, they spent three years in grim orphanages before he remarried (his new wife was a veritable dragon of an ex-army nurse) and Lesley and her older brother were brought home again, to be joined by two other children who were later adopted by her father and stepmother, and a continuing stream of foster children. The impact of constant change and uncertainty in Lesley's early years is reflected in one of the recurring themes in her books: what happens to those emotionally damaged as children. Hers was an extraordinary childhood and, in all her books, Lesley has skilfully married the pain and unhappiness of her early experiences with a unique gift for storytelling.

'She was three when her mother died under tragic circumstances'

Lesley's desperate need for love and affection as a young girl was almost certainly the reason she kept making bad choices in men in her youth. A party girl during the swinging sixties, Lesley did it all – from nanny to bunny girl to designing clothes. She lived in damp bedsits while burning the candle at both ends as a 'Dolly Bird' with twelve-inch mini-skirts. She was married, fleetingly, to her first husband at twenty and met her second, John Pritchard, a trumpet player in a rock band, soon after. Her debut novel, *Georgia*, was inspired by her life with John, the London clubs, crooked managers and the many musicians she met during that time, including David Bowie and Steve Marriot of the Small Faces. Lesley's first child, Lucy, was born in this period, but with John's erratic lifestyle and a small child in the house, the marriage was doomed to failure. They parted when Lucy was four.

This was a real turning point in Lesley's life – she was young and alone with a small child – but in another twist of fate, Lesley met her third husband, Nigel, while on her way to Bristol for an interview. They married a few years later and had two daughters, Sammy and Jo. The following years were the happiest of her life – she ran a playgroup, started writing short stories and then opened a card and gift shop in Bristol's Clifton area. Writing by night, running the shop by day and fitting in all the other household chores, along with the needs of her husband and children, was tough.

'Some strange compulsion kept me writing, even when it seemed hopeless,' she says. 'I wrote three books before *Georgia*, then along came Darley Anderson, who offered to be my agent. Even so, a further six years of disappointment and massive re-writes followed before we finally found a publisher.'

There was more turmoil to follow, however, when Lesley's shop failed in the 90s recession, leaving her with a mountain of debts and bruised pride. Her eighteen-year marriage broke down, and at fifty years old she hit rock bottom. It seemed she was back where she had started in a grim flat with barely enough money for her youngest daughter's bus fares to school.

'Lesley did it all – from nanny to bunny girl to designing clothes'

'I wrote my way out of it,' she says. 'My second book, *Tara*, was shortlisted for the Romantic Novel of the Year, and I knew I was on my way.'

Lesley's own life is a rich source of material for her books; whether she is writing about the pain of first love, the experience of being an unwanted abused child, adoption, rejection, fear, poverty or revenge, she knows about it first hand. She is a fighter, and with her long fight for success has come security. She now owns a cottage in a pretty village between Bristol and Bath, which she is renovating, and a creek-side retreat in Cornwall. Her three daughters, grandson, friends, dogs and gardening have brought her great happiness. She is president of the Bath and West Wiltshire branch of the NSPCC – the charity closest to her heart.

ABOUT *STOLEN*

What was your inspiration for *Stolen* and the nameless girl on the beach?

I was just walking along a beach with my dogs one day and I imagined finding a girl washed up. That led me to think of all the different reasons she could've been in the sea: fallen from a ship, pushed or trying to kill herself. Then of course I started imagining what led up to that.

A key backdrop to the story of Lotte and Dale is how they met while working together on a cruise ship. What made you choose this setting of a cruise?

One of the possible scenarios I came up with was that the girl had been pushed overboard on a cruise ship. So I booked on to a cruise going around South America, in the hopes that I would get some inspiration. Unfortunately, I have never been keen on writing about the seriously rich, and this cruise was full of them, and mostly as dull as ditchwater! I found my attention turning instead to the staff and crew. They had to work very long hours, they had to be dynamic and pleasant at all times, and most of them were only sticking it out just until they'd earned enough money to further their personal dream of a hairdresser's or beauty salon of their own. I liked many of these young women; they were brave, funny and go-getters, I liked the way they formed close friendships with other staff, the way they didn't whinge. So before long I had Lotte and Dale's characters sorted! I just had to find another way that the body ended up on the beach.

Lotte seems so fragile and beautiful, and yet she reveals herself to be strong and a tower of support to Dale. Do you think people often defy expectations?

Almost always. I have also found that those who had the toughest childhoods are the bravest, the kindest and by far the most resourceful.

Stolen is set in modern times, although many of your books have been set in the past, in fascinating historical periods. Do the two types of novel require very different approaches in the writing?

Very much so. In one respect it's easier to write a modern-day book because it doesn't need the same depth of research, but I actually prefer writing historical stories. Part of this is because I love history. It isn't a chore to me to read dozens of books, trawl through museums and libraries, and certainly not to go to places like the Crimea or Alaska to recreate events which happened there long ago.

But more than that, there is so much more available drama in historical settings, because ordinary people really were up against it then. There was terrible poverty, lack of medical care, and little or no education. It was the survival of the fittest. To illustrate this, imagine I was writing two books side by side, both set in the same basement flat in London's East End, one in the present day and the other at the turn of the century. Now in the historical one I could have a young mother of six children dying of tuberculosis, the flat is unheated and damp, the children forced to beg on the streets just to get her medicine and good food. We know only a major twist of fate is going to improve their lot. Now the present-day story could be just as compelling if it was about a young woman on drugs or an immigrant family who can speak very little English. Yet we would all realize that however sad and grim their lives are, they aren't going to starve or die for lack of medical treatment, because of the safety net of social security. This is a great thing of course for mankind, but in a story it reduces the compassion and the scare factor.

On top of this I also have to worry about forensic science in present-day books. A hundred years ago crime was solved by plodding police work, now the police can catch someone just by finding one of their hairs at the scene of the crime. I find all that rather restrictive.

Lotte, like so many of the characters in your books, has gone through some unbelievable hardships, right from childhood, and yet remains courageous, on which subject, you have recently judged 2009's Women of Courage Award. Can you tell us more about the women you have met?

I have met so many extraordinary and courageous women over the years that the award has been running. Wonderful women who think far more of others than they do themselves, make light of the huge burdens put upon them and never complain. Some have children with serious and permanent health problems that require care twenty-four/seven. Others have lost a child through sickness or injury, yet offer support and help to other mothers with sick children. We had a wonderful woman who, while sick herself with a rare blood disease, at her own expense brought children from Chernobyl over to Scotland for respite care. There were severely disabled young women who have studied hard against all the odds to gain qualifications so they can get a good job to support themselves. So many inspirational carers, others who have pulled their relatives through drink and drug abuse, and some who were abused by their partners and now help other women going through the same thing.

'Amongst Friends'

The Lesley Pearse Newsletter

A fantastic new way to keep up-to-date with your favourite author. *Amongst Friends* is a regular email with all the latest news and views from Lesley, plus information on her forthcoming titles and the chance to win exclusive prizes.

Just go to **www.penguin.co.uk** and type your email address in the 'Join our newsletter' panel and tick the box marked 'Lesley Pearse'. Then fill in your details and you will be added to Lesley's list.

THE BOOKS

GEORGIA
Raped by her foster-father, fifteen-year-old
Georgia runs away from home to the seedy
back streets of Soho ...

TARA
Anne changes her name to Tara to forget her
shocking past – but can she really become
someone else?

CHARITY
Charity Stratton's bleak life is changed for ever
when her parents die in a fire. Alone and pregnant,
she runs away to London ...

ELLIE
Eastender Ellie and spoilt Bonny set off to make
a living on the stage. Can their friendship survive
sacrifice and ambition?

CAMELLIA
Orphaned Camellia discovers that the past she has
always been so sure of has been built on lies. Can
she bear to uncover the truth about herself?

ROSIE
Rosie is a girl without a mother, with a past full of
trouble. But could the man who ruined her family
also save Rosie?

CHARLIE
Charlie helplessly watches her mother being
senselessly attacked. What secrets have her parents
kept from her?

NEVER LOOK BACK
An act of charity sends flower girl Matilda on a trip
to the New World and a new life ...

TRUST ME
Dulcie Taylor and her sister are sent to an
orphanage and then to Australia. Is their love strong
enough to keep them together?

FATHER UNKNOWN
Daisy Buchan is left a scrapbook with details about
her real mother. But should she go and find her?

TILL WE MEET AGAIN
Susan and Beth were childhood friends. Now
Susan is accused of murder, and Beth finds she
must defend her.

REMEMBER ME
Mary Broad is transported to Australia as a convict
and encounters both cruelty and passion. Can she
make a life for herself so far from home?

SECRETS
Adele Talbot escapes a children's home to find her
grandmother – but soon her unhappy mother is on
her trail ...

A LESSER EVIL
Bristol, the 1960s, and young Fif Brown defies her
parents to marry a man they think is beneath her.

HOPE
Somerset, 1836, and baby Hope is cast out
from a world of privilege as proof of her
mother's adultery ...

FAITH
Scotland, 1995, and Laura Brannigan is in prison
for a murder she claims she didn't commit.

GYPSY
Liverpool, 1893, and after tragedy strikes the Bolton
family, Beth and her brother Sam embark on a
dangerous journey to find their fortune in America.

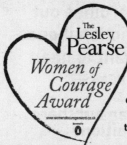

The Lesley Pearse
Women of Courage Award

was launched in 2006 to celebrate the extraordinary achievements of ordinary women; women who have done something special for themselves or someone else; women of courage.

THE 2006 WINNER NICOLE GALLAGHER

'Winning the inaugural woman of courage award was a unique experience which I shall always remember'

NICOLE GALLAGHER from Kent was nominated by her best friend because of her care and devotion to her children who both suffer from rare medical conditions.

THE 2007 WINNER KAREN BAKER

'I still have to pinch myself to remind me that I did actually win the award'

KAREN BAKER from Harrow was nominated by her colleague. She provides full time support for her disabled daughter, Nicky, gives support to her colleagues in a busy role, looks after her father who has Alzheimer's disease and is the key support for her husband who has epilepsy. As if that wasn't enough, Karen has been living with cancer for years.

THE 2008 WINNER KERRY-ANN HINDLEY

'Winning Lesley's Woman Of Courage Award has not only filled me with great pride but given me time to stop and reflect on the achievements I have made throughout my life, it has filled me with renewed enthusiasm to continue working hard towards my goals and to assist others in achieving theirs.'

KERRY-ANN HINDLEY from Glasgow was nominated by her partner because she has overcome personal tragedies, hardship and a terribly troubled youth to take her experiences and turn them into something positive – helping others. After hitting rock bottom, Kerry-Ann stayed in a women's homeless hostel and made a conscious decision to turn her life around and dedicate all her time to helping kids who have shared similar experiences to hers. Kerry-Ann now works for the council in local schools teaching kids life skills and keeping them on the right path, off the street and out of trouble.

PLEASE TURN OVER TO FIND OUT HOW YOU CAN NOMINATE SOMEONE FOR THE AWARD

'I know there are real heroines out there who would put my fictional ones to shame, and I really want to hear about them' LESLEY PEARSE

Is there an amazing woman out there who deserves recognition?

Whether it is someone who has had to cope with problems and come out the other side; someone who has spent her whole life looking out for other people; or someone who has shown strength and determination in doing something great for herself, show her how much she is appreciated by nominating her for an award.

The Lesley Pearse Women of Courage Award gives recognition to all those ordinary women who show extraordinary strength and dedication in their everyday lives. It is an annual event that was launched by Lesley and Penguin in 2006.

The winner and her family will be invited to London for a sumptuous awards lunch with Lesley, where she will be presented with a specially crafted commemorative award, a framed certificate and £200 of Penguin books.

Let us know about an amazing lady you know and make a difference to her life by nominating her for this prestigious award.

To nominate someone you know:

Complete the entry form, or send us the details required on a separate piece of paper, and post it to:

The Lesley Pearse Women of Courage Award, Penguin Michael Joseph, 80 Strand, London, WC2R 0RL

or visit:

www.womenofcourageaward.co.uk

where you can print out a nomination form, enter your nomination details on to our online form and read all about the award and its previous nominees and winners.